UNDER the BOARDWALK

LINDA HOWARD

UNDER the BOARDWALK

POCKET BOOKS
New York London Toronto Sydney

Pocket Books
A Division of Simon & Schuster, Inc.
1230 Avenue of the Americas, New York, NY 10020

This Pocket Books paperback edition July 1999

For information about special discounts for bulk purchases, please contact Simon & Schuster Special Sales at 1-800-456-6798 or business@simonandschuster.com

Cover photo by Ross Anania / Getty Images.

Manufactured in the United States of America

10 9 8 7 6

ISBN-13: 978-0-671-02794-0
ISBN-10: 0-671-02794-8

Contents

Blue Moon

Linda Howard

Chapter 1

ONE FULL MOON A MONTH WAS BAD ENOUGH, SHERIFF Jackson Brody thought sourly; two should be outlawed. Nature's rule of survival of the fittest had been all but negated by humans, with advances in modern medicine and the generally held view that all life was worth saving, with the result that there were a lot of very weird, and/or stupid people out there, and they all seemed to surface during a full moon.

He was not in a good mood after working a car accident on a county road. As sheriff, his duties were not supposed to include working wrecks, but damned if every full moon he didn't find himself doing exactly that. The county was small and poor, mostly rural, and couldn't afford the number of deputies he needed, so he was always juggling schedules anyway. Add the madness of a full moon to an understaffed department, and the problems multiplied.

The accident he had just worked made him so furious he had been stretching the limits of his willpower not to cuss at the participants. He couldn't call them *victims*, unless it was of their own stupidity. The only victim was the poor little boy who had been in the passenger seat of the car.

It all started when the driver of the first vehicle, a

pickup truck, woke up and realized he had missed his turn by about a quarter of a mile. Instead of going on and finding a place to turn around, the idiot began backing up, going the wrong way down a narrow two-lane blacktop, around a blind curve. He was an accident waiting to happen, and he hadn't had to wait long. A woman came speeding around the curve, doing over sixty miles an hour on a road with a posted speed limit of thirty-five, and plowed into the rear of the pickup. She wasn't wearing a seatbelt. Neither was the four-year-old sitting in the front seat. For that matter, neither was the driver of the pickup. It was nothing less than a miracle that all three had survived, though the little boy was severely injured and Jackson had seen enough accident victims to know his chances were no better than fifty-fifty, at best. The car had had airbags, at least, which had kept the two in the car from going through the windshield.

He had given the woman citations for reckless driving, not wearing a seatbelt, and not properly securing her child, and she began screaming at him. Had he ever tried to make a four-year-old sit down and wear a seatbelt? The blankety-blank things chafed her blankety-blank neck, and the state had no business telling people what they could do on their private property, which her car was, and the car had airbags anyway so there was no need for seatbelts, blah blah blah. There she was, with bulging eyes and unkempt hair, a living testament to the destructive power of recessive genes, throwing a hissy fit about getting traffic tickets while her screaming child was being carried away in an ambulance. Privately, Jackson thought people like her had no business having children in their care, but he made a heroic effort and kept the observation to himself.

Then the driver of the pickup, he of the bulging beer belly and breath that would fell a moose at fifty paces, added his opinion that he thought her driver's license should be taken away because this was all her fault for rear-ending him. When Jackson then gave *him* citations for reckless driving and driving in the wrong lane, he was enraged. This accident wasn't *his* fault, he bellowed, and damned if he was going to get stuck with higher insurance premiums because a stupid hick sheriff didn't know an accident was always the fault of the one doing the rear-ending. Any fool could look at where his truck was hit and tell who was at fault here.

Jackson didn't bother explaining the difference between the truck's hood being pointed in the right direction while the truck itself was going in reverse. He just wrote the tickets and in the accident report stated that both drivers were at fault, and seriously pondered whether or not he should lock these two up for the safety of the universe. Terminal stupidity wasn't on the books as a chargeable offense, but it should be, in his opinion.

But he restrained himself, and oversaw the transportation of both furious drivers to the local hospital to be checked out, and the removal of the damaged vehicles. When he finally crawled back into his Jeep Cherokee it was pushing four o'clock, long past lunch time. He was tired, hungry, and both angry and discouraged.

Generally he loved his work. It was a job where he could make a difference in people's lives, in society. Granted, it was usually scut work; he dealt with the worst of society, while having to maneuver on tippy-toes through a tangle of laws and regulations. But when everything worked and a drug dealer got sent away for a few years, or a murderer was put away forever, or a burglary gang was rounded up and an old lady on Social Security got her 19-inch television back, that made it all worthwhile.

He was a good sheriff, though he hated the political side of it, hated having to campaign for office. He was just thirty-five, young for the office, but the county was so poor it couldn't afford someone who was both good and with a lot of experience, because those people went where the pay was better. The citizens had taken a chance with him two years ago and he'd been doing his best at a job he loved. Not many people had that chance.

During full moons, however, he doubted his own sanity. He had to be a fool or an idiot, or both, to want a job that put him on the front lines during the periods of rampant weirdness. Cops and emergency room personnel could all testify to the craziness that went on during a full moon.

A nurse at the local hospital, after reading a report that the tales about full moons were just myths, that the accident rate didn't really go up, kept a record for a year. Not only did the number of accidents go up, but that was when they got the really strange ones, like the guy who had his buddy nail his hands together so his wife wouldn't ask him to help with the housework on his day off. It was obvious to them: a man couldn't very well work with his hands nailed together, now could he? The scariest thing about it was that both of them had been sober.

So one full moon a month was all Jackson felt any human should be called upon to endure. A blue moon, the second full moon in a single month, fell under the heading of cruel and unusual punishment.

And because it was a blue moon, he wasn't surprised, when he radioed in that he was finished with the accident and heading for a bite to eat, that the dispatcher said, "You might want to hold off on the food, and check in on a secure line."

Jackson stifled a groan. A couple of clues told him he really didn't want to know what this one was. For one thing, though the radio traffic was usually businesslike, for the benefit of the good citizens who listened in on their scanners, the dispatcher had fallen into a more personal tone. And they didn't bother to check in on a secure line unless there was something going on they didn't want the listeners to know about, which meant it was either something sensitive like one of the town fathers acting up, or something personal. He hoped the issue was sensitive, because he sure as hell didn't feel like dealing with anything personal, like his mother running amuck at her regular Wednesday bingo game.

He picked up his digital cell phone and checked whether or not he had service in this part of the county; he did, though it wasn't the strongest signal. He flipped the cover open and dialed the dispatcher. "This is Brody. What's up?"

Jo Vaughn had been the dispatcher for ten years, and he couldn't think of anyone he would rather have on the job. Not only did she know just about every inhabitant of the small south Alabama county, something that had been a tremendous aid to him, but she also had an eerily accurate instinct for what was urgent and what wasn't. Sometimes the citizens involved might not agree, but Jackson always did.

"I've got a bad feeling," she announced. "Shirley Waters saw Thaniel Vargas hauling his flat-bottom down Old Boggy Road. There's nothing out that way except the Jones's place, and you know how Thaniel is."

Jackson took a moment to reflect. This was one of those times when growing up in west Texas instead of south Alabama was a definite handicap. He knew where Old Boggy Road was, but only because he had spent days looking at county maps and memorizing the roads. He had never personally been on Old Boggy, though. And he knew who Thaniel Vargas was; a slightly thick-headed troublemaker, the type found in every community. Thaniel was hot-tempered, a bit of a bully, and he liked his beer a little too much. He'd been in some trouble with the law, but nothing serious enough to rate more than a few fines and warnings.

Other than that, though, Jackson drew a blank. "Refresh me."

"Well, you know how superstitious he is."

His eyebrows lifted. He hadn't expected that. "No, I didn't know," he said drily. "What does that have to do with him taking his boat down Old Boggy Road, and who are the Joneses?"

"Jones," Jo corrected. "There's just one now, since old man Jones died four—no, let's see, it was right after Beatrice Marbut's husband died in his girlfriend's trailer, so that would make it five years ago—"

Jackson closed his eyes and refrained from asking what difference it made how long ago old man Jones died. Hurrying a Southerner through a conversation was like trying to push a rope, though sometimes he couldn't stop himself from trying.

"—and Delilah's been out there alone ever since."

He took a wild stab at getting to the point of Jo's anxiety. "And Thaniel Vargas dislikes Mrs. Jones?"

"Miss. She's never been married."

The wild stab hadn't worked. "Then old man Jones was—"

"Her father."

"Okay." He tried again. "Why does Thaniel dislike Miss Jones?"

"Oh, I wouldn't say he *dislikes* her. It's more like he's scared to death of her."

He took a deep breath. "Because . . . ?"

"Because of the witch thing, of course."

That did it. Some things just weren't worth fighting. Jackson surrendered and let himself go with the flow. "Witch thing," he repeated. That was twice in one minute Jo had surprised him.

"You mean you never heard about that?" Jo sounded surprised.

"Not a word." He wished he wasn't hearing about it now.

"Well, folks think she's a witch. Not that I think so, mind, but I can see where some would be uneasy."

"Why is that?"

"Oh, she keeps to herself, hardly ever comes to town. And old man Jones was strange, didn't let anyone come around. Even the mail is delivered by boat, because there's no road going out to the Jones place. The only way to get there is to hike in, or by the river." Background established, she settled into her explanation.

"Now, if Thaniel was going fishing, the best fishing is down river, not up. There's no reason he'd be launching a boat from the Old Boggy ramp unless he was going up river, and there's nothing up there but the Jones place. He wouldn't have the nerve unless he'd been drinking, because he's so afraid of Delilah, so I think you need to go out there and make sure he's not up to no good."

Jackson wondered how many sheriffs were bossed around by their dispatchers. He wondered just what the hell he was supposed to do, since Jo had just told him the only way to get to the Jones place was by boat. And he wondered, not for the first time, whether or not he was going to survive this damn blue moon.

Well, until it killed him, he had a job to do. He assessed the situation and began solving the most immediate problems. "Call Frank at the Rescue Squad and tell him to meet me at the launch ramp on Old Boggy—"

"You don't want one of the Rescue Squad boats," Jo interrupted. "They're too slow, and the guys are all helping with the clean-up at the tractor-trailer wreck out on the big highway, anyway. I called Charlotte Watkins. Her husband's a bass fisherman—you know Jerry Watkins, don't you?"

"I've met both of them," Jackson said.

"He's got one of those real fast boats. He's gone to Chattanooga on business, but Charlotte was going to hook up the boat and take it to the ramp. She should be there by the time you get there."

"Okay," he said, "I'm on my way." He pinched the top of his nose, between his eyebrows, feeling a headache beginning to form. He wished he could ignore Jo's intuition, but it was too accurate for him to doubt her. "Send some backup as soon as someone comes available. And how in hell do I find the Jones place?"

"Just go upriver, you can't miss it. It's about five miles up. The house is hard to see, it kind of blends in, but it's dead ahead and you'll think you're going to run right into it, but then the river curves real sharp to the right and gets too shallow to go much farther. Oh, and be careful of the snags. Stay in the middle of the river." She paused. "You *do* know how to drive a boat, don't you?"

"I'll figure it out," he said, and flipped the phone cover down to end the call. Let her stew for a while, wondering if she had made a bad mistake sending the sheriff out alone into a possibly dangerous situation, on a river he didn't know and in a piece of powerful equipment he didn't know how to operate. He'd driven a boat for the first time at the age of eleven, but Jo didn't know that, and it would do her good to realize she wasn't omnipotent.

He didn't use his lights or siren, but he did jam his boot down on the accelerator and keep it there. By his estimation he was at least fifteen minutes from Old Boggy Road, and he had no idea how far down the road the launch ramp was. In a powerful boat he could easily go sixty miles an hour, putting him at the Jones place in five minutes or less, once he was on the water. That meant it would take him at least twenty minutes to get there, probably longer. If Thaniel Vargas was up to no good, Jackson was afraid he would have plenty of time to accomplish it.

He felt a surge of adrenaline, the surge every law enforcement officer felt when going into a potentially dangerous situation. He hoped he wouldn't find anything out of the ordinary, though. He hoped like hell he wouldn't, because if he did, that would mean Miss Jones—had Jo actually said her name was *Delilah?*—was either hurt or dead.

Witch? Why hadn't he heard anything about this before? He'd lived here for three years, been sheriff for two, and in that time he thought he'd learned about all the county's unusual citizens. There hadn't been a peep about Delilah Jones, though, not from his deputies, not from the mayor or her secretary, who was the most gossipy person Jackson had ever met, not from the bar crowd or the women he dated, not from the blue-hair bingo circuit, not even from Jo. He hadn't missed the fact that Jo seemed well-informed on how to get to the

Jones house. How would she know that, unless she'd been there? And why would she go, considering everything she'd said about the Jones woman being reclusive and her father being strange?

If anyone was practicing witchcraft in his county, he should have known about it. It was all bullshit, in his opinion, but if anyone else took it seriously then there could be trouble. From the sound of things, that was exactly what was happening.

First there was the general blue moon craziness, then the wreck between the two idiots, and now this. He was hungry, tired, and had a headache. He was beginning to get severely pissed.

Chapter 2

JACKSON REACHED OLD BOGGY ROAD IN RECORD TIME and churned down it, his tires digging in and throwing sand. The river was to his right so he kept an eye in that direction, looking for the launch ramp. The old road narrowed and became one rutted lane, with massive live oaks on each side intertwining their branches to form an almost solid canopy. The dense shade gave relief from the heat for about a hundred yards, then he drove out into the sunlight and there the ramp was, down a shallow slope that curved back to the right and was hidden from view by the thick trees until that moment.

He spun the wheel and headed down the slope, the rear end of the Jeep slewing around before he deftly corrected. A blue Toyota pickup, with an empty boat trailer hooked to it, was pulled to the side. Another truck, a red extended cab Chevy, was backed onto the ramp and Charlotte Watkins was standing on the bank, one hand holding the rope to a long, sleek, red and silver fishing boat and the other hand slapping at mosquitos as they swarmed around her bare arms and legs.

Jackson grabbed his shotgun and Kevlar vest and vaulted out of the Cherokee. "Thanks, Mrs. Watkins," he said as he took the rope from her. He put his right foot on the nose of the boat and pushed off with his left, agilely transferring his weight back to his right foot and stepping up into the boat as it floated away from the bank.

"Any time, sheriff," she said, raising her hand to shade her eyes from the sun. "Mind the snags, now. If you get too far to the left, there are some mighty big stumps just under the water, and they'll rip the lower unit right off the boat."

"I'll watch," he promised as he carefully stowed the shotgun so it wouldn't bounce around, then slid into the driver's seat and hooked the kill switch to his shirt. As an afterthought, he tossed her the keys to his Jeep. "Drive the Cherokee home. I'll bring your truck and boat back as soon as I can."

She deftly caught the keys, but waved off any concern about the boat. "You just be careful upriver. I hope everything's all right." Worry etched her face.

Jackson turned the ignition switch and the big outboard coughed into deep, rumbling life. He put it in reverse and backed away from the bank, turning the boat so he was headed upriver. Then he pushed the throttle down and the nose of the boat rose out of the water as it gained speed, before dropping down and settling on plane, skimming across the water.

The river was slow-moving and marshy, filled with snags, shoals, and weed beds ready to snare anyone unfamiliar with its obstacles. Mindful of Charlotte Watkins's warning—another woman who seemed to know an awful lot about the way to the Jones place—Jackson kept the boat dead center and prayed as he tried to balance urgency with caution, but urgency kept getting the upper hand. Maybe Miss Jones was having a peaceful summer afternoon, but maybe she wasn't.

The rush of air cooled him, drying the sweat on his body and making the thick heat of summer feel almost comfortable. As he skimmed past the little sloughs and cuts in the river he looked at all of them, hoping to see Thaniel doing nothing more sinister than feeding worms to the fish. No such luck.

Then he rounded a bend in the river and saw a flat-bottom boat pulled up on the bank and tied to a tree. Thaniel was nowhere in sight.

Jackson didn't slow. The Jones place couldn't be much farther up the river, because it looked as if Thaniel had decided to walk the rest of the way, so he could approach unnoticed. That gave Jackson a little more time, maybe enough time to head off any trouble.

Even as he had the thought he heard the shot, a deep retort that boomed out over the water and was easily audible over the sound of the outboard motor. Shotgun, he thought. He eased up on the throttle and reached for the Kevlar vest, slipping it on and fastening the Velcro straps. Then he shoved the throttle down again, the boat leaping forward in response.

Fifteen seconds later the house was in sight, taking form dead ahead of him, just as Jo had said. The river seemed to end right there. The house was built of old, weathered wood that blended into the tall trees surrounding it, but in front of it was a short dock with an old flat-bottom tied to it, and that was what he saw first.

He had to back off the power to bring the boat into the dock. He reached for his shotgun as he did, holding it in his left hand as he steered the boat. "This is Sheriff Brody!" he bellowed. "Thaniel, you stop whatever the hell it is you're doing and get your ass out here." Not the most professional way of speaking, he supposed, but it served the purpose of announcing him and letting Thaniel know his identity wasn't a secret.

But he didn't really expect things to settle down just because he was there, and they didn't. Another shotgun blast boomed, answered by the flatter crack of a rifle.

The shots were coming from the back of the house. Jackson nosed the boat toward the dock and killed the engine. He leaped out while the dock was still a foot away, automatically looping the mooring rope around one of the posts as he did so, ingrained training taking hold so everything was accomplished while he was in motion.

He ran up the short dock, the thudding of his boots on the wood in time with the hard beating of his heart. The old familiar clarity swept over him, the by-product of adrenaline and experience. He'd felt the same thing every time he jumped out of a plane during airborne training. Lightning-fast, his brain processed the details he saw.

The front door of the old wooden house was standing open, a neatly-patched screen door keeping out the insects. He could see straight through to the back door, but no one was in sight. The porch looked like a jungle, with huge potted plants and hanging baskets everywhere, but there wasn't any junk sitting around like there was at most houses, his included. He took with one leap the three steps up to the porch, and flattened himself against the wall.

The last thing he wanted was to get shot by the very person he was trying to help, so he repeated his identity. "This is Sheriff Brody! Miss Jones, are you all right?"

There was a moment of silence in which even the insects seemed to stop buzzing. Then a woman's voice came from somewhere out back. "I'm fine. I'll be even better when you get this jackass off my property."

She sounded remarkably cool for someone who was under attack, as if Thaniel was of no more importance than the mosquitos.

Jackson eased around the corner of the wide, shady porch that wrapped around three sides of the house. He was now on the right side, with thick woods both to the right and ahead of him. He couldn't see anything out of the ordinary, not a patch of color or a rustling of bushes. "Thaniel!" he yelled. "Put your weapon down before you get your stupid ass shot off, you hear me?"

There was another moment of silence. Then came a sullen, "I didn't do nothin', Sheriff. She shot at me first."

He still couldn't see Thaniel, but the voice had come from a stand of big pine trees behind the house, practically dead ahead. "I'll decide whose fault it is." He edged closer to the back of the house, his shotgun held ready. He was safe from Miss Jones's shots, for the moment, but Thaniel would have a straight bead on him if he chose. "Now do what I told you and pitch out your weapon."

"This crazy bitch will shoot me if I do."

"No, she won't."

"I might," came Delilah Jones's calm voice, not helping the situation at all.

"See, what'd I tell you!" Thaniel's voice was high with anxiety. Whatever he had planned, it had gone sadly awry.

Jackson swore under his breath, and tried to make his tone both calming and authoritative. "Miss Jones, where exactly are you?"

"I'm on the back porch, behind the washing machine."

"Put down your weapon and go back inside, so I can have a little talk with Thaniel."

Again that little pause, as if she were considering whether or not to pay any attention to him. Accustomed to instant response, be it positive or negative, that telling little hesitation set Jackson's teeth on edge. "I'll go in the house," she finally said. "But I'm not putting this shotgun down until that fool's off my property."

He'd had enough. "Do as you're told," he said sharply. "Or I'll arrest both of you."

There was another of those maddening moments of silence, then the back door slammed. Jackson took a deep breath. Thaniel's whiny voice floated from the pine trees. "She didn't put down the shotgun like you told her to, Sheriff."

"Neither did you," Jackson reminded him in a grim tone. He eased to the corner of the house. "I have a shotgun too, and I'm going to use it in three seconds if you don't throw down that rifle and come out." The mood he was in, it wasn't a bluff. "One . . . two . . . th—"

A rifle sailed out from behind a huge pine tree, landing with a thud on the pine-needle cushioned ground. After a few seconds, Thaniel slowly followed it, easing away from the tree with his hands up and his face sullen. A thin rivulet of blood ran down his right cheek. The wound didn't look like anything from a shotgun, so Jackson figured a splinter must have caught him. The tree trunk sported a great raw gouge level with his chin. Miss Jones hadn't been shooting over Thaniel's head; she had been aiming for him. And, from the look of that tree, she wasn't shooting bird shot.

Immediately the back screen door popped open and Delilah Jones stepped out, shotgun held ready. Thaniel hit the ground, braying in panic. He covered his head with his hands, as if that would do any good.

God, give me strength, Jackson prayed. The prayer didn't do any good. His temper shattered and he moved fast, so fast she didn't have time to do more than glance at him, certainly not time to react. In two long steps he reached her, his right hand locking around the barrel of her shotgun and wrenching it out of her hands. "Get back inside," he barked. *"Now!"*

She stood as rigid as a post, staring at Thaniel, paying Jackson no more mind than if he hadn't been there at all. "You're dead," she said to Thaniel, her voice flat and calm.

Thaniel jerked as if he'd been shot. "You heard her!" he howled. "She threatened me, Sheriff! Arrest her!"

"I'm of a mind to do just that," Jackson said between clenched teeth.

"I didn't threaten him," she said, still in that flat, monotonous tone. "I don't have to. He'll die without me lifting a finger to help." She looked up at Jackson then, and he found himself caught in eyes the dark green of a woodland forest, watchful, wary, knowing eyes.

He felt suddenly dizzy, and gave a short, sharp jerk of his head. The heat must be getting to him. Everything kind of faded, except her face at the center of his vision.

She was younger than he'd expected, he thought dimly, probably in her late twenties when he had expected a middle-aged, reclusive country woman, by-passed by modern inventions. Her skin was smooth, tanned, and unblemished. Her hair was a mass of brown curls, and her shorts stopped north of mid-thigh, revealing slim, shapely legs. He inhaled deeply, fighting off the dizziness, and as his head cleared he noticed that she had gone utterly white. She was staring at him as if he had two heads.

Abruptly she turned and went inside, the screen door slamming shut behind her.

Jackson took a deep breath, gathering himself before turning back to the problem at hand. He propped her shotgun against the wall and cradled his on one arm as he finally turned his attention back to Thaniel.

"Son of a *bitch!*"

Thaniel had taken advantage of his splintered attention. The ground where he had lain was bare, and a quick glance told Jackson the rifle was gone, too.

He jumped off the porch, landing half-crouched, the shotgun now held ready in both hands. His head swiveled, but except for a slight waving of some bushes there was no sign of Thaniel. Silently Jackson slipped into the woods close to where the bushes swayed, then stood still and listened.

Thaniel, for all his other faults, was good in the woods. It was about thirty seconds before Jackson heard the distant snap of a twig under a careless foot. He started to follow, then stopped. There was no point in chasing him through the woods; he knew where Thaniel lived, if Miss Jones wanted to file charges against him for trespass and any other charges Jackson thought were applicable.

He turned and looked back at the house, nestled among the trees and blending in so well it looked part of the woodland. He felt oddly reluctant to go in and talk to Miss Jones, a sense of things being subtly altered, out of control. He didn't want to know anything more about her, he only wanted to get in Jerry Watkins's boat and go back downriver, safely away from that strange woman with her spooky eyes.

But his job demanded he talk to her, and Jackson was a good sheriff. That was why he was here, and that was why he couldn't leave without seeing her.

The uneasy feeling followed him, though, all the way to the porch.

Chapter 3

THE WASHING MACHINE SHE'D BEEN HIDING BEHIND was an old-fashioned wringer-type model, he noticed with faint astonishment as he paused in front of the screen door. He couldn't see inside the house; there were no lights on, and the trees provided plenty of shade to keep the interior cool and dim.

He lifted his fist to knock, paused, then gave two firm taps. "Miss Jones?"

"Right here."

She was near, standing in the room just beyond the door. There was a strained quality to her voice that hadn't been there before.

She hadn't asked him to come in. He was glad, because he would just as soon never set foot in that house. And then, irrationally, it annoyed him that she hadn't asked him in. Without waiting for an invitation, he opened the screen door and stepped inside.

She was a pale figure in the dim room, standing very still, and staring at him. Maybe his vision needed to adjust a bit more, but he had the impression she was downright horrified by him. She even backed up a step.

He couldn't say why that pissed him off, but it did, big time. Adrenaline was pumping through him again, making his muscles feel tight and primed for action, but damned if he knew what he could do. He had to take her statement, read her the riot act about shooting at people, and leave. That was all. Nothing there to make him feel so edgy and angry.

But that was exactly how he *did* feel, whether or not there was rhyme or reason to it.

Silence stretched between them, silence in which they took each other's measure. He didn't know what conclusions she drew from his appearance, but he was a lawman, accustomed to taking in every detail about a person and making snap judgments. He had to, and he had to be pretty accurate, because his and others' lives depended on how he read people.

What he saw in the dim light was a slim, toned young woman, neat in a pale yellow, sleeveless shirt that was tucked into khaki shorts, which were snugly belted around a trim waist. Her bare arms were smoothly tanned, and sleekly muscled in a feminine way that told him she was stronger than she looked, and accustomed to work. She was clean, even her bare feet—which, he noticed, sported pale pink polish on the toes; toes that were curling, digging into the floor, as if she had to force herself to stand there.

Her hair was a brown, sun-streaked mass of curls. She didn't hurt the eye, though she wasn't beauty-queen material. She was pleasant-looking, healthy, with a sweet curve to her chin. Her eyes, though . . . those eyes were spooky. He was reluctant to meet them again, but finally he did. They were her best feature, large and clear, fringed with thick dark lashes. And she was watching him now with . . . resignation?

For God's sake, what did she think he was going to do?

He didn't know how long he'd been standing there staring at her. The same thing had happened on the porch, only this time he didn't feel dizzy. He needed to take care of business and get going. The summer days were long, but he wanted to be off the river well ahead of sundown.

"Thaniel slipped away," he said, his voice unaccountably rough.

She gave a brief, jerky nod.

"Do you make a habit of shooting at visitors?"

The green eyes narrowed. "When they stop downriver and sneak the rest of the way on foot, yes, that makes me a bit suspicious about their reason for calling on me."

"How do you know what he did?"

"Sound carries a long way over water. And I don't hear many boats coming my way except Harley Whisenant's, delivering the mail. Since Harley was here this morning, I knew it wasn't him."

"You shot first."

"He was trespassing. I fired in the air the first time, as a warning, and yelled at him to scat. He shot at me then. There's a bullet hole in my washing machine, damn him. My second shot was to defend myself."

"Maybe he thought he was defending himself, too, since you shot first."

She gave him a disbelieving look. "He sneaked onto my property, up to my house, carrying a deer rifle, and when I yell at him to leave he fires from cover, and that's *defending* himself?"

He didn't know why he was giving her a hard time, except for the edginess that had him as prickly as a cactus. "You're right," he said abruptly.

"Well, thank you so much."

He ignored the sarcasm. "I need to take a statement."

"I'm not going to press charges."

She couldn't have picked anything to say more likely to rile him. In his opinion, a good deal of additional harm was done because people declined to bring charges against criminal actions. Whatever their reasoning, they didn't want to "cause trouble," or they wanted to give the perp "another chance." In his experience all they were doing was letting a criminal go free to commit another crime. There were circumstances that called for a little mercy, but this wasn't one of them. Thaniel Vargas wasn't a teenager caught on his first misdemean-

or; he was a thug who had intended serious harm to another person.

"I beg your pardon?" He said it softly, reining in his inclination to roar, giving her a chance to re-think the situation. When he'd been a sergeant in the Army, enlisted men had immediately recognized that softness for the danger sign it was.

Either Delilah Jones wasn't as attuned to his mood as his men had been, or she wasn't impressed by his authority. Whatever the reason, she shrugged. "There's no point in it."

"No point?"

She started to say something, then stopped and gave a slight shake of her head. "It doesn't matter," she said, as if to herself. She bit her lip. He had the impression she was arguing with herself. She sighed. "Sit down, Sheriff Brody. You'll feel better after you've had something to eat."

He didn't want to sit down, he just wanted to get out of here. If she wasn't going to press charges, fine. He didn't agree, but the decision was hers. There was no reason for him to stay a minute longer.

But she was moving quietly and efficiently around the old-timey kitchen, slicing what looked like homemade bread, then thick slices from a ham, and a big chunk of cheese. She dipped a glass of water from a bucket, and placed the simple meal on the table.

Jackson watched her with narrowed eyes. Despite himself, he admired the deft, feminine way she did things, without fuss or bother. She made herself a sandwich too, though not as thick as his, and minus the cheese. She sat down across from the place she had set for him, and lifted her eyebrows in question at his hesitancy.

The sight of that sandwich made his mouth water. He was so hungry his stomach was churning. That was why he removed the Kevlar vest and set the shotgun aside, then sat down and put his boots under her table. Without a word they both began to eat.

The ham was succulent, the cheese mellow. He finished the sandwich before she had taken more than a few bites of hers. She got up and began making another one for him. "No, one was plenty—" he lied, not wanting to put her to any more trouble, not wanting to stay any longer.

"I should have thought," she said, her voice low. "I'm not used to feeding a big man like you. Pops was a skinny little thing; he didn't eat much more than I do."

In thirty seconds another thick sandwich was set down in front of him. She sat down again and picked up her own sandwich.

He ate more slowly this time, savoring the tastes. As he chewed, he took stock of his surroundings. Something about this house bothered him, and now he realized what it was: the silence. There was no refrigerator humming, no television squawking in the background, no water heater thumping and hissing.

He looked around. There was no refrigerator, period. No lamps. No overhead lights. She had dipped the water from a bucket. He looked at the sink; there were no faucets. The evidence was all there, but he still asked, "You don't have electricity?" because it was so unbelievable that she didn't.

"No."

"No phone, no way of calling for help if you need it?"

"No. I've never needed help."

"Until today."

"I could have handled Thaniel. He's been trying to bully me since grade school."

"Has he ever come after you with a gun before?"

"Not that I remember, but then I don't pay much attention to him."

She was maddening. He wanted to shake her, wanted to put his hands on those bare arms and shake her until her teeth rattled. "You're lucky you weren't raped and murdered," he snapped.

"It wasn't luck," she corrected. "It was preparation."

Despite himself, he was interested. "What sort of preparation?"

She leaned back in her chair, looking around at the silent house. It struck Jackson that she was very comfortable here, alone in the woods, without any of the modern conveniences everyone else thought they had to have. "To begin with, this is my home. I know every inch of the woods, every weed bed in the river. If I had to hide, Thaniel would never find me."

Watching her closely, Jackson saw the secret smile lurking in her green eyes and he knew, as sure as he knew his own name, that she doubted she would ever be reduced to hiding. "What about the other stuff?" he asked, keeping his tone casual.

She gave him a slow smile, and he got the feeling she was pleased with his astuteness. "Oh, just a few little things that give me advance warning. There's nothing lethal out there, unless you step on a water moccasin or fall in the water and drown."

He stared at her mouth, and felt a little jolt, like another kick of adrenaline. Despite the coolness of the house he broke out in a light sweat. God almighty, he hoped she didn't smile again. Her smile was sleepy and sexy, womanly, the kind of smile a woman gave a man after they had made love, lying drowsy on tangled sheets while the rain beat down outside and there were only the two of them, cocooned in their private world.

The sexual awareness wasn't welcome. He had to be careful in situations like this. He was a man in a position of authority, alone with a woman to whose house he had gone in an official capacity. This wasn't the time or the place to come on to her.

Silence had fallen again, silence in which they faced each other across the table. She took a deep breath, and the inhalation lifted her breasts against the thin cotton of her blouse. Her nipples were plainly outlined, hard and erect, the darkness of the aureolas faintly visible where they pressed against the fabric. Was she cold, or aroused?

The skin on her arms was smooth; no chill bumps.

"I'd better go," he said, fighting the sudden thickness in his throat, and in his pants. "Thank you for the sandwiches. I was starving."

She looked both relieved and reluctant. "You're welcome. You had that hungry look, so I—" She stopped, and waved a dismissive hand. "Never mind. I was glad to have the company. And you're right about going; if I'm not mistaken, I heard thunder just a minute ago." She got up and gathered their glasses, taking them to the sink.

He got up, too. There was something about her unfinished sentence that pulled at him. He should have let it go, should have said good-bye and got into the boat and left. He hadn't heard any thunder, though his hearing was pretty good, but that was as good an excuse as any to get the hell out of there. He knew it, and still he said, "So you—what?"

Her gaze slid away from him, as if she were embarrassed. "So I . . . thought you must have missed lunch."

How would she know that? Why would she even think it? He didn't normally miss a meal, and how in hell would she know if he looked hungry or not, when she had never seen him before today? For all she knew, ill-tempered was his normal expression.

Witch. The word whispered in his mind, even though he knew it was nonsense. Even if he believed in witchcraft, which he didn't, from what he'd read it had nothing to do with telling whether or not a man had missed lunch. She had noticed he was grouchy, and attributed it to an empty stomach. He didn't quite follow the reasoning, but he'd often seen his mother ply his father with food to gentle him out of a bad mood. It was a woman thing, not a witch thing.

"Meow."

He almost jumped a foot in the air. Now was *not* the time to find out she had a cat.

"There you are," she crooned, looking down at his feet. He looked down too, and saw a huge, fluffy white cat with black ears and a black tail, rubbing against his right boot.

"Poor kitty," she said, still crooning, and leaned down to pick up the creature, holding it in her arms as if it were a baby. It lay perfectly relaxed, belly up, eyes half-closed in a beatific expression as she rubbed its chest. "Did the noise scare you? The bad man's gone, and he won't bother us again, I promise." She looked up at Jackson. "Eleanor's pregnant. The kittens are due any time now, I think. She showed up about a week ago, but she's obviously tame and has had good care, so I guess someone just drove into the country and put her out, rather than take care of a litter."

The cat looked like a feline Buddha, fat and content. Familiars were supposed to be black, weren't they, or would any cat do, even fat white pregnant ones?

He couldn't resist reaching out and stroking that fat, round belly. The cat's eyes completely closed and she began purring so loudly she sounded like a motor idling.

Delilah smiled. "Careful, or you'll have a slave for life. Maybe you'd like to take her with you?"

"No, thanks," he said drily. "My mother might like a kitten, though. Her old tom died last year and she doesn't have a pet now."

"Check back in six or seven weeks, then."

That wasn't exactly an invitation to come calling any time soon, he thought. He picked up the shotgun and vest. "I'll be on my way, Miss Jones. Thanks again for the sandwiches."

"Lilah."

"What?"

"Please call me Lilah. All my friends do." She gave him a distinctly warning look. "*Not* Delilah, please."

He chuckled. "Message received. I guess you got teased about it in school?"

"You have no idea," she said feelingly.

"My name's Jackson."

"I know." She smiled. "I voted for you. Jackson's a nice Texas-sounding name."

"I'm a nice Texas guy."

She made a noncommital sound, as if she didn't agree with him but didn't want to come right out and say so. He grinned as he turned to the door. Meeting Delilah Jones had been interesting. He didn't know if it was good, but it was definitely interesting. The blue moon mojo was at full strength today. When things settled down and he had time to think things over, when he could be entirely rational about the weirdness and come up with a logical explanation, maybe he'd come back to visit—and not in any official capacity.

"Use the front door," she said. "It's closer."

He followed her through the small house. From what he could tell there were only four rooms: the kitchen and living room on one side, and each of those had another room opening off it. He figured the other two rooms were bedrooms. The living room was simply furnished with a couch and a rocking chair, arranged around a rag rug spread in front of the stone fireplace. Oil lamps sat on the mantle and on the pair of small tables set beside the couch and chair. In one corner was a treadle sewing machine. A handmade quilt hung on one of the walls, a brightly colored scene of trees and water that must have taken forever to do. On another wall a bookcase, also handmade from the looks of it, stretched from floor to ceiling, and was packed with books, both hardback and paper.

The whole house made him feel as if he had stepped back a century, or at least half of one. The only modern appliance he saw was a battery-operated weather radio, sitting beside one of the oil lamps on the mantle. He was glad she had it; both tornadoes and hurricanes were possible in this area.

He stepped out on the porch, Lilah right behind him, still holding the cat. He stopped dead still, staring at the dock. "The son of a bitch," he said softly.

"What?" She pushed at his shoulder, and he realized he was blocking her view.

"The boats are gone," he said, stepping aside so she could see.

She stared at the empty dock, too, her green eyes wide with dismay. Her flat bottom was gone, as well as Jerry Watkins's bass boat.

"He must have doubled back and cut the boats loose while we were eating. They can't have drifted far. If I walk along the bank, I'll probably find them."

"My boat had oars in it," she said. "I always have them in case I have motor trouble. He didn't have to cut them loose, he could have rowed mine out, and towed yours. That would save him the trouble of hiking back to his boat, and once he got to his boat he'd probably let the current take them. I figure they're at least a mile downstream by now, maybe more. That's if he doesn't decide to sink them."

"I'll call in—" he began, the notion so automatic that the words were out before he realized he didn't have his radio. He didn't have his cell phone. They were both in the Cherokee, which Charlotte Watkins had driven home. And Lilah Jones didn't have a phone.

He looked down at her. "I don't suppose you have a short-wave radio?"

"Afraid not." She was staring grimly at the river down which her boat had vanished, as if she could will it back. "You're stuck here. We both are."

"Not for long. The dispatcher—"

"Jo?"

"Jo." He wondered how well she knew Jo. Jo hadn't talked as if they were anything more than distant acquaintances, but Lilah not only knew who his dispatcher was, she had called her Jo instead of Jolene, which was her given name. "She knows where I am, and she was supposed to send backup as soon as some was available. A deputy should be along any time."

"Not unless he's already on his way," she said. "Look." She pointed to the southwest.

Jackson looked, and swore under his breath. A huge

purplish black thunderhead had filled the late afternoon sky. He could feel its breath now in the freshening wind that fanned him, hear its voice in the sullen bass rumble of thunder as it marched toward them.

"A thunderstorm probably won't last long." At least he hoped it wouldn't. The way things were going today, the storm's forward progress would stop just as it was on top of them.

She was staring worriedly at the cloud. "I think I'd better turn on the weather radio," she said, and went back inside, Eleanor cradled in her arms.

Jackson gave the empty river another frustrated glance. The air felt charged with electricity, raising the hair on his arms. The blade of lightning slashed down, flickering and flashing, and thunder rumbled again.

He was stuck here for at least a few hours, and maybe all night. If he had to be stuck anywhere, why couldn't it be in his own home? There was always a rash of accidents on a stormy night, and the deputies would need him.

Instead he would be here, in a house in the back of nowhere, keeping company with a witch and her pregnant cat.

Chapter 4

LILAH PUT ELEANOR ON THE FLOOR AND TURNED ON the weather radio, then went into her bedroom, which opened off the living room, and pulled down the side window. The front window was protected by the wide porch, so rain wasn't likely to come in there. With an ear cocked toward the radio, she then did the same in the back bedroom. She knew that Sheriff Brody had come in from the porch, but she deliberately ignored him, doing what needed to be done. He was entirely too big for her small house, too stern, too authoritative, too . . . too *male.*

He disrupted her peaceful life far more than Thaniel Vargas had ever dreamed of doing. What on earth had Jo been thinking, sending him out here? But of course Jo didn't know, and she had, rightly, been worried about Thaniel.

Well, poor Thaniel wouldn't be bothering her again, and there was nothing she could do about it. If he hadn't run she might have—well, whether or not she could have helped him was a moot point, because it was too late now. Still, regret filled her. Whatever Thaniel's faults—and they were many—she didn't wish him any harm. And though she would have tried to help if, if he hadn't run away, years of painful experience had taught her there was very little she could do to alter fate.

That was why the sheriff filled her with such panic. She had known, the moment she saw him, that he was fated to destroy her safe, comfortable, familiar life. She wanted to get as far away from him as she could, she wanted to push him out of her house and lock the door, she wanted . . . she wanted to walk into his arms and rest her head on a broad shoulder, let him hold her and kiss her and do anything else he wanted to her.

In all her life she'd never met a male, boy or man, who elicited even the slightest sexual response on her part. She had always felt isolated from the rest of the world, forever alone because of what she was. The thought of spending her life alone hadn't bothered her; quite the opposite. She enjoyed her solitude, her life, her sense of completion within herself. So many people never achieved wholeness, and spent their entire lives searching for someone or something to make them whole, never realizing that the answer was within themselves. She liked her own company, she trusted her own decisions, and she enjoyed the work she did. There was nothing—*nothing*—in her life that she wanted changed.

But Jackson Brody changed everything, whether she wanted him to or not.

It wasn't just his aura that attracted her, though it was so rich she was almost spellbound by it. All his colors were clear: the dark red of sensuality, the blue of calm, the turquoise of a dynamic personality, the orange of power, with fluctuating spikes of spiritual purple and yellow, healing green. Nothing about him was murky. He was a straightforward, confident, healthy man.

What had so stunned her, however, was the sudden flash of precognition. She didn't have them often; her particular talent was her ability to see auras. But sometimes she had lightning bursts of insight and knowledge, and she had never been wrong. Not once. Just as she had looked at Thaniel and known he would soon die, when she first focused on Jackson Brody the wave of precognition had been so strong she had almost slumped to her knees. This man would be her lover. This man would be her love, the only one of her life.

She didn't *want* a lover! She didn't want a man hanging around, getting in her way, interfering with her business. He would; she knew he would. He struck her as impatient, used to giving orders, slightly domineering, and, oh my, sexy as all get out. He certainly wouldn't want to live out here, without any of the modern conveniences to which he was accustomed, while she much preferred her uncluttered life. She *felt* better without hustle and bustle, without electrical machines incessantly humming in the background. Nevertheless, he would undoubtedly expect her to move to town, or at least to someplace less isolated and more accessible.

Once he realized she couldn't be relocated, he would give in, but with bad grace. He'd argue that he wouldn't be able to see her as often as he could if she lived closer. He would visit whenever it was convenient for him, and expect her to drop whatever she was doing whenever he pulled his boat up to the dock. In short, he would be very inconvenient for her, and there wasn't a damn thing she could do about it. For all the success she'd had in evading or altering fate, she might as well strip off her clothes right now and lead him into the bedroom.

That was another worry. She was rather short on experience in the bedroom department. That hadn't been a bother before, because she hadn't felt even an inkling of desire to get that experience. Now she did. Just looking at him made her feel warm and sort of breathless; her breasts tingled, and she had to press her thighs together to contain the hot ache between her legs. So this was lust. She had wondered, and now she knew. No wonder people acted like fools when they were afflicted with it.

If Thaniel hadn't stolen the boats, the sheriff would have already been gone, and she likely wouldn't have seen him again for quite a while, if ever. She would have gone about her quiet, very satisfying life. But she should have expected that trick with the boats; how else could Fate have arranged for Jackson to stay here? And of course a storm was coming up, preventing any of his deputies from arriving. All of it was inevitable. No matter how inconceivable her visions, almost immediately there would set in motion a train of events that brought about the conclusion she had foreseen.

Not for the first time, she wished she wasn't different. She wished she didn't know things were going to happen before they did; that was asking a lot of a person. She couldn't regret seeing auras, though; her life would feel colorless and less interesting if she no longer saw them. She didn't have to speak to someone to know how he or she was feeling; she could *see* when someone was happy, or angry, or feeling ill. She could see bad intentions, dishonesty, meanness, but she could also see joy, and love, and goodness.

"Is something wrong?"

He was standing right behind her, and the sharpness of his tone told her she had been standing in one place, staring at nothing, for quite a while. Getting lost in her thoughts was no big deal when she was alone, but probably looked strange to others. She blinked, pulling herself back to reality. "Sorry," she said, not turning to face him. "I was daydreaming."

"Daydreaming?" He sounded disbelieving, and she didn't blame him. A man had tried to kill her less than an hour ago, they were stranded, and a whopper of a storm was bearing down on them; that should be enough to keep her thoughts grounded. She should have said she was thinking, instead of daydreaming; at least that sounded productive.

"Never mind. Have there been any weather bulletins or warnings on the radio?"

"Severe thunderstorm warning until ten tonight. High winds, damaging hail."

Hours. They would be alone together for hours. He would probably be here until morning. What was she supposed to do with him, this man she was going to love but didn't yet? She had just met him, she knew nothing about him on a personal level. She was attracted to him, yes, but love? Not likely. Not yet, anyway.

Fresh, rain-fragrant wind gusted through the screen door. "Here it comes," he said, and she turned her head to watch sheets of rain sweeping upriver toward the house. Lightning speared straight downward, and a blast of thunder rattled the windows.

Eleanor meowed, and sought shelter in the cardboard box which Lilah had lined with old towels as a bed for the cat.

Jackson prowled restlessly around the small room. Lilah looked at him in exasperation, wondering if he ever just went with the flow. It was irritating to him that he couldn't affect the weather somehow, either postponing the storm or sending it speeding off, so one of his deputies could risk getting upriver to him.

She gave a mental shrug. Let him fret; she had work to do.

The first sheet of rain hit the house, drumming down on the tin roof. The late afternoon sunlight was almost completely blotted out, darkening the rooms. She moved through the gloom to the oil lamps set on the mantel, her hand setting surely on the match box. The rasp of the match was unheard in the din of rain, but he turned at the sudden small bloom of light and watched as she lifted the globes of the lamps and touched the match to the wicks, then replaced the globes. She blew out the match and tossed it into the fireplace.

Without a word she went into the kitchen and duplicated the chore, though there were four oil lamps there because she liked more light when she was working. The fire in the stove had been banked; she opened the door, stirred the hot coals, and added more wood.

"What are you doing?" he asked from the doorway.

Mentally she rolled her eyes. "Cooking." Maybe he'd never seen the process before.

"But we just ate."

"So we did, but those sandwiches won't hold you for

long, if I'm any judge." She eyed him, measuring him against the door frame. A little over six feet tall, she guessed, and at least two hundred pounds. He looked muscled, given the way his shoulders filled out his shirt, so he might weigh more. This man would eat a lot.

He came on into the room and settled at the table, turning the chair around so he faced her, his long legs stretched out and crossed at the ankle. His fingers drummed on the table. "This irritates the hell out of me," he confessed.

Her tone was dry. "I noticed." She dipped some water into the wash bowl and washed her hands.

"Usually I can do *something*. Usually, in bad weather, I *have* to do something, whether it's working a wreck or dragging people off of flooded roads. I need to be out there now, because my deputies will have their hands full."

So that was the cause of his restlessness and irritability; he knew his help was needed, but he couldn't leave here. She liked his sense of responsibility.

He watched in silence then as she prepared her biscuit pan, spraying it with nonstick spray. She got her mixing bowl and scooped some flour into it, added shortening and buttermilk, and plunged her hands into the bowl.

"I haven't seen anyone do that in years." He smiled as he kept his eyes on her hands, deftly mixing and kneading. "My grandmother used to, but I can't remember ever seeing my mother make biscuits by hand."

"I don't have a refrigerator," she said practically. "Frozen biscuits are out."

"Don't you want to have things like refrigerators and electric stoves? Doesn't it bother you, not having electricity?"

"Why should it? I don't depend on a wire for heat and light. If I had electricity, the power might be off right now and I wouldn't be able to cook."

He rubbed his jaw, brow furrowed as he thought. She liked the sight, she mused, eying him as she continued to knead. His brows were straight and dark, nicely shaped. Everything about him was nicely shaped. She bet all the single women in town, and a few of the married ones, were hot for him. Short dark hair, bright blue eyes, strong jaw, soft lips—she didn't know how she knew his lips were soft, but she did. Oh, yeah, they were hot for him. She was a bit warm herself.

She thought of walking over to him and straddling his lap, and an instantaneous flush swept over her entire body. Warm, my foot; she thought she might break out in a sweat any minute now.

"Running a gas line would be even harder than running power lines," he mused, his mind still on the issue of modern conveniences. "I guess you could get a propane tank, but filling it would be a bitch, since there aren't any roads out here."

"The wood stove suits me fine. It's only a few years old, so it's very efficient. It heats the whole house, and it's easy to regulate." She began pinching off balls of dough and rolling them between her hands, shaping them into biscuits and placing them in the pan. If she kept her eyes on the dough, instead of him, the hot feeling cooled down somewhat.

"Where do you get your wood?"

She couldn't help it. She had to look at him, her expression incredulous. "I cut it myself." Where did he think she got it? Maybe he thought the wood fairies chopped it and piled it up for her.

To her surprise, he surged up out of the chair, looming over her with a scowl. "Chopping wood is too hard for you."

"Gee, I'm glad you told me, otherwise I'd have kept doing it and not known any better." She edged away from him, turning to the sink to wash the dough from her hands.

"I didn't mean you couldn't do it, I meant you shouldn't have to," he growled. His voice was right behind her. *He* was right behind her. Without warning, he reached around her and wrapped his fingers around her right wrist. His hand completely engulfed hers. "Look at that. My wrist is twice as thick as yours. You may be strong, for your size, but you can't tell me it isn't a struggle for you to chop wood."

"I manage." She wished he hadn't touched her. She wished he wasn't standing so close that she could feel the heat from his body, smell the hot man smell of him.

"And it's dangerous. What if the ax slips, or the saw, or whatever you use? You're out here alone, a long way from medical help."

"A lot of things are dangerous." She struggled to keep her voice practical, and even. "But people do what they have to do, and I have to have wood." Why hadn't he released her hand? Why hadn't she pulled it away herself? She could; he wasn't holding her tightly. But she liked the feel of his hand wrapped around hers, liked the warmth and strength, the roughness of the calluses on his palm.

"I'll chop it for you," he said abruptly.

"What!" She almost turned around; common sense stopped her at the last minute. If she turned around, she would be face to face, belly to belly, with him. She didn't dare. She swallowed. "You can't chop my wood."

"Why not?"

"Because—" Because, why? "Because you won't be here."

"I'm here now." He paused, and his tone dropped lower. "I can be again."

She went still. The only sound was the storm, the boom of thunder and wind lashing through the trees, the rain pounding down on the roof. Or maybe it was her heart, pounding against her rib cage.

"I have to be careful here," he said quietly. "I'm acting as a man, not a sheriff. If you tell me no, I'll go back to the table and sit down. I'll keep my distance from you for the rest of the night, and I won't bother you again. But if you don't tell me no, I'm going to kiss you."

Lilah inhaled, fighting for oxygen. She couldn't say a word, couldn't think of anything to say even if she had the air. She was feeling hot again, and weak, as if she might collapse against him.

"I'll take that as a yes," he said, and turned her into his arms.

Chapter 5

HIS LIPS WERE SOFT, JUST THE WAY SHE'D KNOWN THEY would be. And he was gentle, rather than bruising her lips by pressing too hard. He didn't try to overwhelm her with a sudden display of passion. He simply kissed her, taking his time about it, tasting her and learning the shape and texture of her own lips. The leisurely pace was more seductive than anything else he could have done.

She sighed, a low hum of pleasure, and let herself relax against him. He gathered her up, wrapping his arms around her and lifting her onto her toes so that they fit together more intimately. The full press of his body against her made her catch her breath, and that now-familiar wave of heat swept over her again. She looped her arms around his neck, pressing even closer, shivering a little as his tongue moved slowly into her mouth, giving her time to pull away if she didn't want such a deep kiss. She did, more than she had ever thought she would want a man's kiss.

Her heart thudded wildly in her chest. Pleasure was a siren, luring her to experience more, to take everything he could give her. His erection was a hard ridge in his pants; she wanted to rub herself against it, open herself to it. Knowing herself to be on the verge of losing control, she forced herself to pull away from the slow, intoxicating kisses, burying her face instead in the warm column of his throat.

He wasn't unaffected. His pulse hammered through his veins; she felt it, there in his neck, just where her lips rested. His lungs pumped, dragging in air. His skin felt hot and damp, and he moved restlessly, as if he wanted to grind his hips against her.

He didn't say anything, for which she was grateful. Innate caution told her to slow down, while instinct screamed at her, urging her to mate with him; it was fated, anyway, so why wait? What would waiting accomplish? The outcome was the same, no matter the timetable. Torn between the two, she hesitated, not quite willing yet to take such a large step no matter what the fates said.

"This is scary," she muttered against his throat.

"No joke." He buried his face against her hair. "This must be what it feels like to get hit by that famous ton of bricks."

The knowledge that he was as rattled as she wasn't very reassuring, because she would have liked for one of them to be in control.

"We don't know each other." Neither did she know with whom she was arguing, him or herself. All she knew was that, for one of the few times in her life, she wasn't certain of herself. She didn't like the feeling. One of the foundation bricks of her life, her very self, was her knowledge of herself and other people; *not* to know was if that foundation was being shaken.

"We'll work on that." His lips brushed her temple. "We don't have to rush into anything."

But when he *did* know her, would he still want her? She worried at that, feeling, not for the first time, the weight of her differentness. She came with so much excess baggage that a lot of men would think she was more trouble than she was worth.

That thought gave her the strength to push gently at his shoulders. He released her immediately, stepping back. Lilah took a deep breath and pushed her hair out of her face, trying not to look at him, but the clear, dark red of passion emanating from him was almost impossible to ignore. "I'd better get those biscuits in the oven," she said, stepping around him. "Just sit down out of my way and I'll have supper ready in a jiffy."

"I'll stand, thank you," he said wryly.

She couldn't help it; she had to look, meeting his rueful blue gaze in perfect understanding. The dark red of his aura was still glowing hot and clear, especially in the groin area, though more blue was beginning to show through in the aura around his head.

But he did move out of her way, leaning against the wall by the door. She put the biscuits into the oven and opened a big can of beef stew, dumping the contents into a pot and placing that on top of the stove. The simple meal would have to be enough, because she wasn't about to go out into the storm to chase down a chicken for supper. The biscuits could cool, and the beef stew could simmer until he got hungry again.

He was watching her. She felt his gaze, his utter male focus on her. Being female wasn't something to which she gave a great deal of thought, but under that intent study she was suddenly, acutely aware of her body, of the way her breasts lifted with each breath, of the folds between her legs where he would enter. She didn't have to look down to know her nipples were tightly beaded, or at the front of his pants to know his erection hadn't yet subsided.

His unabashed arousal did more to turn her on than any sweet nothing he could have whispered. Something had to be done to lessen the sensual tension, or she would shortly find herself on her back. She cleared her throat, mentally searching for a neutral topic.

"How did a nice Texas boy end up in Alabama?" She already knew; Jo had told her. But it was the only thing she could think of, and at least the question would get him to talking.

"My mother was from Dothan."

No further explanation followed. Deciding he needed

more prodding, Lilah said, "Why did she move to Texas?"

"She met my dad. He was from west Texas. Mom and a couple of friends from college were driving to California after graduation, and they had car trouble. My dad was a deputy then, and he stopped to help them. Mom never did get to California."

That was better; he was talking. She breathed an inner sigh of relief. "Why did she come back to Alabama, then?"

"Dad died a few years ago." He settled his shoulders more comfortably against the wall. "West Texas isn't for everyone; it can be hot as hell, and pretty damn empty. She never complained while Dad was alive, but after he died, the loneliness got to her. She wanted to move back to Alabama, close to her sister and her friends from college."

"So you came with her?"

"She's my mother," he said simply. "I can be in law enforcement here as easily as I could in Texas. Mom and I don't live together, haven't since I was eighteen and went away to college, but she knows I'm nearby if she needs anything."

"It didn't bother you at all to leave Texas?" She couldn't imagine such a thing. She loved her home, knew it as intimately as she knew herself. She loved the scent of the river in the early mornings, the way it turned gold when the dawn light struck it, she loved the dramatic weather that produced violent thunderstorms and torrents of rain, the hot, humid days when even the birds seemed lethargic, and the gray winter days when a fire in the fireplace and a cup of hot soup were the best she could ask of life.

He shrugged. "Home is family, not a place. I've got some aunts and uncles in Texas, a whole herd of cousins, but no one as close to me as Mom. I can always visit Texas if I feel the need."

He loved his mother, and was unabashed about it. Lilah swallowed, hard. Her own mother had died when she was five, but she cherished the few memories she had of the woman who had been the center of life in the isolated little house.

"What about you?" he asked. "Are you from here originally?"

"I was born in this house. I've lived here all my life."

He gave her a quizzical look, and she knew what he was thinking. Most babies were born in a hospital, and had been for the last fifty years. She was obviously younger than that, but too old to have been part of the birth-at-home fashion that was making a comeback in some sections.

"Didn't your daddy have time to get her to the hospital?"

"She didn't want a hospital." Was now the time to explain that her mother had been a folk healer, like her? That she too had seen the bursts of color that surrounded people, and taught her daughter what they meant, how to read them? That she had known everything would be all right, and thus hadn't seen any purpose in spending their hard-earned money on a hospital and doctor she didn't need?

"That was one tough lady," he said, shaking his head. A small smile curved his mouth. "I delivered a baby when I was a rookie. Scared the hell out of me, and the mother wasn't too happy, either. But we got through it, and they were both okay." The smile turned into a grin. "My bedside manner must have been a tad off, though; she *didn't* name the baby after me. As I recall, her exact words were: 'No offense, but I never want to see you again for the rest of my life.'"

Lilah threw back her head on a gusty laugh. She could just see a young, inexperienced rookie deputy, sweating and panicky, delivering a baby. "What happened? Did the baby come early, or just fast?"

"Neither. West Texas does get snow, and that was one of the times. The roads were in really bad shape. She and her husband were on the way to the hospital, but their car slid off the road into a drift not a mile from their house, so they walked back home and called for help. I was in the area, and I had a four-wheel drive, but by the time I got to their house the weather was even worse, so bad I wouldn't risk the drive." He rubbed his ear. "She cussed me, called me every name I'd ever heard before, and a few that I hadn't. She wanted something for the pain, and I was the one keeping her from getting it, so she made sure I suffered right along with her."

His grin invited her to laugh at the image his words conjured. Lilah snickered as she checked on the biscuits. "What about her husband?"

"Useless. Every time he came around he got an even worse cussing than I did, so he stayed out of sight. I'm telling you, that was one unhappy lady."

"How long did her labor last?"

"Nineteen hours and twenty-four minutes," he promptly replied. "The longest nineteen hours and twenty-four minutes in the history of the world, according to her. She swore she'd been in labor at least three days."

Under the amusement in his tone was a thread of . . . joy. She tilted her head, wondering if she read him correctly. "You liked it." The words weren't quite a question.

He laughed. "Yeah, I did. It was exciting, and funny, and amazing as hell. I've seen puppies and calves and foals being born, but I've never felt anything like when that baby slid into my hands. By the way, it was a girl. Jackson just didn't seem to suit her."

His aura was glowing now with more green in the mixture, shot through with joyful yellow. Lilah no longer had to wonder when she would fall in love with him. She did in that moment, something inside her melting, growing hotter. She knew her own aura would be showing pink, and she blushed, even though she knew he couldn't see it.

She felt trembly, and had to sit down. This was momentous. She'd never thought she would love the way others did, not romantically. She loved many people and many things, but not like this. Always, mixed in with her feelings, was the knowledge that she was set apart from them, a caretaker rather than a partner. Even with Pops she'd been the rock on which he leaned. But Jackson was a strong man, both mentally and physically. He didn't need anyone to take care of him; rather, he did the caring.

If she hadn't been able to see his aura, she would eventually have loved him anyway. But she could see it, and she knew the essence of the man. That, and her own precognitive recognition of him as her mate, destroyed her sense of caution. She wanted to throw herself into his arms and let him do whatever he wanted. Instead she got up and checked the biscuits.

She stood there with the oven door open, letting heat escape, staring blindly at the biscuits. Jackson came up behind her. "Perfect," he said with approval.

She blinked. The biscuits were a golden brown, perfectly risen. She had a good hand with biscuits, or so Pops had always said. She took a deep breath, and, using a dish cloth, took the hot pan out of the oven and set it on a cooling rack.

"Why does Vargas think you're a witch?"

That brought her to earth with a thud. The change in his tone was subtle, but there: He was the sheriff, and he wanted to know if anyone in his county was practicing witchcraft.

"Several reasons, I suppose." She turned to face him, her expression cool and unreadable. "I live alone out in the woods, I seldom go into town, I don't socialize. The witch rumor started when I was in fourth grade, I think."

"Fourth grade, huh?" He leaned against the cabinet, blue gaze sharp on her face. "I guess he'd been watching too many *Bewitched* reruns."

She lifted one eyebrow and waited.

"So you don't cast spells, or dance naked in the moonlight, or anything like that?"

"I'm not a witch," she said plainly. "I've never cast a

spell, though I might dance naked in the moonlight, if the notion took me."

"Do tell." The gaze warmed, and moved slowly down her body. "Call me if you need a dancing partner."

"I'll do that."

He looked up, met her eyes, and as simply as that, there was no longer any need for caution.

"Are you hungry?" he asked, moving closer, stroking one finger up her bare arm.

"No."

"So the biscuits and beef stew can wait?"

"They can."

He took the dish cloth and set the pan of stew off the eye. "Will you go to bed with me, then, Lilah Jones?"

"I will."

Chapter 6

LILAH LIT THE LAMP IN HER BEDROOM AND TURNED IT low. The storm and heavy rain made the room as dark as night, lit briefly by the flashes of lightning. Jackson seemed to fill the small room, his shoulders throwing a huge shadow over the wall. His aura, visible even in the low light, pulsated with that deep, clear red again, the color of passion and sensuality.

He began unbuttoning his shirt, and she turned back the bedcovers, neatly folding the quilt and plumping the pillows. Her bed looked small, she thought, though it was a double. It was certainly too small for him. Perhaps she should see about getting a larger one, though she wasn't certain how long he would use hers. That was the problem with the flashes of precognition; they told her facts, but not circumstances. She knew only that Jackson would be her lover, and her love. She had no idea if he would love her in return, if they would be together forever or only this one time.

"You look nervous." Despite the sharpness of his desire, which she could plainly see, his voice was quiet. His shirt was unbuttoned but he hadn't yet removed it. Instead he was watching her, his cop's eyes seeing too much.

"I am," she admitted.

"If you don't want to do this, just say so. No hard feelings—well, except for one place," he said wryly.

"I do want to do this. That's why I'm nervous." Looking him in the eye, she unfastened her shorts and let them drop, then began unbuttoning her shirt. "I've never been so . . . attracted to anyone before. I'm always cautious, but—" She shook her head. "I don't want to be cautious with you."

He shrugged the shirt off and let it drop to the floor. Lamplight gleamed on his shoulders, delineating the smooth, powerful muscles, and the broad chest shadowed with dark hair. Lilah inhaled deeply through her nose, feeling the warmth of arousal spread through her. She forgot what she was doing, just stood there looking at him, greedily drinking in the sight of her man undressing.

He sat down on the edge of the bed and leaned forward to pull off his boots. Now she could admire the deep furrow of his spine, the rippling muscles in his back. Her heartbeat picked up in speed, and she got even warmer.

The boots thunked on the wooden floor. He stood and unfastened his pants, let them drop, and pushed down his shorts. Totally naked, he stepped out of the circle of clothing and turned to face her.

Oh, my.

She must have said the words aloud, breathing them in hunger and lust and maybe even some bit of fear, because he laughed as he came to her, brushing aside her stalled hands and finishing the job of unbuttoning her shirt. He put his hands inside the shirt and smoothed them over her shoulders and down her arms, slipping the shirt off so easily she scarcely knew when it left. She wasn't paying attention to her clothing anyway, only to the jutting penis that brushed her belly when he moved.

She wrapped her hands around it, lightly stroking, exploring, delighting in the heat and hardness and textures, so different from her own body. Now it was he who sucked in a breath, his eyes closing as he stilled for a moment. Then he moved even closer, pushing his hands inside her panties and gripping the globes of her bottom as he pulled her to him. She had to release his penis and she made a sound of . . . disappointment? Impatience? Both. But there was reward in the pressure of his hard, hairy chest on her breasts, in the rasping sensation to her nipples. Her entire body seemed to go boneless, melting into him, curving to fit his contours.

His breathing was ragged. "Let's get you naked so I can look at you," he muttered, releasing her bottom long enough to push her panties down her thighs. She wiggled until they dropped to her feet, and his breathing caught on a groan.

"God! You're a natural born tease, aren't you?" He pulled her up on her toes, welding her to him.

"Am I?" She had never thought about teasing a man before, never wanted to; but if what she was doing was teasing him, then that was only fair, because she was driving herself crazy too. The feel of their bare bodies brushing together was so delicious she wanted to moan. She kept moving against him, rubbing her nipples against his chest and turning them into hard, aching peaks.

He stroked his hands over her bottom and back, his hands so hot and rough she wanted to purr. Then one hand went lower, curving under her bottom, and his fingers dipped between her legs. She gasped, arching into him as an almost electric sensation sparked through her. One finger explored deeper, slipping a little way into her. A soft, wild noise erupted from her throat, and she all but climbed him, one leg wrapping around him as she levered herself up so he could have better access.

Panting, she buried her face in his throat, clinging for dear life while she waited in agony for him to deepen the caress. Slowly, so slowly, that big finger pressed deeper and she rocked under the impact. That wild little noise sounded again, and her hips surged, trying to take more of his finger. Pleasure and tension coiled in her, tighter and tighter, until it was pain and something more, something beyond anything she had imagined.

"Not yet," he said urgently. "Don't come yet." He turned and half-fell with her onto the bed, cradling her against the full impact of his weight as he landed on top of her. With a twist of his hips he settled between her thighs, and his erection prodded at her folds, briefly seeking her entrance before finding it and pressing inward. Her entire body contracted, tightening around that thick intrusion, though she couldn't tell whether her body's reaction was in welcome or an effort to limit the depth of his penetration.

His hips recoiled, his buttocks tightened, and he pushed deeper, deeper, until her inner resistance was gone and in one long slide he was all the way inside her.

She would have screamed, but her lungs were compressed with shock and she could barely breathe, much less scream. Her vision blurred and darkened. She hadn't realized. . . . His penis felt almost unbearably hot inside her, burning and stretching her. She ached deep inside, where he was.

He lifted up on his elbows, panting, the expression in his blue eyes both incredulous and ferociously intent. "Lilah . . . God, I can't believe this—Are you a virgin?"

"Not now." Desperately she clutched his buttocks, her back arching as she tried to take him deeper. "Please. Oh, god, Jackson, please!" She bucked her hips at him, her head thrown back as she wrestled with the almost savage pleasure that held her on the edge of release. He was still hurting her, but her entire body was throbbing with a need that overrode any pain. She wanted him deep, she wanted him hard, she wanted him to pound into her and hurl her over that edge.

He gave in to her sensual imploring. "Shhh," he soothed, though his voice was rough with his own need. "Easy, darlin'. Let me help . . ." He reached between their bodies, his callused fingertips finding the bud of her clitoris and gently pinching it up. Again and again he squeezed it, catching it between two of his fingers, and with a sharp cry she imploded, her body twisting and heaving in the paroxysm of climax.

A harsh sound tore from his throat. He gripped her hips, his fingers digging into her buttocks, and thrust hard, driving into her so fiercely the bed thudded against the wall. He climaxed convulsively, grinding down on her for long seconds before collapsing, shaking, on top of her.

She wrapped her arms around his sweaty shoulders and held on tight, partly to comfort him in the aftermath and partly to anchor herself. She felt as if she would fly into a hundred pieces if she let him go. Tears burned her eyelids, though she didn't know why. Her heart still galloped in a mad race to nowhere and her thoughts swam, a kaleidoscope of impressions and wishes and disbelief.

She hadn't known making love would be so hot, so uncontrolled. She had expected something slow and sweet, building to ecstasy, not that headlong dash into the fire.

His heart pounded against her breast, gradually slowing, as did his breathing. His weight crushed her into the mattress. Her thighs were still spread to accommodate him, and he was still inside her, though smaller and softer now.

Now that the storm within was over, she became aware again of the storm without. Lightning cracked so close by that the thunder rattled the entire house, and rain drummed on the roof, but that was nothing compared to what had just gone on in her bed. Storms came and went, but her entire life had just been changed.

Finally he lifted his head. His dark hair was matted with sweat, his expression strained and empty, the expression of release. "Okay." His voice sounded rusty, as if his vocal cords didn't want to work. "When you said 'not now,' did you mean that you didn't want to talk, or that you had been a virgin until then, but now you weren't?"

She cleared her throat. "The second choice." Her own voice sounded rusty, too.

"Holy hell." He let his head drop again. "I never expected—Damn it, Lilah, that's something you should tell a man."

She moved her hands over his shoulders, closing her eyes in delight at the feel of his warm, sleek skin under her palms. "Things happened kind of fast. I didn't have a lot of time to consider the shoulds and should nots."

"There are no should nots, in this case."

"What would you have done differently, if you'd known?"

He considered that, and sighed against her shoulder. "Hell, probably nothing. There's no way in hell I would have stopped. But if I'd known, I'd have tried to slow things down, and given you more time."

"I couldn't have stood it," she said starkly. "Not one minute more."

"Yes you could. You will. And you'll like it."

If that was a threat, it failed miserably. A tingle of excitement shot through her, sending a spark of life into her exhausted muscles. She wiggled a little. "When?"

"God," he muttered. "Not right this minute. Give me an hour."

"Okay, an hour."

His head came up again and he gave her a long, level look. "Before we get carried away again, don't you think we need to talk about birth control? Specifically, our lack of it? I doubt you're on the pill, and I don't generally carry rubbers around with me."

"No, of course I'm not on the pill, but I won't get pregnant."

"You can't be sure."

"I just finished my period two days ago. We're safe."

"Famous last words."

She sighed. She *knew* she wouldn't get pregnant, though she didn't know how to explain to him how she knew. She wasn't certain, herself. It wasn't a flash of precognition, at least not like the usual flash. It was more a sense than a knowing, but there wasn't a pregnancy in her immediate future. Next month, maybe, but not now.

She sighed. "If you're so worried, then we won't do this again, all right?"

He regarded her for a minute, then grinned. "Some chances," he said, leaning down to kiss her, "are just meant to be taken."

Chapter 7

THEY HEARD THE OUTBOARD MOTOR NOT LONG AFTER dawn, when the sun had just turned the eastern sky a brilliant gold. The storms of the night had lasted longer than expected, until almost three o'clock in the morning, but now the morning sky was absolutely cloudless.

"Sounds like the cavalry is arriving," Lilah said, tilting her head to listen.

"Son of a bitch," Jackson said mildly. "I was hoping rescue would take a little longer." He took a sip of coffee. "Do I look like an enraged, frustrated sheriff who was left stranded by a turnip-brain two-bit thug, or a man who's had a night-long orgy and whose legs are as limp as noodles?"

She pretended to study him, then shook her head. "You could use some practice on the enraged and frustrated look."

"That's what I thought." Putting his cup down on the table, he stretched his arms over his head and gave her a lazy, contented grin. "Instead of arresting Thaniel, I may give him a commendation."

"What are you going to arrest him for?" she asked in surprise. "I told you I'm not pressing charges."

"Whether or not you do, he stole two boats, not just yours. What happens depends on what he's done with

Jerry Watkins's boat, and what Jerry wants to do about it. If Thaniel was smart, he left the boats at the launch ramp, but then again, if he was smart he wouldn't have taken them in the first place."

"If he left them out, the amount of rain we had last night would have sunk them," Lilah pointed out. "It takes a lot of rain to swamp a boat, but I think we had enough to do the job, don't you?"

"Probably." Getting up from the table, he walked into the living room and looked out the window. "Yep, it's the cavalry."

Lilah stood beside him and watched the boat carrying two deputies approach her small dock. The river was high and muddy after the night's storms, so high her dock lacked only a few inches being underwater. They carefully tied the boat to the post and stepped out, both wearing Kevlar vests and carrying shotguns. They cautiously looked around.

Jackson quickly bent and kissed her, his mouth warm and lingering. The look he gave her was full of regret. "I'll come back as soon as I can," he said, keeping his voice pitched low. "I doubt it'll be today, and whether or not I can make it tomorrow depends on how much damage the storms did, and if there are any power outages or cleanup to do."

"I'll be here," she said, her manner calm. She smiled. "I have no way of going anywhere, without my boat."

"I'll either get it back, or I'll make damn certain Thaniel buys you a new one," he promised, and kissed her again. Then he picked up his vest and shotgun, which he had placed by the front door in anticipation of his "rescue," and walked out on the front porch.

Both of the deputies visibly relaxed when they saw him. "You okay, Sheriff?" the older of the two called.

"I'm fine, Lowell. But Thaniel Vargas won't be when I get my hands on him. He stole both the boat I was using, and Miss Jones's boat. But he'll wait; how much damage was there last night?"

Lilah stepped out on the porch behind him, because it

would look strange if she didn't. "Good morning, Lowell." She nodded to the other deputy. "Alvin. I just made the sheriff some coffee; would y'all like a cup?" She saw Jackson's brows rise in surprise that she knew his deputies, but he didn't comment.

"No thanks, Lilah," Lowell answered. "We need to get on back. Thanks for offering, but I've drunk so much coffee since midnight I doubt I'll sleep for two days."

"The damage?" Jackson prompted, taking charge of the conversation again.

"Power was out over most of the county, but it's back on now all except for Pine Flats. A lot of trees went down, and there's roof damage to a bunch of houses, but only one actually went into a house, the LeCroy place out near Washington High School. Mrs. LeCroy was hurt pretty bad; she's in the hospital in Mobile."

"Any car wrecks?"

Lowell gave him a weary look. "More than you can count."

"Okay. Sorry I wasn't on hand to help."

"I'm just sorry it took us so long to get out here, but with the storms the way they were, only a fool would have gone out on the water."

"I didn't expect anybody to risk their lives coming after me. I was okay, just stranded."

"We weren't sure, what with Jo telling us she sent you here after Thaniel Vargas. But Thaniel seemed okay, not nervous or anything, and he played dumb, said he hadn't been up here and hadn't seen you."

"You saw him?" Jackson asked sharply.

"He helped us get a tree out of the highway. Anyway, we figured the storm had caught you. We didn't want to take any chances, since you could have run into some other kind of trouble out here, so we came looking."

Jackson shook his head. He never would have figured Thaniel capable of that much brass; maybe that thick-headed act was more of an act than fact. If so, he'd have to take Thaniel a lot more seriously than he had before.

Walking down to the dock, he handed the shotgun to Alvin and stepped into the boat. "Well, let's go to work," he said. He turned and raised his hand. "Thanks for feeding me, Miss Jones."

"You're welcome," she called, smiling as she hugged her arms against the early morning chill. She waved them good-bye, a wave both deputies returned, then went back into the house.

Jackson settled onto a boat seat. "Y'all seem to know Miss Jones pretty well," he said, driven by curiosity.

"Sure." Lowell got behind the wheel. "We went to school together."

It was such a prosaic answer that Jackson felt like smacking himself in the head. Of course she had attended school; she hadn't lived her entire life marooned upriver. He had a mental image of a small, solemn Lilah sitting in that little flat-bottom boat, clutching her schoolbooks, being ferried back and forth in all kinds of weather.

Because he wanted to know, he asked, "How did she get back and forth to school?"

"Boat," Alvin said. "Her daddy brought her. He'd take her to the Park ramp, closest to school. If the weather was good, he'd walk her the rest of the way. If it was raining, a teacher would meet them and give her a ride."

At least he wouldn't have to fret about that young Lilah being left alone at the boat docks, Jackson thought; her father had been concerned for her safety. Though why he would fret about something so long in the past was beyond him.

The trip down river was much more leisurely than his risky dash up it the day before. The swollen river was full of trash, making caution necessary. Jackson hoped he'd see two boats tied to the shore when they got to the ramp, but no such luck.

"I wonder what Thaniel did with Jerry Watkins's boat," he growled.

"No telling," Lowell said. "The damn fool probably just turned it loose. Jerry will be fit to be tied; he set a store by that boat."

At least Jerry Watkins would have insurance on his boat; Jackson very much doubted Lilah would have it on hers. How would she replace it? He gave his bank account a quick mental check; one way or the other, Lilah would have another boat—by tomorrow, if he couldn't find hers. He couldn't bear the thought of her being completely stranded out there, though she was so damn competent he could see her hiking into town if necessary, even though it had to be twenty, maybe thirty miles around. But what if she got sick, or injured herself. She chopped her own wood, for God's sake. He went cold at the thought of an ax buried in her foot.

She had become more important to him, faster than anyone he had ever known. Twenty-four hours ago he hadn't known she existed. Within two hours of meeting her, he'd been in bed with her, and he'd spent the most erotic, exciting night of his life in her arms. He had climaxed so many times he doubted he'd get a hard-on for days. Then he thought of Lilah, waiting for him, and a sudden pooling of heat in his groin told him he had miscalculated. He jerked his thoughts back to the day's work before he embarrassed himself.

The Watkins truck was still sitting where Charlotte had parked it, boat trailer still hitched to it. At least a tree hadn't come down on the truck during the storms; that would be the final insult to a good deed. He looked around; there were some small branches scattered around the parking area, but nothing substantial.

Lowell eased the boat into the bank and both Jackson and Alvin climbed out. While Alvin went to the truck to back the trailer into the water, Jackson surveyed the area. Yesterday he'd been in too much of a hurry to think about details, but now his cop's eye swept the launch ramp, not missing a thing. The parking area was surprisingly large, given how isolated and little-used the launch ramp was. But . . . was it little-used? The area was free of weeds, showing that there was a good bit of traffic. The sandy dirt showed evidence of a lot of different tire tracks, more than he expected. That was strange, given what Jo had said about the best fishing being down river.

Lowell and Alvin competently took the boat out of the water. They had come in two vehicles, one county car and then the truck pulling the boat, which Jackson assumed they had borrowed from the Rescue Squad. That made five vehicles he could count since yesterday afternoon: his, Thaniel's, Charlotte Watkins's, and now these two. The rain had destroyed all but the deepest tracks, but he could still make out at least three more sets of tracks besides the ones he knew about.

Now, why would there be so much river traffic up here? The fishing wasn't good, and right past Lilah's the river got too shallow for boat traffic. He tried to think of a logical explanation for the tracks. Being in law enforcement, his first thought was that maybe drug dealers were meeting here, but he discarded that idea. It was too open, and though Old Boggy Road wasn't the busiest road in the world, there was occasional traffic on it. As if to prove it, at that moment a farmer drove by in a pickup truck, and he craned his neck to see what was going on.

No, drug dealers would find a place where they were less likely to attract attention. So . . . who was coming here, and why?

He strolled over to Lowell and Alvin. "This little ramp gets a lot of use, doesn't it?"

"A fair amount," Lowell agreed.

"Why?"

They both gaped at him. "Why?" Alvin echoed.

"Yeah. Why does it get so much use? Only someone who doesn't know the river would come up here to fish."

To his surprise, both deputies shifted uncomfortably. Lowell cleared his throat. "I guess folks go to visit Lilah."

"Miss Jones?" Jackson clarified, wanting to make certain there wasn't another Lilah in the area.

Lowell nodded.

Looking around the area, Jackson said, "From all these tire ruts, I'd say she gets a lot of company." He tried to picture a steady stream of visitors to Lilah's isolated little house upriver, but just couldn't.

"Some," Lowell agreed. "A lot of women go to see her." He coughed. "And—uh, some men too, I guess."

"Why is that?" A variety of wild reasons ran through his mind. Marijuana? He couldn't see Lilah growing marijuana, but the place was certainly isolated enough. He didn't let himself seriously consider that. Women didn't go to backwoods women for abortions anymore, either, so that was out. Nothing illegal, for sure, because his deputies obviously knew about whatever was going on up there, and had done nothing to stop it. The only thing he could think of that made sense was so ridiculous he couldn't believe it.

"Don't tell me she really is a witch!" He could just see it now, boat after boat making its way upriver for spells and potions. She had denied the witch thing, said she didn't know anything about spells, but in his experience people lied all the time. He dealt with serial liars on a daily basis.

"Nothing like that," Alvin said hastily. "She's kind of an old-timey healer. You know, she makes poultices and stuff."

Poultices and stuff. Healer. Of course. It was so obvious, Jackson wondered that he hadn't seen it. Relief spread through him. His imagination had been running wild, a sick feeling congealing in his gut. He had just found her, a woman who appealed to him on every level, and he couldn't bear the thought of her being involved in something shifty. He didn't know where this thing between him and Lilah was going, but he intended to follow it to the end.

"It's how she makes her living," Lowell said. "People

buy herbs and things from her. A lot of folks go to her rather than a doctor, because she's so good at telling them what's wrong."

He wanted to grin. Instead he collected his vest and shotgun from the boat, and said, "Well, let's go round up Thaniel Vargas. Even if we get the boats back and Jerry Watkins doesn't press charges against him, I want to scare about ten years off the bastard's life."

Chapter 8

THANIEL VARGAS WAS NOWHERE TO BE FOUND. HE HAD gone to ground somewhere, Jackson figured, waiting for the trouble to blow over. Because things were still kind of busy in the county, with the continuing power outage in Pine Flats and cleaning up from the storm, Jackson couldn't devote a lot of time or manpower to finding him.

More than anything, he wanted to get back upriver to Lilah's house, but it just wasn't possible that day. Besides the problems from the storm, the blue moon craziness was still in full force. At traffic court that day, a woman totally lost it and tried to get out of paying a speeding ticket by holding the judge hostage. Why anyone in her right mind would want to trade a simple fine of fifty bucks for a felony charge was beyond Jackson. Getting the courthouse settled down took several hours out of his day, hours when he needed to be somewhere else.

He got home at midnight that night, tired and disgruntled and aching with frustration. He wanted Lilah. He *needed* Lilah, needed the simple serenity of her, the quietness of her home that was such a contrast to his hectic days. They had known each other for such a short period of time, he wasn't certain that they had anything more than a one-night stand, brought about as much by circumstance as by mutual attraction. But he had been her first lover, her only lover; Lilah wasn't the type of woman to have a one-night stand. For her, making love meant something. It had meant something to him too, something more than any of his other love affairs.

Lilah was special: honest, witty, with the bite of irony he enjoyed, and gutsy. She was also sexy as hell, with her well-toned, femininely muscled body and her cloud of curly hair that just begged to have his hands in it.

Though he was her first lover, she hadn't shrank from anything he wanted to do. She had met him halfway in everything, enjoying what he did to her as much as he enjoyed doing it, and returning the favor. He couldn't imagine such uncomplicated joy ever getting boring.

Until now, his house had suited him perfectly. It was an older house, with high ceilings and cranky plumbing, but he'd had the main bathroom completely redone, and the kitchen, not that he was much on cooking. It had just seemed like a smart thing to do. His bed was big enough for him, not like Lilah's too-short, too-narrow bed. They'd had to sleep double-decker, when they slept—not a big sacrifice. He'd liked having her sprawled on top of him, when he wasn't on top of her.

But now his house felt . . . empty. And noisy. He hadn't realized until now how much noise a refrigerator made, or a water heater. The central air system blotted out the night's sounds of crickets and the occasional chirp of a bird.

He wanted Lilah.

He took a cold shower instead, and crawled into his big, cold, empty bed, where he lay awake, muscles aching, eyes burning with fatigue, and thought of that first searing, electric moment when he pushed into Lilah's body. That got him so hard he groaned, and he tried not to think about sex at all. But then her breasts came to mind, and he remembered the way her nipples had peaked in his mouth when he sucked her, and how she had moaned and squirmed when he went down on her.

Sweat sheened his body, despite the air conditioning. Swearing, he got out of bed and took another cold shower. He finally got to sleep about two o'clock, only to dream erotic dreams and wake up needing, wanting, Lilah even more than before.

At eight twenty-one in the morning, Thaniel Vargas's body was found floating in the river. He was easily identified because his wallet was still stuffed in his jeans pocket, along with a can of chewing tobacco. If it hadn't been for his wallet, his own mother would have been hard pressed to identify him, because he'd been shot in the face with a shotgun.

"I don't think he's been dead long," the coroner said, standing beside Jackson as the body was wrapped and loaded in a meat wagon. "The turtles and fish hadn't been at him much. As fast as the river's flowing, the current would have kept him on the surface, plus that dead branch his arm was tangled in gave him added buoyancy."

"How long?"

"It's just a guess, Jackson. I'd say . . . twelve hours or so. Hard to tell, when they've been in the water. But he was last seen night before last, so it couldn't have been much longer than half a day."

Jackson stared at the river, a sick feeling shredding his guts into confetti as he thought this through. He plainly remembered Lilah staring at Thaniel and saying, "You're dead," in that flat, unemotional tone that had been even more chilling than if she had screamed it at him. And now Thaniel *was* dead, from a shotgun blast. Lilah had a shotgun. Had Thaniel gone back to her house yesterday, or even last night? Had she made good on her threat, if it had indeed been one?

That was the best-case scenario, that Lilah had been forced to defend herself, or even that she had shot

Thaniel at first sight. He didn't like it, but he could understand if a woman alone shot first and asked questions later when a thug who had been shooting at her the day before came back for more target practice. He doubted the district attorney would even indict under those circumstances.

Worst-case scenario, however, was the possibility that Lilah was lying in a pool of blood at her house, wounded or even dead. The thought galvanized him, sending pure panic racing through his bloodstream.

"Hal, I need that boat!" he roared at the captain of the Rescue Squad, referring to the boat they had used to retrieve Thaniel's body from the river. He was already striding toward the boat as he yelled.

Hal looked up, his homely face showing only mild surprise. "Okay, Sheriff," he said. "Anything I can help you with?"

"I'm going up to Lilah Jones's place. If Thaniel went back to shoot up the place again, she might be hurt." *Or dead.* But he didn't let himself dwell on that. He couldn't, and still function.

"If she's hurt, she'll need medical attention, and transport. I'll call for another boat and follow you." Hal unclipped the radio from his belt and rapped out instructions.

The Rescue Squad boats were built for stability, not speed, which was a good thing in the roiling river, with all the broken limbs and debris floating downstream, but Jackson still cursed the lack of speed. He needed to get to Lilah. Desperation gnawed at him, tearing at him with the knowledge that, if she had been shot, if she still lived, every second help was delayed could mean she wouldn't survive. He knew gunshot wounds; damn few of them were immediately fatal. A head or heart shot were about the only ones that could kill on contact, and that wasn't guaranteed.

He couldn't think of her lying bleeding and helpless, her life slowly ebbing away. He couldn't. And yet he couldn't stop, because his experience gave him graphic knowledge. Images rolled through his mind, an endless tape that made him sicker and sicker.

"Please. God, *please.*" He heard himself praying aloud, saying the words into the wind.

Getting to Lilah's house took forever. He had started out much farther down the river than from the ramp on Old Boggy Road. He had to dodge debris, and a couple of times the boat shuddered over submerged limbs. The engine stalled the last time, but it restarted on the first try. If it hadn't, he probably would have jumped into the river and swam the rest of the way.

At last the house came into view, nestled under the trees. Heart pounding, he searched for any sign of life, but the morning was still and quiet. Surely Lilah would have come out on the porch when she heard the outboard motor, if she was there. But where else could she be? She had no means of transportation.

"Lilah!" he yelled. "Lilah!" She had to be there, but he found himself hoping she wasn't, hoping she had gone for a walk in the woods, or borrowed a boat from some of the multitude who evidently found their way to her house for folk remedies. He hoped—God, he hoped almost anything at all had taken her away from the house, rather than think she didn't come out on the porch because she was lying somewhere dead or dying.

He nosed the boat up to the dock and tied it to the post. "*Lilah!*"

Boots thudding, he raced up the dock just as he had two days before, but the adrenaline burn he'd felt then was nothing compared to the inferno he felt now, as if he might burst out of his skin.

He leaped onto the porch, bypassing the steps. The windows on this side of the house were intact, he noted. He wrenched open the screen door and turned the knob of the main door; it was unlocked, and swung inward.

He stepped into the cool, dim house, his head thrown up as he sniffed the air. The house smelled as before: fragrant and welcoming, the faint odor of biscuits lingering, probably from last night's supper. The windows were up and pristine white curtains fluttered in the slight morning breeze. No odor of death hung like a miasma, nor could he detect the flat, metallic smell of blood.

She wasn't in the house. He went through it anyway, checking all four rooms. The house seemed undisturbed.

He went outside, circling the house, looking for any signs of violence. Nothing. Chickens clucked contentedly, pecking at bugs. Birds sang. Eleanor waddled out from under the porch, still fat with kittens. He stooped to pet her, his head swiveling as he checked every detail of his surroundings. "Where is she, Eleanor?" he whispered. Eleanor purred, and rubbed her head against his hand.

"Lilah!" he roared. Eleanor started, and retreated under the porch again.

"I'm coming."

The voice was faint, and came from behind the house. He jerked around, staring into the trees. The woods were almost impenetrable; he could be right on her, and not be able to see her.

"Where are you?" he called, striding rapidly to the back of the house.

"Almost there." Two seconds later she emerged from the trees, carrying a basket—and the shotgun. "I heard the outboard," she said as he reached her, "but I was a couple of hundred yards away and—uumph."

The rest of her words were lost under the fierce assault of his mouth. He hauled her up against him, unable to hold her close enough. He wanted to meld her into his very flesh, and never let her go. She was okay. She was alive, unharmed, warm and vibrant in his arms. The wind blew her soft curls around his face. He drank in her smell, fresh and soft, womanly. She tasted the same, her mouth answering his. He heard the basket drop to the ground, and the shotgun, then her arms were around him and she was clinging tightly to him.

Need roared through him like an inferno, born of his

desperate fear and relief. He tore at her clothes, stripping down her jeans and panties and lifting her out of them.

"Jackson?" Her head lolled back, her breath coming in soft pants. "Let's go inside—"

"I can't wait," he muttered savagely, lifting her up and backing her against a tree. Her legs came up and locked around his hips as she automatically sought to balance herself. He wrenched his pants open, freed himself, and shoved into her. She was hot and damp and tight, her inner flesh enveloping and clasping. She wasn't ready for him; he heard her gasp, but he couldn't stop. He pulled back and thrust again and he went all the way in this time. On the fifth thrust he began coming, his body heaving against her as he spurted for what seemed like forever, until his head swam and his vision blurred and darkened, and still the spasms took a long time to die down, small bursts of sensation rocking him. He sank heavily against her, pinning her to the tree. His legs trembled, and his lungs heaved. "I love you," he heard himself muttering. "Oh, God, I was so scared."

Her hands were clasping his head, stroking, trying to soothe him. "Jackson? What's wrong? What happened?"

He couldn't speak for a minute, still in shock from what he had said. The words had just boiled out, without thought. He hadn't said those words to any woman since his high school days, when he fell in love on a regular basis.

But they were true, he realized, and that shocked him almost as much as saying them. He loved her. He, Jackson Brody, was *in love.* It had happened too fast for him to come to terms with it, to think about it as they gradually became enmeshed in each other's lives. Logic said he couldn't possibly love her after so short a time; emotion said to hell with logic, he loved her.

"Jackson?"

He tried to pull away from that emotional brink, to function as a sheriff instead of a man. He had come here because a man had been murdered, and somewhere along the line he had forgotten that and focused, instead, on the woman at the center of the situation. But he was still inside her, still dazed from the force of his orgasm, and all he could do was sink more heavily against her, pressing her into the tree trunk. Birds sang around him, insects buzzed, the river murmured. Bright morning sunlight worked its way through the thick canopy of leaves, dappling their skin.

"I'm sorry," he managed to say. "Did I hurt you?" He knew he had entered her far too roughly, and she hadn't been aroused and ready.

"Some." She sounded remarkably peaceful. "At first. Then I enjoyed it."

He snorted. "You couldn't have enjoyed it very much. I think I lasted about five seconds." The sheriff still hadn't made an appearance; the man held full sway.

"I enjoyed *your* pleasure." She kissed his neck. "It was actually rather . . . thrilling."

"I was scared to death," he admitted baldly.

"Scared? About what?"

Finally, belatedly, the sheriff lifted his head. Jackson discovered he couldn't question her, or even talk about Thaniel, while in his present position. Gently he withdrew from her and eased his weight back, holding her steady while her legs slipped from around his hips and she was once more standing on her own two feet.

"We'd better hurry," he said, picking up her clothes and handing them to her, then pulling up his own pants and getting everything tucked back in place. "The Rescue Squad could be here any minute."

"Rescue Squad?" she echoed, brows lifting in surprise.

He waited until she was dressed. "I was afraid you'd been hurt."

"Why would I be hurt?" She still looked totally bewildered.

As a man, he hated having to question her. As a sheriff, he knew he had to do it or resign today. "Thaniel Vargas's body was found this morning."

A stillness came over her, and she looked at him but somehow she wasn't seeing him, her gaze turned inward. "I knew he'd die," she finally said.

"He didn't *die,*" Jackson corrected. "He was murdered. Shot in the face with a shotgun."

She came back from wherever she had gone, and her green eyes focused sharply on him. "You think I did it," she said.

Chapter 9

"I WAS AFRAID HE'D COME BACK AND Y'ALL STARTED shooting at each other again. I was afraid I'd find you dead, or dying." His voice was remarkably calm, considering how shaken he felt.

She shook her head. "I haven't seen Thaniel since day before yesterday, but I don't have any way to prove it."

"Lilah." He gripped her shoulders, shaking her a little to get her attention. "You seem to think I'm going to take you in for murder. Baby, even if you did kill him, after what happened no D.A. would prosecute, at least not the D.A. here. But I don't think you could murder anyone, not even Thaniel, and he was one worthless jackass. If you say you didn't kill him, then I believe you." The man was speaking again. The sheriff struggled to regain his detachment, though he thought it was a losing cause. He would never be detached when it came to Lilah.

She stared at him, a sense of wonderment coming to her eyes. In a flash of intuition he knew then she hadn't believed him when he blurted out that he loved her. Why should she? Men said "I love you" all the time in the heat of passion. And they had known each other less than two days. He was acutely aware that she hadn't said anything about love in return, but that would wait.

"But one thing keeps eating at me. Day before yesterday, you looked at him and said, 'You're dead,' and damn near scared him to death right then." He didn't ask anything, didn't try to form her answer in any way. He wanted her response to come from her own thoughts.

To his surprise, she went pale. She looked away, staring at the river. "I just—knew," she finally said, her voice stifled.

"Knew?"

"Jackson, I—" She half-turned away from him, then turned back. She lifted her hands in a helpless gesture. "I don't know how to explain it."

"In English. That's my only requirement."

"I just know things. I get flashes."

"Flashes?"

Again the helpless gesture. "It isn't a vision, not exactly. I don't really *see* anything, I just *know.* Like intuition, only more."

"So you had one of these flashes about Thaniel?"

She nodded. "I looked at him when I came out on the porch and all of a sudden I knew he was going to die. I didn't know he was going to get killed. Just . . . that he wasn't going to be here anymore."

He rubbed the back of his neck. In the distance he could hear the droning of an outboard motor: the Rescue Squad was getting close.

"I've never been wrong," she said, almost apologetically.

"No one else knows what you said." His voice was as somber as he felt. "Just me."

She bent her head, and he saw her worrying her lower lip. She saw his dilemma. Then she raised her head and squared her shoulders. "You have to do your job. You can't keep this to yourself, and be a good sheriff."

If he hadn't already known he loved her, that moment would have done it for him. And suddenly he knew something else. "Are these 'flashes' the reason Thaniel thought you're a witch?"

She gave him a rueful little smile. "I wasn't very good at hiding things when I was young. I blabbed."

"Scared him, huh? And all these people who come to you for treatment—you just look at them and have flashes about what's wrong with them?"

"Of course not," she said, startled. Then she blushed. "That's something else."

The blush both intrigued and alarmed him. "What kind of something else?"

"You'll think I'm a freak," she said in dismay.

"But a sexy freak. Tell me." A little bit of the sheriff was in his tone, a quiet authority.

"I see auras. You know, the colors that everyone has around them. I know what the different colors mean, and if someone's sick I can see where and know what to do, whether or not I can help them or they need to see a doctor."

Auras. Jackson wanted to sit down. He'd heard all that New Age mumbo-jumbo, but that's just what it was, as far as he was concerned. He'd never seen a nimbus of color around anyone, never seen proof such a thing existed.

"I haven't told anyone about the auras," she said, her voice shaking. "They just think I'm a . . . a medicine woman, like my mother. She saw them too. I remember her telling me, when I was little, what the different colors meant. That's how I learned my colors." She gave a quick look at the river, where the boat had come into view. Tears welled in her eyes. "You have the most beautiful aura," she whispered. "So clean and rich and healthy. I knew as soon as I saw you that—"

She broke off, and he didn't pursue it. The Rescue Squad boat had reached her dock, and the two men in it were getting out. One was Hal, who had come along himself to take charge if the Squad was needed, and the other was a tall, thin man Jackson recognized as a medic, though he didn't know his name.

Lilah did, though. She left Jackson's side and walked out of the trees into the open, her hand lifted in a wave.

Both men waved back. "Glad to see you're okay," Hal called as they started up the dock.

"Just fine, thanks. Thaniel hadn't been here, though."

"Yeah, we know." Hal looked past Lilah to Jackson. "You left about a minute too soon, sheriff. I still can't believe it."

"Believe what?"

"Jerry Watkins drove up just as you went out of sight. We were just getting the boat in the water. I tell you, Jerry looked like hell, like he'd been on a week-long bender. He looked at the body bag in the meat wagon and just broke down, crying like a baby. He's the one killed Thaniel, Sheriff. He jumped Thaniel about his boat, and you know how Thaniel was, too stupid to know when to back down. He told Jerry he sunk the son of a bitch. Beg pardon, Lilah. Jerry set a store by that boat. The way he tells it, he lost all control, grabbed the shotgun from his truck, and let Thaniel have it."

After years in law enforcement, little could surprise Jackson. He wasn't surprised now, because dumber things had happened. And though the full moon was waning, weird things would continue to happen for another couple of days. He did feel as if he'd dropped the ball, however. He should have thought of Jerry. Everyone who knew Jerry knew how he loved that boat. Instead he'd been so focused on Lilah that he hadn't been able to see anything else.

"He sat down on the ground and put his hands on his head for your deputies to arrest him. Guess he saw that on television," Hal finished.

Well, that was that. Thaniel's murder was solved before it had time to become a real mystery. But one little detail struck him as strange. Jackson looked at the medic. "If you knew Lilah was okay, that Thaniel hadn't been killed in a fight here, why did you come along?"

"He came to see me," Lilah said. She shook her head.

"I can't help you, Cory. You've got gallstones. You're going to have to see a doctor."

"Ah, hell, Lilah, I haven't even told you my symptoms!"

"You don't have to tell me, I can see how you look. It hurts like blue blazes every time you eat, doesn't it? Were you afraid you were having heart problems, maybe?"

Cory made a face. "How'd you know?"

"Just a hunch. Go see that doctor. There's a good gastro specialist in Montgomery. I'll give you his name."

"Okay," he said glumly. "I was hoping it was an ulcer and you could give me something for it."

"Nope. Surgery."

"Damn."

"Well, that's taken care of," Hal said. "We'd better get back, we still got some more work to do in Pine Flats. Will you be along soon, Jackson?"

"In a little while," Jackson said. From the way Hal winked, he figured the older man had cottoned on to the fact that there was something between him and Lilah. Frankly, Jackson didn't care if the whole county knew.

He and Lilah watched the two men get back into the boat and head back down river. Jackson squinted his eyes in the bright sun. "Auras, huh?" What the hell. If he believed she could have flashes of precognition, why not auras? If you loved someone, he thought, you accepted a lot of stuff that you never would have considered before. Privately, he'd check on Cory's diagnosis from a doctor, just to make sure, but for some reason he figured Lilah had been right. Auras were as good a reason as anything.

She reached for his hand. "I told you that you have a beautiful aura. I probably would have loved you just because of what I saw in it. But I had another flash when I saw you the first time."

He closed his hand warmly around hers. "What did that one tell you?"

She gave him a somber look. "That you were going to be the love of my life."

He felt a little light-headed. Maybe it was just the culmination of a very stressful morning, but he remembered that feeling of dizziness the first time he'd seen *her*. "Didn't you say those flashes had never been wrong?"

"That's right." She rose on tiptoe and kissed him. "They're one-hundred percent accurate."

He needed to get back to work. He needed to do a lot of things. But he didn't need to do them as much as he needed to hold her, so he wrapped his arms around her and held her tight, breathing in the essence of the love of *his* life, so happy he thought he might burst.

"We're going to do this up right," he said aloud. "The whole enchilada. Marriage. Kids."

"The whole enchilada," she agreed, and hand in hand they walked into the house.

Linda Howard is the *New York Times* bestselling author of *Kill and Tell, Son of the Morning, Shades of Twilight, After the Night, Dream Man, Heart of Fire, The Touch of Fire, Angel Creek,* and *A Lady of the West.* Her many awards include the Silver Pen from *Affaire de Coeur* and the *Romantic Times* Reviewer's Choice Award for Best Sensual Romance.

Castaway

Geralyn Dawson

Chapter 1

Wild Horse Island, Texas
1883

NAKED, DREW CORYELL EMERGED FROM THE LAZY SURF and strode across the warm sand toward the spot where he'd left the jug of fresh water. Pulling the cork, he lifted the stoneware crock to his lips and tilted back his head. The cool, sweet water slid down his throat like nectar. Swimming always gave him a powerful thirst.

He lowered the jug with a satisfied sigh and gazed out at the gunmetal gray waters of the Gulf of Mexico. A smile lifted the corners of his mouth as he rolled his shoulders, the pleasant ache of fatigued muscles a welcome sensation. "You've been spending too many hours behind a damned desk," he muttered to himself.

Then he sighed loudly and scowled. The thought had painted a dark cloud across his personal sky. He'd come to this secluded island to fish, to get away from the pressures of his business for a time. He didn't want to think about the Castaway Bait Company.

Just then, movement out on the water snagged his attention. A small sailboat cut across the swells headed inland. Curious, Drew sauntered back toward the dunes where he'd dropped his knapsack upon deciding to take a swim. From the knapsack, he removed his great-grandfather's slim brass spyglass, which he carried with him out of habit while here on the island. He lifted the glass to his eye and twisted the lens, bringing the vessel into focus.

He saw a sailor at the wheel and a woman in the bow. A very shapely woman, judging by the way the sea breeze flattened her clothing against her generous curves. She stood in the bow of the boat, a figurehead worthy of the finest of ships.

Long and blowing loose, her golden hair obscured his view of her face. Hoping for a better angle, he climbed to the top of a dune. "Turn this way, sweetheart," he willed.

Minutes ticked by as Drew observed the sailboat's approach. A subtle, unusual tension filled him as he acted the Peeping Tom and spied upon the woman. He wanted to see her face. Badly.

She pointed toward the beach, and the sailboat veered in that direction. Drew realized she'd gestured toward the mouth of the path intersecting the island between his bayside fishing cabin and the gulfside beach. "Curious," he murmured, taking his eye from the spyglass to glance toward the trail through the brush-covered dunes. Was it just coincidence, or had this woman been here before? He'd seen a sign or two of intruders when he'd returned for his annual visit to the small log structure where he had spent his youth. Had this woman been one of them? Was his fishing camp being used as a trysting place, perhaps?

He peered intently through the glass and saw her reach for something. A moment later, she'd brought a pair of field glasses to her eyes. He watched her scan his beach, then he held his breath as her glasses drifted his way. He knew the moment she spotted him because her mouth dropped open. Then the binoculars fell away and he got his first good glimpse of her face.

Drew froze. "Hannah?"

All the breath seemed to whoosh from his lungs. All the blood seemed to rush to his loins. Hannah. It *was* her. Here. Why?

Hannah.

His mouth went dry as she once again blocked his view of her face by bringing up her field glasses. He felt her gaze as the optical instrument shifted slowly downward.

That was when Drew remembered he was naked. Glancing around for a fig leaf, he settled for a clump of grass. Then, while reaching to pluck the clump of concealment from the ground, he had second thoughts. He tossed away the grass, braced his hands on his hips, and played the peacock, displaying himself in all his natural glory. "Let her see what she gave up, by God."

Drew stood facing the gulf, dripping wet, naked, and aroused.

Hannah dropped the field glasses overboard.

Years ago, they had been married.

Never once had they made love.

"Well, well, well," he drawled, speaking to the sandpiper scurrying along the water's edge. "This isn't shaping up to be just another day at the beach."

Hannah Mayfield considered following her binoculars into the water, but when she looked off the sailboat's starboard bow and saw the sandy bottom only a few feet below the surface, she realized drowning would take some work. "Might as well die of embarrassment," she muttered.

Since the moment she'd decided to make this trip, she'd pictured her reunion with Drew in a hundred different variations. Never once had she imagined anything like this. Maybe one of her fantasies did include a certain amount of bare skin, but never *that* much bare skin. Of course, considering her untouched state, Hannah hadn't known a man could be that . . . naked.

Were she not so busy being mortified at the moment, she might have been downright intrigued.

"I reckon you won't be making the return trip to Galveston after all, Missy," observed the sailor whom she'd hired to sail her down to this isolated beach.

"Looks like your husband's home, at that, and plenty happy to see you."

Happy? Hannah sincerely doubted Drew Coryell was the least bit pleased to see her. Hadn't he been mad enough to chew bullets the day she left him? Hadn't he bellowed after her, thundering bitterness and hostility as her father hoisted sail and headed out into the bay? No, Drew wouldn't be happy to see her.

"He probably walks around in that condition all the time," she muttered beneath her breath, tempted to take another peek. She didn't do it, though. If he caught her at it again she'd never be brave enough to leave the boat.

So as the small craft approached the beach, Hannah kept her gaze fastened securely on her hands, fingers laced and resting in her lap. Idly, she thought the contrast between her white knuckles and her suntanned hands a fascinating study in color.

Moments later, momentum sent her swaying forward as the rudder dragged the bottom. "This is as close as I can get," said the sailor. "Looks like you'll be getting your feet wet."

"I'll carry her," came the voice that had haunted her for a decade.

Hannah held her breath, waiting to wake from the dream. Then a hand reached into the sailboat and touched her, grabbed her by one wrist. She knew that touch. Drew. This wasn't a dream. He really was here and not a figment of an overactive imagination.

For the first time, she admitted to herself she truly had not expected to find him on Wild Horse Island. After all, it had been ten years. The doubts planted in her mind by her father's accusations and predictions on the day of their wedding had lasted no longer than the sail home. In her heart, Hannah always believed Drew Coryell would prove her father wrong. She had believed he'd leave the beach life behind and make something of himself.

Apparently not.

Drew was here. Now, this minute. Beside the boat. Touching her. *He's touching me.* Her embarrassment evaporated beneath the wonder of the moment, and her pulse pounded like the surf during a blow.

She wouldn't look at him, not even when he tugged her toward him and into his arms. Cradling her against his body, holding her high and dry, he stepped away from the sailboat.

I'm in Drew's arms again. Instinct had her snuggling against him. Sensation assaulted her. The solid, steely strength of the muscles that held her. The soft rasp of his breathing and the familiar sunshine-and-sea scent of the man who once had been her husband. I'm home, she thought. "Drew," she said with a soft, breathy sigh.

"Hannah." He spoke her name without emphasis or inflection.

"Drew," she repeated, her mouth lifting in a smile.

"Hannah?"

The question in his voice pulled at her. She wanted to ignore it, to savor this moment, but finally, she braved a glance at his face. He stared not at her, but toward the departing sailboat. She vaguely heard the sailor call, "I'll be back in three days."

The question burst from her lips. "Are you married?"

"No, I'm not. Are you?"

"No."

"Hannah?"

Her fingers itched to reach up and trace the strong line of his jaw. "Yes?"

"This is a dream come true for me."

"It is?" Her mouth went dry as a dune.

"It is." One corner of his mouth lifted in a crooked grin. "The hours I've spent over the past ten years imagining this moment . . . and now it is actually happening . . . why, it all but takes my breath away."

"Oh, mine too, Drew. Mine, too."

"It does? Well, that could be a problem. You're gonna need your breath, Hannah. I'm a fisherman, and you know what fishermen do with a catch they don't want." He looked down at her then, and the gleeful heat in his green-eyed gaze warned her even before he spoke. "They throw it back."

Then he dropped her, tossed her, actually. Like a dead red snapper. She opened her mouth to scream, but got out only a squeak before she had to shut it when the cool gulf water closed over her head.

Almost immediately, her behind hit the bottom. Salt stung her eyes and bubbles burst from her mouth as she blew a frustrated breath before climbing angrily to her feet. Humiliation drenched her.

The confounded man was strolling . . . *strolling* . . . from the water. Whistling!

Hannah spat saltwater from her mouth, wiped it from her eyes, and wrung it from her hair. She swished sand from her skirt and washed it from her hands. All the while, her gaze never left the retreating rogue. She searched within herself for her backbone, found it, and muttered, "Fisherman, is he? Well, I'm no catch to throw back. He never caught me. That's the problem, isn't it? I'm the one that got away."

As if he'd heard her, he stopped and glanced back over his shoulder. Standing on the beach, the surf lapping gently at his ankles, rivulets of water trickling down his back and over his bare, sculpted buttocks, and with a wickedly satisfied grin slashed across his face, the man could have been one of God's own fallen angels. Hannah shivered.

Oh, the temptations of sin.

And he's not married.

"Oh, hush," she scolded her own conscience. She hadn't made this trip to discern his marital status or lust after his manly physique. She dare not forget it. She was on a truly important mission, and the only man who could ensure its success was Drew Coryell.

Hannah sighed, gathered up her skirt, and started to slog her way forward. Dismay at the inauspicious start to her endeavor added to the weight of her steps. Unfortunately, the sight of all that skin had distracted her and temporarily scrambled her brains. She would need to do a better job of keeping her wits together if she expected to achieve her goal.

His reaction had done more than cool her off. It had tipped her to the fact that he held a grudge or two against her even after all these years. Well, she'd known when she decided to make this trip that might be the case. She'd known she'd set a difficult task for herself.

But now she knew what to expect; she'd be on her guard. She could deal with Drew Coryell. Besides, what could possibly be more shocking than what had already occurred? What more could the man bare? His soul?

"That's about as likely as snow in Texas in August," she murmured.

Drew never had been one to reveal his innermost feelings. Maybe if he'd been more forthcoming, she would have found it easier to fight her father and stay.

Reaching water's edge, Hannah paused to wring her skirts again and gather her composure. Personal considerations came a distant second to the noble quest that had brought her here today, and she needed to remember that. Hannah had come to Drew representing not herself, but the people of Texas. Her former husband had the opportunity to make a grand contribution to this great state, and she intended to do anything and everything within her power to ensure that he granted the request she had traveled here to make.

To that end, she was well prepared to rock Drew Coryell's boat. "So button up your hatches or your breeches or both, fisherman. There's a hurricane blowing ashore and its name is Hannah."

Hannah.

Drew was lost in a fog as he buttoned the placket of his lightweight cotton trousers, then reached for a shirt. Hannah Mayfield. When he went to slip his arms through the shirt sleeves and couldn't, he finally saw he'd lifted a second pair of pants from his trunk instead of a shirt. The woman had him even more confused than he'd realized.

Questions whirled like a waterspout in his brain. Why had she come? What did she want? Where had she been living the last ten years? Not Galveston, he knew. The Mayfield family had sold their home and moved away the very day she secured her damned annulment.

Having followed her to Galveston, Drew had hidden on the pier and watched the ferry take her away, then he'd washed his hands of the entire affair. He'd been full of anger and hurt pride, not to mention the broken ribs and assorted bruises Roger Mayfield's hired thugs had bestowed upon him. Still, young fool that he was, for months afterward he had expected her to come to her senses and return to him.

He had loved Hannah, truly, deeply loved her. He had honestly believed she loved him in return. That proved how stupid young men can be. It had taken her ten long years to come back.

Anger surged through him as Drew found a shirt and yanked it on. *Well, you are too damned late, darlin'*. Any tenderness he'd felt for her had died long ago.

Hadn't it?

He grimaced and tugged his shirt collar away from his neck. Damned thing wasn't even buttoned and it still felt like a noose. Hannah Mayfield. Hell.

"Why?" he muttered aloud. Why was she here? How had she found him? Only two people at the Castaway Bait Company knew where he intended to spend his holiday. Neither of them would have shared his business with a stranger.

And Hannah Mayfield was a stranger, he told himself as he slowly buttoned his shirt. Nothing more than that. He hadn't thought of the woman in years. Well, in months, anyway. He'd put that part of his past behind him. He was a successful businessman now. A wealthy man. Hannah Mayfield was nothing more than a bad memory.

A bad memory who had sailed up to his beach today. She was all grown up, a woman, not a girl, and more beautiful than sunrise over the gulf. *A bad memory who isn't wearing a wedding ring—not mine or anybody else's.*

Drew made a grunting noise. No wedding ring. Why had he even noticed? "It doesn't matter to me," he told himself. He certainly didn't want her now.

His gaze drifted toward the corner of the cabin where a decade ago the bed had sat, before he'd moved it to the other side of the room. Back then he had wanted her desperately, and Hannah had returned his desire. As if it were yesterday, he recalled the passion in her eyes, the heat in her touch, the little mewling sound of need she'd made when he'd laid her upon their bed. And he had no sooner gotten her naked when the door burst open and her father stole Drew's bride away, then sicced his goons on the distraught groom. It had taken his body weeks to mend. His heart, a month of Sundays.

He'd had a hard time accepting that she'd actually left him. He couldn't believe she hadn't stood up to her father. She should have resisted. She had married Drew.

But in the end, that hadn't meant a damn thing.

Now Hannah Mayfield was back. Why? Why had she sought him out after all this time?

Drew gazed out the cabin's window and spied the woman in question marching purposefully his way. "Well," he said softly, "I guess it's time I asked her."

Having taken the path from the beach, Hannah stood gazing at Drew's home, trying to work up the nerve to knock. In the end, she didn't need to because Drew stormed from the cabin, slamming the door behind him. She frowned, not liking the look in her former husband's eyes as he approached. The words *hard, deliberate,* and *ruthless* came to mind at the sight of him. Add an earring and a cutlass and go back in time two hundred years and the man could have passed for a pirate—a furious pirate. Temper radiated off him in waves.

Hannah shifted her gaze to the blue sky above the bay where snow-white gulls swooped and dove for their supper. She easily imagined what those poor fish felt like in the instant before the predator plucked them from the sea. Her gaze slipped to Drew's bare feet and she checked just to make certain he hadn't grown talons during the past ten years.

No talons. However, his steps certainly appeared determined. She braced herself for the attack she fully expected him to launch.

He didn't disappoint her. "Why have you come?" he demanded, finally halting within arm's reach of her.

Calm, Hannah. Remain calm. "I have something to ask you."

"So ask." He folded his arms and leaned closer.

Hannah forced herself not to take a step back. Licking her lips, she tucked a damp strand of hair behind her ear and tried to overcome her dismay. Calm, ha. The man could intimidate a shark.

And I'm more shrimp than shark at the moment.

What had happened to the storm that had blown ashore—blustery, powerful, and forceful? This wasn't going at all as she had planned.

"Well?" he said, a definite sneer in his tone.

"Drew, I . . ." Her voice trailed off as she searched for words. *I'm glad you put your clothes on? I missed you? I was wrong to leave you? I wish I could turn back the clock?*

"You what?"

No, she couldn't say that. She had not come here for that. Besides, speaking those words would be ten times more difficult than getting out the request she'd come so far to make. She looked him in the eyes, swallowed hard, and said, "I represent the Texas Historical Preservation Society. We are a group of concerned citizens dedicated to ensuring that the history of our state is not lost to the annals of time. As you probably know, the capitol burned two years ago, and in addition to the building, that ravaging fire claimed a number of historically significant documents, including the state's only copy of the

1836 Republic of Texas Declaration of Independence from Mexico."

Drew started to laugh, softly and, Hannah thought, bitterly. "That's why you've come? The Declaration of Independence?" His laughter grew louder. "The irony of this moment slays me."

"Irony?"

He nodded. "That you of all people would value that particular document enough to make this particular request."

She felt a breeze of strength whisper through her. "Maybe, Drew, it's because of who I am and what I've done, or more importantly what I *failed* to do, that I recognize the value of independence more than most."

This time he was the one who looked away. Drew shoved his hands in his back pockets and turned to face the water. For a long moment the only sound to be heard was the gentle wash of the waves against the sand and the high-pitched call of the seabirds from on high. Finally, he spoke. "Do you remember the story behind that piece of paper?"

Sensing his need to repeat it, Hannah answered, "Bits and pieces. Would you tell me again?"

He drew a deep breath, then said, "It's been almost fifty years now since my grandfather stood as witness to the signing of the declaration at Washington-on-the-Brazos. The new government kept one copy, then President Sam Houston asked for volunteers to take the other four to leading towns around the country in order to spread the news more quickly. My grandfather jumped at the chance to do his part and almost immediately, he left for Bastrop. He did his duty and showed the declaration to every person he met along the way. Three days after the fall of the Alamo, he finally made his way home—just in time to die. Turned out he showed the prized document to a Mexican spy. They fought and my grandfather killed him, but he received a mortal wound in the process."

Drew kicked a tuft of grass with a bare foot and

continued, "My grandmother packed up the declaration with the rest of her husband's things and fled her home barely ahead of the Mexicans."

"In the Runaway Scrape," Hannah added, remembering the term for the time of mayhem when a large part of the Texas population abandoned their homes to escape the advancing enemy army.

Drew nodded. "They eventually settled along the coast. Over time, accidents and illness have taken every Coryell but me. That's how the declaration came to me, and I have kept it safe ever since."

"So you do still have it?"

"Of course. It's no longer on this island, however. I won't risk it to a gulf storm."

He paused for a moment, his gaze following the white splash against brilliant blue of a seagull in flight. "It is my most prized possession, Hannah. That's why I shared it with you when I made you my family. It's all I have left of them."

He turned his head and stabbed her with a stare. "And you want to take it away from me."

Chapter 2

DREW'S FEET POUNDED AGAINST THE SAND AS HE RAN along the edge of the lapping surf. Emotion rolled through him, providing fuel for the physical exertion he demanded of his body. Anger, bitterness, disappointment—each were part of what drove him. But the underlying energy, what added the most fuel to his fire, was self-disgust.

Damn him for a fool for thinking she might regret having left him.

At various times throughout the past decade he had indulged in fantasies in which Hannah spent her life pining away for him. Whenever he got to feeling lonely, missing her and wondering about her, he'd tell himself she undoubtedly spent the majority of her days regretting her choice. He'd imagined meetings with her at which she'd fall at his feet and beg his forgiveness. He'd daydreamed of reunions at which she threw herself into his arms and begged him to take her back. He'd visualized coming home from the office one day and finding her naked in his bed, naked in his bath, even naked on his boat, pleading with him to save her from a sorry life by taking her and making her his own.

Instead she showed up wanting not him, but his family heirloom.

"Idiot," he puffed out. You'd think a man would outgrow childish fantasies. You'd think he'd put the ache of a broken heart behind him. "Sap-skull."

Drew picked up his pace, running full speed to keep from thinking, until his lungs gave out and forced him to slow to a walk. Finally he stopped, bent over, and breathed deeply, collecting both his breath and his thoughts.

This was ridiculous. All these feelings were ten years old. It was foolish to allow them to plague him still. Of course, seeing Hannah again had stirred them up, but it was time to put them to bed.

Bed. The word hit him like a sailboat's boom.

Slowly, he straightened. He focused his gaze on an ungainly brown pelican taking flight from the beach in front of him as a deliciously wicked idea took root in his mind. *Why not? Why the hell not?*

Turning around, he headed back toward his cabin. He turned the notion over in his mind, weighing the pros and cons, debating the sense of the entire idea.

It was mean. Ungentlemanly. Contemptible, even.

But the woman owed him.

Hannah Mayfield owed him for the broken ribs, the broken dreams. She had cured him of falling in love. Since he'd never fallen in love again, he'd never married again. Never fathered children. He liked children, liked them a lot. Hannah had cost him a family. She owed him.

"And I know just how to make her pay."

Approaching his cabin, he saw her sitting primly atop the three-legged stool he liked to sit on while whittling. When she saw him, she stood and faced him. Looking at her without a fog of anger clouding his vision, Drew was caught by surprise at the picture she presented. Hannah could easily have been a mermaid come ashore.

Her wet dress clung to her like a second skin, outlining her generous, eye-candy curves. Her blue eyes sparkled like sunlight on the surf. Her chin was up, her shoulders back, and her lips . . . oh, her lips . . . were pursed in a delicious little pout that shouted to a man, *Kiss me!*

It took all Drew's strength not to comply that very instant.

She licked those lips and said, "Drew, please. Can we talk?"

Talk. Yeah, they could talk. That could be part of it. Talking was good. Touching was better. Lots of touching was lots better.

Because that was his price.

The woman owed him that much. She owed him the touching and the wedding night he'd been denied and the honeymoon that had been stolen from them. Maybe then, finally, he could get her out of his system once and for good.

It was, he thought, an inspired idea.

Drew sauntered over to the water-filled washtub where earlier he had dropped the wooden creel containing the speckled trout he'd caught that morning. Removing the wooden box from the water, he carried it and his polished oak tackle box down toward the water. Only then did he condescend to speak to his former wife, calling over his shoulder, "All right, Hannah. If you want to talk while I'm cleaning my lunch, feel free."

She followed him to the board propped between two rocks at water's edge where he set down his slight burdens. He threw back the creel lid, revealing the fish, then from the tackle box he removed a razor-sharp fillet knife. Glancing up at her, he said, "Well?"

Hannah inhaled a deep breath that attracted his gaze to her bosom. This time, Drew licked his lips.

"About the declaration," Hannah said. "I knew it was special to you, but I admit I didn't realize how special. I bet we could come up with a way to make it palatable for you to turn it over to the state if we put our heads together and gave it some thought."

Heads wasn't what Drew had in mind to put together.

"Actually, I've already figured it out," he told her, lifting the fish from the creel.

Hope, relief, and the flash of another emotion he couldn't put his finger on bloomed in her expression. "You have? What is it? Are you going to give me your copy of the Republic of Texas's Declaration of Independence?"

"That depends." He placed the trout on the cutting board.

"On what?"

"You, Hannah. On how bad you want it. On the price you are willing to pay."

The intelligent woman took a wary step backward. "Price?"

Drew nodded. "I heard your sailor say he would return in three days. I'm curious as to why you thought you needed that particular amount of time, but all in all, it suits my purposes."

"Purposes?" she said with a squeak.

He nodded and waited, drawing the moment out, savoring the sweet taste of retaliation mixed with anticipation until she put her hands on her hips, blew a frustrated sigh, and demanded, "What purposes?"

He buried the fillet knife in the board. "It's my price, Hannah. I want you to be my wife—in every sense of the word—until that sailboat comes back to get you."

Her chin dropped and her arms fell to her side. Shock rang in her voice as she asked, "Are you saying you want . . . ?"

"Sex, Hannah. I want three days with you in my bed."

For a long moment, she simply stared at him. Then, seconds before she reacted, her eyes flashed a warning. Hannah reached for the cutting board, but surprisingly, she didn't go for the knife. In one fluid motion, she lifted the speckled trout by the tail and drew back her arm.

Drew didn't believe she'd actually do it so he didn't move at first, and then it was too late.

She slapped him in the face with the fish. "All in all, Mr. Coryell, I'd rather sleep with a shark."

* * *

Hannah didn't run along the beach like Drew had, but she certainly walked hard. She stopped once just long enough to strip off her wet and clinging petticoat, then continued on her way. Fury fueled her pace and worry plagued her mind. She couldn't believe Drew actually proposed such a scandalous liaison.

She was ashamed at how badly she'd wanted to accept his offer.

"Hussy," she muttered. "Strumpet."

Woman.

Hannah groaned and sank down onto the sand, gazing out at the bay. What was the matter with her?

Other than the fact that you're a twenty-seven-year-old virgin?

She groaned and buried her head against her knees. The damp, gritty material of her dress plastered against her forehead, reminding her she had another problem with which to deal. She'd forgotten to get her satchel off the sailboat. She didn't even have a change of clothing with her.

If you were to take Drew up on his offer, you wouldn't need any clothes.

"Aargh!" She flopped backward on the sand and closed her eyes. Sunlight warmed her face. "Hannah Mayfield, you are staring down the barrel of a real dilemma."

Her thoughts darted back and forth like a school of minnows. She could not play the wife to Drew Coryell. She could not share his bed. How dare he make such a proposition. How scandalous. How disgraceful.

How delicious.

She groaned. *What did you expect, Hannah? What were you hoping for?*

Unprepared to answer that question, Hannah sat up. She scooped up a handful of sand and let it drain in a narrow stream from her closed fist. Over and over she repeated the action while she consciously worked to wash her mind free of troublesome thoughts. Eventually, she succeeded and slowly, she relaxed.

She'd finally made it back to Wild Horse Island, a spot she'd dreamed of for a decade. No matter what happened or didn't happen between her and Drew, she would enjoy this moment out of time here in this place of such beauty.

Standing, she brushed ineffectually at the sand clinging to her dress, then continued her walk, angling her path off the beach. She threaded her way into and around the dunes for a time, then aimed for the line of trees growing atop a rocky embankment. Finding herself back at the water, only this time some twelve feet or so above it, she halted beneath a partially shaded grassy spot that appeared so inviting she couldn't pass it up.

And so, refreshed by the peace of her walk, her face shaded by the trees, her body warmed by the sun, and her spirit soothed by the sound of the surf, Hannah slept.

Darned if she didn't dream of Drew Coryell.

Wild Horse Island was little more than a spit of sand, rocks, and trees marking the main passage to the brackish water of Wilson's Lake, where a fresh water bayou yawned into the Gulf of Mexico. Marine life occupied the waters in abundance, making the island an avid fisherman's little slice of heaven. It was also the perfect place to test Drew's most recent designs—personal and professional. He had both in mind as he followed his former wife's trail.

He'd gone about this all wrong, he could see that now. His goal was to bed Hannah. He didn't want to destroy her spirit, and forcing her surrender would do just that. Therefore, if he wanted a willing woman in his bed and not a hellcat or a martyr, he needed to take a more subtle approach. He must convince her that bedding him was the right thing for them both. In other words, he needed to seduce her.

Drew knew just how to go about it.

She'd walked a quarter of the way around the island before veering away from the beach. As he climbed the rise and spied her slumbering beneath the shade of a salt cedar tree, a grin cracked his face. For all her wandering, she'd ended up back within a hundred yards of the cabin. Drew doubted she'd done that intentionally.

Approaching the slumbering, soppy beauty, he nudged her with a bare foot. "Wake up, woman, and take off your dress."

Her eyes flew open and she sat up. "What!"

"Take off your dress." The shock on her face was priceless, and Drew couldn't help but chuckle. "You're all wet, Hannah. I think you should change."

She narrowed her eyes and glared at him. "Go away. I'm not ready to talk to you again yet."

His mouth settled into a grin. She'd always been cute when grumpy. "You need to get out of that dress. Wouldn't want you to catch a chill and fall ill."

"A chill?" She rolled her eyes. "It must be ninety degrees this afternoon. I'm not going to catch a chill. Really, Drew. If this is your idea of trying to get me to fall in with your wicked scheme, then you need a lesson or two in subtlety."

"I'm simply watching out for my guest. You can't be comfortable in that dress. Doesn't the saltwater make it stiff and scratchy?"

She grimaced and plucked at her skirt. She mumbled as she stood. "I left my satchel on the sailboat."

He'd known that, of course. It was part of what made this so much fun. "What did you say?"

Her chin came up. "I left my satchel on the sailboat."

Drew studied his fingernails. "You mean you don't have any clothes to change into?"

"No, I don't. As you undoubtedly have realized."

"Hmm . . ." Drew dragged a hand along his jaw and studied her. "Well, that's a problem. I'm afraid that just won't do. I need you naked from the knees."

"Excuse me?" She blew a sigh filled with frustration. "Drew, I know I didn't say it in so many words, but surely you understood I refused your proposition."

"Oh, yeah. I got that. But I still want you to get rid of

that skirt. Here, you can wear this." He unbuttoned his shirt and tossed it to her. "You'll be more comfortable while we're negotiating an agreement about my document and demands."

"Negotiating?" She glanced down at the shirt, then back up at him. "Drew, I won't change my mind. What would that make me, agreeing to such a thing? You must understand—"

"I understand everything I need to," he interrupted. "You may have changed some over the past ten years, but you can't have changed that much. I know you want the thrill and the excitement. You want your pulse to pound." He stepped toward her, reached out, and trailed a finger down her cheek.

She visibly shuddered. "No. Really. I—"

"I know you, Hannah Mayfield," he said, his voice low and soft as the surf on a windless night. "You may claim to have made this trip on behalf of Texas, but I know another reason why you've come to my island."

"You do?" she breathed.

"Yep, so get out of that dress, sweetheart." He flashed her his pirate's grin and gestured toward the bay. "We can't go fishin' till you do."

Fishing. Hannah tugged on the tail of Drew's shirt and wished herself three inches shorter. In her younger days, she'd often bared her calves and sometimes even her knees when she waded into the surf with pole or net in hand. Never before, however, had she shown this much thigh. She couldn't believe she was doing it now, especially with Drew acting so strangely.

Fishing. He'd spoken no more about the declaration or his shameful proposition as they returned to the cabin and set about gathering up gear. When she tried to bring it up, he started talking hot spots and bait varieties and casting methods, and half of what he said sounded downright . . . fishy. Who ever heard of a lure called an eight-inch Throbbing Bob?

No, the man was pulling her leg, all right. *And he has plenty of leg to pull, considering the shortness of his shirttail.*

Hannah bit back a groan. A modest woman wouldn't be seen wearing something this scandalous. But then, a modest woman wouldn't jump at the chance to wade knee-deep in brackish water to wet a hook or sling a hoop. And when it came to angling, Hannah Mayfield was never modest.

The best times of her life had been spent with a baited hook in the water. Curse the man for knowing her so well.

The road to sin, in Hannah's case, was paved with fish scales. She'd been six years old when she landed her first snapper, and from that moment on, she was hooked. She spent all her free time down on the piers, and when she grew older she saved up enough money to buy her very own rowboat. Her parents had considered fishing unfeminine, but relatively harmless, and they didn't object to their daughter's spending an occasional evening in pursuit of bounty from the sea. Of course, busy as they were with social life on Galveston Island, they didn't know that "occasional" was actually every day.

Nor were they aware when a certain young man took to tossing out a line on the pier at Hannah.

What began as innocent competition for red drum quickly changed to something else. Drew and Hannah talked over trout, flirted over flounder, and stole quick kisses while filling their nets with blue crab. Still, things didn't heat up until he gave her a firsthand lesson on how to cook hoop stew.

Now it was the memory of that fire between them that filled Hannah with a combination of longing and regret as she watched him test a fishing rod's feel. How filled with emotion she had been back then. How empty she had been ever since.

Some of what was running through her mind must have showed in her expression because she saw speculation in the look Drew drilled her way. "So," he said, canting his head to one side. "Did you do much stewing after you left me?"

She froze. "What?"

"Do you make hoop stew very often?" he said, his expression filled with innocence.

Hannah sucked on her lower lip and considered him. The man was driving her crazy. He used to call the kisses and caresses they shared "stewing." Did he remember? Of course he did. He was a man, and men didn't forget such matters. At least, that's what Hannah had been told.

Besides, she was far from oblivious to the undercurrents eddying between them. The look in his eyes when he'd tossed her his shirt had been downright . . . challenging. The gleam in his smile when she approached him wearing it over her damp underwear had been an out-and-out leer.

But with this latest question she sensed a darker emotion flowing beneath the affable facade. Did she make hoop stew very often? She'd best step carefully here with her answer. "My family moved inland to San Antonio. Freshwater fish makes a different tasting stew, so I called it something else."

His lips twisted as he added, "Besides, you left your hoop net back on the island, didn't you?"

She heard a taint of bitterness in his tone and decided it was advisable to change the subject. Knowing Drew, she asked about the snapper fishing of late.

He gave her a look that said he recognized her purpose, but agreed to go along with it. "Haven't done much with the snapper. Day before yesterday, though, I saw a flounder leap."

"You did?" Envy washed through Hannah. She'd heard of such a phenomenon, but she'd never seen it herself. "What was it like?"

His eyes took on a faraway cast and he slowly shook his head. "I've seen smaller schools do this, but never one this big. They'd fly into the air, fish after fish after fish, must have been hundreds of them. It was like they were part of some aquatic-air ballet. Damnedest thing I've ever seen." Glancing out toward the water, he added, "Didn't even try and catch any that day. Spent all my time looking at them. I want to change that today."

Suddenly, Hannah couldn't wait to get her line wet.

Drew loaded his arms with tackle, then motioned for Hannah to get the hoop net. The contraption consisted of a billowy sock of light rope netting laced to the perimeter of a large metal hoop some four feet in diameter. She grabbed the metal with one hand, the coiled retrieval rope with the other, and lifted.

The net smelled briny and fishy and familiar, and the scent brought a smile to Hannah's lips. Contentment descended upon her. She felt a rightness with the world she had not experienced for a very long time. She had missed the salty tang of the air, the cries of the gulls, the hissing foam of a surf as it washed against a sandy beach. San Antonio lay over a hundred miles from the coast, and while she'd found it a nice place to live, she'd never called it home. Home was the beach, the gulf, the pelicans, and crabs.

Home was where Drew lived.

She started at the thought.

Why would she think something silly like that? She had never made a home here with Drew. This had been their dream, but not their reality. The reality was that she'd left him before they had a chance to make a home.

A pang of emotion stabbed through her chest and she closed her eyes as the peace she'd so briefly enjoyed evaporated. It was true. She'd been a coward and a fool and a child afraid to take a stand against her parent. She'd vowed to love Drew forever, and the first chance she got she broke that promise. She'd thrown him away, thrown *them* away. It was the single most shameful thing she'd ever done.

I'm lucky all he did was throw me in the water.

"What's the matter, Hannah?" he asked. "You're looking a little green just when the time has come to bait your hook. Don't tell me you've gone and gotten queasy in your old age."

"No, I'm fine. Just thinking."

She tugged yet again at the shirt she wore and Drew took note of her actions. "You surprise me," he said, eyeing her legs. "What would your father say if he could see you now?"

Her staid and very proper father wouldn't say anything. Roger Mayfield, current president of the Texas Historical Preservation Society, would just kill her. "I don't care to discuss my father."

Drew shrugged and changed the subject. "Follow me, Hannah. There's good wade fishing off the point just up the beach. I keep a stewpot handy there all ready to go. There's a freshwater pond a short walk from here and a patch of wild onions a little beyond that. I'll gather the water and greens if you want to get to hooping."

Hannah frowned. She'd been looking forward to fishing, not tossing the hoop. She gestured toward the load he carried in his arms. "I was hoping to give your fancy reel a try."

"I sort of figured that when I saw your eyes stroking my rod," he said dryly.

"I did not stroke. I simply studied."

"My mistake." Drew shrugged. "Sometimes I get fantasy mixed up with reality."

She cut him a suspicious look.

He smiled blandly and said, "How about we get the stew on first? I'm working up a powerful hunger, and we'll have better luck hooking them later in the day. Besides, if you're interested in using my E. F. Meek reel, I've a whole selection of lures to show you."

"Lures?" she replied. "I don't use lures. I've always used live bait."

For a moment he watched her as if debating a question with himself. Then he wrapped his fingers around the handle of the stewpot and shrugged. "Be daring, Hannah. Try something a little different. I promise you

you'll be glad you did." Tossing her a wink, he turned and headed off into the trees.

Hannah frowned as she watched him go. What a strange exchange that was. In fact, nothing had made much sense to her since he'd dropped her in the water this morning. That she understood. The rest of it . . . well . . . she might as well be a rowboat missing its oars, and Drew the strong current carrying her toward an unknown destination.

"Oh, quit being a fool and just fish," she muttered.

With hoop net in hand, she waded out into the briny water. Ten years having passed since she'd last handled the bulky contraption, Hannah found it difficult to maneuver at first. It took a few attempts to get a feel again for the motion, but once she did she was able to give the hoop a good throw.

Drew was correct about the abundance of sea life at this spot. The first throw netted a red drum and a sand trout. The second, a croaker, a flounder, and three blue crabs. The third toss captured so many fish that Hannah had a devil of a time pulling it up. But she laughed with delight when she finally landed her haul, and by the time Drew returned she had seafood to fill three kettles and a pair of tired arms. She was having the best time she'd had in years.

"Uh, Hannah," he said when she drew back her arm to let fly another toss. "Don't you think you have enough already? We'll be cleaning fish until dark as it is."

Glancing at her catch, Hannah grinned ruefully. "I'd forgotten, Drew. It's like a treasure hunt. You never know what bounty you'll pull from the sea."

"Well, it looks like you have about a galleon of oysters, there."

She groaned at the joke and set the hoop net aside. Despite the wit—or lack thereof—he was right. It would take some time to clean all this fish. And she still wanted to try out that reel. She eyed her catch, then judged the size of the stewpot. Before Drew had a chance to stop her, she'd dumped two thirds of her haul back into water. Shrimp sank and flounder fled. Drew let loose a groan. "Why in the world did you do that? No, wait. Let me guess. You're still Love-to-catch-'em-but-hate-to-clean-'em Hannah, aren't you?"

Hannah flashed him a smile and spoke without thinking. "That's why I fell in love with you, Drew. You always cleaned my catch for me."

"Love? If that's what it was it lasted about as long as a fish in the summer sunshine."

Her smile faltered. How did she reply to that?

Thankfully, he didn't appear to need a response. Instead he picked up a trout and went about the task of cleaning. "There's another knife in my knapsack if you want to peel the potatoes."

Soon the fish were cleaned, the oysters shucked, and the shrimp and potatoes peeled. Hannah added ripe tomatoes and a pound of rice to the stewpot hung from a steel hook off an oak limb. As Drew knelt on one knee and set about starting a fire, Hannah excused herself to change into her stiff but dry dress. She'd felt the need for the protection. Traditionally, after they hung the pot was when Drew and Hannah got to "stewing."

She suspected that was why she nearly jumped from her skin when he rose, turned to her, waggled his brows and said, "So, Hannah. You ready for me to show you my Musky Wriggler?"

Chapter 3

DREW CHEWED THE INSIDE OF HIS CHEEK TO KEEP FROM laughing. Hannah's eyes bugged out and her mouth moved silently open and shut like a fish out of water. Yep, he was going to have a lot of fun with this plan he'd concocted.

The trout slap had given him the idea of how to go about getting what he wanted from Hannah Mayfield. The longer he considered the notion, the more he warmed to it. After all, fishing was his business. He'd made a fortune from knowing how to lure his quarry onto a line.

Only this particular Catch of the Day he intended to lure into his bed.

He removed a small container from his tackle box and opened it. Removing the three-inch, copper-bodied lure, he held it up for Hannah to see. "The Musky Wriggler. It's one of my favorites. Do you want it, Hannah?"

"A lure? You're talking about a fishing lure?"

Innocently, he nodded. "Of course. What did you think I was talking about?"

She sputtered a moment before scoffing. "I told you before I don't like fishing lures. They're so . . . false. Besides, why bother? It's not like you've a shortage of live bait here on the island." She slowly shook her head.

"And to think you accused me of developing an aversion to baiting my hooks."

"Oh, I'm not afraid to get my hands slimy. In fact, at times, that can be downright fun. But there's a lot to be said for bait casting. It can be so . . . sporting."

Hannah sniffed. "Well, you'll never convince me."

"Don't be so closed-minded. Try it. I guarantee you'll be wishing you'd made this choice years ago." He held the lure out, swinging it gently in front of her face.

She studied the bait with a skeptical expression. Still, Drew could tell she was tempted. "Come on, Hannah. Let me take you out in the boat. We don't have to go for long. Just while we're . . . stewing."

Before she jerked her head up, he had schooled his expression into its most guileless form. "Tell you what, I'll fish with shrimp, and you use the Musky Wriggler. I'll bet you catch more than me."

In the old days Hannah never once backed down from a challenge—at least, not a fishing challenge. Now she hesitated, and Drew could tell she needed a little more prodding. He knew just the thing. "After that, over supper we can talk about my copy of the declaration."

With that, the woman literally took the bait.

Holding the lure by its single-pronged hook, she said, "I do want to try out that Meek reel."

"Of course." It was all Drew could do not to rub his hands together in glee. He'd bet his top-selling scalloped spoon that she hadn't changed *that* much over the years. Put a fishing pole in the woman's hands and she got so wrapped up in the moment she forgot to think. Catch her when she had an eight-pound fighter on the end of her line and she'd agree to damned near anything. After all, she'd agreed to marry him while landing a snapper, had she not?

Drew watched her eye the Wriggler with veiled interest. That particular lure had always been lucky for specs. *Yep, I'll have her in my bed by sunset.*

But Hannah surprised him.

"I'm no green girl anymore, Drew Coryell." She

lobbed the bait toward him, and despite the unexpectedness of her actions, he caught it softly in his hand. "I know what you're about."

"You do?"

"You think if you take me fishing and I get caught up in the excitement, you'll be able to convince me to do any wicked thing you wish."

Hell, the woman hit it right on the head. "Why, Hannah, that's not a very nice thing to say."

"It's not a very nice thing to attempt."

"You wound me."

"Not yet, but I think I'll carry the fillet knife with me just in case I need it."

"Hannah!" he protested. Frowning and scowling and acting extremely put out, he returned the Musky Wriggler to its small wooden box, careful to shield the instruction flier inside from Hannah's gaze. The message printed there would expose him, and he didn't want her linking him with the Castaway Bait Company just yet. "I was trying to be nice here, you know."

"Uh-huh," she dryly replied. "Nice and seductive."

He laughed. "Honey, seduction is candlelight and romance. I asked you to go fishing."

"You think I don't remember all those hours on the fishing pier at Galveston? You think I don't recall what happened the first time we made hoop stew? You think I don't remember how you proposed marriage to me?"

"You got awfully worked up over that snapper."

"No, not the snapper." She canted her head and studied him, her mood growing serious. "You never saw it, did you? It was never the fishing. It was always you, Drew. You were the attraction."

He blinked. What was she saying?

But before it could all soak in, she continued. "I didn't figure it out myself until years later. I started falling in love with you the first day we met. If alligator baiting had been your hobby, I'd undoubtedly have developed an affinity for it, too."

Drew was having trouble getting past the shock of all

this. Nothing was going as he had planned. With a few short sentences, she'd up and changed everything. "Wait just a minute. You're not standing there telling me you don't like to fish."

"No, I love to fish. I've always enjoyed it. But I enjoyed you more. I wanted to be with you, Drew."

The words slipped out before he thought to stop them. "Then why did you leave me?"

A bittersweet smile spread across her face. "Because I was young. Because you were my first love and I didn't know to trust my feelings. Because I listened to my father when he told me I wouldn't be happy married to a ne'er-do-well with sun-bleached hair and beach sand between his toes."

Drew looked down at his bare, sand-encrusted feet and asked, "And was he right?"

"Partially, perhaps," she replied, following the path of his gaze. "I think for myself I could have been happy here forever. The two of us living here together like we'd planned—it would have been paradise. But my father was right in some ways. It would not have been just the two of us forever, and this . . ." She made a sweeping gesture that encompassed the fishing cabin, beach, and bay. "This is no place to raise a family."

Never mind that he agreed with her, Drew bristled at the criticism. "Wild Horse Island is a fine, safe place."

She shrugged. "Wild Horse Island has no schools or neighbors or other children. This is eighteen eighty-three. Texas is no longer the frontier. I want my children to have the benefits of a settled, established society. They'll need a good education to help them fulfill their destiny in the new century."

Drew's blood chilled. She spoke as if those children existed. "You said you weren't married. I assumed you had no children."

She took a step back and turned away. Quietly, she said, "I'm not married and I have no children. I was simply trying to explain . . ."

"How you would feel if you and I had had children." Hot anger and a fair share of hurt replaced the cold pulsing through his veins. "This life wouldn't be good enough for you. *I* wouldn't be good enough for you."

"No, Drew. That's not what I—"

Suddenly, he had to get away from her. He didn't give her a chance to finish, but turned on his bare heel and stormed away, emotion seething inside him. He'd check the snares he'd set earlier that day thinking rabbit would be a nice change from fish. Not that he had an appetite now. If he so much as tried to eat he thought he'd gag.

You're acting crazy as a bullbat, Coryell. He agreed with everything she said—Wild Horse Island wasn't the place to raise a family. But still, hearing it from her rankled a man, rode like a burr beneath the saddle.

Sometimes the truth was a bitter pill to choke down.

He found the first snare empty and headed for the second, grimacing when he stepped on the razor edge of a broken clamshell. He stopped and rubbed his foot and admitted that maybe she had done the proper thing in leaving him all those years ago.

Her father had been right back then. When he married Hannah, Drew's greatest ambition had been to take his wife to his bed and keep her there. He'd had no thought for the future, no dreams or goals or aspirations. Her leaving had changed that. Hannah's desertion had given him a purpose.

Drew had wanted to show her, to prove to her he could be a success. On the day he'd received her annulment papers he'd vowed to make a success of himself and rub the Mayfield family's face in the fact. After watching her sail away from him, he nursed his sorrows by going fishing, and that's when the idea for the Castaway Bait Company had been born.

Drew picked up the clamshell and chucked it at the trunk of a salt cedar tree. He'd worked hard ever since. He'd made some costly mistakes in the beginning, for instance, not knowing to patent his early designs. But he'd learned, and the business had grown. Now he held the patent on thirty-seven baits, and his company manufactured and shipped their products all over the country.

"But damned if I want her to know." He turned his face into the sea breeze and gazed out toward the gulf. In the distant sky, storm clouds billowed and the surf rolled onto the beach rougher than normal for this time of day. Perhaps the wind would blow away the confusion that plagued him. Why was it that now that he'd been handed the perfect opportunity to prove himself, he didn't want to do it? Why was he holding back?

Because you don't want what you do for a living to matter. You want Hannah to love you for yourself.

Wait a minute. Love? Where the hell did that come from? Love had nothing to do with this. His goal was to seduce her, nothing more. What she thought of him didn't matter. It shouldn't matter.

It did matter.

He muttered a curse and picked up his pace along the path leading to the second snare. Ten-year-old doubts and insecurities rolled over him, fresh and new and uncomfortable. Minutes ticked by as her words played over and over in his mind. *It was always you, Drew. You were the attraction.*

Finding this trap empty also, he lost the desire to check the other two he'd set. Tonight's stew must be about ready. He needed to stop running away, return to the cabin, and quit acting the fool. He shouldn't have let her get to him like that. None of what she had said negated the fact that she'd left him, that she'd denied her marriage vows on the very heels of having made them. She owed him a honeymoon. "And I intend to collect."

Not retaliation, he told himself, but simply good business.

Drew had learned how to succeed in business, and that was what she'd wanted, wasn't it? The woman would have no room to complain.

He covered the distance to the cabin in less than five

minutes. He found her standing at the stewpot, stirring the mixture with a long wooden spoon. At his approach she looked up. Dismay dimmed her blue eyes. "Drew, I'm sorry if what I said hurt you. I didn't mean to rehash the past. That isn't why I came."

"Oh, I know that. You came for my declaration. But since I don't want to give it up, it seems we have a problem."

She rested the spoon across the top of the kettle. "I can't agree to what you asked."

"My price is too high, hmm?"

"Yes, yes, it is. I'm not willing to prostitute myself for the sake of the Declaration of Independence."

Drew folded his arms and stood with his feet braced wide. "I think prostitution is too harsh a word."

"I don't," she replied, giving him a quelling glance. "Now if you'd care to place a monetary value on the document, we might come to terms."

"Money?" He made a show of rubbing his jaw. "That is an idea. What do you suggest?"

She licked her lips, drawing his attention to her mouth. "I don't know. I hadn't thought about it, actually. I'd hoped an appeal to your patriotism would be enough."

"My patriotism isn't for sale," he said with a shrug. Frustration tightened the corners of her eyes, and Drew started enjoying himself again. "Hmm . . . how to go about placing a value on my family heirloom."

"It's more than that, Drew. It's a piece of Texas's heritage, too. I remember the conversations we used to have about the heroes of the Republic of Texas. I'm betting if we scratch the surface, we'll find some of that patriotism after all."

"So you are offering to scratch my surface?" He rocked back on his heels, inhaling deeply. The delicious aroma of hoop stew teased his senses. "I do like the sound of that."

"Drew!"

He couldn't help but laugh. "Honey, your bargaining

skills could use some work. It is not in your best interests to remind me how valuable that document is."

Sighing, she said, "I know, but I don't want to cheat you. I wouldn't feel right about it."

"Because I so obviously need the money," he replied flatly, his amusement evaporating like steam off the stew.

She hesitated a moment, then looked him in the eyes. "No, because you are right, I did cheat you once before, and I'm sorry for it. It's bothered me ever since. When I leave here this time, I don't want any regrets. For either of us."

No regrets? *Oh, you can count on that, sweetheart.*

Pretty words and apologies couldn't change what went before. Subtle seduction was still in order. That goal hadn't changed. Drew decided the time had come to get down to business. Lifting the spoon from its resting spot across the kettle, he stirred the pot. "I won't sell the Declaration of Independence for any amount of money, Hannah. It wouldn't be right."

"But, Drew—"

He scooped up a spoonful of stew, then tipped it, dribbling the brew back into the pot, testing its thickness. Almost done. "Neither," he announced, "will I insist on the terms I offered you earlier, no matter how great the appeal."

She watched him, a speculative look on her face. So damned beautiful, he thought. He could all but see the wheels turning in her head. "You won't demand I have relations with you."

"That's right."

"But you're not going to give it to me outright."

"No, I'm not." The woman always did have a quick mind. "I can't do that. It's a family heirloom, Hannah. My course of action in this matter must uphold the beliefs of my ancestors. It's a question of Coryell honor."

That one stumped her, obviously. Drew lifted a spoonful of hoop stew to his lips for a taste, as much to hide his smile as to sample the cooking. She must be remembering all the stories he'd told her about the skeletons in the family closet.

"Any onion left? I think it could use a little more." As Hannah added the flavoring, he continued, "In keeping with family tradition, I can't give the declaration to you, nor can I sell it. That brings us to the third possibility—gambling."

"What?" She fumbled the last of the onion, dropping it onto the ground.

"Yep. I come from a long line of gamblers, Hannah. The Coryell family has a distinguished history when it comes to making bets."

"I thought you had pirates in the family tree."

"That's on my mother's side. The Coryells are gamblers from way back."

Her eyes widened as the light dawned. "You want to *bet* the declaration? You won't sell or give it to me, but you'll use it as a wager?"

"Uh-huh."

Aghast, she shook her head. "What game are you playing? For what stakes? And if you say my virtue, Coryell, I'll find another fish to hit you with."

No longer able to hold back his grin, Drew tsked and said, "Hannah, Hannah, Hannah. You wound me. I told you I wouldn't insist on my earlier terms. No, I don't want your virtue, not anymore."

"You don't?" she squeaked, her spine going straight.

Very subtle seduction, Drew reminded himself. "That's right. What I'm referring to at this particular moment are some of your other womanly skills. You probably noticed earlier that I could use some domestic assistance here on Wild Horse Island. My cabin is screaming out for a good cleaning. The pile of dirty laundry in the corner smells worse than the bait bucket, and when I'm not having hoop stew for supper, I live on canned beans. I have the fixings in my cupboard for fresh bread, but I can't bake worth a darn."

"I bake delicious bread," she said suspiciously.

"I remember." He folded his arms and rocked on the

balls of his feet. "You see, Hannah, it occurs to me—belatedly, I admit—that wifely duties involve more than sex. I'm thinking perhaps a little cooking and cleaning could be part of our deal for the declaration."

Her eyes narrowed. "Fresh bread and clean sheets? That's putting an awfully high value on my domestic skills. What mischief are you about here?"

"No mischief. A bet. A contest, if you prefer the term." Drew dipped the spoon into the stew for a second taste. "Umm . . ." he murmured. "That's as fine a fish stew as I've made in years. Did you add something to this when I wasn't looking?"

"No," she said, frustration vibrating in her tone. "Drew, what are you trying to say?"

"I'm challenging you to a contest, Hannah. A fishing competition, live bait versus lures. Me with my artificial bait, you with the real thing. You pick the fish and I'll set a time limit and the greatest total weight gains the victory. If you win, I'll hand over the declaration."

"And if you win?"

"If I win, you play my wife until your sailor comes back for you."

"Play your wife," she repeated. "Drew, don't make me go find a speckled trout."

"I know, I know. I mean cooking, cleaning, and laundry type things. I'm willing to agree that all bets are off when it comes to any possible intimacy between us." Drew was proud of the way he'd worded that. He'd made it sound good without promising a thing.

Anticipation lit her eyes and painted a swash of pink across her cheeks. So beautiful, he thought. Desire for her warmed his blood and hardened his loins. He shifted position, shielding his body's reaction from her possible notice. No sense calling attention to the fact he didn't consider that particular battle done. "So are we on? Do we have a bet, Miss Hannah?"

She pursed her lips. "A contest fair and square? No tricks?"

"No tricks. You have my word. I'll even let you use my

Meek reel if you'd like, although I warn you it needs an educated thumb to prevent backlash. We can work out the particulars over our stew."

Hannah looked from him out toward the bay. Her lips moved and he thought he heard her whisper, "Eight-inch Throbbing Bob."

After a moment's thought, she nodded abruptly. "I accept your challenge, Drew Coryell." She held out her hand. "Shall we shake on it?"

Despite his noble intentions, the heat in his blood got the better of Drew. He took her hand, but instead of shaking it, used it to pull her toward him. "Nah," he said, lowering his mouth toward hers. "I prefer to do it this way."

Chapter 4

The peck kept Hannah tossing and turning a good portion of the night. She wouldn't go so far as to call it a kiss. She had experienced Drew Coryell's kisses in the past. They were long, passionate, ravenous events that stirred her juices and left her hungering for more. This was nothing like that. This had been brief, passionless, and indifferent. He'd no more than brushed his lips across hers. He hadn't stopped to nibble, hadn't paused to savor. He certainly hadn't coaxed his way inside with that talented tongue of his.

A peck, not even a smooch. He might as well have been kissing his sister.

Hannah couldn't help but feel a bit insulted, especially since The Peck had been but the first of a number of such assaults to her confidence in her feminine charms.

During supper he'd never once made a suggestive remark about the two of them "stewing." He'd talked to her about fishing and the sailing trips he'd taken over the years. He'd even gone so far as to politely ask after her father. Then, claiming the role of gentleman, Drew had given up his bed for the night, stringing up a hammock outside between two trees in which to sleep. He never once suggested he share her bed, never tried to charm his way past her defenses. Never even acted as if the idea had occurred to him.

He should have kept his bed. Hannah might as well have been plopped into the kettle and hung over the fire, so much did she stew. Why didn't he want her? Never mind that she should be glad of the fact. That had nothing to do with her current insecurities.

From eleven until midnight, she fretted about her physical appearance. From midnight until one, she brooded that men found her intelligence off-putting. From one to two, she wept over the loss of her womanly allure. Then, somewhere around three the light dawned in the darkness, and she realized he'd played her for a fool.

Nothing was wrong with her. She wasn't unattractive or unlovable. The man wasn't immune to her. That daunting display at the beach upon her arrival put that particular anxiety to rest.

No, Drew was up to something, and she suspected it involved this contest he'd proposed. A fishing contest for a piece of Texas history. How very bold of him.

"Bold, hah," she grumbled into the darkness. She'd show him bold. He likely thought to lure her into complacency, then net her when she wasn't looking. She'd bet her own favorite fishing pole that Drew Coryell still wanted her in his bed.

If she were smart she would forget about the declaration, appropriate his rowboat, and head for home. But she wouldn't do that. Historical documents aside, she felt the need to discover what motivated the man to make his wicked demand. She refused to believe he'd go to the trouble to scheme if all he wanted was to bed her. The Drew Coryell she'd fallen in love with was not that shallow and callous a person. Surely he hadn't changed that much.

No, Drew was up to some bit of mischief, so she would remain on her guard. He wouldn't catch her unawares. She would make certain of that. She would simply outangle the angler.

With that pleasant thought uppermost in her mind, Hannah finally drifted off to sleep. She dreamed of mermaids and pirates and treasure chests filled with riches. She awoke to the stink of dead fish.

"Rise and shine, my little Kidney Spoon," Drew said in a sing-song tone. A match scratched and lamplight flared.

Hannah wrenched opened one eye and worked up the energy to glare. In a voice raspy with sleep, she repeated, "Kidney Spoon?"

"It's a bait. Kidney-shaped blade with a treble hook. J. T. Buel out of Whitehall, New York, filed the patent on it originally."

"What time is it?"

"Four A.M. Time to fish. I've already cut your bait." He sent the bait bucket swinging from side to side. "You can thank me later."

"I'll thank you to leave me alone."

"Leave you alone? Why, Hannah, what's this? Are you trying to welch on our bet?"

She sighed heavily and started to sit up, but remembered just in time she had slept naked after washing out her underclothes before turning in. Clutching the sheet to her chest, she grumbled, "I'm not welching on anything. I need privacy to dress."

"Just be quick about it or you'll miss the boat. This contest starts at five A.M. sharp whether you're on the water or not." He sauntered out the door, bucket in hand, whistle on his lips.

"That blasted whistle of his," Hannah muttered, throwing back the sheet and padding across the room to the fireplace where she'd hung her clothing to dry. It was probably the real reason he didn't kiss her. Likely he'd used up all his pucker power on his silly little ditties.

Her pique mellowed when she spied the mug of steaming coffee sitting on the table. She sipped it while she dressed in one of Drew's shirts and a pair of his pants that she appropriated from a trunk placed at the foot of the bed. The clothes all but swallowed her, the shirtsleeves and pants legs rolled up, the waist gathered and tied with a rope belt, but they served the purpose. The coffee stole through her, chasing the fatigue from her bones. Soon she felt better. Despite the lack of sleep, by the time she donned her shoes she looked forward to the upcoming contest.

"Musky Wrigglers and Throbbing Bobs," she murmured as she quickly made up the bed. No matter what bait he pulled from his tackle box, she intended to win this competition. She had no reason to fear a loss. Hadn't she always been a more successful fisherman than he? Besides, the man intended to fish with artificial lures. Did he honestly think a peculiar-shaped piece of metal would attract more game than a nice, smelly piece of fish flesh? Especially when the woman wielding the rod was as experienced as she? "I sincerely doubt it."

And so, determined to go out and win the priceless Declaration of Independence away from the man so foolish as to put it up as stakes in a scheme, Hannah exited the cabin.

Half an hour later, they were drifting in a rowboat in the middle of the bay. They'd bickered over details of the competition on the trip out, mainly because Hannah had tried to toss out her line and troll while Drew was busy rowing. She hadn't honestly expected to succeed at that gambit, but she had enjoyed needling the man. Now as he stowed the oars and picked up his rod, she waited impatiently to signal the contest's official start. Finally, he nodded toward her and she said, "Begin."

For Hannah, "begin" didn't mean start talking. Drew apparently didn't see it that way. The moment her shrimp-baited line hit the water, he opened his mouth and gave her an unsolicited inventory of the contents of his tackle box.

"In addition to my Musky Wriggler, I've got your Blue-Headed Spinning Squid Bait, the Musky Minnow, the Perfect Plug, the Ball Bearing Troller, the—"

Hannah interrupted. "Hush, Coryell. You'll scare away the fish."

"Don't be silly. This isn't some calm, quiet lake where every sound echoes." He lifted an artificial lure from his tackle box and held it by its two-pronged hook. "I think I'll start off with my Texas Doodle Spring Hook. I've always had good luck attracting live ones with it."

Hannah wrinkled her nose, seeing only a long, thin hunk of black metal with a dangling hook. "That's an ugly piece."

"Ugly! Why, I beg to differ. This fella is a beauty. The design is an improvement on the Sockdolager and it works like a charm."

"Uh-huh," she drawled. "If that's the case, then why don't you quit talking and start fishing." At that moment, she felt a tug on her rod and a grin split her face. "You are already behind."

For the next few minutes, Hannah worked to land her fish. He was a fighter, and she enjoyed the battle, but when she brought him to the boat, she had to bite back a groan of dismay.

Drew eyed the small trout and smirked. "Maybe you should keep it for bait."

"Very funny," she replied, tossing the fish back. She only momentarily considered keeping that particular catch. Terms of the contest declared the winner to be the one with the most weight from the combined poundage of five fish caught in a two-hour period. Giving up the two-pounder was a risk Hannah felt compelled to take, a bold declaration to the man seated in front of her. She had no fear of not catching her quota in weights sufficient to beat his socks off.

Her gaze dropped to his feet. Not that the man bothered to wear socks. "What is it you're wearing on your feet?"

Grinning, he held up a sandaled foot. "Like 'em? A friend brought them to me from the South Seas. They're made from the hide of a wild boar, and they're perfect for the beach. Sand slides in, then right back out again. Why, I—" Drew broke off abruptly as the rod in his hand bowed. "Well . . . well . . . well. Looks like my

Texas Doodle Spring Hook has done its job." Minutes later, he boated a redfish. "What do you think, Hannah? Six pounds? Seven?"

She scowled at him and turned her attention to her line, willing something big to bite. Over the next two hours Hannah pulled in her share of fish, but to her dismay, Drew always managed to bring in one a little bigger, a little heavier. As the clock counted down to the last fifteen minutes, she felt herself growing desperate. While Drew switched out his lures, attaching the Perfect Plug to the end of his line, she baited her hook with an extra big chunk of cut gizzard shad. Five minutes later, she pulled in what she guessed to be a ten-pound snapper. "Hurrah," she shouted. "That'll win it for me. I just know it."

Drew frowned and for the first time that morning looked a little worried. After casting and reeling in four more times, he said, "Hmm . . . I think I'd better pull out the big guns now."

She mocked. "You mean the eight-inch Throbbing Bob?"

He glanced down, then back up at her, a strange, strangled expression on his face. "No. It's better suited to beach fishing. I think I'll use my Musky Wriggler."

Her stringer weighted down with her catch and the time limit quickly approaching, Hannah indulged in a smug moment. "Go ahead, Coryell. Try to beat me. Show me what that Musky Wriggler can do."

"Honey, that's been my fantasy for years."

Casting his line, he smiled at her, and that, along with the warmth in his eyes, made her feel rather like prey herself. Hannah found the sensation reassuring. He wasn't so indifferent to her. Now that the pressure of the contest was behind her, she had a little time to spare to remind him of the fact.

She lifted her hand to the placket of the shirt she wore and flapped the material briskly. "With the sun up, it's getting hot, don't you think?"

The man was so easy.

Drew dragged his gaze up from her bosom. "Hot. Yeah."

"I'll be glad to get off the water, won't you?" She leaned over and the shirt gaped. Slowly, she rolled up the bulky leg of the pants she had donned, displaying her leg halfway up the calf. He nodded, his attention focused on her, and Hannah reveled in her feminine power.

"My rod is wiggling," he murmured.

Good, she thought wickedly. Then, seeing his fishing pole bow toward the water, immediately exclaimed, "Oh, no!"

The fishing pole bowed toward the water as Drew took it firmly in hand. Hannah watched the fight between man and fish with alarm. *Please let it simply be a fighter like my first one. Please let it be a little one.*

The water bubbled as the fish surfaced, then dove once more. Hannah prayed the brief glimpse she got of it would prove wrong, but as Drew won the battle and lifted his prize from the bay, she saw her prayers had not been answered. The fish assuredly topped twelve pounds.

She'd lost the bet.

Smiles wreathed Drew's face as he held up his fish. "God bless that Musky Wriggler. He never lets me down."

Afternoon sun dappled the rope hammock hung between two live oaks outside the fishing cabin on Wild Horse Island. Drew lay sprawled in the contraption, his fingers laced behind his head, elbows akimbo, one leg dangling, his bare big toe digging into the gritty sand beneath him just often enough to keep him swinging. Having awakened from a nap a few short moments ago, he watched his one-time wife hang wet laundry along a makeshift rope clothesline. He believed he could lie there watching her forever.

Sunlight caught streaks of red in her golden hair,

causing it to shine like old gold. Her day outdoors had painted her cheeks pink, and as he watched her profile, he was struck by her appeal. Prettiness had matured into true beauty during the years they'd been apart. The woman had good bones. She would age with grace and style and undoubtedly turn men's heads until the day she died.

Drew's gaze drifted down her body, savoring the sight of her full, high bosom, her tiny waist, and the flare of shapely hips as outlined by a dress dampened by contact with wet laundry and clinging to her form. Her shape stirred his lust, but when she turned to look at him, her mouth flattened in a frown and her eyes narrowed into a blue-fire glare.

Drew bit back a groan. The woman's body stirred his lust, but it was her spirit that inflamed his passion.

He wanted desperately to rise from his hammock, march across the yard and sweep her off her feet. He needed to lay her on his bed and strip away her clothes. He ached to bury his body deep within hers and slake the hunger she'd roused within him.

Patience, Coryell, he told himself. *She's not ready yet.*

So he set about making her so. He set the hammock swaying with a push, then settled into the contraption like a lazy pasha. "Hey, honey?" he called. "Would you bring me a glass of lemonade?"

What he got was a sopping pillow case thrown at his face. He caught it just before it slapped him and he chuckled. It was just the sort of response he'd hoped for. "Now, now, Hannah. Don't be a poor loser. I beat you fair and square."

"I'd like to beat you," she grumbled just loud enough for him to hear.

He watched her struggle to get a sheet hung evenly on the line and figured a gentleman would offer his help. However, since it was in his best interests to keep her temper up, he stayed right where he was. He wanted her own passions aroused, her emotions aflame. He wanted her worked up to the point of explosion because he knew that when Hannah lost control he'd have his opportunity to get her into his bed.

The wedding night due him. The honeymoon stolen from him. Sex. That's what he needed from Hannah Mayfield. *But is that all you need?* asked a little voice in his head.

Drew firmly quashed that voice and turned his attention to the matter at hand. He needed to turn up Hannah's annoyance heat a little higher. This day was ticking away and she'd be leaving tomorrow. The time had come to quit playing this catch. It was time to bring her to boat.

Drew climbed from the hammock and approached Hannah, silently offering a hand with the laundry. She accepted his assistance with ill-concealed bad humor.

"So," he said, throwing one end of the bed sheet over the rope. "Tell me about your life in San Antonio. Are you happy there?"

Suspicion clouded her eyes. "What do you mean?"

"It's a simple question, really. I thought it would be good to get to know you a little better."

She gave an unladylike snort. "Why would you want to get to know the laundress?"

"Oh, Hannah, you're more than a laundress."

In the middle of pinning his shirt to the line, she paused and sent him a questioning look.

"You're also a cook and a charwoman, are you not?"

"Funny, Coryell. You are very funny."

It was in his mind to say something unpleasant about her father, something to get her hackles up, but instead he was distracted by the purse of her pink, pouty mouth. Reaching out, Drew traced a finger across her luscious lower lip. Words appeared from out of nowhere in his mind, and he allowed them to roll off his tongue. "You, Hannah Mayfield, are as pretty as sunrise after a storm."

And then, dammit, he kissed her.

Really kissed her. Not a brief brush of mouths like

before. Completely unplanned, without prior thought, this was a kiss with a capital K.

He put his hands around her shoulders and slowly pulled her toward him. As the inches separating them disappeared, the air surrounding them thickened. Her tongue snaked out and wetted her bottom lip, and all Drew's plans and schemes took flight like seabirds from the shore, leaving behind only the truth that dwelled within his heart.

Lowering his head, he moved his lips against hers, wet and soft and gentle. It was a tender *Hello again, I've missed you* that quickly became more, so much more.

He wrapped his arms around her, their bodies touching, remembering, sighing. Eager and edgy, he traced the seam of her lips with his tongue, seeking entrance. Demanding it. She yielded to him on a little moan of pleasure and he thrust his tongue inside.

Hannah. She smelled of sand and sea and sunshine, of happy days long ago and dreams long denied. She tasted of lemon drops. She must have found his store of candy in the kitchen.

Hannah. Hungry now, Drew deepened the kiss, plundering her mouth, stroking his tongue roughly against hers. Desire, heavy and hot, pooled in his loins and he pulled her closer. Her arms lifted and slipped around his neck. She opened her mouth wider, her tongue dancing with his.

Drew shuddered at her response and clasped her even more tightly. Oh, God, he ached for her. How long had it been? How long since he last experienced this extreme degree of need? Ten years, that's how long. Not since Hannah.

He released her mouth just long enough to steal a breath, then he was back sucking and nipping and nibbling at her lips. His hands swept down her back, cupping the sweet curve of her buttocks and pulling her close, agonizingly close, but not nearly close enough. Instinctively, he pushed himself against her, seeking, throbbing, needing to claim.

Her hands drifted down from his neck, sweeping across the breadth of his shoulders, drawing circles down his back. When her hips joined in the rhythm, rocking with his, Drew discarded all pretense of control. He gathered her skirts in great, impatient handfuls, pulling upward, desperate to bare her skin to his touch.

Ahh. She was naked beneath her skirt, and he remembered seeing her laundered chemise and drawers hanging next to the sheets. He slid his fingers across the silk of her skin, touching her, kneading her, teasing her. So intent was he upon the taste of her, the scent of her, the experience of her, that at first he didn't register her resistence. It took her stammered "No!" to break through the sensual fog clouding his mind.

He loosened his hold and Hannah tore away from him, stepping backward. She stared at him, a tormented light haunting her eyes, cutting him like a bowie knife. Then she blinked. Once. Twice. She shut her eyes and visibly shuddered.

Time spun out like spider's silk. Drew's heart pounded; the heat in his loins provided a constant ache.

"You shouldn't have done that," she said softly.

"Hannah," he said in a rough, ragged tone. "I don't know . . . I didn't mean . . ." How had things gotten so out of hand so fast? When had he lost all control? Why had he veered so completely from his scheme? What had happened?

Hannah happened.

Oh, hell.

In that moment Drew again heard that nagging voice ask, *Is a wedding night all you need from this woman?* This time, he couldn't deny the answer. No. He did want more from Hannah Mayfield than simple, uncomplicated sex. Damn it all, it was true. Despite the hurt and heartache of years gone by, despite the mistakes they'd both had made, he wanted more than the honeymoon that hadn't happened.

Drew still wanted the life she had promised him a

decade ago. He wanted the feeling of completion he'd lost and never found again in another woman's arms. He wanted the laughter and the bickering and the love. Oh, God, the love.

He wanted the marriage.

The realization left him raw and reeling. Wonderful. Just wonderful. Didn't he remember the lessons of the past? Didn't he remember the pain? Only a dolt would want any more of her than what she owed him beneath the sheets. Only a masochistic sap-skull would open himself up to the same pain she'd caused once before. *Damn me for an idiot sonofabitch.* He muttered softly, "To think I thought this was just about sex."

He didn't know he'd said it aloud until he saw her body stiffen. Her chin came up, her shoulders went back. Fire lit her eyes.

"What is this all about, Drew?" she asked, her voice icy and betraying a slight tremble. "Tell me. It's about more than a silly honeymoon, isn't it? You have some secret agenda, so tell me what it is."

He all but quit listening after the words *silly honeymoon.* How could she deny what they'd had together that way? His temper flared, red-hot and steaming, and he struck out, wanting to hurt her as she had hurt him. "I told you what I wanted, dammit. Sex. That's it. Nothing more. Just sex."

The words echoed on the breeze swirling between them. Hannah's eyes went wide and wounded. "I don't believe that," she whispered.

Now Drew was running on pure emotion, thought having little to do with anything that came out of his mouth. "Well, you should, because it's the truth. You hurt me when you left. I wanted to get back at you. I'm a damn fine lover, Hannah Mayfield, and I intend to ruin you for any other man. You'll look back on leaving me as the biggest mistake of your life."

She sucked in an audible breath. "Revenge. That's what this was—the contest, the kiss. It was a game for you, wasn't it? A mean-spirited game of Pay Hannah Back." Before he could respond, she added, "I never thought you could be so cruel."

Then she turned and fled to the cabin, slamming the door shut behind her.

Drew's stomach sank like a Brass Minnow bait and he pushed both hands through his hair in exasperation. What the hell had just happened? How had everything gone so awry so quickly? If marriage to Hannah Mayfield was what he wanted, he and his vile temper had just set it back at least a dozen years. "You are smooth as a starfish, Coryell."

He stood staring at the cabin door, his heart pounding, his breathing hard. Damn him for his lies, curse him for speaking from emotion rather than thought.

If he had taken a moment to think about it, he could have told her the truth. He could have explained what a fishing trip, a kiss, and a bowl of hoop stew had taught him.

"I could have told her that I've never stopped loving her."

Hannah shut the cabin door behind her, then leaned back against it and exhaled a shaky sigh. Her knees went watery and the tremble in her heart worked its way out to her arms and legs, and she slid to the floor in an undignified heap.

Curse Drew Coryell. He had fooled her hook, line, and sinker. "That slimy eel. That barnacle. The man belongs on the sea floor sucking up silt like the other bottom feeders."

And she should be boiled in fish oil for letting him get the better of her.

As quickly as it came, her temper dissipated, leaving despair in its wake. He'd never had any intention of handing over the declaration. He'd set out to seduce her from the start. The Peck, the gentlemanly behavior, the hoop stew, the fishing contest, his goading superiority guaranteed to stir her passions—he'd formatted a battle plan and set it into motion like a West Point general. And she, fish-brained woman that she was, fell without a fight.

Agitated, Hannah pushed to her feet and started pacing the room, her mind spinning like a whirlpool. What should she do now? Should she stand and fight back? What did she want?

His love.

"No!" The denial burst from her lips like a cry of pain. She wouldn't think that. She would not allow her mind to go in that direction.

She had come to Wild Horse Island as a representative of the Texas Historical Preservation Society. She'd made this trip for one reason alone: to obtain on behalf of the citizens of Texas the only known surviving copy of the Republic of Texas's Declaration of Independence.

If that's the case, whispered that wicked little voice in her head, *then why did you lie to your father about where you were going?*

Hannah shut her eyes and pressed her palms hard against her forehead. "No. No. No. No. I won't. I won't think that." Drew admitted to being out for revenge. He was nothing more than a predator. He was a shark who did his swimming on land, and she'd better remember it.

Seconds ticked by as she debated what to do. Until now she hadn't believed he'd send her away from here without the declaration—contest or no. The young man she'd married had been proud of his heritage, proud to be a Texan, and she had felt in her bones that he'd be honored to present the document to the State of Texas on behalf of the Coryell family.

Apparently, she'd been wrong. Apparently, the man cared more about avenging the blow she'd dealt to his masculinity by recognizing him for the beach ne'er-do-well he was, than about preserving the history of Texas, of honoring the men who fought and died for the ideal of independence.

Or did he?

The question whispered through her mind like a

gentle ocean breeze. As the minutes ticked by, Hannah stopped trying to ignore it.

Was Drew being truthful when he made those hurtful claims? Did he feel nothing for her but lust? If so, why all the passion in his kiss, in his words? Why all the emotion?

Maybe his attempted seduction was more than cold-blooded revenge.

Hannah pondered the question a moment, then shrugged. Her mind was a muddle. She needed to clear it before she could do any proper thinking. To that end, she decided she'd finish up the laundry and then go swimming. She also decided Drew deserved to donate a shirt to the cause.

Hannah crossed the room to Drew's trunk and threw open the lid. She dug to the bottom for the pristine white silk businessman's shirt she'd spied and wondered over earlier. Removing it, she held it up before her. Saltwater would ruin this beautiful cloth.

Hannah smiled. Sometimes a girl simply had to take her pleasures wherever she could find them.

Chapter 5

JUST AS HE'D DONE FOR THE BETTER PART OF HIS LIFE, Drew took his problems fishing.

The noontime sun beat down upon him as he drifted in the rowboat some thirty yards offshore in the bay. He wished he'd grabbed his hat before shoving off; he'd be much cooler. Or maybe not. Grabbing his hat would have meant entering his cabin and facing Hannah. At that point the idea of *hot* took on a whole new meaning.

Drew reeled in his line, then cast it out again. He used a Maybug Bait for tackle this time, mainly because he never caught anything on that particular lure, an idea that suited his fancy. This fishing trip was for therapeutic purposes only. He had some heavy thinking ahead of him. Alone in a boat surrounded by water was the best place to do it.

If he wanted to win Hannah's love, especially after today's debacle, he would need a damn fine plan.

Of course, the obvious solution was to tell her the truth. He could march up to the cabin and explain how it had taken him some time to understand the motivation behind his actions. He could tell her about the Castaway Bait Company and list his patents like a pedigree. He could lay all his cards on the table and declare his love for her.

"But I don't want to do it that way," he grumbled, sending his line flying with the flick of a wrist. His pride balked at the idea.

Drew wanted to win Hannah as the man who had lost her. He needed to know that she loved him for himself, not for the financial success he'd achieved. Sure that made his task more difficult, but he considered the potential gain worth the risk. Besides, if he couldn't manage it this way, he could always resort to the truth later on. After all, the sailboat wasn't scheduled to return until sometime tomorrow.

Probably the first thing he should do was tell her she could have the declaration. He couldn't in good conscience keep it now that he knew his was the only known surviving copy. "You should have told her that up front," he muttered. Had he been honest then, he might not be in this current mess.

A little self-honesty from the beginning wouldn't have hurt anything, either. Too bad he'd been too busy trying to get even. "Idiot," he groused. Hindsight often made a man appear the fool, and this instance was no exception.

However, it did him no good to worry about what had gone before. He needed to devote his attention to figuring out how to proceed from here.

"So," he said, then scowled when the fishing pole bowed toward the water. He immediately stopped reeling in, allowing the line to go slack. Sure enough, the fish slipped off the hook. "How should I . . . ?" his voice trailed off as motion on shore grabbed his attention. He did a double take. "Hannah?"

He grabbed for his ever-present knapsack and yanked out his great-grandfather's spyglass. Bringing it to his eye, he stared toward the splash of white in front of his fishing cabin. Then he damned near swallowed his tongue.

She'd donned one of his shirts again. He watched her hang her wet dress on the makeshift clothesline, next to her underclothes. His stare moved from her underclothes to her bare legs, and he realized she must be naked beneath his shirt.

His mouth went dry. He lowered the spyglass with hands that shook. He tried to resist—tried hard—but a moment later he succumbed and brought the glass back up to his eye.

Hannah had disappeared. While he wasn't looking, she'd disappeared from the campsite. A sixth sense told Drew he'd best find out where she had gone.

Grumbling, he stowed his pole, picked up his oars, and headed ashore. Upon reaching Wild Horse Island, he dragged his boat away from the water, then checked the cabin. Nothing.

Outside again, he stood beside the laundry flapping in the gentle ocean breeze and gazed around the camp. The yeasty fragrance of baking bread drifted from the cabin as he debated what to do. Should he follow her or wait for her return? Surely with bread in the oven she didn't intend to disappear for long. Which did she want him to do?

Knowing Hannah, she probably wanted him to follow her. Knowing Hannah, he'd probably be better off staying right where he was. He studied the ground, discovered her trail, and set off tracking her across the island.

Fifteen minutes later, he figured out where she was headed. On the gulf side of the island, he wove in and around and over the dunes and eventually arrived at the beach. Footprints led across the sand toward the water, but it was the pile of white silk lying just beyond reach of the waves that grabbed his attention. "Oh, Hannah."

Almost against his will, he lifted his gaze toward the gulf. There she was, some thirty yards out, a mermaid cavorting in the surf. A naked mermaid, he knew. She dove, her bare legs rising above the surface of the waves and in seconds, Drew went hard as a harpoon.

It made him angry that she had that kind of power over him, so when she surfaced, he called out, "Hannah, come back in. It's not safe to swim alone."

"Go away, Coryell. It's not safe to swim with sharks, either, and that's what I'd be doing if you were in the gulf. Now leave me alone, I'll be fine. I don't want you around." Firing that salvo, she abruptly sank beneath the waves and swam away.

Drew watched the surf, and as the seconds ticked by and she failed to reappear, his heart began to pound. "Damn it, Hannah," he said, stripping off his shirt and starting to tug off his heavy denim pants in preparation for going in after her. Then he spotted her farther out than where he'd been looking, and he breathed a huge sigh of relief.

He cupped his hands around his mouth and yelled, "Get back here. You're too far out. The current gets dangerous out there." When she disappeared for a second time, he stripped off his pants while cursing, "Blasted woman."

Dressed only in his drawers, he ran into the water, then dove when it was deep enough and started swimming toward the spot where he'd last seen her. Was this her way of getting back at him? Getting swept out into the gulf and drowning? Or maybe serving up an arm or a leg to a goddamned shark? Furious and fearful, he cut fast, smooth strokes through the water.

Halting periodically, he searched the water for sight of her. Where did she go? Fear twisted his belly and threatened to steal his breath. When he got hold of her he'd . . .

"Help! Drew, please help me."

Fear stung like a jellyfish. Treading water now, he whipped his head around, trying to trace the sound. Left . . . somewhere left of him. He twisted around and heard a gurgled shout.

There. A hand. Her hand with something around it . . . a fishing net?

A chill slithered down his spine. Damn. Damn. Damn. Hannah was tangled in a fishing net. He swallowed a mouthful of saltwater and fear as he struck out swimming, pulling and kicking with all his strength, knowing she could drown before he reached her. Knowing he couldn't let her die. Knowing such an outcome would destroy him, too.

Be smart, honey. Don't fight it. Try to float. He lifted his head, trying to spot her, but saw only the rolling blue waves of the gulf. Panic welled inside him, but he grimly controlled it. He didn't have time for panic.

Where are you, honey? Show me. For God's sake show me.

As if she had heard him, she surfaced, just long enough for him to catch sight of her. Even as she sank once more, he reached her, his fingers first brushing her hair, then an arm. Careful to avoid tangling himself in the net, he grabbed her by the shoulders and propelled her head toward the surface.

He heard her sputter, cough, and draw a breath. It was the sweetest sound he had ever heard.

Supporting her head above the water, Drew kicked toward shore. With the net swirling around them, the going was difficult. He'd have given up every one of his lure patents for a knife right then. At least Hannah knew better than to fight him and compound one stupid act with another.

It felt like forever before he reached water shallow enough in which to stand. He shifted Hannah into his arms, then carried her out onto the beach. He strode to the spot where he'd left his clothes and gently set her down. From his pocket, he removed a knife. His hand trembled as he cut the offending net away. "Damned shrimpers throw everything overboard. You wouldn't believe some of the trash that washes ashore."

Finally free, Hannah rose onto her hands and knees, coughing hard. Then she rolled onto her back and collapsed onto the sand, eyes closed, her chest rising and falling as she continued to suck in deep breaths.

That was the first time the fact registered with Drew that she wasn't naked, as he had previously believed. She wore strips of cloth—torn pieces of one of his bedsheets, perhaps—tied to conceal her from her breasts to her thighs. She might as well have been naked; the cloth had ripped, and she had rope burns across her belly.

The sight sparked his temper all over again.

He ranted. "What the hell were you thinking, Hannah? Of all the stupid, idiotic, foolish things to do. Do you know how close you came to dying just then? And it wasn't only that hunk of fishing net. The current out there gets nasty due to the pass into the bay. And let's not forget the danger of shark attacks. It's tarpon season here, and their migration up and down the coast attracts sharks by the dozens. And a shark is the most accommodating fish in the gulf. One of 'em could easily accommodate a trio of you. It's rare they'll swim in where it's shallow, but out there where you were . . ." He shuddered, then finally shut up.

Hannah opened tired eyes. "You saved my life, Drew. Thank you."

His knees turned to water and he sank down onto the sand beside her. "I have never been so frightened in my entire life."

She reached out and touched him, placing her hand on his thigh. "I wasn't. I knew you'd save me. That's what kept me from panicking."

He got a lump the size of an oyster in his throat. "You trusted me that much?"

She smiled sadly and shut her eyes. "Yes. Amazing, isn't it, that I'd trust you to save my life on the very heels of your having told me you wanted to hurt me."

"Ah, Hannah, don't. I never . . ." His voice trailed off. He didn't know what to say. He'd acted petty and foolish and mean and he *had* wanted to hurt her. God, what a fool he'd been. Failing to find words with which to heal the pain his blindness had caused her, he tried to tell her another way.

Leaning over, he kissed the rope burns on her stomach.

* * *

At the touch of Drew's gentle lips against her skin, Hannah thought she was drowning all over again. This time, however, the tide sweeping over her was pure emotion. How could he be so mean and vicious one moment, and so sweet and tender the next?

"Please, don't hurt me any more."

He lifted his head. "It stings?"

"No, you hurt my heart." Then, blinking back tears, she added, "But I guess I hurt your heart, too, didn't I?"

Drew nodded solemnly. "Cleaved it right in two."

"And that's why you asked me to sell myself for the declaration."

He responded with a half-dozen invectives muttered under his breath. "Look, that was wrong. I'm sorry I ever brought that up. I was angry, Hannah. I've been angry for years because you walked out on my love."

"Yes, I did. And it was wrong of me and cruel of me and undoubtedly the dumbest thing I've ever done in my life." Sitting up, she met and held his gaze. "I loved you, too, Drew, and I shouldn't have listened to my father. I should have stayed with you. I should have at least suggested you leave the beach life behind. But I didn't and I've regretted it and I haven't been able to put you behind me."

Her lips lifted in a tremulous smile and her eyes pleaded for him to listen and to believe. "That's why I had to see you again, why I really made the trip to Wild Horse Island. I couldn't marry Jeremy without seeing you again."

Drew went still as beached driftwood. "Jeremy? Who the hell is Jeremy?"

"He's my beau."

"Your beau."

"Yes. He's asked me to marry him. I knew I needed to see you again before I could tell him yea or nay."

He glanced away, looking out toward sea. She watched his shoulders rise as he drew a deep breath, then softly asked, "And now that you've seen me?"

She shrugged. "I want a family, Drew. I want children."

He grabbed her arm, his grip fierce. "You will *not* marry him."

Hannah saw something in his face, some truth he wouldn't admit shining in his eyes. Her heart pounded as if she stood poised on the edge of a precipice, except Drew was the one who needed a good push. So she pushed by trying to tug her arm from his steely grip. "Let me go."

"Say it, Hannah. Say you won't marry this Jeremy person."

"Let. Me. Go."

Seconds passed. Long, pregnant flashes of time. Then Drew's eyes blazed. "Never, dammit. Never again."

And he kissed her. His mouth was hard on hers, driven and demanding as he forced her lips apart and plundered her mouth.

Hannah ravished right back. As he buried his fingers in her hair, her hands swept hungrily up and down his back. When his mouth finally released hers to trail down her neck, kissing and nipping along the way, she arched against him. And as he rose above her long enough to strip away the bands of cloth shielding her breasts, she lifted her head and licked him, tasting salt and sea and Drew. His deep-throated groan sent a shiver of excitement racing up her skin.

Hannah felt daring and desperate, her actions ruled by passions that had simmered inside her for so long. She gave herself up to the heat he roused within her. She wanted this. She wanted him. This was the real reason why she had come to Wild Horse Island. She knew that now.

She had never stopped loving Drew Coryell.

In that moment, the world surrounding Hannah faded away. The seagulls quit calling, the surf stopped rolling, the sea breeze ceased to blow. *I love you,* she silently vowed as his hands streaked across her skin. *I love you* thrummed in her heart as he dipped his head and suckled her breast.

Those three words played a litany through her mind over and over and over as he stroked, laved, kneaded, and teased her body to a fever pitch. And when—finally, thank God—he claimed her, joining his body with hers and sweeping her higher and higher with every long, luscious thrust until she convulsed beneath a tidal wave of pure sensation, Hannah said them aloud. "I love you."

Seconds later she felt his climax deep in her womb and she rejoiced. But it was the words he whispered next that sent her spirit soaring.

"I sure as hell hope you meant that, sweetheart, because I love you, too."

Long minutes later when they could breathe again, Drew rolled to his feet, then bent and lifted her into his arms. Cradling her against him, he walked out into the water and washed away the sand that now coated their skin. They frolicked in the surf like children, then loved like adults in waist-deep water. Wonderfully tired and temporarily sated, they exited the water and donned their clothes as protection against the late-afternoon sun. "We should go back to the cabin and get you a hat," Drew told her, scowling as he thumped the tip of her nose. "You're starting to resemble a lobster."

"Well, thank you so very much for the compliment," she dryly replied.

They walked hand in hand along the edge of the softly rolling surf, their conversation comfortable and limited to inconsequential matters. A couple of times Drew attempted to turn the talk to more serious subjects, but Hannah refused to cooperate. Time enough for that later; now she wished to simply enjoy the moment.

Then, suddenly, time ran out.

They returned to the fishing cabin to fetch Hannah a hat and found a sailboat pulling up to the end of the fishing pier.

"Oh, no," she fussed, tugging on the hem of her shirt in embarrassment. "He's early. Why? I specifically told him to pick me up in three days. In fact, he told me that suited him just fine because he wanted to make a run down to Corpus Christi to visit his sweetheart." After a moment's pause, she added, "Maybe they had a fight."

"Go on to the cabin, honey," Drew said, giving the small of her back a slight shove. "That's not the same boat."

"What? Were you expecting company, Drew?"

He shook his head. "No. Only a couple people know I'm here. I hope there's not trouble at the factory."

Trouble at the factory? What factory? Hannah wanted to ask, but taking the time now wasn't worth the risk of getting caught by a stranger half-naked and thoroughly ravished. Darting for the shelter of the fishing cabin, she spared the sailboat one last curious look . . . and froze. She blinked and looked again. "Jeremy? And my father!"

Drew whipped his head around. "Jeremy?"

Hannah's eyes closed. "Yes. Oh my. And Papa, too."

Seconds ticked by in silence before Drew cleared his throat and asked, "Shall I send them away?"

Yes, her heart cried, though her mind knew better. She had to face this sometime. Might as well get it over with. "No. I'll talk to them."

Drew took her by the arm and started tugging. "Better get in the house and get some clothes on in that case." Then, as he grabbed her dress and underwear off the line, he muttered just loud enough for her to hear, "I can't believe this is happening all over again."

Inside, he, too, quickly pulled on clean clothes. Then he walked to a large wooden box that sat in one corner of the room and carried it over to the table. Drew threw open the box lid and sat down.

"What are you doing?" Hannah asked, aghast. She knew what was in that box. She'd snooped in it yesterday. She might have understood if he'd reached for a gun or something, but fishing lures? Really!

Drew lifted one of the two dozen or more small wooden boxes inked with the words Castaway Bait Company from inside the larger container. "What am I doing?" Drew repeated. "I'm doing what every man should do when his father-in-law comes to call." Then he flashed her a pirate's grin. "I'm fixing to go fishing."

Chapter 6

DREW WAS STRUNG TIGHTER THAN TANGLED FISHING line on a rusty reel. Daddy Mayfield on Wild Horse Island. The man was about as welcome here as a hurricane. And, to make matters even more unpleasant, he had to go and bring ol' Jeremy with him.

At least this time Mayfield had the good manners to show up after the bedding—or beaching, in this case—rather than beforehand. Still, Drew would rather strap a steak on his butt and take a swim in shark-infested waters than go through another outraged-father scene. *Yep,* he thought as the pounding on the door commenced, *this is shaping up to put a real damper on what has been a mighty fine afternoon.*

Bang bang bang bang. "Drew Coryell, this is Roger Mayfield. I wish to speak with you."

The moment took on a surreal cast. Drew had been in this place before, played this same scene in the past. It had ranked as one of the most miserable days in his life.

How would today's theater play out?

Drew glanced at Hannah, whose sun-kissed complexion had gone dead-fish-belly white, and found he could use a little reassurance. "Did you mean it?"

Smoothing back her hair, she met his gaze. He saw in

her eyes that she knew what he meant. "I love you, Drew."

The knot in his gut eased just a little.

"It's open," he called, his stare locked with hers, even as the door swung wide and Roger P. Mayfield stepped inside. When he caught sight of his daughter, he briefly closed his eyes and swayed as if in relief.

"Hannah Elizabeth Mayfield. You *are* here."

"Hello, Father."

Drew's gaze slid right over Roger Mayfield, noting only in passing that gray hairs now outnumbered dark ones on the fellow's head, and focused on the man who trailed in behind him. *Jeremy,* he silently sneered.

A woman would think him handsome, Drew thought, taking in the coal black hair, aristocratic features, and solemn brown eyes. Good tailor, too. Drew detested the man on the spot.

Roger advanced toward his daughter. "Come along, Hannah. Let's go outside. We need a private place to talk."

He reached for her arm, but she shrugged him off. "Father, wait."

"Keep your hands off her," Drew warned, dismissing ol' Jeremy and turning his attention toward Hannah, ready to jump to the rescue if need be.

Mayfield shot him a glare. "I believe that's my line, Coryell. Hannah? Outside, now."

"No, Papa."

The firm tone of her voice shocked everyone in the room. Ol' Jeremy winced. Mayfield's mouth fell open. Drew sucked in a breath and studied Hannah. She had regained some color in her cheeks. Considering the hue was a shade of green, he didn't take that as a good sign. He also watched Hannah's eyes. That was where she would betray her feelings first, Drew knew, because he had seen it happen on their wedding day. The brightness in her eyes first dimmed, then dulled. When doubt sparked to life, Drew had wanted to die.

"No?" Mayfield repeated. "You said 'no' to me, Daughter?"

She nodded. "Anything I have to say may be said in front of Drew."

Mayfield went red. "You stubborn girl. I never thought to hear such disrespect from my own daughter's mouth. To think what your dear, departed mother would say at a time like this. She would be sorely disappointed, Hannah. The humiliation of having a daughter who . . ."

While Mayfield continued to expound on his late wife's opinions, ol' Jeremy crossed the room and took a seat at the table opposite Drew. He glanced at the fishing lures and lifted one small box from inside the larger one. Drew resisted the urge to bat his hand away and concentrated on Hannah instead.

Despite the fact that her father was busy scolding her like a child, she looked a little better. Pink had replaced the seasick coloring in her cheeks. In fact, the longer her father talked, the brighter her complexion grew, and by the time Roger paused to take a breath, she appeared downright flushed. Was she embarrassed or angry? He couldn't tell.

". . . your mother's memory. And your parents are not the only people you have shamed with this behavior. To treat your fiancé so shabbily is—"

"Fiancé?" Drew questioned sharply.

"Fiancé!" Hannah protested.

"Nothing official," Jeremy hastened to explain. "I asked. She never answered."

Good. Drew wouldn't have to kill the man, then. However, when he saw Jeremy wink at Hannah, he decided it wouldn't hurt to hurt him a bit.

. . . reprehensible," Hannah's father continued. "Last time was bad enough, but at least you had married the scoundrel. What about now, Daughter? Are you wife again or simply harlot?"

"That's enough," Drew snapped, shoving himself to his feet. Seconds later he had Roger Mayfield by the lapels and up against the wall. "Speak of her again in such a manner and I'll—"

"Don't, Drew," Hannah said, laying a hand on his arm as her father sputtered and spewed. "This is my battle."

"It's my island."

"He's my father."

"My sympathies, my dear."

She laughed, a clear peal of amusement that floated in the air like the scent of spring following a long, harsh winter. "Oh, Drew, go sit back down and play with your Texas Doodle Spring Hook."

"Hannah!"

"Father, you need to hear a few truths and I'm the only one who can say them."

It was then that Drew saw what he'd hoped to spy in her eyes. Confidence. Full-blown conviction. None of that nasty doubt that took her away from him before. For the first time since spying the sailboat, Drew was able to draw a full breath.

Slowly, he loosened his hold on Mayfield, patting out the wrinkles he'd made in the man's jacket with a little more force than was necessary. In a tone too soft for anyone else to hear, he warned, "Watch yourself."

Mayfield looked as though he wanted to hit him. Drew would have loved to oblige him with a fight. Instead he backed away and resumed his seat, casting a suspicious look toward Jeremy, who appeared intent upon studying Drew's lures.

Then Hannah addressed her beau. "It seems my family owes you an apology, Jeremy. I don't know what excuse my father used to drag you down here, but I doubt he included much truth."

Drew's hand fisted when Jeremy flashed her a grin and winked again. "Don't mind me, love. You know how much I enjoy good theater."

"She's not your love." Drew shot a glare across the table.

Jeremy folded his arms and leaned back in his chair. "Is that so?"

Drew put his hands flat on the table and leaned forward. "Yes. And if you feel the need to discuss it further, you and I can step outside."

Roger Mayfield opened his mouth, but Hannah spoke first. "Enough," she said. "Drew, behave."

"Me? What about him?"

Her lips twisted in a rueful grin. "Jeremy always conducts himself like a gentleman. You, on the other hand . . ."

A gentleman, hmm? Drew relaxed a little more. Then, wanting to get on with it, he took the conversation to the heart of the matter. "I'm a scoundrel, but that's why you love me. Right?"

Hannah eyed him sharply. Their gazes held, his breathing stopped. She smiled and said, "Right."

Drew exhaled. Jeremy winced. Roger Mayfield groaned. "Oh, Hannah. Please, no. Listen to me. Perhaps I've gone about this poorly, but that doesn't negate the fact that nothing has changed. The man still lives on this island. He's still a ne'er- do-well, he just admitted as much."

"No," Drew corrected. "Scoundrels and ne'er-do-wells are two different animals altogether."

Mayfield ignored him and pleaded with Hannah. "Think of your future. Think of your children. What kind of father will this man make?"

"Drew will make a wonderful father," she replied. "However, you are rushing things, Father. I haven't had the opportunity to ask him to marry me yet."

Drew almost missed the last bit since he was busy preening over the part where she said he'd make a good father. However, the word *marry* did register, and he sat up straight at that. "Hannah?"

"You asked last time," she said, offering a nervous smile. "It's my turn."

Roger Mayfield slumped into a chair.

Marriage. Drew dragged his palm down the side of his

face. Marriage. With Hannah doing the asking. Without knowing the Castaway Bait Company had made him a wealthy man.

And here I thought this day had taken a dive toward the bottom.

He squelched a smile and asked, "So, are you asking me now?"

"No. Not in front of . . . company."

"You afraid of my answer?"

She shrugged. "Maybe a little bit."

Across the table from him, Jeremy started stacking lure boxes into two different stacks and whistling under his breath.

"Just a little?"

'Yes, just a little."

"Hmm . . ." Damn, she looked cute standing there all nonchalant. If they were alone he'd kiss her witless right now. Drew slanted a look toward ol' Jeremy. Maybe he'd do it anyway.

While he debated the idea, Hannah's father moaned. "Oh, Hannah. You do love him, don't you? A woman's love, not a girl's."

"Yes, Papa."

"I feared as much. You never got over the man. You've not been happy since our move to San Antonio. I recognized the fact, but I didn't want to admit it." He yanked a white handkerchief from his jacket pocket and blew his nose. "I thought I was doing what was best for you, Daughter. I thought you were too young to know your own mind. I wanted more for you than the struggle of a life as a fisherman's wife. I didn't mean to ruin your happiness. I didn't begin to guess the degree of my mistake when I forced an annulment upon you."

Drew couldn't believe he was hearing the man correctly. How long would these wonders keep on coming? Even as he wallowed in the pleasure of the moment, the sheer misery painted on Roger Mayfield's face propelled him to his feet and prodded him to say, "That's enough. You were a father protecting his daughter from a man who wasn't good enough for her. I hope I'll be that vigilant if I'm ever so lucky as to have a daughter of my own."

Mayfield gazed at him in shock. Jeremy pursed his lips in a soundless whistle, then took a Spinning Squid Bait from its box. Hannah protested, "What do you mean, not good enough?"

"It's true, honey. I had no ambition. I was content to spend my days fishing and beachcombing, picking up work in Galveston only when I needed it. I had no business marrying you."

"Well, thank you very much," she replied, folding her arms in a huff.

Drew couldn't help but grin at the picture of peeve she presented. "Ah, honey, you can't get snitty about the truth. You were smart enough back then to question my ability to provide for you and any children we might have. Don't discount that intelligence now."

That appeared to give Mayfield a new bit of wind for his sails. "So what about it, Coryell? Are you willing to leave this island and find a position to support my daughter in a manner in which she deserves?"

"I don't believe that'll be necessary," Jeremy piped up.

Drew glanced at him, saw what he was doing, and realized the jig was literally up.

"This is a Castaway Hannah Jig," Jeremy continued, dangling the lure. "Quite a selection of baits you have here, Coryell. I wouldn't be surprised if it wasn't one of everything the Castaway Bait Company has produced."

Mayfield snarled. "What does that have to do with anything, Judge?"

"Judge?" Drew inquired. "I thought your name was Jeremy."

"The name is Jeremy Eckler. I'm an attorney by profession and am serving a temporary stint as a state court judge. But I'm a fisherman by avocation."

Hannah's brows arched. "Is that right, Jeremy? I never knew that about you."

Drew was aghast. "You were going to marry the man and you didn't know he liked to fish?"

"She never would have married me. I've known that for quite some time now. I do consider her a great friend, however, so I was happy to accompany Roger on this trip to serve in whatever capacity he required." Nodding toward Mayfield, he added, "Your concerns as to his financial status can likely be put to bed." Then, looking at Drew, he tossed the jig on the table and said, "Am I right?"

Glumly, Drew nodded. "This is not how I imagined all this happening."

"All *what* happening?" Impatience riddled Hannah's voice.

When Drew didn't answer, Jeremy took the bait. Lifting the top box from one of the stacks of lures, he read aloud, "Presented by Castaway Bait Company. The Castaway Hannah Trolling Spoon." Setting that box down, he picked up a second. "The Castaway Hannah Cock-Tail Kicker." A third. "The Castaway Hannah Spinning Squid Bait." Now, the dates on the lure boxes indicate these were all produced during the company's first year. As the years pass, the number of Hannah baits drops to . . . ?"

"One," Drew said with a sigh. "We're doing one Hannah bait every year now."

"Drew, explain yourself," Hannah demanded, her voice soft and suspicious.

All in all, he thought, he'd rather sit down to supper with sand sharks. He scratched his stubbled beard and took just a moment to wax philosophical. For years he'd worked every day from dawn till dusk dreaming of this very moment. He'd thrown himself into the effort to build Castaway Bait Company with the intention of one day rubbing his success in the Mayfield family's collective face.

Now that the day had finally arrived, success wasn't what he had it in mind to be rubbing.

"Drew?"

Ol' Judge Jeremy apparently decided to help him along. "Hannah, Roger," he said. "Have you ever taken time to peruse the pamphlet that comes folded inside the lure boxes? You should. It makes interesting reading. In the case of these lures, it includes a personal quality guarantee from the founder and president of the Castaway Bait Company . . ." he paused dramatically and met Drew's gaze. ". . . a Mr. Andrew Coryell of Wild Horse Island, Texas."

Roger Mayfield gasped audibly. "I don't believe it. You're not a beachcombing bounder after all?"

Jeremy settled back in his chair, an amused grin stretching across his face. "I keep my eyes on Texas business. It's a safe bet that Hannah's honey is a wealthy man."

Drew winced as Hannah's mouth dropped open, her complexion flushing red, then draining white, then brightening all the way to crimson.

"Castaway Hannah this," she said, taking a threatening step in Drew's direction. "Castaway Hannah that. Castaway Hannah Cock-Tail Kicker? What sort of message were you sending?"

He shrugged. "Well, in hindsight, I wonder about that myself. Since lures are snapped on the end of a line, doesn't matter that you can cast them away because they almost always come back. Funny how the mind works, isn't it? That's not at all what I was thinking when I came up with those names."

"Your company." Roger stood, his face glowing with delight. "Castaway Bait is your company. Why, that's wonderful. Isn't it, Hannah?"

"Wonderful?" Eyes narrowed, she advanced on Drew. An intelligent man, he pushed from his seat and backed away. "Wonderful?" she repeated. "That's not the term I would choose, Father. Words that pop to my mind are sneaky, underhanded, liar . . ."

She backed him up against the wall. Drew offered up, "Justifiable."

She snorted. "Mean."

"Broken-hearted."

"Wicked."

"Repentant."

She paused at that, then continued with a sniff. "Cagey."

She stood so close to him, her breasts brushed his chest. His body reacted, growing hard, and he shifted forward just enough to touch her. "Lover."

Hannah stared deeply into his eyes, gazing all the way to his soul.

"Lover," he repeated in a whisper, his nostrils flaring as he drew in the scent of sand and sea and sex still clinging to her. "My lover."

He waited a long, tense moment, then her eyes softened, and he breathed a sigh of relief. But he sighed too soon.

"Why didn't you tell me?"

"You assumed I'd stayed here on the island all this time. I might have told the truth if you'd asked."

"Drew," she protested.

"Well, it's true. Besides, I didn't want to win you with my wealth. I wanted to do it with—"

"Your Musky Wriggler?"

Her father chimed in. "Hannah Mayfield!"

Drew cracked a grin, his gaze never leaving Hannah's as he addressed her father. "It's a Castaway Musky Wriggler and it's one of our best-sellers. I used it to trounce your daughter in a fishing contest earlier today."

She wrinkled her nose. "Well, don't take it personally, Coryell, but I still prefer live bait."

A crude suggestion came to mind, but he managed to swallow the words.

Her father cleared his throat. "Well . . . um . . . yes . . . uh. Oh my. Jeremy, I think it would probably be better all around if we finished our business here right away. It's shaping up to be a fair evening for sailing."

Drew's head came up and he drilled Mayfield a glare. "Hannah is not leaving, not this time."

"No, I expected as much when I made this trip, and

it's one reason I asked Jeremy to come along. My Hannah hasn't been happy these past ten years. And while I know she dreams of a home and family of her own, she hasn't allowed herself to fall for any of the men I've encouraged her to see."

"Not even me, and I'm a great catch," Jeremy pointed out. "Dealing with rejection has been difficult, I'll have you know."

Hannah laughed and turned around, facing the others, but remaining within the shelter of Drew's arms. "You are a wonderful catch, Jeremy, and had my heart not already been committed elsewhere, I'd have surely cast my line your way."

"Fine, fine, fine," Drew said impatiently. "What does that have to do with sailing?"

Roger Mayfield folded his arms. "If it's all the same to you, I'd just as soon not share a shelter with my daughter on her wedding night."

"Wedding night?" Drew and Hannah asked in tandem.

Jeremy hooked his thumbs behind his jacket lapels. "I'm a judge, remember? It's why your father asked me to come along. The paperwork is all taken care of, save for your signatures, of course."

Hannah stepped toward her father, wonderment in her voice as she asked, "You planned for me to marry Drew? That's why you came to Wild Horse Island?"

He shrugged. "It's my duty as a father to see that he makes an honest woman of you."

"You mean I'm going to marry Drew today? Here? Now?" Horror rose in her tone as she glanced down. "In *this* dress?"

"Here and now, yes. But I brought along your mother's wedding gown just in case you'd like to wear it."

Her chin slowly fell and she silently mouthed the words, *Mama's dress.* Then she looked at Drew, her eyes moist and filled with hopeful joy. "Is this all right with you?"

"Ah, honey, it's more than all right. It will be my

greatest joy." He paused, then added, "Although I do have one condition."

"Condition!" Mayfield exclaimed, his tone ripe with offense as Drew scrounged a pencil from the depths of the tackle box, then wrote a string of numbers on the bottom of a lure box.

He handed the box to Mayfield. "Yep, a condition. This is the combination to my safe in the Castaway Bait Company's offices. I want you to sail up to Galveston and retrieve my wedding gift to my bride and take it with you back to San Antonio or Austin or wherever you think it belongs."

Hannah's eyes widened, then filled with tears. "Oh, Drew."

"What is this?" her father asked. "I don't understand."

"Oh, Daddy," she said, her gaze locked with Drew's. "He's giving me—giving us all—the most wonderful gift." Then she threw herself into Drew's arms and gave him the kind of thank you kiss most men can only dream about.

Mayfield's brows knitted. "What gift?"

"It must be a damned good one," Jeremy observed as the kiss went on and on and on.

Hannah finally came up for air, then laughed and looked toward her father. "He's giving it to me to give to Texas, Papa. Drew has one of the missing copies of the Declaration of Independence."

Epilogue

A GENTLE SURF LAPPED AT THE BEACH WHERE HANNAH and Drew stood to take their vows before Judge Jeremy Eckler, Roger Mayfield, and a pelican perched on a driftwood log. The bride wore her mother's powder blue silk wedding gown, the groom a set of clothing taken from the clothesline before being completely dry. Neither bride nor groom wore shoes; both wore smiles of utter joy.

Roger Mayfield cried with unabashed fanfare when his daughter promised to love, cherish, and never, ever again leave her husband. Judge Jeremy watched the seagulls diving for their supper and whistled softly when the groom took his direction "Now kiss your bride" to record lengths.

The mood was rushed as Mayfield and Jeremy boarded their sailboat for the trip to Galveston. As father of the bride, Roger wanted to be well away from Wild Horse Island before his baby girl went to her marriage bed. Such things did a father no good to consider. At the same time, as president of the Texas Historical Preservation Society, he was near bursting with excitement at the thought of retrieving the Declaration of Independence from his new son-in-law's safe.

Jeremy Eckler was in a hurry to leave, too. As payment

for his judicial services, Drew had gifted him with an entire set of Castaway Bait Company fishing lures. Jeremy intended to turn the wheel over to Mayfield on the trip up the coast and get in a few hours' trolling. "I like the looks of that Lone Star Bobber," he called to Drew as the boat slipped its mooring.

"It's a good one," Drew agreed, keeping his arms wrapped around his bride.

"I prefer the Musky Wriggler, myself," Hannah said, snuggling back against her husband.

They watched and waved until the sailboat disappeared from sight. Drew turned to his wife and said, "Well, Mrs. Coryell. We have about an hour before dark. Any ideas on how you would like to spend the time?"

"As a matter of fact, I do."

He grinned, took her hand, and started to lead her toward the cabin. Hannah, however, planted her feet and refused to go. "I want to go fishing."

"You what?" he snapped.

"Yes." She tugged his tie free, then began to work the buttons of his shirt. "You see, Mr. Coryell, I am an avid angler, and I am searching for that perfect lure, a unique bait that will be mine and mine alone."

Drew both relaxed and tensed as she pushed the shirt off his shoulders, then turned her attentions to the button at his waistband. "I suspect that as president of the Castaway Bait Company, you might have just what I've been looking for."

"You think so?" Drew rasped as her fingers worked her magic and his pants dropped to the ground.

"Oh, my. Oh, yes. I knew it." Hannah's eyes twinkled wickedly as she dropped to her knees before him and said, "Now that, Drew Coryell, is what I call an eight-inch Throbbing Bob."

Geralyn Dawson lives in Fort Worth, Texas, with her husband and three children. She loves college football, hates sorting socks, makes a mean bowl of chili, and wishes her sons would shave their sideburns.

Geralyn won the National Readers' Choice Award for *The Wedding Raffle* and was a finalist for Romance Writers of America's prestigious RITA award for *The Wedding Raffle, The Bad Luck Wedding Dress,* and *The Bad Luck Wedding Cake. Romantic Times* magazine has recognized her work with nominations for a Career Achievement Award and Reviewers' Choice Awards.

Her books reflect her strong belief in the power of love and laughter. You can write Geralyn at P.O. Box 37126, Fort Worth, Texas 76117, S.A.S.E always appreciated, or e-mail her via her homepage at http://www.GeralynDawson.com

Ruined

Jillian Hunter

Chapter 1

Cornwall
1843

PEOPLE IN THESE PARTS STILL TALK ABOUT THE RUINA-tion of Miss Sydney Eloise Windsor, a lovely professor's daughter from London.

Her downfall had been Wicked DeWilde's saving grace.

Some of the older villagers swore she was the spirit of a drowned Burgundian princess. They said she had been brought back to life by an ancient warlord whose ghost haunted the cove of St. Kilmerryn. The desolate knight had waited for centuries for this woman. On foggy nights his figure stood sentry on the cliffs, searching the sea for her lost ship.

Sydney looked nothing like a Burgundian princess. At least not until the warlord gave her the gold torque, which she only wore to bed, with nothing else, to seduce her husband.

Still, this was Cornwall, the land of maidens turned to stone on the moor for dancing on Sundays, the land of giants and the Secret Folk. Anything could happen here, and often it did.

People in these parts did like to talk over a furze fire, and DeWilde Manor with its unconventional master and mistress had provided plenty of fodder for that.

There was that great black dog who adored her ladyship for one thing, and the terrifying stories that poured from Lord DeWilde's pen. Not to mention the demon that her ladyship had ghost-layed in a burial cairn, and the duel his lordship had fought, over her honor, in his drawers.

With only an apple pie as a weapon.

It had all started with a shipwreck.

Sydney had been taking a nap when Jeremy had run the yacht onto the rocks. So, apparently, had Jeremy, or he would have been paying more attention. But the four passengers were wide-awake now, wondering if they were to be drowned or dashed to death on a spine of submerged rocks. Sydney thought of her family and how they would miss her.

She didn't have time to be afraid when they ran aground. She was too busy bailing water out of the yacht with a soup tureen. She could hear her friends, trapped somewhere above, shouting for help. Twilight had just fallen. A wave of icy water knocked her across the cabin. She fell into the wall and started to lose consciousness.

Her last impression was of a blue light flooding the cabin and the sense of a man's gauntleted hand lifting her to safety.

She never saw his face. Nor did the others when she thought to ask them about it. The light had disappeared by the time the yacht had washed ashore, and she decided she'd probably imagined the whole thing after all.

It had been a recipe for disaster, Sydney thought as she fished her soggy reticule from the wreckage: a full liquor cabinet and four young fools in a racing yacht blown off course by a squall into a treacherous crosscurrent on the Cornish coast. Her friends might be good fun, but they had a total disregard for common sense, and Sydney was never going to get in a situation like this again.

"Who put all these rocks here where I couldn't see 'em?" her friend Jeremy, Lord Westland, shouted.

Jeremy's young wife, Audrey, a trim blonde whose father owned the yacht, gave him a shove. "Freddie's lying in his cabin half-dead. Save him and stop that shouting like a woman."

Sydney shoved her dripping hair from her face. "He isn't half-dead. He's half-drunk. I tried to lift him, but he refuses to be budged. I left his head resting in the commode. At least he can get air."

"It's a wonder we weren't all killed," Audrey exclaimed, emptying water from the tiny heels of her fashionable silk shoes.

Her cousin Freddie popped up between the ruins of mast and auxiliary sails. "I say, did we beat His Grace?"

"Not only did we not beat him, Freddie, but we're shipwrecked," Jeremy said.

"Shipwrecked?" Freddie stared in disbelief at the ocean breakers crashing over the damaged wooden hull. "Well, blister me. I had no idea."

Sydney picked a path across the silk-tasseled cushions and splintered timber to take refuge on the rocky shore. "My father predicted something like this would happen."

"Well, if you knew we were going to be shipwrecked on the godforsaken coast of Cornwall, you should have warned us," Audrey said sourly.

Freddie wobbled up between the two women, a bottle of gin under each arm. "Exactly where on the godforsaken coast of Cornwall are we?"

"The locals call it Devil's Elbow," a deep voice said behind him.

"Devil's Elbow?" Jeremy scratched his head. "I don't suppose they have a decent supper room or hotel here."

"They do not," the deep voice said, openly amused this time.

"Who said that?" Sydney whispered.

"Maybe it was the devil," Freddie ventured. "After all, this is his elbow."

The foursome turned in unison, heads lifting to the bleak wall of cliff that rose before them. Fog drifted in swatches across the cove. Dusky shadows distorted shapes and made everything look out of proportion.

The dog sitting on the shelf of overhanging rock, for example, looked like the mythical monster Cerberus guarding the gate to the underworld.

Audrey gasped and backed into her husband.

Her husband rubbed his eyes at the apparition, or whatever it was.

Freddie took a drink, gaping like a carp.

"Oh, dear," Sydney said, hiccoughing loudly.

The dog wagged its tail and began to bark.

"Look," Audrey whispered, "there's a house on the cliff. The dog must belong there."

A brooding granite Georgian mansion with corner turrets sat on the cliff edge in lonely grandeur. Gaslight glowed behind the leaded windows, creating an aura of seclusion and mystery.

"Civilization," Freddie said, sighing in relief.

"That," the deep voice said dryly, "is a matter of opinion."

The tall form of a man detached itself from an unseen path carved into the cliff. He wore an unbuttoned black overcoat with narrow trousers and polished boots, and he moved with power and purpose. His lean face tightened in amusement as he came close enough to examine the four survivors.

Sydney suppressed the urge to stare at him and marvel over his athletic build. They were going to need a strong man to repair the yacht. The fact that he was as handsome as sin was completely irrelevant. She was betrothed to another man, and she had no business noticing such things as a square jaw and compelling gray eyes and shoulders of granite.

"What good luck that you've found us, sir," she said energetically. "Our yacht is—"

"—ruined." He strode around her, poking his ebony cane at a brass chandelier that glinted like a mermaid's offering in a tidal pool. "Ruined beyond the slightest hope of redemption."

"Does that mean we're out of the race?" Freddie said, lowering his bottle.

Jeremy blinked, suddenly sober. "Do you mean she can't be fixed?"

"Not by me," the stranger said. His gaze cut back to Sydney, lingering for several seconds on her pale face before it dropped to the bloodstains that had blossomed on her wet skirts.

A wave crested on the shattered hull and threw cold spume into the air. The sea sounded suddenly calm and rhythmic, as if by ruining the yacht some unseen spirit had been appeased.

"Where is that blood coming from?" the man demanded in a voice one could hardly ignore.

"I banged my knee up a bit when we ran aground," she said meekly, responding to his masterful tone.

Audrey looked at her in concern. "Sydney doesn't weigh a shilling. She flew across the cabin when we ran aground, but she's too well-mannered to complain."

"Or too drunk," Freddie said.

The stranger came up to Sydney, gently lifting her skirts up to her knee. Sydney knew she ought to protest this impropriety, but no sound came out of her throat. Audrey was watching her in horror. But all Sydney could think was, *Oh! His touch is making me tingle all over, and what luck I'm wearing my new stockings.*

Sydney realized that she wasn't behaving like a young woman betrothed to a duke should behave. She rarely did behave in a proper manner, which made it all the more a mystery why Peter wanted to marry her in the first place.

She knew why she had wanted to marry him. Her fiancé was young, wealthy, and as charming as a prince when he chose to be. He brought Sydney's ancient aunt little presents. He took her sisters on outings, but lately she'd been disturbed by the way his eye lingered when he spotted a pretty shopgirl, and she would have to be a total idiot not to have noticed the long, meaningful look he'd exchanged with Lady Penelope Davenport at last month's Mayfair dinner party.

Sydney realized she wasn't sophisticated. Her father had recently retired from the university. She and her three sisters now lived with their parents in Chelsea, comfortable but certainly not well-off. Sydney knew she didn't have much experience with the opposite sex. She had definitely been swept off her feet by the Duke of Esterfield. But what girl wouldn't have been, especially when she would probably have ended up as a governess otherwise?

Still, even a girl who had no worldly experience, so to speak, sensed certain things, and although Sydney had never breathed a word of this aloud, she wasn't totally persuaded that Peter loved her with his whole heart, or that she even loved him at all.

The yacht race, away from Peter, had given her time to reconsider their engagement. It was actually a relief to escape him because lately he was always finding fault with things she said or did, and his friends weren't much better. They were thoughtless, fickle, and amusing, but Sydney wasn't thinking of marrying them so their flaws were really neither here nor there.

"Does this hurt?" the stranger asked, his deep voice jarring her thoughts. He pressed his thumb into the back of her knee.

She sighed. "No. It feels wonderful."

"Sydney!" Audrey said, scandalized.

The man smiled faintly. "And this?"

"Oh," Sydney cried, flinching as he fingered her kneecap. But the deep pain soon dulled in contrast to the warmth she felt when his fingers slid down her stockinged calf, and he seemed to know what he was doing even if Sydney had relinquished complete control of the situation.

He had strong, competent hands and the devil's own

eyes, full of humor and self-confidence. Sydney sighed again.

"Are you a physician?" Jeremy asked, frowning at this peculiar turn of events.

"No." The stranger lowered her skirts, straightening to regard the shipwreck with a resigned look. "I suppose I shall have to offer you lodging. This woman should have a doctor look at her knee. It's deeply gashed and that swelling is only going to get worse."

"I am Jeremy, Lord Westland," Jeremy said, prompted by a poke from Audrey. "This is my wife Audrey."

"Freddie Matheson," Freddie said, stomping his sodden shoes to get warm.

The stranger looked at Sydney. "And you are—"

"Sydney. Sydney—" She hiccoughed, her other hand flying to her mouth.

"Sydney Hiccough." He raised his eyebrow. "What an unusual name. I don't think I'm liable to forget it."

Sydney shivered as a gust of cold air chased across the cove. "It's Windsor, actually. Your name, sir?"

"I know who you are," Jeremy said suddenly, pointing his index finger up at the man's face. "You're Lord DeWilde. We shared Henley's opera box last summer."

Freddie gasped. "One of *the* DeWilde brothers?"

"The literary DeWildes?" Sydney asked, so impressed that for a moment she forgot she was freezing to death and had just allowed a man to peep under her skirts. "One of the three brothers famous for writing tales of the Wondrous and Terrible?"

Freddie gaped up at him. "Why, I stayed up all night reading *Confessions of a Scottish Corpse.* Nearly scared myself to death."

"My personal favorite was *A Ghost Chats from the Grave,*" Sydney said warmly. "Oh, golly, this *is* an honor, Lord DeWilde."

Only Audrey remained unimpressed, studying the dark stranger in cynical silence.

Sydney nudged the woman, annoyed at Audrey's lack of enthusiasm. "Audrey, I know for a fact that you couldn't sleep an entire week after reading *The Elixir of Death.* Isn't that a fact, Audrey?"

Audrey blinked. "Yes. It's a fact. But I'm wondering which DeWilde brother—"

The rest of her sentence was lost in a sudden clamor of bells ringing across the cove from the parish church. The deafening sound reverberated against the cliffs. It throbbed to a painful pitch in the air.

The dog on the rocks above them threw back its head and let loose an unholy howl in protest.

"Ye gods." Freddie groaned in pain. "Bells."

"Hell's bells," DeWilde said, clapping his hands over his ears.

Sydney raised her voice to a shout. "What do they mean? Are we being invaded by the French navy?"

DeWilde took her hand to guide her over the rocks and shipwreck debris. Almost as an afterthought, he looked back to motion the others to follow. "The bells were meant to warn you," he said as he drew her into a relatively quiet crevice in the cliff.

"Warn us?" Sydney said, shoving a strand of dripping hair from her face. She wished she had a comb. Imagine looking like a drowned mouse when you were rescued by a man like Lord DeWilde. "Warn us against what?"

He stared at her in amused concentration for several seconds. He seemed to be contemplating his answer.

She smiled to show she wasn't intimidated, which of course she was. She was spellbound, drawn to the magnetism of his dark gray eyes. His gaze bespoke a depth of experience and a self-control she could only envy. Sydney was sure her own emotions were written all over her face. She could never hide her secrets from anybody, but then again, she didn't have any secrets to hide.

"The cove looks harmless, but it is not," he said, his voice low with mischief. "There is a treacherous crosscurrent in the channel. It doesn't take much to run aground. A strong wind, a miscalculation—"

"Or four foxed idiots in a yacht," Sydney said ruefully.

He laughed. The low vibration of his voice did amazing things to Sydney's system. The sexual resonance gave her the shivers and made her feel as though she'd just drunk three glasses of brandy in a row.

"The villagers would tell you that the ghost of the Blue Knight lured you here," DeWilde said. "Well, perhaps he did. The bells were meant to warn you away, but it's too late now."

Too late. He turned. His words echoed in Sydney's mind as she limped after his tall figure onto the cliffside path. She couldn't say why, but she understood he was talking about something more than the shipwreck. He was every bit as intriguing as his novels, as those tales of the Wondrous and Terrible, and if she was sensible, she would have closed this book before she was drawn in any deeper.

She should have taken his warning to heart. She should have resisted. She definitely should *not* be clambering after him in the shadows with this delicious sense of adventure, wondering how the chapter would end.

Rylan Anthony DeWilde, Baron DeWilde of Harthurst, strode ahead of the struggling group, whistling in a carefree fashion. He didn't usually whistle after shipwrecks. But then again, shipwrecks usually didn't wash beautiful young brunettes with soulful brown eyes to his shore. No one he'd ever rescued before had made such a powerful impression. Small, sweet, a lovely girl.

Miss Sydney Hiccough would have to stay in his house until her knee felt better. Knees were tricky joints. They took a long time to heal, and relapses were common. She'd need looking after. In bed.

He whistled louder.

His dog brushed against his long legs, begging for a run

across the moor. Rylan knelt and took the hound's ugly face in his hands.

"Listen to me, you spoiled beast. No frightening off that young lady back there like the last female who was brave enough to come visiting. I rather fancy Miss Sydney Hiccough."

The dog stared at him in plaintive silence.

"All right," Rylan said. "Frighten the others if you must. But be gentle with the lady."

The dog bounded off like a rocket toward the dark expanse of moorland that stretched beyond the cliffs.

Rylan straightened. His angular face amused, he watched the four unsteady figures weave their way toward him. He shook his head as his gaze lit on the woman. There was something soft and uncomplicated about her. She had an openness that could be used as a weapon or a weakness. It would depend on the man she gave herself to.

Rylan knew without doubt he was that man.

He smiled to himself, watching her eyes widen as she looked up at him, whatever she'd been saying to her friends forgotten. She might know it, too. She didn't bother hiding what she felt. For no reason at all, Rylan felt more hopeful then he had in a long, long time.

Audrey and Jeremy were supporting Sydney on either side, depriving Rylan of the chance to offer his help. She was such a slight thing, he could have carried her up the cliff without taking a breath. In fact, it was a wonderful idea—a stroke of genius—and quite the gentlemanly thing to do.

He turned, strode right up to Sydney with his cane under his arm, and swept her up off the sand. Audrey couldn't manage a single word; she elbowed her husband in the side, and Freddie just stood there, looking half-hopeful, as if DeWilde would offer to carry him, too.

"Honestly, this isn't necessary," Sydney said, not quite able to hide a grin.

"But you are hurt, and I don't want you to fall. The path is steep."

He reached the top of the cliff long before the others. His footsteps were certain and he knew this path, walking it alone for inspiration when his work wasn't going well. Still, in all his months here, he'd never imagined anything quite as wonderful as the woman who weighed practically nothing in his arms.

"I shall set you down here," he said.

"Do you know something, Lord DeWilde?"

Rylan stared down into her face. "I know many, many things, Miss Windsor." However, at the moment, he couldn't recall a single one of them.

Sydney smiled. "It has always been my secret wish to meet you."

It was unexpected, the power of her honesty, her innocence, and the way he reacted. She might as well have reached into his chest and torn out his heart. He was hers from that moment on, and, naturally, being an arrogant DeWilde, he didn't doubt the favor would be reciprocated.

He kissed her lightly, lingeringly, on the mouth before he set her down on the sandy grass. Sydney just stared at him, speechless, but not for one instant was he sorry for what he'd done. If he was sorry about anything, it was only that her three friends had finally reached the top of the path, and he couldn't kiss her again.

He glanced over his shoulder at the somber Georgian mansion, thinking of the privacy it afforded. He'd lived there for thirteen months now. Thirteen months to reassess the unsatisfying course he'd charted for his life. Thirteen months of penance for losing his temper and almost killing another man, who clearly deserved to be killed, but not at Rylan's hand.

Time enough to brood over a new book and search his soul, to realize he didn't need constant excitement or dangerous women to make him happy. Pursuing pleasure alone had never appealed to him, but somewhere there had to be a balance between boredom and self-destruction.

He'd chosen this isolated Cornish parish for his self-exile because it suited his purposes to research superstitious lore. Some of the legends he'd begun to investigate predated pagan times. There was magic here, if one believed in it, which he didn't.

The villagers claimed that no outlander was washed ashore by accident. Ghosts, they said, lured the seafarers onto the rocks. St. Kilmerryn was said to be haunted by an ancient knight who grieved for a lost princess.

The church bells might have sounded too late to warn the woman.

But Rylan thought she had come just in time for him.

"It's too late for what?" Freddie kept asking Sydney after Rylan gently deposited her on the path to his house. "And did he say something about a ghost?"

The effects of the alcohol they'd so freely imbibed was wearing off. The chilly sea air cut through their wet clothing. The high spirits of an hour ago were rapidly deflating. She felt like belting Freddie for the sheer hell of it, which wasn't at all like Sydney, and she couldn't stop thinking about that kiss, which had probably meant nothing at all to DeWilde, but she certainly wasn't liable to forget it.

"It's too late for what?" Freddie said again, huddling against her.

"It's too late for tea," Sydney said crossly. Her knee ached. Her head pounded, and she was still perplexed by Audrey's cryptic response to the fascinating man who strode ahead of them, and by her own response to him. She was tingling all over.

"Why were you so rude to him, Audrey?" she asked. "It's a great honor to be rescued by a DeWilde."

Audrey snorted. "If one ignores the fact that he examined your knee in public and carted you up the cliff like a captive."

"Tea?" Freddie sniffed. "I should hope not. I want something much stronger."

"Wait here a moment," DeWilde called over his

shoulder. "I need to make sure the other hounds aren't running loose. We weren't expecting visitors."

"No wonder," Freddie said, frowning up at the atmospheric Georgian manor house that seemed to have been spawned from the rocks forming its foundation.

The estate was edged with thorn-laden brambles and Cornish elms that the wind had twisted into weird shapes. A loose shutter banged in the wind. A hound howled. The gables and leaded windows gave the house a gothic appearance.

"Egads," Jeremy said. "I'm not surprised he comes up with those warped stories, living in a creaking old tomb like this."

"Does it have a laboratory in the cellar, do you reckon?" Freddie whispered.

"If it does," Sydney said, "I shall ask his lordship to grow you a brain and have it immediately implanted inside the hollow cavity of your head."

"Hush," Audrey said. *"He's* coming."

Lord DeWilde hurried down the overgrown path toward them. "It's all right now," he said. "The infamous Danger Hounds are secured in their kennel."

"The Danger Hounds," Sydney murmured. "Goodness, not the very dogs that hunted down Squire Elliot in *Sinner from the Netherworld?* Not the bloodthirsty dogs who did their master's evil bidding?"

"What evil bidding?" Jeremy asked.

"I don't know," Sydney said. "I was too frightened to read that part."

Freddie looked around the grounds. "We're not going to get ate, are we?"

DeWilde raised his brow. "Not by me."

An hour later they were comfortably ensconced before a cheerful fire in a large gaslit drawing room. The middle-aged housekeeper, Mrs. Chynoweth, served hot tea and scones with clotted cream.

Sydney sat on a black silk sofa, her second cup of laudanum-laced tea in her lap. Lord DeWilde had sent for a physician. He must have suspected she was in pain even though she tried to cover it.

"I expect Peter is halfway to the Lizard by now," Jeremy said, slouched on the sofa in his rumpled suit with his cravat twisted to one side.

Freddie reached for another scone. The hound, planted in the middle of the carpet, growled in warning. Freddie drew his hand back to his lap. "Peter will fetch us, won't he, Sydney?"

Sydney was staring across the room at Lord DeWilde. His dark hair was brushed back onto his shoulders. He seemed to be looking into the fire. But every now and then, Sydney caught him studying her with an intensity that made her toes curl. Which, of course, she wouldn't have noticed if *she* hadn't been sneaking peeps at him and wondering why he'd kissed her in the first place and why she had read so much into what was probably an impulsive gesture on his part.

Handsome man, she thought with a sigh. The laudanum had begun to take effect. Brilliant writer. Why does he live alone in this broody old house? Does he have a wife? Her thoughts were blurred. She started to close her eyes only to open them wide and look directly into his gaze. Awareness jolted through her like an arrow.

He gave her a slow personal smile. No one else in the room noticed it, thankfully, but it set Sydney's nerve endings on fire. She wriggled back against the sofa.

And sent her teacup flying to the floor.

"Oh, goodness."

"It's all right," DeWilde said, not quite suppressing a grin.

Sydney leaned down to get the cup, feeling a blush creep up her neck. "I hope our shipwreck hasn't disturbed Lady DeWilde," she said impulsively.

Conversation stopped. Lord DeWilde's head lifted from the hearth. Audrey shot her an annoyed look. Sydney, after all, was not really one of them. She was a professor's daughter, practically of the working class. Trust her to put her foot in her mouth.

"Alas, there is no Lady DeWilde," Rylan said, looking more amused than saddened by this announcement.

Sydney felt rather stupid, but she felt relieved too. "Well, I—"

Freddie's voice interrupted her, undoubtedly saving her from saying something even more socially unforgivable. "I said, 'Do you think Peter will come and fetch us?' "

All of a sudden Sydney looked down and saw that the dog had settled itself at her feet. "Well, hello," she said softly. "You're not really a big beast, are you?"

DeWilde smiled. "You've made a friend, Miss Windsor. Consider yourself honored. That hound would rather bite off someone's head than behave."

"I like animals," Sydney said.

And that animals liked her didn't surprise Rylan. She'd had that same effect on him. He'd probably run and fetch a stick if she asked him.

"That dog is a demon," Freddie whispered. "And you never did answer my question about Peter."

Sydney tore her attention away from DeWilde's face. He made her feel so self-conscious. "Peter?" she said, trying to rebalance her empty saucer on her good knee.

"Peter, the Duke of Esterfield," Audrey said sharply. "Peter, your beloved and betrothed, your One and Only. You do remember him, Sydney?"

"Gadzooks," Freddie said. "Do you think a spar thwacked her on the skull?"

Sydney noticed something flicker in DeWilde's eyes. A cold glitter of regret or disdain, she didn't know, but it told her he didn't approve of her engagement.

"Of course I remember Peter," she said in a crisp voice. "And, yes, he'll probably fetch us." She bit her lip, and added, "If he thinks of it, that is. He isn't exactly known for his charitable instincts. We have a better chance of being rescued by my father. Papa will probably swim here to rescue me."

Silence fell over the small group. DeWilde pretended to poke at the fire. Sydney knew he was pretending because the fire was perfectly fine as it was. He was pretending just so he wouldn't have to look at her again. She stared, rapt, at his brooding profile and thought again of his eyes and the wonderful stories he wrote that frightened and uplifted her at the same time.

Mrs. Chynoweth came in to clear away the dishes. She brought in Lord DeWilde's outercoat and cane, her voice low with concern. "Must you go out again tonight, my lord? Samhain is almost here, and there are dangerous wicked spirits in . . ."

Sydney lost the end of the sentence. She was eavesdropping and couldn't very well ask the woman what sort of wickedness Lord DeWilde might encounter. Where *was* he going this late at night anyway?

It seemed to be a regular ritual. The hound was already at the door, whining to get out.

"Where's he off to at this hour?" Freddie whispered in her ear.

"No doubt he's a practicing necromancer," Sydney said dryly.

DeWilde turned at the door, pulling on a pair of black leather gloves. Shadows hid his expression from Sydney. Yet she knew he was looking straight at her. "I have business on the moor and won't be back until after dawn. Mrs. Chynoweth will see you to your rooms. And Miss Windsor, don't be alarmed if the physician arrives late tonight. He has a long ride to reach us. I do not think your injury is serious, but one must be careful. If you wish to write a letter to your papa, I will have it posted in the morning."

Then he was gone, leaving Sydney staring at the door with a strange compulsion to follow after him and the realization that her life was about to be changed forever.

The worst part was, she couldn't wait to learn how.

Rylan galloped across the bleak moonlit moor. He cantered around the circle of standing stones, the black dog running at his side.

If he could ride off his anger, he would have to keep

going until the sun rose and he rode to the lonely cliffs of Lizard Point.

The Duke of Esterfield.

He bellowed a string of curses into the air.

The beautiful woman he coveted belonged to one of the biggest swines in all of England. Charming on the outside, Peter was one of the most amoral and unprincipled men Rylan had ever met. Yet most people did not see Peter's dark side. They were besotted by his wealth and boyish charisma.

He could see why Peter had fallen in love with Sydney, defying convention to marry a woman beneath his class. Sydney was in a class of her own, and wasn't black attracted to white, the perverse to the pure?

Oh, Rylan knew plenty about Sydney's betrothed. He'd avoided any personal association with Peter, though, aside from almost killing Peter's cousin in a duel.

It hadn't exactly made them best friends.

What nasty secrets Rylan knew about Peter had come from researching a private club of noblemen that had recently sprung up in London and was rumored to be based on the Hellfire clubs of the previous century. Not that there were any Black Masses or murders, but there was a lot of drinking and seducing of young women and the lewd behavior that Prince Albert bemoaned.

Rylan felt sick at the thought of Sydney falling into the hands of a man who would defile her innocence.

He slowed his horse, and his anger simmered down into resolve. The matter was settled. She wasn't leaving his house. He didn't know yet how he'd keep her, but he'd figure it out. A man didn't write tales of the Wondrous and Terrible without having a devious mind, and Rylan's plot twists left his readers biting their nails to the quick.

He came to the base of a hill where a bonfire blazed and cloaked figures danced in a circle, chanting into the night.

Witchcraft. Demons. Supernatural wonders. He had

set out to prove that there was no such thing as magic. Yet the heathen rituals he had witnessed here in no way resembled the cruel tendencies of human nature.

He slid off his horse and moved into the shadows of the hill where he could watch the pagan ceremony.

Rylan was really beginning to believe there was no real magic to be found. Only the fantasies and imaginings and wishful thinking of deluded people. He'd traveled the world over searching for proof, for inspiration. The closest he'd come to magic was the sight of Sydney Windsor washed up in his cove and spilling her tea on his carpet.

He leaned against a boulder and stared up into the undulating flames before he opened his saddlebag. It held a meat pie, pen and paper, a pistol. He had to smile. The weapon had been packed by his housekeeper, who was concerned that a Samhain spirit would possess her master's soul. Or that the villagers might rough him up if they caught him observing their secret practices.

He wasn't worried about his life being threatened at all. He'd won a wrestling match against the three strongest men in the village his first week here. Hell, he'd barely exerted himself. And since then he'd not only commanded respect but made some new friends.

Mrs. Chynoweth kept warning him that the strange goings-on after midnight on the moor were another matter. She said even the gentlest souls were subject to bewitchment. And how did anyone know it wasn't Lady Tregarron or Squire Pendarvis dancing about for the devil under those silk hoods?

Rylan wasn't worried about supernatural things either. Interested, yes, for research purposes.

He was more worried about how to break the news to Sydney that she wasn't going to be the Duchess of Esterfield after all. He hoped she didn't have her heart set on living in a big manor house or on attending royal functions.

If he could ensnare her with magic, he'd do it in a

second. For now, though, he'd have to fall back on the age-old spell of male-female attraction.

Fortunately, he thought with a grin of pure arrogance, there appeared to be more than enough of that between them. Sydney hadn't taken her beautiful eyes off him all evening, and if they had been alone, he would have satisfied her curiosity in more ways than one.

"What kind of business could DeWilde have on the moor?" Freddie wondered aloud.

"Perhaps he's going to dance naked with a coven of witches," Sydney said irritably. "The man is a writer. Who are we to question where he finds inspiration?"

Jeremy stood from the sofa and stretched. "As long as he didn't use *us* for his research. Anyone else for bed?"

Audrey looked across the room. "Miss Hiccough is. She can barely keep her eyes open. Go on up, Sydney. We'll wait here until the doctor arrives."

"Just in case it's Dr. Frankenstein," Freddie said, throwing his arms up to limp around the sofa with a hideous grin. "In case he wants to perform a nasty operation on our hapless Miss Windsor while she lies, drugged and helpless, in the body snatcher's bed."

Sydney didn't argue. She was too drowsy to tell them they were behaving like proper idiots. They'd just argue back that it was time she started behaving like an aristocrat and not a social mushroom, seeing that she would become a duchess in two short months.

"A duchess," she said to herself as she limped from the room. "Can you believe I'm going to be a duchess?"

Mrs. Chynoweth appeared out of the shadows, mumbling under her breath. "You could believe anything, miss, after living with Lord DeWilde for over a year."

The doctor came and went, having examined Sydney's knee under the eagle-eyed supervision of Audrey and Mrs. Chynoweth. Sydney slept, strangely relaxed in the unsettled atmosphere.

The doctor told Audrey at the door, "She's to stay off it for a week. Apply liniments of deer grease twice a day. Dulse tea will improve her circulation. It's good for constipation, too."

"I am sure Sydney will appreciate that very much," Audrey said in a tart voice. "Are you sure she can't walk?"

"No weight on that leg for at least two days," he said. "She'll be feeling the pain of it in the morning."

"Two days," Audrey murmured. "It will be too late then. Oh, poor Sydney. There's no hope to save her, it would seem."

As soon as the doctor left, Audrey hurried back downstairs where Jeremy and Freddie were helping themselves to liberal amounts of his lordship's port and sausage pies.

Freddie sprawled across the sofa with a bottle balanced between his bare feet. Jeremy was examining the bag of Celtic runes he had found on the card table.

Freddie yawned in boredom. "What does his lordship do for proper entertainment? This ain't rustication. It's embalmment. This place is as lively as a crypt."

Audrey swept into the center of the room, bristling with agitation. "The doctor just left. We have a genuine crisis on our hands."

"Has Sydney gone fatal on us?" Freddie asked in alarm.

Jeremy's mouth dropped open. "Good God. I didn't know a knee injury could turn deadly. Well, not that quick anyway. What are we going to tell Peter?"

"Sydney is perfectly fine." She paused for effect. Then she looked around, lowering her voice. "Our host is another matter. He isn't what you think. Or whom."

Freddie blinked. "He isn't a DeWilde?"

"He is a DeWilde," Audrey said, glancing uneasily at the door. "But there are three brothers—Valentine, Geoffrey, and Rylan. Valentine and Geoffrey are invited everywhere, but Rylan, well, the name Rylan DeWilde is synonymous with scandal. The man does just as he pleases."

Jeremy tossed the runes on the table. "As long as he's a DeWilde, I don't see what all the drama is about."

Audrey compressed her lips. Sometimes she couldn't believe what a clot he was. "He almost killed Peter's cousin Edgar in a duel last year over a shopgirl who claimed she was carrying Edgar's bastard."

Freddie burped. "Is that all? I thought you were going to tell us DeWilde was a vampire."

"The whole affair was hushed up by Peter's family," Audrey said. "Nobody really knows how Rylan got involved, or why. Rumor has it that the shopgirl's unborn child was a DeWilde."

"Do you think I should get one of them pedicures?" Freddie asked, examining his toes.

Audrey sighed. "Of course, rumor also has it that the same child was sired by Peter."

"I thought Peter's cousin fathered the creature," Freddie said in confusion.

Jeremy snorted. "I'd like to meet this shopgirl. Imagine getting impregnated by three men at once."

"I can't imagine getting impregnated at all," Freddie said.

"Peter was Edgar's second in the duel," Audrey said quietly. "He hates Rylan."

"Well, we won't sit them together at the supper table, or ask them to dance with each other," Freddie said.

"Are you both as thick as a brick?" Audrey said. "Don't you understand what this means?"

The two men glanced at each other, then said, "No," in unison.

"If Peter won't stay in the same room with DeWilde," she said slowly, "he's not going to be delighted that his fiancée and three best friends are having a cozy holiday in Cornwall together. Is he?"

Jeremy and Freddie exchanged alarmed looks. Peter was not only the social link that connected them to the upper, upper crust, he was the purse that paid the way.

"I see what you mean," Jeremy said grimly. "We do owe Peter our loyalty."

"Not to mention several thousand pounds," Freddie said.

Audrey turned from the fire. "Therefore, being Peter's dearest friends, we must leave the house of his enemy."

Freddie sat bolt upright. "In the middle of the night?"

"Where will we find a carriage?" Jeremy asked.

"We'll walk," Audrey said resolutely.

"Walk?" Freddie gazed in horror at his pampered white feet. "Across a moor? And to where, I ask."

"To the village," Audrey said. "This is Cornwall, you dolt, not darkest Africa."

"Is there a difference?" Freddie asked.

A door slammed somewhere behind them, echoing through the house. Jeremy rubbed his haggard face. "Does Sydney know any of this? Does she know that Peter was carrying on with a shopgirl?"

Audrey glanced away. "No. She doesn't know about him and Lady Penelope either."

"That's still going on?" Freddie said in shock. "God."

"Yes," Audrey whispered. "And we're not going to breathe a word of it to our little Sleeping Beauty upstairs, or she'll break off the engagement and end up marrying someone awful like a clerk or a retired sailor. Then Peter will end up marrying someone deadly dull, and we'll be cut off like poor relatives."

Jeremy looked bewildered. "What do we do, then?"

"We rescue her." Audrey tossed Freddie his socks. "We spirit her as far away from DeWilde as we dare. One night in his house, and she'll be ruined whether he lays a hand on her or not."

Rylan held the hound by the scruff of the neck. Master and dog stood together in the unlit hall, eavesdroppers in their own home.

"Stay," Rylan said, his voice low and gruff. "You might have a chance to indulge your killer instincts later, but not yet."

He ducked his tall frame under the stairs as the three conspirators in the drawing room tiptoed out into the hall.

Rylan would have been amused by their idiotic antics if he weren't so furious. He'd be delighted to show them the door, but he'd be damned if he was going to allow them to abduct a half-drugged and inexperienced young woman.

They weren't going to take Sydney back to the man who was more of a monster inside than the tortured characters Rylan and his brothers had created.

He was just going to have to protect her. He hadn't realized how urgent a problem it was until he'd overheard the conversation in the drawing room.

Ruining Miss Windsor's reputation wouldn't just clear the field for him to capture her. It would probably save her from making the biggest mistake of her life.

Chapter 2

"WAKE UP, SYDNEY." AUDREY LEANED OVER THE BED.

"I can't find her clothes," Freddie said, bumping into the bedpost.

"Lord, Audrey, the woman is harder to move than a beached whale."

"She never looked that heavy," Freddie said. "She's so little."

"Sydney, *wake up.*"

Sydney surfaced from her dream long enough to scowl at the three familiar faces that hovered about her.

"What?" she whispered.

"We're leaving," Audrey said. "Get up. Get dressed."

"Leaving where?" Sydney whispered, burrowing like a caterpillar under the covers.

"Leaving Lord DeWilde's house."

"Lord DeWilde." Sydney smiled a mysterious smile. "Lovely man. Did you see the cleft in his chin?"

"As lovely as Lucifer," Audrey muttered, tugging the quilt off the bed. "Sydney, your very life is at stake."

Sydney sat up, frowning into the dark. "Am I dreaming this?"

Audrey tried to pull her off the bed. "No. Now hurry up before he comes home."

"I like Lord DeWilde." Sydney rolled herself back into the quilt. "Go away, all of you. I need to sleep."

"Did you know he's known as Wicked DeWilde?"

"I didn't know that," Sydney said, yawning loudly. "But I do now. Go away."

Audrey dropped onto her knees beside the bed. "He sailed naked down the Nile with three native women!"

Sydney forced one eyelid open. "On a barge?"

"On a barge, or a steamship, who cares?" Audrey said impatiently. "What matters is that he was naked with the Nubians."

"Naked," Sydney murmured, staring at the ceiling. "That must have been a sight."

Audrey shook her. "Listen to me. The man is a scandal. He shocked Venice last summer by entertaining an exiled prince and his concubine in his apartments."

"Were they naked, too?" Freddie asked.

"How should I know?" Audrey hissed.

Sydney was drifting back to sleep. The laudanum had proven too powerful for her system. She wanted to slip back into the delicious dream she'd been having about Lord DeWilde. He'd dedicated a book to her, and she wanted to thank him.

Audrey dug her nails into Sydney's shoulders. "Sydney, we have to leave before he comes back."

Sydney tried to poke Audrey in the eye. "That isn't polite."

"Never mind polite," Audrey practically shouted. "DeWilde isn't what he seems. There are three DeWilde brothers, Sydney. Rylan is not merely a coauthor of those lurid tales, he's the one upon whom Valentine and Geoffrey have based their most notorious villains. His wild past has been their inspiration. His misdeeds are legend."

Sydney just smiled.

"I think she's gone round the bend," Freddie whispered.

Jeremy opened the window to the windy night.

"Those hounds are howling to raise hell. Let's get out of here before someone comes."

"The Danger Hounds of DeWilde Manor." Sydney sighed. "It's just like the book. How exciting."

Audrey stared at her in desperation. "Don't you understand what I am saying? DeWilde is not the sort of man one can safely associate with. He's Peter's sworn enemy. Your reputation will be ruined if you don't escape tonight. He's a villain, Sydney."

Sydney tried her hardest to awaken. Her head felt as if it were stuffed with wool. Her thoughts kept drifting away before she could hold them. Suddenly she saw herself sailing down the Nile with DeWilde and they were both—

"Naked," she whispered. "Oh, golly."

Audrey and Jeremy joined forces to hoist Sydney from the bed. Then Freddie tried to help, but instead of helping, he fell on Sydney's knee. She let out a yowl of pain that could be heard across two continents.

There were footsteps coming up the stairs, hard and determined. The door shook as someone pounded it from the other side.

DeWilde's voice broke the stunned silence in the room. "What is going on in there? Miss Windsor, are you all right?"

"My God." Freddie turned chalk white. "The body snatcher is back. What do we do?"

Jeremy threw his leg over the ledge. "We escape. Come on, Audrey. I'll catch you."

"What about me?" Freddie said.

"Catch yourself," Jeremy said before he jumped.

"Oh, Sydney." Audrey looked over her shoulder in regret. "We really did try."

Audrey and the two men had just landed in the garden when DeWilde broke through the door. For a horrible moment, when he saw the open window, he thought they'd taken Sydney with them. Then Frankenstein trotted over to the bed and licked the small hand dangling from the bed.

Sydney slept, a smile on her lips, a Sleeping Beauty blissfully unaware of the evil world around her.

Rylan strode over to the bed and reassured himself that she wasn't hurt. The sight of her lying there with her limbs entangled in his sheets almost stopped his heart with desire. His eyes grew dark as he studied her sensuous curves and thought of waking up beside her every morning. Which he would.

He examined her with the proprietary satisfaction of a man who had been entrusted with a rare treasure. He looked forward to the pleasure and privileges of ownership.

He knelt at the side of the bed, resting his chin on her shoulder.

She looked so sweet and defenseless. But wasn't his Sleeping Beauty cold? He frowned in concern, nudging Frankenstein away. Sydney had kicked off the covers and her skin felt too cool. She needed to be warmed up.

He reached for the heavy quilt, then stopped, transfixed by her sensuality. The strings of her night rail had become untied, revealing her shoulder and the swell of her breast.

He needed to touch her. Just once. He was shaking at the thought.

He traced his forefinger over her plump breast. His breath quickened as the nipple hardened, thrusting against the thin linen. Dusky as a rosebud, so responsive to his touch. His gaze lowered to the juncture of her thighs, to the shadowed delta there.

He needed to be inside her. His mouth curved into an unconscious smile of anticipation and for a minute he felt as if had just caught fire.

He closed his eyes. He imagined how it would feel to make love to her, to be so deeply embedded in her body he could not move. A low growl broke in his throat, disturbing the silence.

Sydney stirred, whimpering in her sleep, as if she could sense his restless energy, the male hunger that possessed him. As if she sensed the threat. He smiled tenderly.

"Hush," he murmured, stroking her hair with infinite gentleness. But the impulses he fought were feral and unrefined. He was not surprised she could sense them.

She would never belong to herself again, but to him.

Rylan could hardly wait. He took a breath for self-control.

"It's all right," he whispered, allowing himself to run his hand down her arm. "You're safe here." Then he reached up to pull the quilt around her, protecting her not from the cold but from his own black desire.

She smiled at him in her sleep. Then, just as he tried to pry himself away, she curled her arms around his neck.

"Stay," she ordered him in the softest, the sexiest whisper.

His body responded with a surge of raw arousal that made him suck in his breath.

"You're too good for a snake like Peter, duke or not," he said in a determined voice. "You're going to forget he even existed."

"DeWilde." She gave a sigh. "You have a nice chest, do you know that? So strong."

He swallowed, not certain what to do. So he just stayed in that dangerous position for several seconds, breathing her faint soapy scent, mingled with liniment, feeling the softness of her skin. His body throbbed until the suspense of holding her became unbearable.

"What are you doing?" she whispered groggily.

"Letting you go back to sleep." Lord, his voice sounded rough, but he was so hot for her, he ached with it and could barely force the words from his throat.

"Did I hear Audrey's voice?" she murmured, cuddling against him.

"She jumped out the window," he said distractedly, trying to pry her hands away before he ended up on top of her.

"Jumped out the window?" She made a little snorting sound against his shoulder. "You're teasing me."

"Actually, I'm not," Rylan muttered. "I'd like to, but this probably isn't the time."

She tilted her head back. "I had the oddest dream."

Her mouth was soft and inviting. He wanted to taste it in the worst way. He wanted to brand every inch of her delicious body with his kisses. "Did you?"

"Umm." Her hands tightened around his neck. Rylan looked down and saw her night rail slide down again off the slope of one ivory shoulder. The sight made him instantly hard.

"I dreamed about you." She gazed up at him. "You touched me."

"I didn't." He gave her an innocent grin while his body went on the warpath.

"You did." She sighed, and he realized she was still half-asleep, too relaxed to censor her thoughts. The quilt slid to the floor. Sydney curled her knees into her body.

"And where did I touch you in this dream?" he asked, his voice deceptively calm.

"I'd be embarrassed to say," she breathed, lowering her eyes.

"Did you like my touching you?"

She smiled against his shoulder, whispering, "Yes. I did, now that you ask."

Rylan swallowed, his face stark with self-denial. He was so aroused it hurt to breathe. "I didn't kiss you, did I?"

Sydney hesitated, and twisted her fingers in his hair. "I—"

"Not like this—"

And his mouth covered hers in a kiss that was only a prelude to all the naughty things he planned to do to her. He kissed her with such devastating skill that she quivered, breathless, in his arms. He teased the corners of her mouth with his tongue, easing her back onto the bed.

"Oh," Sydney said. "Oh."

Her lips were pouting, swollen and red when he finished. A pulse throbbed in the hollow of her throat, and he lay against her, a man in torment and loving every second of it.

He kissed her neck and shoulders until she lay gasping with pleasure. He tugged her night rail down to her belly, exposing her creamy breasts. His face intense, he studied her as he squeezed and pinched her distended nipples between his fingers. Then he tormented each tip in turn with sensuous licks of his tongue. He took his sweet time teasing her. Sydney arched off the bed in shock and anticipation.

She took shorter breaths, letting him have his way. She gave a moan in her throat. The sound sent a shiver of lust down his spine.

"Am I dreaming this?" she whispered.

"I don't know." His voice was hoarse. "It's possible we both are."

"Good," she breathed, "because if I weren't dreaming, I really would have to stop you."

He ran his palm over the mound of her pubis, pressing hard. She drew a breath. He leaned down and kissed her there, tantalized by the scent of her arousal. Musk of virgin. She went still as he raised his head to stare at her.

"I want you very, very badly," he whispered.

"I like this dream," she whispered back. He hesitated before reaching down for the quilt. He could so easily take advantage of her, but there wasn't much pleasure in seducing a half-awake woman, no matter how badly his body throbbed to possess her.

He wanted her to be fully aware when he loved her.

He wanted her to always remember the moment he'd made her his.

"Go back to sleep," he said.

"Hmm," she said, closing her eyes.

The hounds in the garden below were howling again. He settled Sydney back in the bed and got up to investigate. From the window he could just make out three shadowy figures running hell-for-leather toward the moor.

"That takes care of that," he said grimly.

He'd gotten rid of his first obstacle.

"Don't dream about anyone else but me, Sleeping Beauty," he said from the door.

Sydney awakened and heard the wind whistling outside the window. She'd heard the hounds too, but she was too achy and drugged to investigate. Besides, it was still dark outside, and she could hear the sea, restless and rough.

She touched her forehead, wondering if she had developed a fever.

DeWilde's virile scent hung in the air, dangerous, erotic. The scent of brandy and male desire. His face rose in her thoughts, tauntingly sensual, and she began to shake. Why did she ache and flush with these bewildering sensations? Her breasts felt engorged, and her mouth was so tender.

She sat up on her elbow, frowning into the dark.

Odd voices kept echoing in her brain. She shouldn't have read the first chapter of *The Elixir of Death* before falling asleep. Fear was playing tricks on her imagination.

He sailed naked down the Nile . . .

Your reputation will be ruined . . .

The door creaked open slowly.

Sydney peered up through her eyelashes, hesitant to breathe. She pulled the cover up to her neck.

A dark bulky shape pushed into the room. It panted and paddled over to the bed like a horrible beast.

He's a villain, Sydney. A villain . . .

"Frankenstein," Sydney whispered in relief. "What do you want?"

The dog stared at her for several seconds with pleading eyes. Then it jumped up on the bed and settled on Sydney's chest, breathing doggy breath in her face before laying down its head.

Sydney grinned and closed her eyes again, knowing somehow that both the dog and its master would take care of her through the night.

She limped down the stairs late the next morning and found Lord DeWilde alone in the drawing room. Papers, books, and pens sprouted in piles on the sofa and at his feet. The house appeared to have been furnished in a most haphazard manner. But he looked like a man who spent as much time outdoors as at his desk. That powerful body could have been honed only by hours of hard riding or, to judge by the size of his shoulders, possibly by lifting boulders twice a day.

She stared at his strong forearms in fascination. The sleeves of his white shirt were pushed up to allow him to write. His long, elegant fingers swept across the paper in bold strokes.

Sydney was embarrassed at how easily she could almost feel those fingers stroking her skin, leaving a wake of wonderful shivers instead of words.

She tiptoed up behind him. "Goodness, is that your latest masterpiece?"

The pen stopped. A secretive smile crossed his face as he swiveled around. "I was struck by a sudden inspiration late last night. I've decided to write about a succubus."

"A succubus?" Sydney said in a startled voice.

"It's a female demon who seduces men in their sleep," he explained. "She—"

"I think I should wait to read it when it's published," she said hastily. "I wouldn't want to spoil the suspense."

"You were my inspiration," he said with a low chuckle, looking her in the eye.

"Me?" she said, her voice a squeak of shock.

He rose from the desk, towering over her. He was so blatantly masculine that Sydney stepped back in self-defense. He looked even larger in this cluttered room than he had last night on the beach. His virility had not seemed as intimidating outside against the backdrop of rugged cliffs, and she hadn't spent an entire night in his house.

Something had happened, but she wasn't sure what. She wasn't sure she wanted to know, or what she would do when she found out.

An expectant silence fell. Sydney felt a flush crawl over her body. There was a sizzling tension between them which she had noticed yesterday, although not to such a degree. She could practically taste the change in the air.

This was alchemy.

This was trouble.

"Have you ever sailed naked down the Nile, my lord?" she asked him without thinking.

Rylan dropped his pen in surprise. Then he started to laugh so hard that Frankenstein, who had followed Sydney downstairs, ran to hide behind a chair.

Sydney felt like joining the dog to cover her embarrassment. Where on earth had that question come from?

"I was only half-naked, actually," Rylan said when he managed to get his amusement under control.

Sydney restrained herself from asking which half of him had been naked. In fact, she was wishing she'd never asked such a strange question at all. She didn't know what she'd been thinking, but the thought had to have come from somewhere.

He shook his head, surveying her from top to bottom. That wicked smile kept lurking on his lips. It unsettled Sydney. He seemed to know something she didn't, and she was certain he would use his knowledge to disarm her, although he wasn't the kind of man who would deliberately hurt a woman. He didn't seem to have Peter's hard streak.

"Did you sleep well?" he asked, looking amused all over again.

She blushed without knowing why. "I must have."

"Why do you say that?" he asked with a grin.

Sydney frowned. "Why shouldn't I say that?"

He came around the desk. Dark mischief danced in his eyes. She looked even better to him now than she had last night in bed. He wondered if she was just pretending that nothing had happened. "You don't remember your . . . dream?"

She blinked in disbelief. "Are you telling me it wasn't really a dream, the kissing and the—" She just couldn't finish.

"Of course it was a dream, if that's what you want to believe," he said in a patronizing voice that made her want to throttle him. "A dream come true."

She edged toward the door, but Rylan apparently wasn't going to let her escape with any dignity. He moved behind her, settling his big hands on her shoulders in a proprietary hold.

She froze on the spot, staring down at her shoes. His breath raised a row of goosebumps on her neck. She swore she could feel the power of his hands all the way down her spine, and the only thing she could think about was him sailing down the Nile in the altogether.

"Don't you remember *anything?*" he said in a hopeful voice.

She ground her teeth as his lips brushed her nape. His touch was bringing back all the details that she'd lain in bed this morning musing over in privacy. Only it had really happened, and if she wasn't careful, it was going to happen again.

"Of course I don't remember," she retorted.

His chuckle was annoyingly smug. "Sydney, are you

telling me a fib, or is this just a ploy to get me to refresh your memory?"

She spun around. "I'll tell you what needs refreshing—it's your manners. I've never met such an overbearing man in all my days."

His mouth curled into another teasing grin. "Not even in your dreams?"

"Good heavens," she said.

He slid his hands down her back. "I don't think you should be on your feet," he said gently. "The doctor wants you to rest."

"I feel perfectly fine." But she didn't. Her knee throbbed. Her head felt hot and giddy, and even worse, she half wished he'd keep rubbing her with his big hands.

She backed away.

He followed.

Then somehow, by hoping to evade him, she ended up flush against his hard body. Somehow his mouth captured hers, and the world dissolved in a dreamy mist. The floor rushed up to meet her, and he caught her in an iron grip, saving her the humiliation of falling at his feet.

His features blurred. His mouth demanded more and more. Shivering, she tasted the guttural growl of pleasure he gave as he backed her into his desk. She was drowning in his kisses, dying in little breaths between them, living for the next.

She hesitated for a moment, her gaze lifting to his. Rylan raised his brow questioningly. Then, to his delight, she softened and let her body relax, giving him the permission he needed.

He felt the world dissolve around him in a red mist. The floor rushed up to meet him, and the lust he'd kept at bay all through the night unleashed itself like a gale. He hadn't been sure that she'd really felt the same way as he did, but now that he knew, nothing on earth was going to stop him.

He didn't waste a second in taking advantage of the

situation. He wasn't going to give her a chance to change her mind.

He practically devoured her with kisses that left her gasping in surprise and pleasure. He supported her with one hand while the other was busy unbuttoning her jacket. He ate at her mouth until she clung to him, until she would have done anything he asked her then and there.

They danced around the desk, locked in a heated embrace. They knocked his books and papers to the floor, months of research lost in a moment. They kissed their way in carnal combat across the carpet and ended up entangled together on the sofa, breathing hard, with Frankenstein playfully jumping up to join them.

"Go," Rylan shouted, waving the hound away as he nibbled his way down Sydney's neck. "We're busy."

"No, we're not," Sydney said, coming up for air.

She took a deep breath. Rylan's knee had gotten wedged between her skirts. Her unbuttoned jacket dangled from her wrist. And then he was leaning over her, looking beautiful and wild and downright dangerous. He was a master at this.

There eyes locked in a battle of wills.

"Do you want me to carry you back up to bed?" he said, his voice tender and persuasive. He traced his forefinger across her wet, trembling mouth.

Sydney thought she was about to experience a fatal heart seizure. A violent tremor went through her. She was ashamed to admit to herself that it wasn't a socially acceptable tremor of mortification.

It was more like a tremor of unadulterated lust.

"I am perfectly capable of walking on my own," she said, her heart pounding in her ears. "Furthermore, I am engaged to marry another man."

He leaned down even lower and stared her in the eye. His scowl let her know in no uncertain terms what he thought of that statement. Sydney couldn't help thinking how stunning a specimen of maleness he was, even though she was scared to death of what he was going to do. And of what she would let him.

"If you belonged to another man, you wouldn't have been shipwrecked on my cove," he said coldly.

She raised her chin. "My fiancé can hardly control the weather."

"He obviously can't control you either," he said, "or you wouldn't be sprawled on my sofa with my knee lodged between your sweet thighs." He cupped her breast in his palm, staring at her with a knowing smile. "You're mine now anyway, and I'm not about to let you take such dangerous risks with your life."

There was a rattling sound of a tea cart outside the door.

Sydney gasped, pulling her jacket back on. "Good Lord, if my friends see me, they'll die."

"Friends?" He grunted, allowing her to wriggle to her feet. "What manner of friends would abandon a helpless woman to the mercy of a man with my reputation?"

"Abandon?" Sydney said. "What are you talking about?"

He frowned. "You really don't remember?"

She shook her head. She did recall snatches of a disjointed conversation with Audrey, and that wicked business with Rylan on the bed, but nothing more. The laudanum had obviously addled her senses.

Mrs. Chynoweth knocked at the door. "Tea, my lord."

Rylan regarded Sydney with a ruthless smile. It was time to tell her the truth so that she would understand what he'd saved her from. "Sit down, Sydney. We're going to talk."

Sydney frowned at the teapot. If she understood DeWilde correctly, she didn't need something as weak as tea to drink. She needed a full bottle of his most potent port.

"Are you saying my friends abandoned me?" she demanded.

"Like rats on a sinking ship," Rylan said, holding back a grin. Hell, was it his fault if things were going his way? He hadn't pushed the stupid blockheads out of that window. "They knew I'd fought a duel with Peter's cousin. They figured it would be disloyal of them to stay in my house."

"Well, now I'm unchaperoned," Sydney said, "and I just woke up in the bed of the man who tried to kill my betrothed's cousin. Could it get any worse?"

"I didn't try to kill him," Rylan corrected her. "If I'd tried to kill the worm, he'd be dead. I tried to wound him."

Sydney gave him a sour look. "Does Peter know about the duel?"

"Hell—pardon me for swearing—Peter was the worm's second in the duel. I'll say he knows."

"This is dreadful," Sydney said.

"Isn't it?" Rylan tried to make a sympathetic face, which didn't quite counteract the delighted gleam in his eye. "But what can one do?"

"It's your fault," Sydney added, glowering at him.

"My fault? It's my fault that you were shipwrecked and I, out of the goodness of my heart, gave you shelter in my house?"

"No." She was getting upset, and it didn't help that she hadn't recovered from their sensual tussle on the sofa. "But it *is* your fault you wounded the worm—oh, good grief—Peter's cousin, I mean."

"That wasn't my fault, either." Rylan's voice had grown brittle. "Edgar practically begged me to fight him. In public, I might add. I couldn't very well walk away from that, could I? This isn't the first duel that Peter and his cousin have fought, by the way."

Sydney stared down at the carpet. Her father had warned her that Peter had a dark side, that he liked to drink too much and lost his temper too easily, that he had a reputation as a ladies' man. But Sydney had been so swept up in all his power and attraction that she'd ignored her own instincts—the same instincts that were drawing her to DeWilde.

A coal shifted in the grate. She glanced up and caught Rylan staring at her intently.

"What were you dueling over?" she asked quietly.

He hesitated.

"Was it a woman?" she said, clasping her hands.

"Yes."

Sydney's eyes widened. "All three of you were fighting over the same woman?"

Rylan chuckled. "Well, I wasn't personally involved with her myself. I'd never met her until that night."

"You risked your life for a stranger's honor?" Sydney said dryly.

"There's more to it than that," he said. "At first I believed she was carrying my brother Valentine's love child. Valentine was out of the country at the time." He paused. "As it turns out, the child could also belong to Edgar or even Peter. All three men apparently slept with her in the same month. Valentine, however, is paying the support."

Sydney went deathly still.

Rylan realized he had revealed a secret that had upset her, but he would rather hurt her now than have her ruin her life being married to a man who was more shallow and self-serving than someone like her could imagine. Sydney didn't understand what lay ahead of her. She had no idea how unhappy she'd be as the wife of a man who cared only for his own pleasure.

"I believe Peter must have conducted this affair before we were engaged," she said in a stilted voice.

Rylan snorted at her naive faith. There had been numerous other affairs and, according to Audrey, Peter showed no signs of allowing matrimony to shackle his uncontrollable sex drive.

He looked directly at her. His chiseled face was devoid of any gentleness. "I chase after demons and I write about man's darkest vices and quest for cosmic power. I write about men who make pacts with Satan. It's true that I have a certain reputation, but at least I'm not a hypocrite and I haven't hurt anybody on purpose. I can't say that for your fiancé."

Sydney smiled without humor. "That's preposterous. He's a duke, for heaven's sake, and he hasn't hurt me."

Rylan wanted to shake some sense into her. "Not yet he hasn't," he said, his voice rising. "I saw Peter in a private club when I was researching *The Elixir of Death.* He had a half-naked woman on his lap, and he took her home in his carriage."

"How do you know he took her home? And how do you know it was him?"

"It was him!" he shouted.

Sydney was frightened by his intensity. "You don't even know Peter!" she shouted back.

"I know all of Esterfield I can stomach," he said in contempt. "He's a cad and a womanizer. The man is sowing his wild oats all over London, and shows no sign of stopping, not even for you, Sydney."

"Are Audrey and Lord Westland devil worshippers too?" she said sarcastically. "Is Freddie really a werewolf in a fat man's body?"

He crossed his arms over his broad chest, unmoved by her response. There was no understanding in his heart where another man was concerned. "I've shocked you and now I've hurt you. It was necessary, Sydney." His beautiful mouth lifted in a beguiling smile. "But I am perfectly willing to make your hurt go away."

Sydney scooted to the other end of the sofa. "What about my friends? Don't you want to warn me away from them too?"

"As far as I know, stupidity and selfishness are the worst crimes they've committed," Rylan replied.

She stood decisively. "Thank you so terribly much for all you've done, but I don't think we have anything else to discuss, so if it's all the same to you, I'll be on my way now. Would you be kind enough to make travel arrangements for me into the village?"

"Well," he said, rubbing his chin to control his annoyance. "I'd offer you a horse and carriage, but your friends stole my horses when they ran off last night."

Sydney put her hands on her hips. "How far *is* the village?"

"Ten miles or so across the moor. A little longer if you take the moorland path to enjoy the scenery. The church is on the cliff, but the bell ringer is a bit mad."

She narrowed her eyes. "Are you telling me there's no way for me to leave this house?"

He didn't look at all upset by her predicament. In fact, Sydney thought he was taking her social ruination in stride.

He lifted his large shoulders in a shrug. "If you insist, I can drive you in the coal cart to the village. Of course, the journey across the moor, taking in the ponies' temperament, will probably take two days. And two nights. Three if it storms."

"Two nights?" Sydney said in horror.

He shook his head. "Spent alone together. Isn't it terrible?"

"You're saying we'd have to sleep on the moor?"

"We might find a cave to share."

There was a pause.

"Wicked DeWilde," Sydney said through her teeth. "I remember now. That's what Audrey called you."

"I won't lie to you," Rylan said. "I have been called that in the past."

"I don't wonder why."

"I led a reckless youth," he said. "I did not develop a conscience until after I reached my majority."

"Some men never do," Sydney said.

"Oh, Sydney." His mouth curled in the sexy smile that sent fire down her spine. "I don't know how someone so adorably naive ended up engaged to a snake like Esterfield, but isn't it a good thing I saved you?"

Mrs. Chynoweth came in with a fresh plate of scones, bustling between them to make room on the tea table.

She gave them both a friendly smile as if she were totally oblivious to the chill in the air. Sydney lowered her voice.

"Are you insulting me, Lord DeWilde?"

He reached for a scone. "Actually, I was complimenting you. You don't have the qualities to hold a snake like Peter for long. He would grow bored with your sweetness and lack of sophistication."

"That was definitely an insult," Sydney said. "You're a smug, opinionated man."

"Now *that* was an insult," he said, pointing his scone at her with an accusing grin.

Sydney backed away from the sofa. "You've been kind to shelter me, but under the circumstances, I can't stay in your house any longer."

Rylan and Mrs. Chynoweth exchanged alarmed looks. They both wanted Sydney to stay. "Where will you go, miss?" the housekeeper asked in concern.

"She can't go anywhere far on that leg," Rylan said confidently as Sydney limped to the door. "And she can't go anywhere because there's nowhere else to go."

Sydney was upset. She threw all her belongings into her valise and hobbled down the stairs. She wasn't as furious with Lord DeWilde as she was with her so-called friends for abandoning her to the overbearing man. They should have stayed to protect her, or at least to offer their support.

The housekeeper and her husband met her at the bottom of the stairs. Sydney braced herself against their well-meaning concern.

"Where are you going, miss?" Mrs. Chynoweth asked in dismay.

Sydney caught a glimpse of Rylan in the drawing room, standing by the fire. He looked straight at her with a knowing smile that sent every thought from her head. Then he blew her a kiss. She glared back. She would show him she was immune to his charm.

How could the man suggest she place herself at his mercy when her reputation was at stake?

A scoundrel like DeWilde probably didn't give a farthing for what the world thought. Why, hadn't all three brothers been denounced by the clergy for their Faustian ventures into a realm that was morally forbidden to man? The DeWildes had always done as they pleased.

"I would like to hire your husband to drive me into the village," she announced loudly.

"He can't do it, miss," the housekeeper said.

"How much?" her husband asked.

Mrs. Chynoweth gave him a discrete little kick in the ankle. "It will take you two days to walk to the village of St. Kilmerryn."

"Three days. Possibly four," Rylan called from the drawing room. "She'll get lost on a bog track or meet up with a local ghost. I predict disaster."

Sydney raised her chin. She would show them all what a Windsor could do when forced to the wall. "I shall find my way."

Rylan dropped onto the sofa, lacing his hands behind his neck. He grinned as he heard the door slam. His Sleeping Beauty wasn't going anywhere. There wasn't anywhere to go. It should take her at most an hour to realize that. He'd welcome her back into his bed with open arms. He'd bring her tea and sympathy, and he wouldn't say "I told you so" when she realized he'd been right all along. He might even take a nap while he waited so he'd be refreshed for their reunion.

A frown banished his complacent grin. Of course, Sydney didn't know there wasn't anywhere to go. He couldn't bear to think of her getting hurt, hobbling around on her knee. She needed him to take care of her. Sooner or later Esterfield would show up, demanding his bride-to-be. It undid Rylan to think of that snake destroying her innocence. Rylan had spent enough of his life studying human nature to predict that Peter would seek pleasure outside the marriage bed.

Rylan would guard her heart and worship her body. However, it seemed he might have to do something about taming her independent streak first, or he'd never get the chance.

He jumped up from the sofa, Frankenstein at his heels. The two of them would just have to follow Sydney until the stubborn darling realized she had only one place to go.

Back to him, where she belonged.

Chapter 3

THE RUINED YACHT. GOOD LORD, THE INTREPID WOMan hadn't wasted her time wandering around on the moor. She'd gone and taken refuge right in the shipwrecked yacht that sat in the cove below the house, flaunting her independence under his very nose.

Score a point for Miss Windsor's resourcefulness.

Rylan shook his head, his gray eyes ruefully amused. It could be worse, he told himself. At least he could keep an eye on her every move, even if he couldn't touch her, and he would go insane. But he did worry about the weather, unpredictable at this time of the year.

He wanted her back.

He missed her terribly.

He paced to the edge of the cliff path and stared up at the sullen morning sky. Clouds massed on the horizon. A gale could blow up and dislodge the yacht before she knew it. The rising wind smelled of a storm.

Sydney could be washed out to sea during the night and lost to him forever, just as the Burgundian princess of legend was lost to the lonely warlord who was said to haunt this very spot. Rylan was beside himself with concern. He wouldn't rest until he brought her back home.

All of a sudden Sydney popped out of the cabin, a

cloth in her hand. She waved gaily up at the cliff from the splintered deck. Her long brown hair danced in the wind. Rylan felt a tug of longing deep in his gut. She made him feel so good.

"Good morning, Lord DeWilde!" she shouted. "We're neighbors now—in a manner of speaking. Perhaps you'll pay me a proper visit after I tidy up a bit. This place is—a wreck."

His mouth tightened in an unwilling smile as he hurried down the path toward her. "What do you think you're doing?"

Sydney walked unevenly over the listing deck to grin down at him. He stared at her moist pink mouth, remembering the taste of it. "How nice of you to come calling, my lord," she said. "Unfortunately, I'm not receiving visitors today."

"I miss you, Sydney."

"I'm sorry to hear that." She was really delighted.

"I haven't eaten a thing since you've been gone," he said.

She tossed her hair back. "It's only been two hours, Rylan."

He gave her a heart-melting grin. "I'm wasting away to a mere shadow of myself."

She made a show of eyeing him.

It was difficult to muster up much sympathy for six feet two inches of solid muscle and sinew.

"Frankenstein misses you, too," he said. As if on cue, the dog dropped its heavy head down on the sand between its paws. "He wants to sleep beside you again tonight. So do I."

He managed to look forlorn for several seconds. Sydney steeled herself against this subtle but potent method of seduction.

"Frankenstein is welcome to sleep in the cabin tonight," she said sweetly. "You, however, are not."

He folded his arms over his chest, and what a masculine chest it was, she couldn't help noticing. The rising breeze lifted his straight black hair from his shoulders.

He stood like a pirate with his powerful legs planted apart, looking arrogant and ready to plunder. Sydney realized she might have quite a fight on her hands, and most of it with herself.

"You can't stay here," he said, frowning.

"Why not?" She bit her lip to break the spell of his sinful appeal. "Do you own the beach, Lord DeWilde? Would you like me to pay you for harboring this ship—shipwreck—in your cove?"

"Come back to the house with me," he said, holding out his hand.

She clutched the cloth to her chest. She wouldn't show him how tempted she was to go anywhere he would take her. "Why?" she asked warily.

"You won't be safe here," he said, tsking in concern. "I'm worried about you."

She backed up against the railing. "You said yourself that there's nothing around here for miles."

"Sydney." He spoke her Christian name with a sensual smile that she almost could not resist. "You might get cold during the night. The sea air. The fog. You're a delicate woman. You need to be sheltered from the elements."

"I'll use an extra blanket."

Rylan gave her a worried look. "What about the ghost?"

"Ghost?" Sydney felt gooseflesh ripple down her forearms. "What ghost?"

"The warlord's ghost. He haunts these cliffs searching for his lost princess."

Sydney shivered as she remembered the strange blue light during the shipwreck, and the gauntleted hand that had saved her. "Perhaps he's a friendly spirit. And what would a warlord's ghost want with me?"

Rylan arched a thick eyebrow. "He might want to mate with you—in an otherworldly sort of way."

Sydney scoffed at this dramatic nonsense. Imagine having sexual relations with a spirit.

"It's the sea that poses the greatest risk," he added

gravely. "A storm could dislodge the yacht and drag you back into the waves. You'd sink before I could reach you."

"Save such dire imaginings for your next novel," Sydney said calmly. "I shall be perfectly safe in my little shipwreck."

Rylan had planned to ride to the moorland burial cairn that night to observe the villagers' attempt to exorcise the warlord's ghost the following morning. The people of St. Kilmerryn blamed the ghost for their poor fishing harvests and stormy weather. The ghost-laying was to provide inspiration for the next scene in *The Raven Never Sleeps,* which Rylan would complete in a rough draft for Valentine and Geoffrey to edit.

But he had no horse. And he was obsessed in watching Miss Windsor from his window with a pair of field glasses.

How could he think about corpses and tormented creatures when that woman was driving him to distraction? Not that he didn't enjoy the distraction. He'd been working too hard lately. A few more months alone in this house and he'd become a permanent eccentric.

His eyes narrowed. "Lord," he said to himself. "She's hanging her stockings out to dry on the mast." And instantly he pictured her undressing for bed in that draughty little cabin. He saw her pointy breasts and heard the helpless sighs of pleasure she had uttered on the sofa. He wanted to feel her legs wrapped around his waist. More than anything he wanted to sink inside her and stay there forever.

He growled aloud, as irate as a caged beast.

Mrs. Chynoweth gave a sniff of disapproval behind him. She'd gotten used to hearing him growl when his writing went wrong, so she didn't jump in horror as she had her first days in this house. " 'Tisn't right, my lord. That young woman alone and unprotected in the ruined cabin. She ought to be sleeping here tonight."

"Indeed she should," he said heartily, although they were both thinking about Sydney's sleeping arrangements in an entirely different context.

He and Sydney would wake up in the middle of the night holding each other. Rylan would make slow, gentle love to her until dawn. He'd kiss her from head to toe and everywhere in between and ask her advice on the scene where his creature seduces a schoolmistress because she was so sweet and innocent and caring, which was exactly the sort of woman Rylan's heroes couldn't resist.

They might discuss their plans for the future and how he'd always hoped to have a big family. He decided to keep her away from his brothers until after the wedding—the *private* wedding. The practical jokers would probably try to abduct her and hold for hostage.

The sky had turned gray. A gust of wind banged at the shutters and a few drops of rain splattered against the windowsill.

"I knew a storm was coming," he said. "She can't stay in that wreck."

Mrs. Chynoweth put down the coal bin she'd brought to the hearth. "My husband took her some hot tea and pasties. Miss Windsor seemed quite determined to stay by herself." She paused. "The villagers are saying that she's the spirit of the Burgundian princess who was drowned at sea while her betrothed waited on the cliff. They think the warlord is going to come and get her tonight."

Rylan threw the field glasses on his chair. "Well, he's not going to take her away from me. I'm bringing her home even if I have to drag her here."

Dusk had fallen over the cove.

Sydney sniffed with emotion as she read the last page of the story; the ending never failed to touch her heart. It was a book with startling perceptions and profound insights that provoked the mind.

The story of the corpse's return to the otherworld after trying to redeem his soul would haunt her for a long time. She felt his need for forgiveness and understanding.

Only a man with deep passions and compassion could write like this.

She closed her moist eyes. She pictured DeWilde's sinfully handsome face. She felt his dangerous male energy. She didn't care if all the villains in the DeWilde books were based on his character. She had developed a weakness for villains.

"Brilliant." She reached blindly for a handkerchief to blow her nose. "The man is not only beautiful but brilliant."

She gave her nose a noisy blow, not hearing the man himself answer from the unhinged cabin door.

"Thank you. I'm glad you liked it."

She clasped her hands over her chest, sniffing loudly. "He speaks to my secret heart."

"Sydney."

She sat up slowly. "I can even hear his voice."

"It is my voice, you nitwit."

Sydney suppressed a shriek. Her brain went into shock. In her unfastened gown, with bare feet and unbrushed hair, she wasn't prepared for his visit. An empty teacup and an embarrassing mound of gnawed apple cores were strewn on the sofa.

She jumped up to confront him.

He was dressed in a white shirt and snug black velvet breeches that were molded to his powerful thighs. His long black hair was tangled from the wind. His lean face wore an expression of chilling urgency. He was the most dangerous thing that she, having had a relatively sheltered life, had ever seen.

"Oh, golly," she whispered.

She realized she was trapped. Not only by his physical superiority, but by her own imagination. She tingled all over with the thrill of anticipation that reached to her toes.

Shipwrecked . . . and now seduced!

"I think we should talk about this first," she said, bumping into the wall.

"We don't have time to talk," he shouted. "We're going to die if we don't act now. Nature doesn't wait for a tête-à-tête before unleashing herself."

Sydney's heart dropped at that. She wasn't sure she could withstand a session of Nature unleashed in the form of Wicked DeWilde. The very foundations beneath her feet seemed to tremble. Blood roared in her head, and she lost her sense of balance.

She closed her eyes. "I realize that a man like you experiences dark passions. And even though I may appear to be a sophisticated woman—"

"You appear to be a cork-brain, Sydney!" he roared.

She gasped as he lunged at her, or at least she assumed he lunged at her. Actually, he was thrown by the impact of a wave against the yacht. Her thought processes stopped as his body slammed into hers. They pitched backward onto the sofa, and stars exploded behind her eyes.

"Tell me this is another dream," she said with a groan, disentangling their limbs.

Rylan picked an apple core out of his hair. "Neither of us is going to live long enough to worry about dreaming if we don't get out of here," he said.

A blast of wind broke through the cracked porthole. The candles in the girandole on the wall went out, plunging the cabin into darkness.

"What was that?" she whispered.

"The sea. There's a storm moving in even faster than I expected. Didn't you notice it?"

Sydney's eyes widened as she felt the violent pounding against the yacht. "I was too caught up in *Confessions of a Scottish Corpse.*"

He grabbed her arm, wrenching her toward the door. "We are going to be genuine corpses if we don't get out of here."

A wave crashed against the cabin door, spraying a

spume of water into the air. A rock appeared behind the porthole.

"Hell's bells," Rylan bellowed. "We're being washed out to sea!"

Sydney stared down at the cold seawater rushing around their feet. "I think you might be right."

The cabin floor lurched to the left. Sydney stumbled back into the solid blockade of Rylan's body.

He clasped her against his chest. "Does that convince you we're in danger?" he demanded.

She stared up into his face. His chest felt like steel. "Oh, I'm in danger, all right."

He steered her toward the door, only to force her back down on the sofa as an enormous wave flooded the cabin. Within seconds chilly water gushed up to their waists. Sydney began to shiver at the shock of the cold.

"Take off your clothes," he ordered her.

"Why?"

"We're going to swim," he said in exasperation. "I can't have your petticoats dragging you down."

"Swim?"

He nodded and ripped off his boots. "If we get pulled into one of the caves, we're lost. The undercurrents are too strong to fight."

"It's so dark outside, Rylan. What happened to the sun?"

He tore off his cravat. "I'm going to tie this rope around your waist and mine. Be strong, Sydney. This isn't called the Devil's Elbow for nothing."

Rylan stripped down to his drawers. Sydney shed everything except her chemise and pantalettes.

She couldn't believe she was going to swim for her life in her unmentionables with Lord DeWilde in a Cornish sea.

Half-naked, bound together at the waist they escaped through the door and plunged into the witch's cauldron of wind-swept sea. The sky was almost black. The storm had already tossed the partially submerged yacht into the current, and Sydney would never have made it out of the cabin without Rylan's strength fighting to keep her at his side.

A small crowd witnessed the rescue.

In a year the story would become legend in St. Kilmerryn.

Farmers on ponies waited to be of assistance, wondering aloud if the Blue Knight had struck again. Ropes and life preservers were lowered from the cliff. Hounds howled over the roar of the dying wind and rain. Housewives held up lanterns whose golden light was reflected on the cove.

Rylan hauled Sydney onto a rocky ledge and took a breath. The yacht bobbed out to sea, truly ruined this time. Sydney stretched out on her side like a waterlogged mermaid and moaned.

Rylan stared down at her wet, shivering body and decided he was no better than an animal. Only an animal would consider having sex at a time like this. Her chemise was torn at one shoulder. Her pantalettes were soaked to the skin. Even in the dark he could see the perfect contours of her breasts and the cleft of her shapely backside. The way her underwear was sheathed to her skin was more sexual than sheer nudity.

And she was still bound to him at the waist, a position he found wildly erotic and to his liking.

He touched her shoulder. He couldn't help it. Then he leaned down and kissed her, rubbing his cheek in her hair. Now that he wasn't worried about saving her life, he felt the most peculiar mingling of gratitude and lust; and he realized he loved her as he'd loved nothing before. He thought suddenly about the Blue Knight and wondered if he'd ever even existed, and for the first time he felt a stirring of sympathy for the man.

"I'll have to carry you the rest of the way. Sydney, do you hear me?"

Sydney was too exhausted to move. His lips felt wonderful, and she welcomed the warmth of his body;

even the spark of desire deep inside her felt good because it told her they were still alive. "My life is ruined," she said, letting out another loud moan. "How will I explain this?"

"I can't let him have you back," he said, leaning down even lower. "I'm sorry."

He shook his head for emphasis, but in fact he didn't look particularly sorry about the situation to Sydney. If anything, he looked pleased with himself, as if he'd plotted everything from the shipwreck to the storm, as if her life were another chapter in one of his infamous books and he'd created her for his private enjoyment.

"Has it ever occurred to you that I might love him?" she asked in annoyance.

He grinned. "Not for a moment. Not after the way you snuggled up to me last night."

Sydney flushed, tempted to shove him off the rock. She surveyed his wide shoulders and bare chest with a sigh. He'd thrown his leg over her hip as if to anchor her. She had a feeling he wasn't ever going to let her go, that he meant what he'd said. She had never felt so safe and so threatened at the same time.

"I doubt any duke in his right mind would want me if he saw us sitting on a rock together in our drawers," she said with a sigh.

"I want you." He laid his hand on her belly. "Very, very badly."

She sat up slowly, trying to pretend she hadn't heard him. "I think my toes are turning blue."

Rylan kissed her again, slow and deep.

Sydney shivered and kissed him back, hauling him back down on top of her. "But only because I'm freezing," she whispered.

The small crowd on the cliffs cheered in the rain.

The kiss had added spice to the legend.

Chapter 4

RYLAN LEARNED SOMETHING THAT NIGHT.

He discovered how difficult it was to carry a woman up a cliff when he had an erection. Her breasts kept bobbing against his bare chest, and her head was wedged under his chin. Her wet body was plastered to his. Torture, every step was sweet torture.

She had wrapped her legs around his waist to keep from sliding, her ankles locked together behind his back.

Under normal circumstances, he would have enjoyed her stranglehold on his private region. But it was bone-numbing cold, and he was, after all, ascending a precarious path carved into a cliff in total darkness.

He plunked her down amid the brambles and twisted elms outside the house. She was an adorable mess. "Do you want me to run in and get you a cloak to cover you up before anyone see us?"

Sydney clenched her chattering teeth together. "N-no. T-too cold."

"Oh, Sydney," he said. Then he kissed her again because he didn't know when he'd have another chance. He kissed her until neither of them felt the bitter wind blowing through the garden. He rubbed his large hands possessively down her back, over her breasts and her soft little bottom, and Sydney didn't even try to stop him because she was a lump of melting ice and his touch was bringing her back to life.

A low chuckle of victory escaped him. The reluctant grin on her face reassured him again that she felt the same way he did, that she knew they were made for each other. She'd been washed up on his beach by a power stronger than either of them could fight.

And he would fight to keep her.

He just didn't realize the chance would come as soon as it did.

There was no one in the house. The Chynoweths had presumably been standing on the cliff with the others to watch the rescue and probably everyone was still there talking about it and embellishing the story.

Sydney said a silent prayer of gratitude to be spared the embarrassment of parading through the hallway like Adam and Eve. She couldn't imagine how she'd explain this to Peter—or to her parents, for that matter.

She ran upstairs to hide. Rylan made a detour into the kitchen for a few meat pasties, a bottle of brandy, and a huge apple pie.

He burst into the bedroom a minute after Sydney did, humming in good humor. He kicked the door shut behind him, locked it, and laid his feast on the night-stand.

He was grinning from ear to ear, obviously delighted with the way everything had turned out. At least Sydney assumed he was grinning. She couldn't tell for sure because she was hiding under the covers.

"Hungry?" he said.

Rylan peeled the covers from her clenched fingers. She was right about the grin. The good-looking devil obviously thought almost drowning was an experience to laugh about.

"Rylan, you're going to catch your death. You're still in your drawers."

"I know." He winked at her. "But I really don't see any point in getting dressed." Then he gathered Sydney in his arms and kissed her, his powerful arms bracketing her body as he began the complicated process of lowering her inhibitions.

Sydney sank into the quilt. His kiss was so deep and intimate that she couldn't defend herself. He drew her lower lip between his teeth, biting gently. Her whole body softened, and a melting sensation swirled in her stomach. His mouth plundered hers until she felt like she was drowning all over again. Only this time Rylan wouldn't save her; he was dead set on ruining her.

"Oh, Sydney." His husky voice was the most arousing sound she had ever heard. "I knew I would make you mine the moment I saw you at the cove."

"Don't say that, Rylan," she whispered.

He rubbed his palm over her breast, squeezing the pink tip between his thumb and finger. It puckered at his touch. "Why not?"

"Because—oh, just kiss me again."

Rylan didn't need to be asked twice. He took her face in his hands, and his mouth claimed hers, tasting her sweet little sigh of surrender. Kissing was only a prelude to what he wanted. It only whet his appetite for more. He thrust his tongue against hers. He needed to be inside her, the deeper the better.

He released a groan into her mouth and wedged his knee between her long white legs. She shuddered at the contact, realizing how vulnerable she was. He slipped his hands under her bottom and molded her body to his, whispering, "That's better. Oh, God, Sydney," he said thickly. "I have to feel you against me. I can't get close enough."

They fit together so well. Sydney waited and wondered why she didn't give way to panic.

"Don't do that, Rylan," she whispered, twisting upward into him.

"Why not?" he said hoarsely.

"Because it feels too good."

He chuckled. "I know what feels even better."

"Rylan."

He moved his mouth down her arched throat to her breasts. He suckled on one nipple through her silk chemise, drawing the peak between his teeth. Sydney's breath caught on a sob. And when he began to move his mouth down to her belly to the cleft between her legs to taste her, she couldn't find the strength to breathe at all. She shook and felt sensations too intense to fight. She was powerless to stop him.

"Sydney?" He raised his face appealingly to hers. The raw sexuality in his deep blue eyes ravaged her to the core. He knew that she would let him do anything now he wished. "Isn't this nice?"

She stifled a whimper. She was trembling too much to talk, she could barely think, and her flesh was throbbing where his tongue had teased her. A door slammed downstairs. She could hear the Chynoweths in the kitchen, and Sydney knew that she would be a thoroughly ruined woman when she saw them again.

"Let me eat you, Sydney." His smile was both angelic and sinful. "Please."

She would probably faint of shame before the night ended . . . if she didn't faint of pleasure first.

She closed her eyes, groaning. "Go away, Rylan."

"I can't go away." He traced his forefinger down into the slit of her pantalettes, probing the folds of her flesh. His finger slid into her damp crevice. Her belly quivered in response. "This is my house."

"Then leave the room," she said, biting her lip to keep from whimpering again, which would only end up encouraging him.

"I can't do that either. I don't have anything on except my drawers. My housekeeper is a decent woman."

"So was I until I came here." She sat up with a moan of remorse. "And I'm an engaged woman. In fact, I'm still wearing Peter's ring—a priceless family heirloom."

Rylan reached up for her hand, lightly tugging at her finger. The ring came off. He flicked it in the air and it went flying out the window, landing with a loud *plink* in the rocks below. He grinned in surprise. "Oh, dear. Look what happened."

His arrogance amazed her. "That was my betrothal ring."

His white teeth nipped her thigh. His tongue quickly soothed the stinging bites he left behind. Sydney clutched his shoulders, pressing the soles of her feet into the bed. "The ring didn't fit you, or it wouldn't have come off like that," he said with a matter-of-fact smile. "Mine will be there to stay. Forever."

He lowered his head. Sydney's moan of self-pity was cut short by the muted clamor of bells ringing across the cliffs.

It was a frantic, wild sound, a warning in the wind.

"What is that?" she whispered.

Rylan looked up to the window, but he didn't loosen his possessive hold on her hips. His eyes were glazed with pleasure. His expression said he didn't give a damn what happened beyond this bed.

"Just another unwary outlander being led to ruination," he murmured, his mind on other, more interesting matters.

"Another shipwreck?" Sydney's eyes widened. "Aren't you going to take action?"

"I will if you'll hold still long enough."

She wriggled off the bed and ran to the window to look outside. Rylan sighed, reaching for the bottle of brandy. His body pulsated with arousal, but it looked as if he still had a little work to do before he wore down her defenses.

"It's too dark to see if there's a ship in distress," she said. She paused, deep in thought. She looked delicious with her long hair drying in serpentine curls over her scantily clad body. Rylan ground his teeth to keep from dragging her back on the bed. He could smell her on his skin and on his sheets.

She sighed. "I suppose the best thing to do is to be honest with Peter. I'll beg his forgiveness."

Rylan frowned, lowering the bottle from his mouth. The only begging she would do was to him, tonight. "Like hell you will. Do you really think that I brought you to my bed so that a snake could have you afterward? I don't even want to hear you say his name again."

She looked at him over her shoulder. "How did I get myself in this mess?"

"Come back to bed, Sydney," he said, rising to draw her back against his broad chest. He began to massage her neck with his hands. There was magic in his touch, and she responded to it.

"I'll join a nunnery," she thought aloud. "Do they take ruined Protestants into convents nowadays?"

He ran his bare foot up and down the inside of her calf. The friction made her feel faint. His long fingers circled her belly button, tickling her and teasing. Sydney couldn't hold out much longer.

She began to shake. The bells were pealing wildly now. She wondered if they were prophesying her downfall, which appeared to be imminent. "I'll throw myself at the Mother Superior's mercy. I'll say I was seduced by the devil—"

He walked her backward into the bed. She fell straight back and he followed, pinning her down beneath him. His eyes glittered in the dark, proclaiming victory.

"You'll have to put some clothes on first," he whispered, blowing in her ear. "You can't go to a nunnery naked."

Sydney blinked. "That's a good point."

Naked or not, she wasn't going anywhere at all, he thought arrogantly. But women needed soothing at a time like this. They needed gentling.

"Poor Sydney," he said. "I'll make everything all right. I'll take care of you."

She closed her eyes. They were both exhausted from fighting the storm.

Rylan glanced at the pendulum clock on the nightstand. Almost eleven. He doubted that the ghost-layers would meet tomorrow on the moor. The storm would probably keep them away.

The damn bells were still ringing, though. He frowned, watching the wind stir the curtains. He ought to investigate, but he couldn't tear himself away from the bed. He wouldn't leave until Sydney was bonded to him in every way, and she was so close to trusting him.

He lowered himself next to her and wrapped her securely in his arms. "You probably shouldn't touch me again," she whispered. "Not if I'm going to become a nun."

"You're not," he said, smiling at the thought.

A soft knock sounded at the door.

Sydney gasped and opened her eyes in alarm. Rylan kept her locked firmly in place.

"My lord?" It was the housekeeper. "Is all well with you? Do you want tea and towels?"

"What do we do?" Sydney whispered.

"Pretend to be asleep." Rylan gave a loud unconvincing snore.

"This is so embarrassing," Sydney whispered, staring at the door.

There was a long pause.

"Shall I launder the clothes you dropped on the kitchen floor, my lord?" the housekeeper asked in a curt voice that told them she knew exactly what was going on in that room.

Sydney smothered a snort of laughter. "She knows," she whispered. "You'd better leave right now."

Rylan grinned, refusing to move. He was silent as the housekeeper finally walked away, obviously resigned to the situation.

Rylan didn't intend to leave, and he didn't want anybody to intrude on what he had just found. God help him, he wanted to keep Sydney to himself as long as he could.

This lonely, wind-swept cove was his retreat from the world. So was the woman who had been brought to him. He had everything he needed now to be happy.

For three more hours he was in heaven. He made love to Sydney with words and with his hands and mouth. He kissed every inch of her body until there wasn't a nerve ending beneath her skin that didn't respond to his sensual expertise.

He rubbed his unshaven cheeks across her breasts like a caress. He explored the secret places of her body without inhibition, preparing her for pleasure.

"I'll never be a nun now," Sydney said with a sigh.

"No." Rylan pinned her down and spread her legs wide, his own body so ready he hurt with it. "But you'll be my wife, and I'll take you naked and ruined any time you ask."

Then he lowered himself between her legs, and the matter was taken out of her hands. There was nothing but the power of his body and the sexual initiation he showed her. There was nothing but a rush of sweet pain as he embedded himself inside her, piercing so deeply that for a moment a red haze filled her mind and stole her breath. Then slowly it eased.

He kissed her face, murmuring tenderly. He laid his cheek against hers and told her how sorry he was that he'd hurt her. Then Sydney dared run her fingers up his chest, tracing the iron-hard muscles that tightened at her touch. He groaned and squeezed his eyes shut, moving inside her again, deep sensual strokes that pressed her into the bed. For a moment Sydney felt as if he would impale her with his shaft. He was big, and she felt herself stretching to accept him. Her back arched before she could stop the instinct. He raised his head, growling in approval, past listening to anything she might have said.

He slid his hands under her bottom, forcing their

bodies even closer together. He ground his mouth down on hers and tasted the groan she gave. In a hazy corner of his brain he knew he must be hurting her again. But he couldn't control the pumping of his hips any more than he could control the waves that pounded the cove.

He was driven to possess her, and he'd never felt anything as good as her tight little body in his life. She was shaking and laughing and sobbing, but he didn't stop. He just moved slower. He sank inside and pulled away, setting a pattern that left her whimpering with pleasure. He teased her like this until she stiffened, and then convulsed in a climax that was the most sensual act Rylan had ever seen.

"Oh, my God, Sydney." He grinned in triumph; he felt every spasm that rocked her. Her response drew him over the edge; he too was falling, ready to explode. He was trembling and pushing inside her, not able to bury himself deep enough. He was thrusting and groaning like a man possessed.

His orgasm shook him to the core. He pumped and pumped, compelled by a force so powerful he knew he would frighten her. But it was Sydney who had unleashed the beautiful fury. It was sweet innocent Sydney who had shown him that every sexual encounter he'd ever experienced before had been a shadow, a charade, compared to this.

Sydney listened to the waves crashing outside the window. She heard the deep, satiated rhythm of Rylan's breathing. She felt the heavy warmth of his leg locked over hers. He didn't want her to forget, even in his sleep, that she belonged to him. Not that she could. There wasn't any inch of her body that didn't bear his brand.

The bells outside had just stopped ringing.

Some poor soul had probably been washed ashore to ruination.

And Sydney had just been rescued from marriage to a

man she did not love and who, evidently, had never loved her.

She touched Rylan's face, snuggling against his muscular chest, her solace and seductor.

It had taken the first shipwreck to bring her to the man of her dreams.

The second shipwreck had brought her to her senses.

Chapter 5

SHE HADN'T BEEN ASLEEP FOR LONG, MAYBE ONLY A FEW minutes, when Sydney heard a voice calling her name. She ignored it for as long as she could. Rylan had worn her out, and she did not want to move.

She opened her eyes, wondering drowsily if he were calling her in his sleep. His relaxed body imprisoned her: his huge leg was locked over her at the knee, his arms were hooked around her waist, and his chin rested on her shoulder. She shivered as she remembered how fiercely he had possessed her. She, who had never been touched by another man, had been taken from head to toe.

"Sydney!" the insistent voice called again. "Sydney, are you up there?"

It was Peter standing below the window. Sydney eased out of bed, full of dread, and hurried to look. He was standing between the rocks and boulders below, drenched to the teeth.

"Let me in the house, Sydney," he demanded when he saw her shocked face. "I have come to rescue you."

"Oh, dear." She glanced in trepidation at Rylan stirring in the bed. "Can you come back in a few hours, Peter?" she whispered. "It's the middle of the night."

"Come back?" he said indignantly. "Audrey has told

me everything. I'm not going to leave you in this den of vice another minute. Meet me at the door, Sydney."

"Keep your voice down, Peter. You'll disturb his lordship's hounds."

Rylan sat up, rubbing his eyes. For a moment Sydney was distracted by the sight of him, a big sensual beast who had made her his own a short while ago. A frisson of desire went through her, disturbing in its power. She remembered the way she had responded to him during the night. The way she responded now as his gaze traveled over her body in patent ownership. She quivered, aware of the sweet throbbing between her thighs, evidence of his possession.

"I love you so much," he said with his irresistible grin. "Come back to bed. I'm missing you."

"Sydney," Peter whispered through his teeth. "Get down here now."

"Just a bloody minute," she said, turning back to the window.

Rylan raised a dark eyebrow. "Cranky, aren't we? Come back to bed and eat some apple pie. You're going to need your strength for what I have in mind."

The sheet slipped off his shoulder, revealing a sinewy torso of steel. He gave her a heavy-lidded look. Sydney caught her breath, seduced by the primal desire in his eyes. The man had far too much power over her. But she would learn, she vowed. She would make him plead for her touch, too.

"I'll feed you, Sydney," he said in a husky voice.

"Are you coming or not?" Peter hissed.

She swallowed a groan. "I have to put on my robe first."

Rylan gave a chuckle. "What for? And why are you shouting, Sydney? You'll have the Chynoweths pounding at the door to rescue you."

Sydney looked down at Peter again.

He was hugging himself in the wind. His face looked blue. She could practically see icicles forming on his ears. "S-S-Sydney."

She shut the window and approached the bed. "Rylan, what would you do if Peter showed up on the doorstep and demanded I go away with him?"

He took a deep swallow of brandy. His eyes gleamed with anger. "Kill him on the spot."

She nodded slowly. "That's what I thought. Rylan, I'm going to run downstairs for a few minutes."

He hooked his fist around her knee and drew her to the bed. "Why?"

"To—to get plates for the pie."

He pulled her onto her knees beside him. He ran his callused fingertips up and down her spine. Sydney drew a breath, shaking with desire. "I don't know if I can stand being away from you that long," he whispered in her ear.

A pebble bounced off the windowsill. Rylan glanced up, his eyes narrowed.

"Listen to that wind." Sydney slid off the bed and grabbed her dressing robe before she could succumb to him again. "Wait here."

He stretched back on the bed like a muscular animal awaiting its prey. "I don't have anything to wear except my drawers. Bring some clothes from my room on your way back, Sydney. And hurry. I want you back soon."

She threw on her robe and rushed downstairs. Frankenstein greeted her at the bottom of the stairs, tail thumping in recognition. The animal, accustomed to its master's nocturnal ramblings, obviously thought they were going to have an adventure.

The dog's friendly demeanor turned to one of aggression, however, when Sydney opened the door to let Peter in from the cold.

He pushed around her with impatience, going straight to the port decanter on the sideboard. His straight blond hair was slicked back from his scalp. His frock coat and tweed trousers were sodden and clinging limply to his lanky frame.

"How did you get here?" Sydney whispered.

"In my yacht." He looked at her, his mouth pinched white. "Which ran aground, I suspect, in the same cove as Jeremy's. I swear I was lured there by a fiendish blue light. This is the devil's own cove."

Sydney couldn't suppress a shiver. "Didn't you hear the bells warning you away?"

"What bells?"

He took two drinks before he could control himself. Then he turned to her, frowning in surprise. "Why aren't you dressed?" He eyed her in suspicion. "You look like a harlot with your hair like that, as if a bird were making a nest on your head."

"It's two o'clock in the morning," she said, her heartbeat loud and uneven.

"Another night in this house." He cursed. "How could you be so stupid, Sydney?"

Sydney frowned. "Lower your voice."

"The hell I will."

"You'll be sorry if you bring his lordship downstairs," she said. "He's . . . a very physical man."

"A physical man, is he?" Peter lowered his glass. He looked her up and down again. "How do you know what kind of man he is?"

Sydney pulled her dressing robe together. Frankenstein was eyeing Peter like a Sunday pork roast. "Don't use that tone of voice, Peter. You're getting on the dog's bad side. He doesn't much like people."

"Damn the dog," Peter said.

"Sydney?" Rylan's deep voice rumbled from the top of the stairs. "What's taking you so long? Are you all right? It's lonely up here without you."

Peter stared at the opened door in shock. "Oh, my God. Audrey was right. You've been ruined, haven't you?"

Sydney reached down to grab hold of Frankenstein. "Yes, Peter, it's true," she said. "I've been ruined. Only a short while ago, actually. It was a lovely experience, and I don't regret it. Your timing is terrible."

Peter swore at the top of his lungs. He came up to

Sydney and gripped her chin between his fingers. "I should have known not to look for a bride in the gutter. You're practically a peasant—a professor's brat, a nobody." He pushed her away, breathing hard. Sydney thought he actually looked hurt by her betrayal, as if the cad hadn't deserved it.

"A peasant?" She was incensed at this insult to her respectable background and her hard-working father, who had always warned her Peter was no good. She let go of Frankenstein and folded her arms in satisfaction as the dog bounded forward to bite Peter on the ankle. He hopped backward into the sideboard and knocked over the crystal decanter.

The glass shattered on the polished wooden floor, and port spread in a puddle. Frankenstein lunged in the air and leapt onto Peter's chest, shoving him into the sofa.

Pinned to the cushions by the massive dog, Peter let out an unearthly yell.

"Shut up, Peter," Sydney said. She couldn't imagine how terrible it would be if he refused to leave. "You're frightening Frankenstein."

Peter made a strangled noise in his throat. "Frankenstein?"

Sydney hauled the dog off the sofa. "He was only trying to protect me."

An angry male voice joined the conversation. "He was doing what he was trained to do."

Sydney spun around, still holding the hound by the scruff of the neck. Peter struggled to rise from the sofa. Frankenstein's tail wagged like a windmill.

Rylan stood in the darkness of the doorway, looking as intimidating as a man can look when he's wearing only a pair of drawers and holding an apple pie. Fury cut deep lines in his face.

Peter stood up slowly, straightening his trousers. "DeWilde. I see you haven't changed your habits at all."

Rylan glanced at Sydney. "Neither have you. You're still the same snake you always were."

"And you're as debauched as ever," Peter said in a

contemptuous voice. "Living in this grave of a house, writing about demons and ghosts." He stared at Sydney. "Ruining young women. My friends warned me not to marry beneath my class, but I suppose I had to witness it with my own eyes. Only a whore would have let this happen. I can't blame it all on you, DeWilde, as much as I'd like to."

Rylan strode up to the sideboard. "If you say another word about Sydney, I'll break your jaw. I've told her what I know about you and *your* late-night vices."

"What has he told you, Sydney?" Peter demanded.

She drew a breath. "He said you're a snake and . . . that you take women home in your carriage."

Peter managed a smile. "Champion of lurid literature and fallen women. What a calling." He turned to Sydney. "And you believe him. How could you do this to me? You didn't exist until I found you."

"Peter." She faced him squarely. "You were always trying to improve me, to change my clothes and the way I behave. I was never good enough for you—"

"You're more than good enough for me," Rylan interrupted.

"Thank you for that," she said. "Now be quiet, Rylan. I want to tell Peter what I think."

"How could you do this to me?" Peter said again, sounding really baffled. "How could you give up a man like me for someone who makes a career of creating ghouls and monsters? He's so . . . different."

"I know about you and your paramour Lady Penelope," Sydney said with a hurt dignity that Rylan couldn't help but admire. "You are a liar and a philanderer, Peter."

Peter glared at Rylan. "You told her this?"

"No." Rylan's eyes narrowed. "But if I'd known, I probably would have. She deserves the truth. She deserves to know what a snake you are."

Peter grabbed Sydney's hand, examining her bare fingers. "What happened to my betrothal ring?"

"Well, I—"

"I threw it out the window," Rylan said.

"The window?" Peter said in horror. "You threw my great-grandmam's heirloom out the window?"

"When Sydney and I were in bed," Rylan said, pulling her hand away from Peter. "It was getting on my nerves when I was trying to—"

Sydney clapped her hand across his mouth before he could finish.

"I've had enough of you, DeWilde." Peter began to circle him.

Rylan began to circle too, Sydney caught in the middle. "Snake," Rylan said. He made a hissing sound. He wiggled his hand up and down. "Serpent. Asp. Adder. Viper. Cobra."

"Python," Sydney added.

Rylan grinned at her. "Thank you."

"I belong here," Sydney said to Peter, who wasn't listening at all. "I was shipwrecked that night for—oh, golly, you're *not* going to fight over me, are you?"

Peter threw the first punch.

Sydney ducked.

Then Rylan threw the pie.

Sydney had never seen two grown men fight before. She expected it at least to begin on a note of chivalry, but this was an embarrassing spectacle, not at all romantic like knights jousting in a tournament over a lady's honor.

It was more like two bears wrestling in the woods. They grunted like gladiators. They called each other dreadful names. They swung and missed, knocking into furniture. Rylan practically pushed her across the room to clear the field. Then he went into action, his sculpted body moving with raw power. Sydney had never seen such a display of strength.

She caught a Wedgwood plate that bounced off the bookshelf. Mrs. Chynoweth, running in to investigate the noise, rescued an inkpot before it ruined the carpet.

Sydney was reluctant to break up the fight. She didn't

want to ruffle Rylan's pride, and, more important, she didn't want to get hurt by a flying fist.

They were destroying the room, though. Rather, Rylan was destroying the room, using Peter's head and shoulders like a plough. She winced as Peter crashed into the card table, staggering around to swing at the air where Rylan had stood seconds before.

Mrs. Chynoweth watched in dismay, but she didn't interfere either. Broken furniture was a small price to pay for his lordship's happiness. The housekeeper worried that he spent too much time chasing ghosts and ghouls. In her opinion he should be chasing his own children and telling bedtime stories.

A wife would bring balance to his life. A wife would keep him home at night performing husbandly duties, instead of his dangerous midnight investigations on the moor. Mrs. Chynoweth firmly believed that the dead should be left alone.

"Smack him a good one, my lord," she shouted, banging her fist into her palm.

Sydney looked at her in disbelief.

It didn't take Rylan long to emerge as conqueror. He'd wanted to impress Sydney with his strength, and it would have been too easy to knock Peter out cold with the first punch. He'd needed an outlet for his anger, and Peter's face served that purpose well.

Sydney didn't look all that impressed. Rylan wondered if it had something to do with the fact that he was wearing only his drawers. It tended to put the situation in a peculiar perspective.

"Did you kill him?" she asked anxiously, peering down at Peter.

Peter grunted, spread out flat on the carpet.

"I guess not," Rylan said, not bothering to hide his disappointment.

He started to look for the port decanter, but stopped as someone pounded loudly at the door. The sound echoed in the silence.

"Who the hell—"

A few seconds later Mrs. Chynoweth ushered a dozen or so of St. Kilmerryn's populace into the darkened drawing room. The housekeeper lit a lamp, and a rosy-gold glow illuminated the battle scene.

"Who are these people?" Sydney whispered in bewilderment, backing into Rylan, whose arms shot out to engulf her without hesitation.

"That's the Reverend Ellis, miss," Mrs. Chynoweth said. "That's Lewis, the stonecutter, and—"

"What is everyone doing in my house at this hour of the morning?" Rylan demanded.

The Reverend Ellis cleared his throat. "What are you doing entertaining company in your drawers, my lord?"

" 'Tis Samhain morn, my lord," Lewis said, taking a seat on the crowded sofa. "You were to lead the expedition to exorcise the warlord's troubled ghost from its grave."

"Samhain," Rylan said. "I thought the storm would keep everyone in bed."

Which was where he certainly had wanted to be.

Mrs. Chynoweth twisted her hands together. "Surely you'll not pursue this folly now that you and Miss Windsor are—"

"—engaged to be married," the Reverend said forcefully. "I'll be performing a November wedding, I see."

The housekeeper turned to Sydney. "Please tell his lordship to abandon this dangerous plan to release the warlord's spirit."

"The warlord?" Sydney asked. "Are you talking about the Blue Knight?"

Lord Tregarron answered her question from the sofa. "Yes, miss. The medieval warlord who watched from the cliffs for the princess who never arrived."

"Her ship was lost at sea," Lewis added, settling his grubby self into the cushions.

Mrs. Chynoweth gave a sigh. "The lady was the love of his life."

"How sad," Sydney said. "What happened to him?"

"He locked himself up in the castle that used to stand

on this very cliff," Lewis said. "He brought all manner of wizards and witches from Wales and Scotland to bring her back. He cast spells in the cove to summon her from her watery grave."

Mr. Chynoweth snorted. "A loose screw, I say."

"Why don't you let the poor man rest in peace?" Sydney asked Rylan.

"He isn't in peace," the Reverend said. "His soul is in torment."

Rylan shook his head. "This isn't my idea. I'm just going along to witness a supernatural event for research purposes. I neither believe nor disbelieve in these things."

"The warlord's spirit is caught between two worlds," Lewis explained. "He's haunting the cove and causing all these accidents at sea. Seven people have died so far this year."

Peter sat up, cradling his jaw. "Oh, God," he said. "I'm mortally wounded."

"Who are you?" Lewis asked in astonishment.

Peter wiped a wedge of pie off his face. "The Duke of Esterfield."

Lewis snorted. "And I'm the Queen of England."

Sydney leaned down to whisper to Peter when Rylan wasn't looking. "If I were you, I'd stay out of Rylan's way. There's no telling what he'll do once he gets his clothes on."

"Where will I go?" Peter asked in bewilderment.

"I don't really know," she whispered. "I don't think I care, either."

Mrs. Chynoweth began to bustle around the room, assessing the damage. She looked up as Sydney offered to help her.

"I feel responsible for the fight, Mrs. Chynoweth."

"Bless you, miss." The housekeeper lowered her voice. "But I'll clean up in here. You just take care of his lordship. Persuade him to stay home. 'Tis dangerous to one's soul to be in a graveyard at cockcrow. Use your influence to keep him safe."

Sydney didn't say anything to this suggestion. She simply slipped out of the room when the housekeeper wasn't looking. Peter had taken her advice to escape, and all she could say was good riddance to the snake. Rylan had already rushed upstairs to his room to dress in something more suitable for a ghost-laying.

Sydney had the same idea. She yanked on her rose woolen gown and jacket. She jammed on her half boots. She wasn't going to miss a supernatural event for anything in the world.

Besides, she felt an inexplicable empathy for the poor warlord who had grieved to death for the woman who'd almost been his wife.

Sydney didn't know why, but she had to be present when his soul was given release. Her engagement to Peter was a thing of the past, and she felt free to do something dangerous if she liked. She wasn't going to be a duchess, and if she wanted to lay a spirit, that was her affair and no one else's.

The ghost-laying party walked by the light of tin lanterns across the treeless moor in the eerie aftermath of the storm. Sydney rode the Reverend's pony, imagining that someone—something—was observing their every move. The hair on her nape prickled, and she sensed a restless energy in the air. Her knee barely hurt, and she kept her attention focused on Rylan standing beside her.

It was dark, and the wind whistled around the stone circle they passed. They trampled over dead cotton grass and gorse. The villagers walked in a solemn group. No one uttered a word.

This was dangerous business, this disturbing the dead, and Sydney was in the center of it. She sensed she was going to play an important part.

At the top of Holy Hill was the chambered burial cairn which, legend said, contained the remains of the lonely warlord. Because it was believed he'd been possessed by demons at the time of his death, he'd been denied a resting place in the churchyard.

He'd lived such a long time ago, and he'd slain giants

to please the king, but his own people had buried him in this prehistoric place. No wonder he couldn't find peace.

No one had ever been able to stand for more than three seconds on the rocking stone that guarded his grave. Children and daring young people had tried over the centuries, only to be thrown off balance to the ground. It was as if a malevolent spirit resided within the lichen-covered granite. A few victims swore they'd felt a powerful hand push them away.

Yet when Sydney stepped upon it, the rocking stone remained still.

"Dear lady," the Reverend said in alarm. "Pray come down off that devilish contraption."

Sydney tossed back her hair. She didn't feel the least twinge of fear, but something compelled her toward the chambered burial cairn. She had to get inside. A power stronger than common sense called her.

"What are we going to do?" she shouted down to the others.

Rylan took out his pen and notebook, standing apart from the others in his black cape with the heavy dog at his side. He was the largest man in the group.

"Come down, Sydney," he said, frowning up at her. "You're going to fall."

The villagers crowded in a nervous circle around the hill, watching the sky for the first glimmer of dawn. A farmer's wife had brought a phial of water all the way from a holy well in Ireland. The church bell ringer had carried a large silver bell, presumably to ring at the ghost. An old man crossed himself. Rylan recorded every detail.

"Come down, Sydney," he said again, his frown deepening.

She shook her head. "I don't want them to hurt him."

"Don't be silly," he said. "He's a ghost. He can't be hurt. He's already dead."

She sighed. The wind stirred her hair into her face, and her skirts whipped around her ankles. A tingle of foreboding crept down her spine. The burial cairn beckoned her.

"I think someone should warn him," she said. "Poor ghost."

"For heaven's sake, Sydney." Rylan started to climb up after her, looking annoyed. "You've been reading too many of my novels."

"I wouldn't go any nearer that burial chamber," the young minister said in panic. "The creature might turn violent if you block his return to the grave. He might take it on himself to possess your body."

Rylan raised a brow at the thought of a warlord possessing Sydney's body. It would make her an interesting wife and bedmate.

He put away his pen and notebook. "Sydney, you're going to fall. Come down this instant."

"I can't," she said. "He wants me."

"I want you, too," he said sternly, irritated by the distant look in her eye.

"Well, you can have me," she called down. "Later."

He started after her. Sydney threw him a grin and disappeared down into the tunnel that twisted into the underground cairn.

The stone rocked crazily when Rylan stepped on it, but he jumped down after Sydney, dropping into a dark vault that smelled of earth and mold. He didn't know what had gotten into her, but all of a sudden, he was frightened and—well, hell, he was jealous, although he didn't know why.

"Sydney?"

He followed her down into a hidden chamber. In the false twilight he saw her standing before a huge stone block that barred further exploration. The tomb of the warlord was believed to lie beyond this closed door. It had been sealed for centuries.

A series of loud thuds sounded behind him. Lewis and the Reverend had braved the rocking stone to join them. The two men landed only inches behind him in the musty crevice between the burrows. Sydney was standing a few feet in front of them, the strangest look on her face.

"This is as far as anyone has ever gone," Lewis said, out of breath and rising stiffly. "That block wouldn't budge for the Lord Himself."

"Move aside, Sydney," Rylan said, eyeing her warily as he approached the cairn. "You'll not want to get bumped when we break into the tomb. This is men's work."

He braced his shoulder on the sealed block and shoved with all his might. The two other men added their support. The block didn't give an inch, men or not.

"Well, that's it, then," the Reverend said, sounding relieved. "I'll sprinkle the holy water here and hold the ritual on the hill. 'Tis almost cockcrow. Hurry, my lord. If we fail, we must endure another year of the warlord's wrath."

"Come on, Sydney," Rylan said, reaching for her hand. "The so-called Hour of Demons is here."

"Demons," she said to herself. "He wasn't a demon at all."

The Reverend climbed back up the stony crevice and began reciting in Latin from the top of the hill. His voice sent a hollow echo through the cairn. Sydney was staring at the sealed block of stone.

"We're going to miss it," Rylan said, curious despite himself. "Let's climb out."

"I'll be right there," she said.

She wasn't though. The moment Rylan left, she touched the stone block that barred the way into the cairn. A jolt of electricity shot through her arm. The block swung open beneath her tingling fingers, and the stone suddenly heated to such a degree that she pulled her hand back in reaction. She stared in awe into the black musty tumulus.

"Rylan," she said in a low voice.

He looked back over his shoulder, halfway up the stones that led outside. The Reverend's voice boomed like a thunderbolt. The wind blew through the standing stones above like a warning. A strange tension vibrated in the air.

He saw her standing at the entrance to the tomb, and for an instant he felt the invisible power that pulled her inside. His fear returned in force. Something was taking her from him. The warlord, or whatever lived inside that grave.

"Sydney," he shouted. "Don't go in there."

The Reverend's voice rose into the wind. Daybreak loomed a breath away. Some of the villagers raised their clubs and pitchforks to protect themselves against the ghost who would be forced to return to his grave.

"Don't be silly," Sydney said. "I just want to look."

He jumped down to stop her, but he was too late. She had stepped into the shadowed chamber. Whatever waited for her in that darkness was claiming her, and Rylan couldn't reach her.

The Reverend's voice grew louder. "In the name of the Father and of the Son . . ."

The earth rumbled for endless seconds. The sky took on an unearthly burgundy-gold glow. The wind rose to a howl. Somewhere outside a woman fainted, and everyone was convinced that Good and Evil were battling for a soul, with the outcome undecided.

"Satan, be gone from this man and let his tormented spirit rest!" the Reverend said in a trembling voice.

"Lord be with us!" Lewis shouted in fright.

Rylan scrambled down the dirt and rocks and reached the stone block just as it swung shut on Sydney. He caught a breath of the air within, stale and redolent of decay. He saw her standing in the tumulus with a smile on her face before darkness claimed her. It was the smile of a woman who was asking for trouble.

"No," he shouted, throwing his whole weight into the block. *"No."*

Chapter 6

SYDNEY WAS SURPRISED AT HOW BRIGHT IT WAS INSIDE the burial chamber. She'd heard the block swing shut behind her. Yet she wasn't frightened. Her heart was beating rapidly, though. She thought it was more from anticipation than fear.

She wasn't frightened even when the figure of the ancient knight materialized out of the brightness, outlined in blue radiance. She had known he was waiting for her, that he had saved her during the shipwreck. She'd wanted to thank him.

He was handsome, she thought. He reminded her of Rylan with his long black hair and powerful warrior's build. He wore a blue tunic that buckled at the shoulder with a scrolled brooch. Yet his smile was infinitely sad, full of centuries' worth of sadness.

"Are you the Blue Knight?" she asked.

He nodded slowly. "Aye, lady, that I am, to my eternal sorrow."

"They're trying to send you away," she whispered. "They mean well. They want to release your spirit."

He heaved a weary sigh. The light of his presence grew fainter, like a candle at its end. " 'Tis time. I am truly ready to find rest."

The stone block groaned open behind Sydney. Rylan

burst into the chamber, looking from Sydney to the apparition in disbelief. He didn't know what he'd expected, but it wasn't this. He was excited and on edge, and somewhere deep inside he sensed that he never would have been allowed to witness this phenomenon if not for Sydney.

"Who—"

The Blue Knight held out a circlet of hammered gold to Sydney. " 'Tis for you, lady, blessed by the magician Merlin himself. Wear it as you wish. I have kept it hidden all these years for my bride."

Rylan moved protectively in front of Sydney and took the piece of jewelry from the ghost's gauntleted hand.

"Say 'thank you' to him," Sydney prompted him.

Rylan stared at the Celtic torque he held. "Thank you." He glanced up, suddenly feeling the creature's torment and wishing he didn't because he was never going to look at anything in the same way after this. "We meant you no harm."

"Nor did I mean harm," the Blue Knight said. "But I have caused trouble with my torment. 'Tis time to go."

He faded before their eyes until only a faint blue glow illuminated the cairn.

"Wait," Rylan said, seeing the chance of a lifetime disappear before his eyes. This was the kind of thing he wrote about, and now he realized he really didn't understand the supernatural at all. He'd only scratched the surface. "Wait. I want to know so many things about dying and the spirits—"

"I brought her to you, friend." The low melancholy voice sounded weak. "Cherish her. And you, lady," he said to Sydney, "pray for my soul."

Only Lewis and the young Reverend had been brave enough to remain on the hill while the earth shook and the sky took on an unholy hue. The others had scattered across the moor, not willing to come face to face with a genuine ghost. What had seemed exciting in theory was damned frightening in fact.

A peaceful light rose over the hill. The wind had died. Rylan helped Sydney climb out of the cairn, his hand grasping hers so hard her fingers went numb.

"It is done," the Reverend said in an unsteady voice.

Lewis pulled out a flask of gin and offered it all around. Only Sydney accepted. " 'Twas the finest ghost-laying I've seen in all my days," he said with a pleased grin.

Rylan stood alone with Sydney on the hill for a few minutes after that. He examined the torque in the light.

"It has a Latin inscription," he said, rubbing his thumb across the tarnish.

Sydney peered over his shoulder. "*'Vivit post funera amor.'* "

"Love lives beyond the grave." Rylan frowned. "I am jealous of a ghost," he said, "and grateful to him at the same time. If that shipwreck hadn't brought you to me, Sydney, I might as well have been buried in that cairn beside him."

Tears stung Sydney's eyes. She knelt, burying her face in Frankenstein's neck. She wasn't the weepy sort at all, but she felt a deep sense of relief and renewed faith.

Rylan knelt beside her and touched her cheek. "Can I take you home now?"

Rylan and Sydney were married three weeks later in the tiny chapel of St. Kilmerryn by the sea.

Church bells rang out across the misty cove, but not in warning this time. They pealed in celebration.

The villagers watched the newlywed couple in awe. By now word of the ghost-laying on the moor had reached as far as Penzance. If Rylan had stirred up a little gossip in the sleepy parish before, he was a full-fledged scandal now.

So was Sydney. The difference between her and her husband, though, was that everybody liked her. They respected Rylan—he had friends—but most people tended to keep a polite distance from the big man with his devil dog.

Sydney had a surprise for her husband on their wedding night. She wore the Celtic torque around her throat, and nothing else. Rylan nearly fell out of bed when she appeared before him. He had never seen such an enticing sight in his life. His dark gaze examined her with a thoroughness that made her turn pink. From her sweet face to the tips of her toes, he studied her in possessive appreciation.

He unfolded his big frame to close the window on the foggy November night. He kept one eye on his wife the whole time. Her long hair tumbled over her full breasts and back. She looked like a pagan Venus, washed up from the sea for his pleasure alone.

"Don't close the window all the way," Sydney said. "I like to hear the waves when I fall asleep."

Rylan grinned, pulling off his shirt. "Who said anything about sleeping?"

Sydney sighed in anticipation as his strong arms locked around her. She couldn't wait to make love with him again. She was really trying to control herself. Perhaps it was the torque she wore. It must be giving her pagan urgings. She had the most powerful desire to explore Rylan's body. A mischievous smile lit her face.

"That smile is going to get you into trouble, Lady DeWilde," Rylan said. "It's too alluring by half."

He pulled her into bed beside him. They cuddled for a few minutes. Then Rylan kissed her, and once that happened, Sydney no longer had any control of the situation.

She was his.

And he was hers.

Her fragrance was the strongest aphrodisiac Rylan had ever known. It drugged his senses. He ran his hands over her body, unable to believe she belonged to him. But she did. Her soft breasts overflowed his palms. The gold circlet at her throat made her look pagan and ripe with sexual power.

He couldn't wait to get her pregnant. A hot rush of

blood surged through him at the thought of her slender belly swelling with his child.

"How sweet you are, Sydney." He nuzzled her shoulder. He slipped his fingers between her legs, probing gently. "How wet and warm in there. I want to be inside you."

Sydney closed her eyes, trying not to gasp. The sensations he aroused made her shudder. She twined her arms around his neck and bit his shoulder. The torque was making her wild. She bit him again.

"God," he said, laughing. "That hurt." He played with her in utter enjoyment, groaning as her excitement grew. He teased her until he was shaking as badly as Sydney. His jaw clenched, he straddled her and thrust inside, sheathing himself in the depths of her body.

Sydney's heart pounded in her chest. She grabbed his shoulders and held on for dear life, lifting herself to meet his erotic thrusts. He braced his hands under her hips as if he couldn't get deep enough inside her. She groaned in satisfaction as he penetrated her to the hilt, driving inside her until neither of them could repeat their own names if asked to do so.

He taught her so much that night. He taught her that love between a man and a woman was a more precious intimacy than she'd ever imagined possible. He was both tender and demanding in bed. She was so glad he'd ruined her.

"Rylan, hold still," she whispered, scooting back against the pillow later that night. "There's something in your hair."

"Lord," he said. "A bug. I'll bet I caught it from Peter."

"No. Not a bug. Snakes don't have bugs, do they? It's a silver hair."

"No wonder." He grunted. "I aged ten years when you vanished into that tomb. Why did you do that to me?"

"I had fun," Sydney said, yanking the shining hair out by the roots.

"Ouch." He sat up, rubbing his head.

"It was rather cruel of you to make Peter walk all the way across the moor to the next village, Rylan," she said, glancing at the window.

He grunted again. "It was kind of me not to kill him."

"I'm sending another letter off in the morning to my parents," she said thoughtfully.

"Do you think they'll like me?" he asked.

"I don't know." She paused. "I have to admit that Papa thinks the books you write are devoid of literary merit. I believe he said you were morally reprehensible."

Rylan scowled at that.

"But Mama thinks you're brilliant, and so do Aunt Agatha and her six children. Did I mention that I want to invite them all to come for Christmas? My grandparents will probably come, too." She ran her fingers through his hair. "No more strands of silver."

Rylan sighed. "Look again after I meet your father."

Sydney knew then why she'd fallen in love with Rylan. It didn't have as much to do with his sinful beauty (although that didn't hurt) or his fame as it did with the kind of man he was.

He was the kind of man who cared about her so much he'd grow a gray hair over worrying if her father would hate him. He was the kind of man who'd rescue and ruin her in the same night.

Dangerous *and* dependable. She couldn't ask for more.

Over the years, their romance became a legend. Mrs. Chynoweth never tired of retelling their tale, even when she reached her retirement, and she would sit at the coal fire with his lordship's children and the family's dogs, descended from Frankenstein. The four little DeWildes loved hearing about their beginnings, about how Mama had been shipwrecked, not once but twice, and how Papa had rescued her.

"Such a story could only have come true in Cornwall," Mrs. Chynoweth would always conclude, sitting back in her chair. " 'Tis the land of King Arthur and all manner of mystical things, and there's nowhere like it in the entire world."

Rylan never wrote about his strange experience with Sydney in the warlord's burial chamber. It was too personal to share with anyone else. As time passed, all he could remember of the Blue Knight was his advice.

"Cherish her."

Which Rylan did, with all his being, and the family of three sons and a daughter she gave him. He loved them more every day, and his life was full of simple pleasures and the usual little struggles.

They never saw the ghost again, although Sydney and her children remembered him every night in their prayers. There was never another shipwreck on St. Kilmerryn's shores, not even during the worst storms. Sailors marveled at how they were guided around the rocks to safety as if by an unseen hand. An aura of peace and protection encircled the brooding house on the cliffs.

The same people who once whispered that the cove was haunted now smiled and said it was enchanted.

Jillian Hunter is the author of eight critically acclaimed novels, including *Daring, Fairy Tale,* and *Delight,* all published by Pocket Books. She has received several awards, including the *Romantic Times.* Career Achievement Award and the Romance Communications Readers' Choice Award. Her work has been nominated for the Holt Medallion, the National Readers' Choice Award, and the Prism Award. She grows miniature roses in the mountain foothills of Southern California with her husband and three daughters.

Buried Treasure

Miranda Jarrett

This one's for all the dedicated "skate moms"
who spend *their* summers inside the
IceLine Twin Rinks in West Chester, Pennsylvania,
watching the next generation of world-champion
figure skaters and hockey players

Chapter 1

Westham, Colony of Massachusetts
July, 1722

"I AM SORRY IF YOU'RE UNHAPPY, ZACH," SAID MIRIAM Rowe as she turned away from the window, "but I *am* going to marry Mr. Chuff, and there's nothing you can say or do to persuade me otherwise."

Miriam paused before the fireplace in her mother's upstairs parlor, smoothing the skirts of her rose-colored gown as she searched for the right words to make Zachariah understand. She had worn all her best clothes today, from the silk ribbons twined through her hair and the embroidered white flounces at her cuffs, down to her neat white stockings and the polished brass buckles on her shoes. It was almost as if she hoped that, through her dress, she could will this conversation with her favorite brother into being equally fine and gracious.

Which, alas, from the expression on Zach's face, she could already guess would not be the case.

The word *unhappy* didn't do justice to what Zach so clearly was feeling at her announcement. *Betrayed, furious, murderous:* any of those would more accurately describe the emotions that were twisting his handsome features.

Miriam sighed with resignation, and disappointment, too. Though there was scant resemblance between them—her half-brother, the only child of their mother's first marriage, was tall and dark and lean while Miriam herself was short and fair and inclined to plumpness—he was still the one member of her family she felt closest to, and the only one whose blessing would truly have mattered to her. She was sorry, very sorry, that Zach felt this way about Chilton Chuff, but not so sorry that she'd break off her betrothal. Zach would simply have to accept it and stop being the most protective older brother in all New England.

"This is generally where a gentleman would offer his best wishes," she said with wounded reproach. "Even a rascal like you, Zach."

"How in blazes am I supposed to offer you best wishes on such a damnable misfortune?" he demanded in return. Though only twenty-four, Zach was already an officer on board a Boston ship, a first mate in a beautifully cut gray coat with pewter buttons down the front. But with that authority he'd also fallen into the irritating habit of expecting obedience, even from his sister. "You scarcely know this fellow, Miriam!"

"That's not true." Miriam's chin rose in swift defense. "I have *known* Mr. Chuff since he came to Westham to visit Dr. Palmer at Whitsuntide, nearly three whole months ago. I *know* that he is a great learned scholar come clear to this colony from Oxford, and I *know* him to be a good, generous gentleman with an income sufficient to support a household and family. His company is most agreeable, and—"

"Oh, ayé, most *agreeable,*" said Zach with withering emphasis. "You forget that I've met your schoolmaster, Miriam, and he's about as agreeable as a sack of wet cornmeal."

"He is not! He is vastly clever, and—"

"He's not Jack," interrupted Zach. "That's what you're really saying, isn't it? He's not Jack."

Now it was Miriam's turn not to answer. How could she, really, with Jack Wilder's name hanging in the air between them? Quickly she turned back toward the window, hiding the emotion that she'd thought she'd long ago buried. But even that was a mistake, for through the half-open window the beach and the rocks and the waves glittered in the morning sun, reminding her all the more of Jack, and of all the other bright summer mornings they'd shared together on that same beach.

"Jack made you laugh, muffin," said Zach softly, giving words to the thoughts she was determined not to speak herself. "God knows he had his faults, but I'd always thought he'd made you happy, too."

Lightly Miriam brushed her fingertips over the windowpane, as if to wave away the past that couldn't be changed. Jack *had* made her happy, deliriously, blissfully happy; she couldn't deny that. But she hadn't been able to do the same for him, or fight the demons that had driven him even then. He'd broken her heart when he sailed away without so much as a farewell kiss, and she'd never forget that, either.

"That was a long time ago, Zach," she said firmly. She wished he'd stayed angry; anger had been easier to answer. "I'm well past the age of running barefoot in the sand after you two, playing the hapless maiden princess for you bold pirate kings to capture."

Her brother smiled, his blue eyes softening with recollections of his own. Jack Wilder had been his friend, too, and as children the three of them had been inseparable. Jack, Zach, and Miriam: the whole town had always spoken of them together in a single breath.

"And how old are you now, Mistress Rowe?" he teased gently. "A grizzled nineteen, isn't it?"

"Twenty last month." She leaned forward to poke a finger into his shoulder. "I'm a grown woman, Zach, and growing older every day, which you'd see for yourself if you bothered to come home more than once a year."

"I would have," he retorted, "if I'd known you'd been up to this sort of mischief."

"You still don't understand, do you?" With a sigh she dropped into the tall-backed Windsor chair before the empty grate, folding her hands over her apron and crossing her feet in an unconscious mimicry of her mother. "I don't want to spend the rest of my life as the innkeeper's spinster daughter, making beds and bowing and scraping and clearing up after other folk. With Mr. Chuff, I'll be more. He respects me, Zach, enough to make me his lady-wife; and take me with him to live in a pretty house in Cambridge, near the college where he's been called to teach. He needs a wife who can make his home a hospitable place for his friends and other gentlemen, and he needs a clever woman who's from this colony to help him learn our ways. And I'll never again have to wipe a table after some spewing sot of a sailor."

"All you'll be doing is trading one sort of spewing sot for another," said Zach with disgust. "You're too clever yourself for such a fool's bargain, Miriam."

"And what lasting marriage isn't a bargain of some kind?" She smiled wryly. "The only time people marry for love alone is in ballads, where there's never bread to buy or children to clothe."

"I thought that once, too," said Zach with uncharacteristic seriousness, "but not now."

She looked at him curiously, her head cocked to one side. Her brother had a long history of charming women in every port he visited, but he never stayed with any one long enough for a genuine attachment to blossom. At least he hadn't before this. "You say that as if you've fallen in love yourself."

"Nay, not I. But among my friends I've witnessed enough of love, real love, not to scoff at it." With a sigh Zach crouched down before her chair, taking her hands in his own so she had to meet his gaze. Since she'd seen him last he'd grown older, too, his responsibilities and the hard life of a sailor stealing away the last of his boyishness, and the changes made her think wistfully of how fast, how forever, their reckless childhood had flown past.

"All I want is for you to be happy, muffin," he said, his hands rough around hers, "and I can't fathom how a merry little creature like you could content herself with a dry stick like Chuff, with or without love."

"I can," she said stubbornly. "I *will.*"

Unconvinced, Zach waited for her to continue, and her heart sank beneath the weight of all she couldn't say. But how she longed to tell her brother the truth, how she'd accepted Chilton precisely because he was dull and well-bred and respectable and reliable, all the things that Jack Wilder hadn't been and never would be, even if he somewhere still lived. Given what he'd chosen to do, the odds weren't strong that he did. But though she'd never be able to love Chilton the same way she'd loved Jack, in return she'd never be hurt by him, either.

"Oh, Zach, it's so different for women!" she cried softly. "You grew restless here in Westham, and so you—and Jack, too—ran off to sea, to chase whatever fortune you pleased. But I must sit and wait for mine to come to me, and now at last it has. No matter what you say, I'm no fool, Zach. Fate brought Chilton here to me, and I'll never meet another man as fine, not in Westham."

"Then come to Boston with me instead," said Zach impulsively. "Or to Appledore, where my father's people are. Think of the first-rate husband you'd be able to catch for yourself there!"

"Oh, aye, as if husbands dangle from the trees like ripe fruit for the picking." She smiled, touched by the blind impossibility of his offer. Perhaps Zach had not grown up so very much after all, if he still could believe that love was all anyone needed. She knew to her own sorrow it wasn't, or else she'd still be with Jack Wilder. "The wedding is set for a fortnight hence, Zach. I hope you'll still be here to help us celebrate."

"A fortnight hence, you say." He released her hands and stood, and sadly Miriam realized that he hadn't agreed. He dug deep into the pocket of his coat, frowning a bit as he fumbled blindly through the contents before he drew out a small bundle, wrapped in a scrap of linen.

"Here, muffin," he said, holding it out to her. "I remembered. This is for your collection. That is, if you're not so very old and sensible that you have put aside your shells as a vain and idle occupation."

She shook her head as she carefully began unwrapping the bundle. For as long as she could remember she'd collected seashells, beginning with the dark blue mussels and fan-shaped scallops that washed up on their beach, to the more exotic conches and whelks and pearly oysters from faraway oceans that Zach and seafaring friends of her father's would bring home for her. She had a special latched wooden box for the shells, lined with the softest sheep's wool, that she kept beneath her bed for safekeeping, so that, whenever she wished, she could take them out when she should have been asleep and spread them across her coverlet. They were her gems, her jewels, her private cache of beauty and dreams in a world that was too often gray with winter cold, endless work, and fireplaces that smoked. Eagerly she unfurled the last strip of linen, and a small white shell tipped into the palm of her hand.

"Oh, it's beautiful, Zach!" she breathed, touching it lightly with her fingertip as she turned it toward the sunlight. The shell gleamed against her skin, as luminescent as the moon, a whorled, flat spiral crowned by tiny knobs and daubed randomly with bright pink spots that almost looked like tiny hearts.

"It's called a Maiden's Wish," said Zach, his head crowded next to hers as together they studied the shell, "or so the old woman who sold it to me in St.-Pierre told me. When I said I meant it for my unwed sister, she swore that you must keep it close—in your pocket by day, and under your pillow by night—for three days and three nights. Then, on the next morning, the first man you clap eyes upon will be your true love."

She glanced up at him, her brows drawn together in a skeptical frown. "You don't believe that, do you?"

He shrugged. "I might, and I might not. What matters is if *you* do."

"Very well, then. I do." She grinned, rewrapping the shell and carefully tucking it into the embroidered pocket that hung at her waist. "And I shall be sure—*very* sure—that Mr. Chuff is the first man I see on Wednesday morn."

"Mind you, three days and three nights, no more, no less." Zach grinned in return, and winked for good measure. "And there before you will stand the luckiest man in Westham."

Chapter 2

"YOU'RE TOO LATE, MY FRIEND," SAID ZACH AS HE dropped onto the wooden bench, kicking his boots disconsolately out before him in the dust. "The rumors we'd heard weren't rumors at all, but the truth. Miriam told me herself. She's going to marry that flap-eared schoolmaster in a fortnight, and nothing's going to change her mind."

"Nothing, that is, but me." Jack Wilder leaned back against the oak tree's trunk, holding his tankard of ale steady on his knee. "I've come too far for Mirry to lose her now."

He beckoned for the barkeep in the doorway to bring Zach a tankard of his own, and the man hurried to obey. Though the night was too warm to sit indoors, the owner of Hickey's ale shop was happy enough to cater to his customers in the yard outside, here beneath the oak tree with a fine view of the harbor. Hickey must be beside himself with joy, thought Jack cynically as he held up the coin for Zach's ale, with a customer—even one with a cutthroat's reputation—who was willing to pay in hard money with the king's likeness. Coins like that usually ended up in the till of Westham's other, more respectable tavern, the Green Lion. But the Green Lion belonged to Miriam's father, and Jack wasn't ready for that meeting just yet.

But Miriam herself—Lord, he couldn't wait to see her again.

"Tell me everything about her," he demanded as Zach took a long swallow of ale. "How she looks, what she said—I want to know it all."

Zach hesitated, wiping his mouth with the back of his hand. "She's changed, Jack. She's turned more serious, more sober, and telling me over and over about how she wasn't a girl any longer until it seemed like an echo."

"She's right," said Jack. "Her twentieth birthday was three weeks past."

Zach groaned. "Oh, aye, *you* go ahead and remind me, too, for I'd clean forgotten. How the devil did you remember, anyway?"

Jack remembered because he'd never forgotten. It had been on Miriam's sixteenth birthday, four summers ago, that he'd coaxed her out alone to walk on the beach. She'd been woman enough for him then, even if her brother had been blind to the difference. Of course she'd laughed and skipped ahead on the sand, and tried to pretend that this was no different from all the other times, when Zach had been there, too. But it had been different, as different as sunshine is from the moonlight that turned her hair to spun silver, and when, in the shadows of her father's dock, he'd drawn her gently into his arms and kissed her and told her she was the only woman in the world for him, they'd both felt the magic of that moonlight in the promises they made and the passion they shared.

And then he'd returned home to find the circle of vultures that had been his pirate father's oldest friends, his crewmates, waiting to carry him off to claim a legacy he hadn't wanted. Too late he'd realized their rum was as poisoned as their lives, and when he'd awakened he was on their ship, far from home and gone without making any kind of decent good-bye to Miriam. Instead he'd begun the journey that had carried him to the far side of hell, and only now, four years later, brought him back to where he'd begun.

His Mirry's sixteenth birthday: no wonder he'd never forgotten it. How could she possibly not feel the same?

"You disremember your own birthday, Zach," he scoffed. "Why should your sister's be any different? As for this new soberness in her, why, most likely her pitiful schoolmaster has given her no reason to smile."

But Zach only shook his head glumly. "I tell you she has changed, and not for the better, either. She fancies this Chuff because he's respectable and dull and because he's learned enough to spout Greek like a—well, like a very Greek. Everything you're not, Jack. I said that to her outright. 'Because he's not Jack,' I said, and she agreed."

Jack stared at him in disbelief. "She agreed? Just like that?"

Zach nodded vigorously. "Aye, aye, just like that. I tell you, she's a whole different Miriam."

"Hah." Jack scowled down at the last of his ale, his own mood turning equally flat. He'd considered it a sign of great good luck that his return to Westham had coincided with Zach's as well, but now he wasn't as certain. How could his Mirry be eager to marry another man? Even though Zachariah Fairbourne was his oldest friend, one whose word he'd trust with his life, he refused to believe that Miriam would be so faithless, and so willing to squander her sweet self upon a schoolmaster at that. Zach might be his oldest friend, but Miriam was the one he loved best.

"Yet I'll wager she's still the fairest lass in Westham," he said firmly. "I'll wager there's still no other that can hold a candle to her."

"You would know her," said Zach with such blunt and unpoetic brotherly honesty that Jack could have throttled him. "She's not changed *that* way."

She wouldn't have changed at all, not to Jack. For four

endless years, as he'd been forced to become harder, tougher, stronger to survive, he'd held tight to the memory of Miriam as she'd been: of the taste of her kiss and the scent of her skin and feel of her, soft and yielding, in his arms, of the round, high curve of her breasts, the pouting ripeness of her lower lip, the teasing, throaty laughter that lit her eyes from within, and how her petticoats pulled taut over her hip when she held them clear of the rocks and sand, her little bare feet pink in the cold seawater.

"She said she was done with running in the sand," said Zachariah mournfully, echoing Jack's own thoughts, "and that she was too old for playing princess with us, hunting treasure on the island. As if we'd still expect her to, the silly muffin!"

"*I* would," said Jack. "And I will."

Yet instantly Zach's jaw tensed, his whole body on guard, enough to make Jack mutter a half-hearted, disgusted oath to himself. What the devil had made him mention piracy and Miriam together like that, anyway, as if Zach needed one more reminder? Likely there wasn't a man, woman, or child in Westham that didn't suspect the wicked, lawless nature of his former ship and crew, and the rest would pretend they did.

It would be common knowledge, just as everyone knew Jack's father had sailed with the infamous pirate Henry Avery in the *Fancy*. Not that Jack would be blamed, or even scorned, for what he'd done. As most Westham folk would be quick to point out, Jack Wilder had never harmed any Englishmen, choosing instead to plunder the richer ships in the Red Sea and Indian Ocean with heathen owners and crews, who all likely deserved whatever they'd gotten. Besides, what else could be expected? Such things ran in the blood, didn't they? *Everyone* knew; but obviously Jack himself had been foolish to hope that his oldest friend wouldn't have been among them.

"I didn't mean it like that, Zach," he said wearily. "I told you before: I'm done with pirating."

"Aye," said Zach with none of the conviction Jack had wanted to hear from a friend. "That you did."

Jack sighed. "Then for God's sake, at least *pretend* that you heard me."

Zach took a long swallow of ale. "Honest men don't rely on deceit, Jack," he said earnestly, "or on words alone. You'll have to show me you've changed. I know you can sail anything that floats. I can get you a place in a Fairbourne vessel by noon tomorrow, if you wish it. But you have to be the one to make that decision, not I."

Jack's smile held more bitterness than humor. He'd come back for Miriam, not charity from her brother and his righteously perfect Fairbourne cousins, and he'd no intention of accepting it. He did have his pride.

Yet he'd often considered how differently their lives might have run if they'd each been born into the other's family. God knows they'd both started out the same, both fatherless boys who loved the sea. But would Zach have been better able to resist the legacy of a dashing pirate father? Or would Jack himself be wearing that elegant gray gentleman's coat instead of gold hoops in his ears if he'd had the power and the wealth of the Fairbournes to steer his choices?

"I'm considering it," he said lightly. "Now you didn't tell Mirry that I'd come here with you to Westham, did you?"

"After I'd sworn to you I wouldn't?" Zach's expression was carefully impassive. "I told you I'd help you for Miriam's sake, not yours. But if you don't love her true the way you claim, or if you make her suffer in any way, why would you then—"

"Why what?" demanded Jack automatically, unable, even with Zach, to keep the reflexive challenge from his tone.

"Why?" With the single word, Zach tossed the challenge back in his face. "Damnation, because she's my sister, that's why, and you're a—"

"A what?" Jack smiled bitterly. "A thief, a scoundrel, a murderer, a black-hearted devil born only to be hung? Do you think I'd have dared come back for Miriam if even half the stories were true? I told you before, Zach, and I'll swear to it in whatever way will make you believe: I'm done with that trade, done for good and the sake of my own tattered soul. And for Miriam."

"For *Miriam?*" repeated Zach with patent disbelief.

"Aye, for Miriam, and what other reason would be better?" Impatiently Jack struck his fist to his knee. "I've come back to make her happy, Zach, and I'd have thought you'd want the same for her."

"I do, but—"

"Wouldn't you rather see her with your oldest mate, the one man who would put her life and joy before his own? Or would you prefer she tossed herself away on this puling schoolmaster, and see her swallowed up into dull old Cambridge, away from the sea and away from us?"

With obvious reluctance, Zach shook his head, and Jack, to his sorrow, could understand. He could wax on endlessly about old acquaintance, but the cold truth was that he wasn't the same man who'd left Westham, and he and Zach both knew it. He'd seen the change himself in every looking glass. Four years of bloodshed and mayhem, typhoons and hurricanes, living with one eye on the hangman's noose and the other on the knives of his crewmates, all of it had left its mark on his face. His pale eyes in particular now held a dangerous, almost wolfish look that made other men keep their distance. It was not the face of an honest New England gentleman, and it was most definitely not a face to trust with a favorite sister.

"Your word of honor, Jack," Zach was now saying. "Give me your word of honor that you'll treat her well."

"Given," said Jack with an impatient sweep of his

hand. Of course he only wanted the best for Miriam, as long as that best included him.

"And that you love her," continued Zach. "The dear little fool still loves you well enough, though she's too stubborn to admit it. God knows that's the only reason I'm even considering acting like some blasted matchmaker on your behalf."

Jack strived to look properly lovesick. It wasn't hard, considering how he really did feel about Miriam. "I do love her, Zach. Always have, and always will."

"Then you'll give me your word that you'll wed her?"

Jack hesitated as the icy finger of respectability traced down his spine. Miriam was the one good thing in his entire misspent life, and what he felt for her went well beyond love the way other people seemed to mean it. In the years they'd been apart, the sharp ache of separation had never lessened. He'd missed her more than if he'd lost an arm or a leg, she was that much a part of him, and he'd no intention of ever leaving her again.

He wanted her back, wanted her more than anything else in this life or the next, yet somehow that wanting had never quite translated itself in his mind into marriage. Marriage was grim and doleful and cheerless, a cold, black pit of duty that swallowed up all the joy and spice between men and women. He wouldn't wish that on his Mirry, any more than he would on himself, but he wasn't about to abandon his chances by confessing as much to her brother, either.

"I told you I'd treat her honorably, didn't I, Zach?" he declared heartily, and that much he meant.

"In every way," said Zach firmly. "Else I'll see you hung myself, friend or no friend."

Jack nodded impatiently. The fine points could be worked out later, once he had Miriam by his side where she belonged. "You did make her a present of the seashell?"

"Aye," said Zach, still eyeing him warily, "though she

thought the part about finding her true love on the third morning was a bit daft."

"In three days it will seem to her the most logical notion under the sun," said Jack with a confident smile as he settled back against the oak's trunk. "And best of all, there won't be a word of that schoolmaster's Greek to any of it."

Chapter 3

CAREFULLY MIRIAM POURED TEA FROM THE POLISHED pewter pot into the cup in her hand, striving to make an elegant arc of the golden brown liquid. Though Mama had insisted she learn such niceties so as to be able to cater to the occasional gentry who stopped at the Green Lion on the road from Boston north to Salem, now she was glad because it pleased Chilton. She smiled as she handed him the teacup, and he beamed back at her with approval.

On so warm an afternoon Miriam herself would just as soon have sipped buttermilk or sweetened lemonade than a steaming dish of tea, but Chilton would never sacrifice his genteel ritual. Besides, this was the one part of the day, after the dinner dishes had been washed and before the preparations for supper were begun, that Miriam—and the Green Lion's single private dining chamber where they sat—could be spared from the tavern. With a weary little sigh she settled herself in the chair beside Chilton's, taking care to hide her dishwater-reddened hands in the folds of her apron.

And she *was* weary, not just from serving dinner to twenty, but from her own restless sleep these past two nights since Zachariah had returned. Instead of convincing her brother of the wisdom of her coming marriage, their conversation seemed to have shaken her own resolution. Of course accepting Chilton was right; of course she'd be happy with him. So why, then, had she taken such care to put that foolish seashell beneath her pillow each night, a small, mischief-making lump that had caused her to toss and turn and dream odd, broken dreams of Jack Wilder?

"Miriam dear, you do not attend me," chided Chilton indignantly.

"But I do, Chilton," said Miriam with guilty haste, thrusting a small tray of biscuits before him. "These lemon ones are your favorites, aren't they?"

"That is not what I meant at all," he answered severely, though he didn't hesitate to take one of the offered biscuits. "You have not listened to a word I have spoken these ten minutes past."

"That's not true," said Miriam automatically, if not truthfully.

"No?" He waved the half-eaten biscuit with dainty elegance between his thumb and forefinger. "If you can repeat to me one fraction of what I was saying of Dr. Hynde and his theory of transmogrification, then you shall have my heartfelt apology. But I rather believe, my dear, that you cannot, and so instead must be obligated to me."

He popped the last of the biscuit into his mouth, his jaws working in neat, rapid bites of triumph. For Miriam, whose errant thoughts had been preoccupied with the memory of Jack Wilder's wickedly rakish grin, those rabbity little bites were a dreadful reminder of what she'd lost. Chilton was a respectable man, even brilliant, but with his ginger-colored brows and lashes and the face around them as pale and round as a pudding, he could not be called handsome, and never, ever rakish.

But Chilton had asked her to be his wife, something Jack had never bothered to do, and for that alone he deserved better from her. "I am sorry, Chilton," she began as inexplicable tears stung her eyes. "I know how much Dr. Hynde's theories do matter to you. But the Lion's been so busy these last days, and I've been working so hard that—"

"Do not distress yourself, my dear, I beg you." Chilton reached for her hand and gently began to pat the back of it. "As soon as you are my wife, my dearest helpmeet, then such troubles will slip from your life."

She sniffed and looked down at his smooth, tapered fingers resting upon her own red knuckles. Gentleman's hands, she thought miserably, just as this was a gentleman's seemly way of comforting a lady. So why, then, did she wish that he'd sweep her into his arms instead and hold her tight against his chest, even try to kiss her? That was exactly the sort of thing that Jack had done, and what good had come from it? Could craving such brash attention mean that she in turn wasn't fit to be Chilton's wife, that all she really deserved was a scoundrel like Jack Wilder?

"You are too good for me, Chilton," she began wretchedly. "I do not know why you—"

"I'll not hear a word more against my choice, or yourself, either," interrupted Chilton. "Once we are wed, I promise I'll grant you a better life. It is, after all, not so very much longer to wait."

Miriam managed a wistful smile. As usual, Chilton was right. Marriage would end her foolish restlessness. It was this dreadful in-between time that was making her look backwards to the past. That, and Zach's meddlesome magic seashell. "I wish our wedding were tomorrow."

"My dear, impatient little bride." Chilton smiled indulgently, his voice as rich and fulsome as clotted cream. He raised her fingers, caressing them gently with his own, and kissed the air over the back of her hand. "I wish it were, too. But until then, Miriam, we must curb our more base desires."

"But that isn't what I mean!"

"I know well enough what you mean, Miriam," said Chilton kindly. "Not that I fault you for it, not in the least. Growing up in such a barbarous land, so close to the savage wilderness and away from the better influences of society, it is not surprising to have, ah, heated and ungovernable impulses. I admit to feeling them myself where you are concerned. But we must not succumb to those passions, and instead must be guided by our sensibilities."

As the long, stiffened curls of his wig brushed over her hand, she thought grudgingly of how he seemed to be doing a much better job of passion-curbing than she. Perhaps it was because she hadn't the faintest idea of what or where her sensibility was, let alone of how to be guided by it. But in this, too, Chilton was right. She must learn to control her passions or she'd never be happy, not with him and, more importantly, not with herself, either.

But it was one thing to make such bold resolutions, and quite another to make them *real.* By the time the last of the Green Lion's tipplers had been pointed toward home and the coals in the kitchen fire were banked for the night, Miriam was so tired she could barely drag herself up the winding back stairs to her room under the eaves. There the air was close and warm, the shingles of the sloping roof overhead still holding the heat of the day though it was nearly midnight, warm enough that Miriam flopped on top of her coverlet in her thin linen shift alone, her arms and legs outstretched to catch any breath of a breeze that might drift in through the tiny casement window.

Tonight, she told herself firmly, *I will sleep, and I will* not *dream.*

But as soon as she closed her eyes, her unconscious mind wantonly ceased to obey.

She was again sitting with Chilton, and once again he was bowing over her hand with his courtier's grace. She smiled and arched her wrist gracefully, her manners for once a match for his, and as she did, he laughed, low and deep in his chest. It wasn't Chilton's laugh, not at all, and when he lifted his face to meet her startled gaze, it wasn't Chilton's face, either, but

Jack's, his wavy dark hair falling across his forehead as it always did, his pale eyes wicked and teasing as his fingers tightened around hers to pull her from her ladylike chair and onto his lap, his thighs hard and muscled beneath her bottom as he tipped her back in his arms to kiss her and—

She jerked awake, her breathing rushed and her heart thumping and the heat of the room pressing down on her with the same force that Jack had in the dream. Another wretched, willful, wrong-headed abomination of a *dream,* and with a groan she pressed her hands to her flushed cheeks.

She hadn't dreamed of Jack in years, and certainly not like this. Why should his memory suddenly come back to haunt her, now that she was promised to another? Her passions were racing away like a team of runaway horses, all right, and she was determined to rein them in. Grimly she squeezed her eyes shut and rolled onto her side, sliding her hand beneath her pillow to bunch it beneath her cheek. As she did she felt the little lump of Zach's seashell, placed there as she'd promised.

"Maiden's Wish, ha," she grumbled as she pulled it out from hiding. "More like Maiden's Torment."

She was not by nature superstitious, but enough was enough. She shrugged a calico short-gown over her shift, not bothering to lace the front closed, and with the shell held tightly in her hand she padded barefoot down the stairs and out the kitchen door.

At the yard's fence, she paused, relishing the peace around her. In a village like Westham, no one else would be awake at this hour, let alone abroad, and the little cluster of houses and shops stood shuttered and silent beneath the stars and the dull gleam of the quarter moon. From the marshes on the far bank of the river she could hear the rhythmic chatter of crickets played against the gentle *shush* of the waves coming in across the sand with the tide. It was cooler here, too, than it had been in the house, and as she turned her face toward the water she already felt calmer and more at peace. This had all been Zach's fault, putting doubts and ideas into her head, and she meant to deal with it now, before it caused her any more trouble.

Purposefully she headed around to the front of the tavern, her bare feet choosing the dry wild grasses along the side instead of the sharp crushed shells of the carefully raked path. She passed beneath the hanging signboard of the emerald-green and gilt lion, and between the now-empty posts for tying horses. It was only a short walk to the tavern's own dock; long ago her grandfather had had the shrewd foresight to realize that travelers on the new road north from Boston would want a dry, comfortable spot to wait for a boat to ferry them across the river to continue their journey, or, coming from the south, a decent bed and a warm supper before the tide shifted in the boatman's favor.

The worn planks of the dock were smooth beneath Miriam's feet, and at the very end, next to the ferry bell, she stopped, hooking her toes over the edge in the daredevil way that she and Zach—and Jack, too—had always done as children. She herself hadn't done it for years now, but somehow, there in the moonlight, it seemed oddly appropriate. After all, in a way, wasn't she still daring the two boys who had ruled her life?

She opened her hand, holding the little shell up to the moonlight. "There, Zachariah Fairbourne," she muttered resolutely as she drew her arm back to heave the shell into the dark water below. "*This* is what I think of your heathenish wishing shell, and *this* is what I think of your wretched true love for—"

"You're too late."

She spun around so quickly she nearly tottered off the edge of the dock, her arms flapping like an inelegant duck as she struggled to keep her balance. But the man didn't move to help her, his long shadow in the moonlight the only thing to reach out toward her.

"It's after midnight, Mirry, the third morning," said Jack Wilder softly. "Now come, and greet your own true love."

Chapter 4

JACK HAD IMAGINED THIS MOMENT TIMES BEYOND counting and in a thousand different ways, but none of them could come close to having Miriam here, really here, before him. She'd so clearly tumbled straight from her bed that it made him ache just to look at her: her plain linen shift sliding off one shoulder beneath the unlaced short-gown, the tantalizing roundness of her breasts and hips so clear beneath the soft fabric, her hair slipping out from its braid into tiny, teasing tendrils around her slender throat, her startled eyes still heavy-lidded with sleep. She had changed, true, but not the way Zach had said. She'd changed subtly, ripened from the girl he'd left behind to the woman he'd come home to, a woman that he wanted very much to claim for his own forever.

And, unfortunately, a woman who right now [illegible]ed madder than the devil's blazes with him.

"You are not my own true love, Jack Wilder," she said as she belatedly clutched the front of the short gown together. "You aren't *my* anything!"

"Aye, I am." He said it as the fact it was, and smiled slowly, his gaze drawn to how ineffectually, and how appealingly, that clutched calico was covering her breasts. She'd grown more plump, her body more openly lush. He approved. "You look good, Mirry. Better than good."

"Then stop looking this instant." She glared at him furiously as she tugged harder at the calico. "What are you doing here, anyway? Why did you come back? Why did you have to come back *now?"*

Impatiently she tossed her bedraggled braid back between her shoulder blades, and his smile widened. She still cared, else she wouldn't let her temper get the better of her this way, her dark eyes flashing and her round, dimpled chin raised with out-and-out belligerence. And he hadn't forgotten all the interesting trouble that temper of hers could lead her into.

"From what Zach's told me," he said evenly, "it's high time I did come back. Forgetting me, throwing yourself away on some puffed-up periwig—that's not well done, Mirry."

She gasped, her small mouth a perfect, charming O of indignation. "I should have known from the first that you two would contrive to do this to me, just like you always did! Zach and you—oh, *you!"*

She threw the shell at him, aiming at his face, but he deftly caught it with one hand.

"A Maiden's Wish, isn't it?" he said as he took one step toward her, then another, lightly tossing the little shell in his palm as if he'd never seen it before. "They say it will always tell the truth of a female heart. And I'd say they were right."

"How long did it take you and Zach to make up *that* crock of nonsense?" she said defiantly, even as she began to back away. "Take care that you stay where you are, Jack Wilder. Don't you come one bit closer."

"Then you stay where you are, Miriam Rowe, and stop making me chase you."

"Jack, please," she said, the first edge of panic creeping into her voice as she inched away from him. "Go away. Leave me alone. Whatever there was between us is done, finished. Go away *now."*

"I've come clear around the world for you," he said, his voice harsh with honesty as he held his hand out toward her. "Do you think I'll clear off now with only an arm's span left between us?"

She shook her head, but as her bare feet slid backwards and away from him she forgot how close she was to the edge of the dock until it was too late. Abruptly she began to topple backwards again, and this time, before she could protest, Jack caught her wrist and pulled her back from the edge, and back into his arms.

Too late Miriam realized what he'd done, too late to choose the dark-running river instead of the infinitely greater danger of Jack. In the water she could thrash her way to shore, but pressed against the hard wall of his chest she was powerless to save herself. Instantly she remembered the dangerous feel of him, and worse, her body remembered, too, shamelessly moulding against his as if four years were no more than last night. Four years, she was discovering, meant nothing: it would take a lifetime for her racing heart to forget the feel of him.

"Let me go, Jack," she ordered breathlessly, scrambling against him. "Blast you, let me *go!*"

"No," he said, tipping her effortlessly back over his arm. "I won't."

"Jack Wilder, if you don't—"

"Hush," he ordered, his voice low as his face came down upon hers, "and not one word more, mind?"

She wouldn't mind, but as she began to tell him so his mouth closed over hers, reducing her protest to a wordless whimper. Sensation raced through her like a flame, and mindlessly she parted her lips for him. All the heat of July was concentrated in his kiss, searing her even as she sought more. He drew her closer, his hands spreading wide over her bottom to pull her tight against his hips.

"You're mine, Miriam," he breathed hoarsely, his words hot upon her throat. "All mine."

But she wasn't, and his arrogant assumption instantly cut through the foggy haze of desire. With her palms square on his chest she shoved hard to break free, reeling back away from him.

"The devil take you as one of his own!" she gasped, struggling to regain what little composure she'd had, or at least as much as was possible under the circumstances. "I am *not* yours, Jack Wilder, and don't you believe otherwise!"

Yet from how he was watching her, his pale gray eyes with their thick lashes at once predatory and possessive in a way that made her shiver despite the heat, she knew he believed exactly that. He was still tall and lean and a trifle unkempt, still the rough-edged orphan boy in town without a mother to keep him tidy: his thick, wavy hair coming untied and his cheeks shadowed with dark stubble, his coat open and his shirt loose, with a patterned bandana knotted carelessly around his throat. But he wasn't the same boy who'd loved her once. He was a man now, a man who'd discovered a whole world of experience and sin, and with her entire being she sensed the difference.

"I am not yours," she said again, more weakly, as she strived to convince herself as much as him. "I'm *not.*"

"Why the hell should I believe that when you don't?" he demanded, raking his fingers impatiently back through his hair. "Didn't that kiss prove as much?"

She shook her head fiercely. "You gave up all right to me when you left, Jack. You took my . . . my innocence, and then you sailed away without a second thought for the consequences."

"Damnation, Miriam, I had no say in that!" he said, his voice rumbling low with the urgency to make her understand. "I was as good as a prisoner on that ship! Do you believe I would have left you of my own will, after the best night of my life—"

"But you did," she said bitterly. "You *did.*"

"And don't you think it grieved me, too?" he demanded roughly. "Those first weeks I thought I'd go mad. God knows I wanted to get back to you, Mirry, but those bastards watched me night and day, swearing it was my father's fondest wish that I be with them."

"Don't blame this on your father!" she cried unhappily, the agony of the day he'd left suddenly fresh again. "He was dead before you were born. You had no reason to follow in his wicked footsteps, none at all!"

"For God's sake, Miriam, it wasn't that simple." He shook his head with frustration. "You, and my father, and every other damned thing that happened—it's so hard to explain, Mirry."

She went very still. He'd never kept secrets from her before, and she felt this one now rising like a wall between them. "Even to me, Jack?"

"Especially to you." He shook his head again, his face oddly expressionless, his thoughts turned inward and apart from her as he stared off toward the river. "I don't even know where to begin."

"Then why did you have to come back, anyway?" she whispered. "Why didn't you just stay in India or China or whatever heathenish place you were?"

"That's one question you shouldn't have to ask." He took her hand to draw her back. "Do you think I'd ever forget what we had, lass? What we still have?"

She stiffened, determined this time not to yield. "You will let me go, Jack. Let me go, or I'll . . . I'll scream."

"You?" he said incredulously. The small gold rings in his ears glinted in the moonlight and made him look every bit as exotically disreputable as he was supposed to be. "Not you, Mirry. You never were the sort of girl to fall into fits and scream. Ringing that bell to raise the dead, now, that's more your manner."

"Very well." With her free hand she grabbed for the rope to the ferry bell. "I'll sound an alarum to wake the whole town."

"Oh, aye, and what would the whole town make of it?" he said. "They'll remember us together, lass, hand in hand, and they'll see no crime in us together again. Except your new lover. *He* might not be as understanding."

Instantly her hand dropped from the bell rope. "No, Jack," she said slowly. "You're the one who must understand."

"And I do, sweet," he said. "I understand that you and I are—"

"No," she said as firmly as she could. "That's not what I meant. It's done between us, Jack, done forever."

Done: the word fell with a grim finality between them, a finality that she felt just as keenly.

"Done?" he repeated with an odd little twist of his shoulders, his expression growing guarded. "Done with me, you say?"

She swallowed hard, and nodded.

"Done." His smile turned into a grimace as he shook his head. Stiff armed, he jammed his hands into the pockets of his greatcoat, so much like the lost boy she remembered that she almost wept. "Done, am I, to be tossed away like an old stocking not worth the mending?"

"Jack, I didn't—"

"Did you never spare a kind thought for me then, lass? Four years, and not one?"

"In four years?" she repeated wistfully. "Oh, Jack, in four years I've granted at least ten thousand thoughts to you, and shed a tear to match each one!"

She saw how his face relaxed with a reassurance she did not want him to feel. "I knew you weren't hard-hearted, love," he said in a rough whisper. "Don't be cruel and pretend otherwise."

Swiftly she looked down at the dock and away from him, and rushed on before he'd say more things, sweet, loverlike things, that she'd no right to hear.

"Don't begin, Jack," she pleaded. "Just . . . just don't. I'm not a girl any longer, and I can't live on wild games and promises you've no intention of keeping."

"But I've never lied to you, Mirry," he said slowly, "not once, and I'm not about to begin now. You'll see. I've plans for us, lass, great dreams and—"

"No more dreams, Jack, I beg of you!" she cried. "I need someone who lives his life honestly and won't go off for years and years and get himself killed for no reason. I need a man who will be there when I need him. Chilton will, and that's why I'm going to marry him, and nothing you do or say now is going to change my mind."

She turned then and ran, not trusting herself to wait for Jack's answer. But the answer didn't come, and he didn't follow her, either, her own footsteps echoing unanswered on the dock, and as she fled alone she couldn't decide whether she was disappointed or relieved.

Still she ran and didn't look back, up the path and around the tavern and through the kitchen door and up the winding stairs to her room beneath the eaves. With a muffled sob she threw herself face down on the bed.

Oh, Jack, why have you come back now? If you had to return at all, why couldn't you have come back in a fortnight, when I'd be wed and safely locked away from you forever?

Her heart was pounding, her lips still burned from his kiss, and her whole body felt heavy with unfulfillment and longing for what was wrong.

Wrong, wrong, *wrong* . . .

"Miriam?" Gently her mother pushed the door open, her face beneath the linen nightcap lined with worry in the glow of the candlestick in her hand. "Aren't you abed, girl?"

"Oh, yes, Mama." Miriam twisted around, taking care to keep her chin tipped down in the shadows so her mother would not see her tears. "I . . . it was so warm a night that I went outside for a breath of air. But I'm back now, and wicked weary, too."

She yawned dramatically, hating herself for being untruthful to her mother.

"Very well." Her mother frowned, her expression a

mixture of doubt and concern. "But your father was sure he'd heard voices down near the dock."

"'Twas nothing, Mama." She pulled her pillow into her arms, hugging it so tightly against her aching, confused heart to keep from crying that she thought her arms would break. "Nothing at all."

Chapter 5

"ARE YOU LOOKING FOR A DRAM OF RUM, SIR?" ASKED the small boy, his voice piping up cheerfully beside Jack. "You'll find a traveler's welcome there at the sign of the Green Lion, and that's the honest truth."

"Is that so?" Jack doubted he'd find any sort of welcome at all at the Green Lion this morning, but that hadn't kept him from coming back to this beach to squint up at the tavern, hoping for another chance to speak to Miriam. Reluctantly he looked away from the tavern down to the boy beside him, and scarcely managed to bite back an oath of astonishment. The boy's round face and shock of tow-colored hair were the very mirror of Miriam's, even to the eager grin framed by Miriam's dimples. Desperately Jack tried to guess the boy's age: five, six, or only four? Blast, he never could tell with children!

"'Course it's so," said the boy staunchly. "My pa keeps the best house north of Boston, and my mam's the best cook, and the devil take the rascal who dares say otherwise."

"Strong words for a whelp your size." Somehow Jack managed a weak smile. So the boy was Miriam's brother, not her son, or his, either. Now that he could breathe again, he could just remember a baby still in skirts toddling about the tavern when he'd left. Besides, Zach would never be so accommodating now if he'd left Miriam to bear his bastard, but for a bewildering moment the possibility had still been there. Strange how quickly his conscience had been willing to claim the boy as his blood, stranger still how disappointed he felt to learn the truth. "I'd wager your mother doesn't like you taunting old Lucifer in her house."

The boy wrinkled his nose sheepishly. "Not exactly," he admitted. "I 'spect she'd paddle me good. But my brother Zach says swearing's not a sin among sailors, as long as you don't do it before ladies."

"Like your mother?"

The boy nodded vigorously. "*Especially* my mother. But since I mean to be a sailor like Zach, I warrant there's no harm in practicing." He squinted up into the sun, carefully considering Jack from the gold rings in his ears to the toes of his well-worn seaboots. "I 'spect you've heard of my brother Zachariah. He's about the best sailor ever came out of Westham, and set to make captain himself by year's end."

Jack would take exception with that "best sailor," but the judgment of worshipful younger brothers could be forgiven. Again he felt an odd twinge of regret for everything he'd missed.

"Oh, aye, I know Zach," he said as he crouched down to the boy's level. From the willow basket half-full of driftwood beside him, it was clear the boy had been sent to gather kindling on the beach, and from the large, dead, and noisomely vile horseshoe crab in his hand, it was just as clear that he was willing to be distracted. He wasn't Miriam, but he was still close enough to her to be a comfort to Jack.

"Zach and I have been mates since we were scarce old enough to find mischief," he continued. "And your sister Miriam—I've been friends with Miriam every bit as long."

"You're friends with Miriam?" The boy scowled uncertainly. "Miriam doesn't keep friends with men, excepting Mr. Chuff, and he can't count as a friend since he's going to be her husband. And he'll never be *my* friend, anyways."

Jack beamed. No wonder he'd taken such a liking to this boy. "Well then, I'd be honored to be considered your friend," he said, his large hand swallowing up the boy's smaller one. "I'm Jack Wilder, and mind you call me Jack."

The boy stared at him with such unabashed awe that Jack wondered uneasily if even he, too, had heard tales about his adventurous past.

"I'm Henry," he managed to gulp at last. "Henry Rowe. Your servant, sir."

"No servant about it," said Jack firmly. "You call me Jack."

"Jack, then." The boy flushed and grinned with adoration. "Good day, Jack."

"Good day, Henry." Jack lowered his voice in confidence. "And I can prove I know your sister, too. I know she likes plums better than apples and puts so much molasses and milk in her tea that the spoon fair stands upright on its own in the cup. I know she sings worse than a donkey, but that she can copy any birdcall so true that the creatures fly straight to her hand, pleased to make her acquaintance. And I know she has three tiny freckles on the back of her left knee, one, two, three, same as the stars in old Orion, rising up north above her garter."

"Lordy," breathed Henry, his eyes round. "I didn't know about those freckles!"

"Then maybe they should be our secret," said Jack, lowering his voice to a gravelly whisper. "You know how ladies can be about such matters."

Henry nodded with seven-year-old sagacity. "She'd tell Mama I'd been spying on her in the privy."

"And there you'd be, flogged again for something that wasn't your fault." Jack sighed dramatically. "It's an unjust world, Henry Rowe, and you're a wise man to watch after your back. But here, here's a safer thing to tell about Miriam: she loves hunting buried treasure."

"Miriam?" asked Henry, truly puzzled. "How could Miriam like hunting treasure when she hates getting dirty?"

"She always got plenty dirty with me," confided Jack. "And sandy, too. Digging for treasure's not tidy work."

Henry wriggled with excitement, the horseshoe crab flopping against his leg as he pressed closer to Jack. "Where'd you go hunting?" he demanded. "How much gold did you find?"

"Carmondy Island, not far from here." With his forefinger, Jack traced a crude map in the sand of the coast around Westham, adding a lopsided circle below the mouth of the river for the island. "Mirry and I—and Zach, too, when he was in the humor—must've dug up half that infernal island, and never found so much as a ha'penny. But drunk or sober, my Uncle Joe, before he died, always swore my father's portion of Avery's treasure was hidden there on Carmondy. 'Fifty paces from the highest water,' he said, and my Uncle Joe never—"

"Henry Rowe." Miriam's voice was frosty as her shadow fell across the treasure map. "You know better than to go talking to every ragamuffin stranger you find on the beach!"

"But he's not a stranger, Miriam!" Henry scrambled back to his feet, clutching the horseshoe crab for reassurance like some foul-smelling weapon. "He's Jack Wilder, and he's a friend of yours and Zach's, and now me, too, and he was telling me all about—"

"Go to the kitchen *now,*" ordered Miriam, pointing toward the tavern for emphasis. "Mother was looking for that wood a half an hour past. Go, Henry. *Now."*

Jack's smile grew with undisguised pleasure. She must have come from the kitchen herself, for her cheeks were rosy from the heat of the fire and there were cross little daubs of flour on her chin. And how he loved hearing her give orders like this, all stern and full of fluster! He could think of several he wished she'd give to *him.*

"Ah, Mirry, don't go blaming the poor little lad so," he said as Henry labored up the path through the dune, the heavy basket thunking clumsily against his bare shins and the dead crab's long, pointed tail dragging forlornly through the sand. "I was the one who kept him, not—"

"I know exactly what you were doing, Jack Wilder!" she said indignantly. "Filling his head with your treasure nonsense, luring him into dreams of growing rich on gold stolen from others instead of working honestly for it! If you hope to reach me through him, why, it won't work, Jack, and I won't have you doing it to Henry!"

"I meant him no harm, Mirry," he said, sweeping off his hat and holding it contritely over his chest. "Besides, Henry's a clever boy, and I doubt he'll take any of what I said amiss."

But her eyes didn't warm to that elegantly swept hat, and her mouth didn't soften. "Cleverness has nothing to do with it. Henry's only seven, and ripe to believe every last lie he hears from a sailor, honest or not."

"Then we haven't one damned thing to quarrel over." He might as well put his hat back on his head for all the good it seemed to be doing him. "I was only telling the boy old stories of when we were children, digging holes out on Carmondy. Happy times, weren't they, lass?"

She hesitated, and he could see the memories flicker through her eyes, clear as day and every bit as happy for her as they'd been for him. Zach had been right: she did still love him, and Jack's hopes soared.

"You do remember the island, don't you, pet?" he continued, his voice dropping low and husky as he spun the past out for her once again. "How the vines hung low from the scrub pines and made shady nests for us away from the sun? Wild roses in June, raspberries in July, pokeweed in August, with those cross old terns overhead, scolding us like nobody's business. And remember how we'd swear to save the cakes and cider we filched from your mother's kitchen until noon, a reward for digging all morning? We never did last the morning, not once. But I've not forgotten the flavor of those orange cakes as you slipped pieces into my mouth with your own dear little fingers, or how you'd laugh with delight when I pulled you close and let me kiss the crumbs away, as if you'd planned it that way from the beginning."

He'd wager his life she hadn't forgotten. From the way her lips had relaxed while he'd spoken he knew she remembered the first tentative kisses they'd shared in that musty green haven, kisses that had tasted of cider-soaked crumbs and innocent inexperience, the sweetest kisses he'd ever known.

He took a step toward her, swinging his hat gently from his fingertips.

"Remember how we'd claim Carmondy for our very own?" he said softly. "And a ruddy fine little kingdom it was, too, with you as the princess-queen on your throne, there on the roots of the single oak? It's still there, you know, that oak. I saw it when I sailed past the other day. We could go back to the island, Mirry, just the two of us. We'll see if I can make you sigh with pleasure again, and if your lips still taste of orange and cider. Happy times, princess, happy times worth remembering."

All they needed was time to talk and to sort out the misunderstandings between them, to find their way back to the things that had bound them so tightly together once before. He knew it was possible, and from the shimmer of unshed tears in her eyes he knew she did, too.

But when, finally, he reached for her hand, she pulled back, and to his sorrow he saw how she'd shuttered those same eyes against him.

"Nothing to do with that island or your father or your Uncle Joe brought any of us happiness, Jack," she said, even as the tremor in her voice betrayed her, "and you're a fool if you remember it otherwise. You hurt me once because of it, but I won't have you hurting me or Henry or anyone else in this family again."

And with one swift sweep of her toe she obliterated the treasure map he'd marked in the sand, and left him alone with his hat hanging in his hands and more hurt than she'd ever know bottled up tight in his heart.

Chapter 6

"A GIFT?" MIRIAM SET THE PEWTER PITCHER ON THE table and turned to smile at Chilton as he came through the doorway of front room. "You've brought a gift for me?"

"Yes, yes, my dear, all for you," said Chilton. The package he handed her was long and flat, swaddled in dun-colored muslin and tied with green ribbons. "Though I must confess I am the mere messenger, obediently conveying the offering of another."

Miriam frowned. "Who's that?"

"I do not know," said Chilton as he patted the package fondly, almost as if it were a pet. "All the boy who brought it would say is that it is a bridal gift for Miss Rowe. But I have my guess: a certain gentleman in Cambridge, a learnéd colleague of mine with exquisite tastes."

Miriam glanced at him uneasily. Westham was too small a town for anonymous gifts, and the giver she had in mind was neither learnéd nor a gentleman. She hadn't heard from Jack since she'd found him with Henry yesterday, but she knew him too well to believe he'd given up already.

"Open it, Miriam!" ordered Henry as his tow-blond

head crowded in beneath her arm with his own sense of urgency. "Open it now!"

With everyone in the front room watching, Miriam had no choice. She wiped her hands on the front of her apron, then carefully untied the ribbons and unwrapped the muslin. Out onto the table slid length after length of pale yellow silk cloth, glistening like gold in the morning sun as it slipped sensuously over her hands.

"Oh, Miriam," exclaimed her mother in awe, leaning over Miriam's shoulder to touch one finger to the fabric. "There must be fourteen, fifteen ells here, more than enough for a full gown! Whoever would give you such a generous gift?"

"I vow that my guess is confirmed," declared Chilton. "Only my esteemed friend Dr. Paxton would send so elegant a gift. This is the finest Canton *senchaw,* my dear, the very best silk in the world, the likes of which come to Britain only in the holds of an East India Company ship."

Miriam drew back from the silk as if she'd been burned. The silk might have begun its trip to Britain in the hold of an East India Company ship, but it certainly hadn't finished its journey there. *Blast* Jack Wilder for making her such a gift! If he'd rung the ferry bell last night he couldn't have made any more of a commotion than he would with this silk.

"Look, Miriam," said Henry, digging through the discarded muslin. "You got a new shell, too."

"Ah, a *Caputa taurina,"* said Chilton importantly as he plucked the shell from Henry's fingers and held it up to the light from the window. "A pretty bauble for a lady, more proof of Paxton's excellent taste. It must have come in the same ship as the silk, for the genus Cerebridae is found only in Indian waters. You do know, Miriam, that the natural sciences are something of a whimsical study with me."

Henry, however, was not impressed. "My sister has heaps of seashells," he said, looking longingly at the shell Chilton had taken away, "and I'd wager she knows lots more about them than you."

"Prideful little rogue," said Chilton with a disdainful snort. "A good whipping would cure you of such impudence towards your betters."

Swiftly Mrs. Rowe pulled Henry to one side for his own protection.

"Surely Miriam has showed you her collection, Mr. Chuff," she said, striving to smooth over Henry's misguided opinions. "In her box she has shells from well-nigh everywhere. Your friend could not have imagined a better gift for her."

Chilton's friend might not, thought Miriam, but Jack certainly would. He knew all about her collection, for he'd helped her find the first shells when they'd all been no older then Henry, digging about in the sand with bits of driftwood.

Including the sand of Carmondy Island, and at once her heart began racing all over again.

And as she looked at the large black shell poised there in Chilton's fingers, she knew, too, that Jack had chosen it to make her think of more things she shouldn't. This was no demure Maiden's Blush, round and pearly white. Though equally beautiful and rare, this was the most embarrassingly *male* seashell she'd ever seen, long and blunt and tipped with coral red. It was a good thing that Chilton had come up with the fancy Latin name for it; God only knew what kind of shameless, common term Jack would have offered.

Double, *triple* blast him!

"Indeed, I did not know you collected seashells," said Chilton with approval, blissfully unaware of Miriam's thoughts. "A most genteel pastime. I was once so fortunate as to view the Duchess of Barrington's famous grotto. Her Grace and her daughters—lovely, elegant girls—had embedded hundreds of seashells into designs in the plaster arches of their summerhouse."

Miriam frowned, appalled by such a suggestion.

"Stick them down into plaster? So I couldn't touch or turn them? I would never do that."

"But you must consider it, my dear!" said Chilton, his eyes bright with enthusiasm for the project. "To bend nature, to tame it to serve art and man is such an admirable goal! You could begin on a small scale, a wall in our garden, with this shell from Dr. Paxton as the centerpiece, and—"

"No," she said irritably, taking Jack's shell from him. "I do not believe I will."

She wished Chilton wouldn't try to *direct* her quite so much; it made her feel very much like those poor seashells trapped forever in plaster. Besides, she'd no intention of keeping this particular shell at all, let alone sticking it into plaster as a constant reminder of the giver. "Mama, have you seen Zach yet this morning?"

"I believe I saw him down by the dock a short while ago," said her mother, clearly perplexed. "But Miriam, Mr. Chuff is here expecting his breakfast."

"Then he shall have it, the same as any other guest, but it cannot come from me." She bobbed a quick afterthought of a curtsy to Chilton, who was looking equally perplexed. "I am sorry, Chilton, but I must speak to my brother directly."

She hurried from the tavern before he could try to stop her, her petticoat sweeping over the path to the dock. She seemed to be hurrying away from one person to another a great deal lately; it was not a pretty habit to fall into, and one more thing to blame upon her brother and Jack. With an impatient sigh to match her temper, she shielded her eyes against the sun with the back of her hand and scanned the shore for Zach.

She spotted him at once, fiddling with the mast of a small boat pulled up on the beach.

"Good day, muffin," he called as she came toward him. He stood upright, his shirt clinging damply to his back and arms as he wiped his sleeve across his brow. "Faith, it's hot already, and the sun's barely risen in the sky. More like Jamaica than Westham."

But Miriam was in no humor for chat about the weather. "Where's Jack?"

He regarded her with a cautiously blank expression. "Jack who?"

"Jack-a-dandy, Jack-a-napes, Jack pudding, Jack sprat." She sighed with exasperation. "Don't play games with me, Zach. You know perfectly well I mean Jack Wilder."

"Jack Wilder?" he said, not doing a particularly good job of pretending to be ignorant. "Why should Jack be here in Westham?"

With frustration she kicked at the side of the boat. "You tell me, Zach. Or are the two of you so busy plotting the next way you mean to humiliate me that you haven't time to bother with the truth?"

He frowned. "Jack didn't want me to tell you," he said. "He wanted to surprise you instead."

"Well, he did that much and more last night, didn't he? Maiden's Blush, my foot. And that was only the beginning, wasn't it?" She held out the suggestive shell for her brother to see. "Look at this foolishness, as if you two haven't been chortling over it already. How can you wonder that I prefer Chilton! You and Jack are no better than Henry and his little pack of knavish boys, chalking rude pictures on the privy door. And as for that silk—"

"Didn't you like it, Miriam?" he asked disingenuously. "I thought the color would favor you most royally. You must grant that Jack knows your taste."

She narrowed her eyes, her fingers closing over the shell. "Where is he?"

Zach hesitated, clearly torn between loyalty to his friend and the wrath of his sister. "He's taken a room over Hickey's," he finally confessed. "But, Miriam, you can't go chasing after him there."

"I most certainly can," she retorted as she turned on her heel in the sand and charged up the dune toward the lane.

She had never been to Hickey's herself, for not only was the alehouse the kind of place that respectable women avoided on principle, but it was also the Green Lion's only spirit-serving rival in Westham, albeit a rival of the lowest possible nature. Her father would thrash her on both counts if he learned she'd gone there. But she couldn't let Jack continue to plague her like this. She had to make him stop it now, and if she had to beard him in his den at Hickey's, then so be it.

And Zach had been right about the heat. The ale shop stood at the opposite end of town, past the fishermen's racks for drying codfish, and by the time Miriam had reached the sandy path that led to it, her petticoats were edged with dust, her shift was sticking damply to her body beneath her stays, and a tickling trickle of moisture was pooling in the hollow between her breasts. In her haste, she hadn't paused for a straw hat to put over her cap, and she could feel the sun baking and blistering the skin on her nose and cheeks. At least this way Jack would find her thoroughly resistible, she thought grimly, and climbed the last few feet to the small alehouse.

From the outside, Hickey's didn't look much like the harbor of all deviltry that its reputation promised: a drab shingled building without so much as a signboard, a cheerless yard of packed sandy soil beneath a single tall oak, and five battered outdoor benches, one of which was occupied by a farmer still snoring away last night's drink. Beyond the far side of the building Miriam could hear the distant murmur of men's voices and laughter, and though she was a bit leery of what she might find, she resolutely marched around the corner.

The group of men beside the stone well stopped talking as soon as she appeared, their heads turning to her in unison. The stout man in the stained leather apron was Mr. Hickey, and to his right was his single employee, a one-armed old sailor named Amos. The others, Miriam guessed, were simply midday customers, eager for tales from Westham's own home-grown pirate himself. From the open-mouthed awe on their faces, they clearly adored Jack, admired him, and probably envied him, too, though it was equally clear from the way they hung back that they were a bit afraid of him as well.

For there in their midst, happy to oblige in his breeches and nothing else, stood Jack. Last night in the moonlight she hadn't noticed how darkly tanned he'd become, his gray eyes and white teeth all the more startling by contrast. Startling, too, was the long, pale scar that slashed across his chest, the mark of some long-ago sword or knife that could have claimed his life. He'd been washing from the bucket beside the well, and glittering droplets from his wet hair trickled down his bare skin, highlighting the scar even more. His chest was broader than she remembered, his arms and shoulders more muscular from the hard work of a deep-water sailor, and the thicket of dark hair that centered it tapered down toward the buttons on his soft, low-slung breeches—so low-slung that she caught herself wondering how exactly he was keeping them there on his hips.

"Miss Rowe!" exclaimed Hickey with an anxious nod. "This is an, ah, honor."

"Good day, sir," she answered brusquely, "but it is Mr. Wilder here that I have come to see."

As soon as she'd spoken she felt herself blushing, her cheeks turning fiery beneath her sunburn. "Come to see," indeed: what devil had made her say *that?*

Jack grinned and flung back his long, dark hair with all the unself-conscious exuberance of a wet dog.

"Friends, friends," he said with a half bow that encompassed them all. "You will excuse me while I, ah, *see* Miss Rowe?"

Wishing countless tortures upon Jack's head, Miriam somehow managed a properly stony face as the men shuffled past her toward the little tavern, all of them chuckling slyly and jabbing one another in the ribs. Not one could meet her eye, and a good thing it was, too.

Not one, that is, except for Jack.

When they were alone together, his grin widened. "So, have you come to thank me for the gifts, Mirry?"

"I most certainly have not," she said swiftly, wishing he would cover himself and stop distracting her wits in such a way. "You should not have sent them, Jack. It's—it's not proper for me to accept anything more from you."

"And why not?" he asked easily, his gaze wandering over her with the same wanton familiarity he'd demonstrated before, so open and appraising that she found herself fighting the desire to cover her already well-covered self with her hands. "Unless you didn't like the silk?"

"Of course I *liked* the silk. What woman would not? Though I don't wish to know how a scoundrel like you could come by something that costly."

His wink wasn't about to tell her. "What matters is that you like it. So why shouldn't you accept such a small token from me? After all that we shared together, pet, certainly we—"

"That's exactly why not," she said, her flush deepening even further as she considered how much of their conversation was drifting through the tavern's open windows. "Mr. Chuff is a most respectable gentleman, and as his promised wife I can't take such gifts from any other man. Including you. *Especially* you."

"It's not as if I'm still wooing you. I've taken your refusal outright, you see, and given up. I'm not what you want or need, and if I care beans about you—which I do, beans beyond counting—I must admit it." He flung his arms out to each side and bowed from the waist in a gesture of full surrender. "I've lost you to the better man."

"But I . . ." She broke off, at a loss, not sure what to say next. She hadn't expected him to give in so readily, nor would she have predicted the unflattering wound it was causing to her pride. Her *pride:* yes, that was it, and not her heart. She nodded as if she understood, and tried to smile. "That is . . . very gracious of you, Jack."

"Damned right." He sleeked back his wet hair, his grin fading. "I know when to cut my losses, Mirry. It's the way it's always been with me. Remember, one more time, that gold my father was supposed to have tucked away on Carmondy Island. Seems like I spent my whole boyhood—with your help—hunting for that treasure, all on account of what my uncle let slip when the rum had him. Then one day I up and realized that that gold never would be mine, and most likely had never existed in the first place, and I quit looking for it. Just like that, it was over."

Miriam swallowed hard. Of course she remembered those endless, exciting treasure hunts on Carmondy; she never forgot anything where Jack was involved. Yet as she stared at the long scar on his chest, she thought of how much else about him she still didn't know, and now, it seemed, never would.

"And so that is how you now feel about me?" she asked in a tiny voice. "Like treasure that didn't exist?"

"Exactly." His expression remained so cheerfully, blandly pleasant that she wondered if she'd imagined the heat that had simmered between them that first night on the dock. "I guess you weren't ever any more mine than that treasure was. You said so yourself."

"That is true," she admitted. "But I didn't mean to sound so . . . so unfeeling."

"You didn't, Mirry, not for a moment," he said firmly as he plucked his shirt from the edge of the well and pulled it over his head. "What's done is done, and done for good, too."

"For good, and for better," she echoed, striving to sound as reasonable as he did. She was, after all, getting exactly what she'd come for. He was relinquishing her to Chilton, and promising never to bother her again. So why, then, did she feel as if she were the one who'd lost? "I never thought of you as being this sensible, Jack."

"Nor you, Miriam. But then we're not children any more, are we?" He smiled as he shook his shirtsleeves down over his arms, almost as if he were shaking himself free of her, too. "Now you keep that yellow silk and make it up into something fancy and fine, and every time you wear it you think of me, mind? There's no sin in remembering, not even when you're grand Madame Chuff of Cambridge. We'll say our farewells here, since I'm clearing off for Boston this forenoon."

"So soon?" She frowned as she stared down at his offered hand, a cold sort of farewell that she'd never thought to see from him. "You cannot stay for the wedding?"

"Oh, aye, wouldn't that be a feast for the gossips?" He winked and leaned down to kiss her cheek, taking her hand since she hadn't accepted his. He frowned as he did so, and turned her palm upwards to uncurl her fingers. There in her palm, forgotten, lay the wickedly suggestive shell that she'd meant to toss back in his face. Jack chuckled, glancing slyly up at her from under his lashes, and carefully folded her fingers back over the shell.

"You can keep that for memory's sake, too," he said. The careless, easy merriment in his eye cut her heart to the quick, and made her dare to ask the one question that still mattered.

"If I hadn't come here this morning, Jack, would you have called at the Lion to say farewell? Or would you just have disappeared again like you did before?"

But he only smiled, no sort of answer at all, and stepped away. "Good-bye, my pirate princess," he said softly. "And may you discover all the love in your life that you deserve."

Chapter 7

ALONE IN HER ROOM UNDER THE EAVES, MIRIAM crouched down on the floor beside her bed to pull the box with her shells out from beneath. Kneeling, she began carefully to arrange the shells across her coverlet in a fan-shaped design, the lightest ones at the edges and the darker ones pointing toward the center. As she placed each shell, she thought of the person who'd brought it to her, or the place where she'd pulled it from the sand herself. It was a ritual she often followed when she felt troubled, for sorting and arranging the shells somehow ordered and calmed her thoughts as well. But when at last she took Jack's shell from her pocket, she realized too late that the only spot she'd left for it was directly in the center of her design, the one place it—and the giver as well—had no right to be.

"I thought I'd heard you come back, Miriam." Mrs. Rowe came to stand beside her, her hands folded over the front of her apron as she studied the fan of shells on the bed. "I don't know why you spoke so strongly to poor Mr. Chuff about making a shell fancy for his garden. What else, really, do you do with your shells now?"

Quickly Miriam began to return the shells to the box, all pleasure and peace in them gone for now. She knew what her mother's lecture would be, just as she knew she deserved every word of it: how she'd abandoned poor Chilton without his breakfast, how a good wife must always look after her husband's welfare and wishes before her own, how nothing else must ever be more important. Coming up here in the middle of the day, shirking her duties in the kitchen to steal a few moments alone to sort out her confused thoughts over her shells, had only made matters worse.

"I'm sorry about Chilton's breakfast, Mama," she said, her head still bowed. "I know I should have stayed to attend him as he likes, and I promise it will never, ever happen again."

"Apologize to Mr. Chuff, not to me," said her mother as she sat on the edge of the bed next to the shells. Clearly she had come from the kitchen herself, for her cheeks were flushed from the heat of the hearth fire, and tiny, wispy curls—the same fine, silvery hair she'd passed on to Miriam—had escaped from beneath her white ruffled cap.

"Mr. Chuff is a good, fair man, Miriam," she continued. "So good that now he believes he has somehow wronged you, and not the other way around. But Mr. Chuff is not the reason that I wish to speak with you."

"I should have begun the onions for supper," said Miriam in a guilty rush, dusting her hands together as she rose to her feet. "I didn't mean to be so—"

"The onions are fine, daughter," said her mother, gently catching her by the wrist to stop her. "Another five minutes will make no difference."

"But I promise that—"

"I heard this morning that Jack Wilder's back," interrupted her mother. "Here, in Westham."

Miriam gasped. "Henry told you, didn't he? What else did he say? Or was it Zach? Oh, when I catch the pair of them, I'll—"

"Then you did know." Wearily her mother smiled. "And I am too late with my warnings."

"Oh, Mama." Miriam sat on the bed close beside her

mother, tucking her hand around the older woman's arm. Mama smelled like the kitchen, of wood smoke and baking apples and grated cinnamon and laundered linen pressed within a hairsbreadth of scorching, and as Miriam leaned against her shoulder she let herself breathe deep of the warm, comforting scents. "There's nothing left to warn me about, not where Jack is concerned."

"With all my heart I pray that is so." Her mother stared down at her hands instead of meeting Miriam's gaze. "If I believe that you're old enough to choose a husband, then I also must not expect you to account to me any longer for your actions."

"But, Mama, he told me that he—"

"No excuses, Miriam, nor explanations." Troubled, her mother hesitated, searching for the right words. "Some would say it is my fault, you know, for letting you and Zach become so close to a boy like Jack Wilder. But the truth is that I felt sorry for the lad, left alone in the world with only that wicked uncle of his for family. Imagine leaving any child in the care of a ne'er-do-well drunkard like Joe Wilder!"

Miriam didn't have to imagine it, for she'd seen the reality of Jack's dismal childhood. When Joseph Wilder had returned to Westham with the sickly baby boy, the only product of his dead brother's brief and faraway marriage, he'd vowed to raise the child like a son. It was a blessing, then, that Joseph had fathered no children of his own, for poor Jack was left to more or less raise himself, with tales of his father's piratical exploits the only real nourishment he found. He'd grown up charming and reckless, as wild as his name, and, in the opinion of most of Westham, born only to be hanged. The sole place that welcomed him was the Green Lion, where Miriam's mother had always managed to find one more piece of bread or chicken leg for him—a kindness that, to Miriam's surprise, her mother seemed now to regret.

"You did the right thing, Mama," she said. "Jack needed friends, and you were always one of his best."

"I wonder." Mrs. Rowe shook her head uneasily. "I meant to be kind to the boy, that was all, not that it has helped him tell wrong from right. A very pirate, merciful heaven! But how could I know such charity would put my own little ones in danger?"

"You didn't," said Miriam slowly. She felt the sands of truth beneath her shifting precariously toward falsehood in a way she didn't wish, not with Mama. "What harm could come from your kindness?"

"No harm to Zachariah, no," her mother answered. "Like most men, he has always been able to look after himself, no matter who his friends might be. But you, lamb, you were different, soft and gentle and trusting, your eyes shining bright whenever Jack came whistling down our path. I would never wish poor Jack ill, of course—he's done enough of that to himself without me—but you cannot know how happy I was to see him go off to sea, or how I would have done anything—*anything*—to keep him from returning to you."

Appalled, Miriam stared at her mother. She'd always thought her feelings for Jack had been a well-kept secret between them, and she guiltily wondered how much her mother might have spied from her bedchamber window the other night. "But, Mama, I didn't—"

"Do you think me blind, Miriam? Do you think that I never saw the looks that passed between you two, or heard how your voice would grow low and breathless with him?" Mrs. Rowe sighed and awkwardly patted Miriam's fingers where they lay curled around her arm. "But you're four years older now and, I pray, four years wiser."

"I am," said Miriam with more sadness than she intended. In her heart she knew Jack would always remain her first love, most likely her only one, but Chilton was the man she'd determined to marry. How could there be a better definition of wisdom and maturity than that?

"You're a good daughter, Miriam," said her mother softly, the highest praise she could give. "And for your sake, I trust that whatever attachment lay between you and Jack is done. With Mr. Chuff you have the opportunity to improve yourself beyond measure, a gentleman's wife of standing and reputation. No woman with an eye to her own welfare and future could wish for more. And yet, and yet, I wonder still."

"What is there to wonder, Mama?" asked Miriam, remembering how blithely Jack was once again sailing from her life. "Everything is as you say."

"I pray that it is." Her mother smiled wistfully. "You know I do not often speak of Zachariah's father, from respect for yours. There's little enough to say, anyway, for we were wed less than a year before he was lost. But I want you to know that I loved him when I married him, Miriam, loved him with all my heart and body, through richer and poorer and sickness and health and even through drowning in a nor'easter off Halfway Rock. I loved him, just as I now love your father."

"But why are you telling me this *now?*" asked Miriam, her voice wobbling with unshed tears. "Don't you believe that I . . . I care enough for Chilton?"

Why, why hadn't she been able to make herself say the same word Mama had used? Why couldn't she love Chilton the way she had loved Jack—loved him still?

"Only you know that, lamb," her mother said gently, all the criticism she'd offer. "And only you know what matters most to your own heart. And now, I think, it's high time we tended to those onions before our guests give us up for lost."

Brusquely Mrs. Rowe brushed her hands down her apron and rose to her feet, pulling Miriam up with her. She gave Miriam's shoulders a quick hug, then bent to sweep the last of the shells into the box.

But Miriam could only watch in miserable silence, striving to turn her thoughts, too, away from Jack and Chilton and her own confused heart, and toward peeling the onions for dinner. Mama was always so good at that, able to decide what needed to be done, then doing it, and moving along to peeling onions or apples or whatever else was waiting in the kitchen. Mama wouldn't weep over things that couldn't be changed. She ordered her life with the same tidy efficiency that she ruled the Green Lion—an efficiency that Miriam, even on her best days, felt hopelessly incapable of copying.

But she would keep trying, just as she'd promised Chilton to keep trying to control her tempers and passions. She *would.*

And try to forget the one man she loved, who'd already forgotten her.

Chapter 8

"TELL ME TRUE, CHILTON," SAID MIRIAM AS, LATER that afternoon, she stared down into the little boat tied at the end of the dock. "Are you quite sure you wish to do this?"

Chilton drew himself straight enough to strain the buttons on his dun-colored waistcoat. "How can you doubt my intentions now, Miriam?"

"I didn't mean it that way," she answered quickly. "I've never doubted your intentions towards me. It's just that—Chilton, do you know *how* to row a boat?"

"Oh, it's a simple enough process," he said dismissively, as if boat-rowing were a mystery too great for her to comprehend. "One merely draws the oars in unison back through the water in a rhythmic arc, thereby propelling the vessel forward. It could not be simpler."

Still Miriam stood with her hands at her waist, dubiously glancing from the boat, bobbing gently at the end of its rope with a lantern in the bow, to Chilton, and back again. This wasn't any ordinary little row upriver: the boat was on loan from her father, the straw hamper with a cold supper was from her mother, and even Henry had made a contribution, a small basket of wild raspberries that he'd gathered himself. It all was carefully calculated to give her and Chilton an unforgettably romantic summer evening together, and Miriam's only regret was suspecting the idea had been Mama's instead of Chilton's.

"After all, Miriam, how difficult could it be?" continued Chilton with an airy wave of his hand. "Considering how one sees even the lowest-born creatures on the Thames maneuver about in their boats with ease? Concentration and application, my dearest, those are the twin secrets to mastering everything in this life."

Miriam cocked a single skeptical brow beneath the wide brim of her straw hat. She did not want to hurt Chilton's feelings, but she'd no wish to be floundering about on the river all night, either.

"I can take the oars for the first bit," she suggested. "Not because I doubt your abilities, of course, but merely because I know our river so well."

"No, no, I shall not hear of it!" he said impatiently. "Zach told me exactly what to do, and certainly the word of a salty old sea dog like your brother must carry some weight, even with you."

"The boat was Zach's idea?" she said suspiciously. She could imagine her brother barely stifling his guffaws as he suggested to poor trusting Chilton that he take the boat. She'd have to check herself to make sure the grips on the oars hadn't been greased or the oarlocks loosened before they began.

"Yes, it was," declared Chilton as he tentatively waved one stockinged leg out behind him to begin backing down the ladder to the boat, "and most helpful your brother was, too. However else would I know where to take you? Now commence your voyage, my dear Cleopatra. Your pleasure barge awaits upon the Nile!"

"Sit *down,* Chilton!" cried Miriam urgently. "You can't stand upright like that in a boat!"

But as the boat rocked perilously from side to side beneath Chilton's unbalanced weight, all he did was flop forward to grab at the sides, leaving his bottom in the air and his coattails flapping like some very inelegant tripod.

"Down, Chilton!" ordered Miriam as she hurried down the ladder herself, her skirts bunched hastily over the crook of her arm. "Sit down *now!*"

And sit he did, finally losing his balance so that he toppled headfirst into the bottom of the boat.

"Chilton!" Miriam reached for his hand just as he popped back up, shoved his wig back from his eyes, and fumbled his way upright before plopping down on the bench behind him. "Chilton, are you unharmed?"

"Perfectly," he sputtered, still clinging tightly to her hand. "Though I do believe your father is in need of a new boat, this one being in such dangerous disrepair."

"It will do for tonight," said Miriam lightly, letting him save face however he could. As she settled herself on the forward bench facing him, she scanned the dock and river and beach, fully expecting to find Zach enjoying his joke. But her brother was fortunately nowhere in sight, and though she would speak to Zach later—speak to him *sharply*—now she must concentrate on soothing Chilton's ruffled manly pride while keeping their boat afloat.

She looked down at his uncallused hand linked with hers. By the time they reached the willows at Tockwotten, where they'd planned to have their supper, those neat scholar's hands of his were going to be in more "dangerous disrepair" than her father's boat ever would be. But how strange that his hand roused no other feelings in her; all Jack had had to do was glance her way and she'd gone soft and warm as butter in the sun.

Not that it mattered now. Now she must be good and useful to Chilton, as she'd promised her mother.

"You can take the oars now," she prompted, slipping her hand free to twist around and untie the boat, shoving it away from the dock. "One in each hand, you know."

"I *do* know, Miriam," snapped Chilton with misplaced indignation. "I am not a fool."

Not exactly a fool, decided Miriam as her temper

began to simmer. Not a fool; but when he grabbed the oars and began to flail them about in the air like lopsided wings, he was certainly executing an excellent impression of one.

"Like this," she said as patiently as she could, leaning forward to lay her hands firmly over his and guide the oars back into the water. "Towards me, then back. Smoothly now, Chilton, or we'll never get anywhere."

He stopped and glared at her, beads of sweat trickling down his forehead from beneath his wig. "You are not to instruct me, Miriam. That is not your role. Such forwardness is disagreeable in a woman, and not to be tolerated."

Miriam gasped indignantly. "If it were not for my 'forwardness,' then we would sit here in this same wretched patch of water all night!"

"My dear Miriam," said Chilton severely. "There will be no place for any forwardness from you at all in our marriage. I shall be the head, as is proper, and you will be the hands, executing my wishes for the benefit of us both."

"Very well." Miriam sat back on her bench, her arms folded tightly over her chest in a posture of mutinous submission. "My hands will be meekly idle and unforward, while your head will row us up the river to Tockwotten. But I vow, Chilton, if you capsize this boat and ruin my clothes, my hands will have a precious hard time ever heeding your head again."

For once he did not deign to answer, or perhaps he was concentrating too hard on making the oars obey to worry about doing the same with Miriam as well. With the help of the incoming tide to ease them upriver, they did finally begin to make progress, but by the time they reached their destination, afternoon had faded into dusk with night near enough that Miriam lit the candle in the lantern in the bow of the boat.

Tockwotten had long been a trysting spot, doubtless back before the English settlers in the last century, back to countless Massachusetts or Nipmuc braves and their sweethearts. The bend in the river slowed the water and made an easy landing place, with a sloping bank covered in meadow grass that grew to a conveniently discreet height.

But what made Tockwotten special was the willows. Clustered together on the bank, their heavy heads bent forward to trail their branches in the water, the trees created mysterious shadows that constantly changed, a nervous, whispering *shush* as the breeze played through the silvered leaves, and gnarled roots that twisted into a score of playful perches overhanging the river's dark surface. There was a seductive sense of danger to those shadows and leaves and twisting roots, too, an undercurrent that warned as much of what wasn't visible as of what was, and that had made countless young women inch closer with a delicious shiver to their young men for protection. As Chilton guided the boat beneath the sweep of the branches, even he was impressed into awed silence.

Miriam held the lantern up in her hand to let the light dance over the restless leaves and branches and dapple over the water's surface. She loved this place. She always had, and Zach rose a few points closer to forgiveness for suggesting it to Chilton.

"I say, Miriam, this is a peculiar spot for supper," said Chilton uneasily as he glanced up at the quarter moon, caught in the tangle of branches overhead. "Might as well take tea in a crypt as dine here."

"Tockwotten only feels that way," said Miriam, her voice automatically dropping to a whisper. "It's every bit as safe as an open field, but much more interesting. And we're only a mile beyond Westham, along the path on the bank."

"That's a comfort, I suppose." He peered over the edge, into the black water. "Would there be serpents in there?"

Miriam nodded solemnly. "Giant ones, a hundred feet

long at least, with great gnashing teeth like swords and spiked scales like a dragon's to help them swim upriver from the ocean."

He recoiled so fast she couldn't help laughing.

"Oh, Chilton, how could there be serpents like that here?" she scoffed merrily. It was really very wicked of her to tease poor Chilton in this way, but she couldn't help it. "This is Massachusetts, not India! Besides, the water's no more than a foot or two deep beneath us, not nearly enough to harbor giant serpents."

But the shocked look remained on his face, his eyes wide as he peered into the shadows. He grabbed the lantern from the bow of the boat, holding it up like a shield against the shifting darkness.

"What is that noise, Miriam?" he whispered hoarsely. "Don't you hear it?"

She paused, listening to the familiar sounds of evening. "Crickets and blackbirds and the breeze running through the leaves. Nothing else."

"Nothing?" repeated Chilton anxiously. "Yet I would vow I heard—"

But what he'd heard or imagined didn't matter any longer, for with a bloodcurdling banshee's wail something large and heavy dropped down from the darkness inside the willow and, with a shower of leaves and breaking twigs, onto the branch directly over their heads. Miriam gasped in startled uncertainty as she peered up into the shifting shadows, but Chilton shrieked with terror, tumbling backwards into the boat so suddenly that Miriam feared he'd somehow been wounded by the unseen thing above them.

"Chilton!" she cried, lurching across the rocking boat to grab his arm. "Oh, dear God, *Chilton!*"

"Oh, I fancy he's well enough," said the voice overhead. "No more than a dollop of maidenly distress, eh, Master Chuff?"

"Jack!" Miriam gasped again, but this time not with fear but with outrage that, fortunately, wasn't quite

speechless. She still couldn't make him out in the shifting shadows, but she hadn't any doubt that he was there. "What are you *doing?*"

"I'm merely plying my humble trade, lass," he answered, his voice barely more than a low, disconcerting growl. "And a good thing I am, too, from the sorry look of your affairs here."

"How dare you speak to a gentleman so!" sputtered Chilton as he struggled upright in the boat. Somehow, despite all his thrashing, he'd managed to keep the candle in the lantern lit, and he raised it now, a quavering, quaking beacon. "Begone, you—you foul, ill-bred specter!"

But whatever bravado Chilton had mustered evaporated the instant the lantern light found Jack, and even Miriam, who'd thought she'd known what to expect, felt her blood chill in her veins.

He stood balanced on a branch with all the coiled ease of a panther, swaying gently with the tree as the breeze ruffled his long black hair and white linen shirt. The half-light hid his eyes and made his face all angles and harsh planes above an unforgiving slash for a mouth, a face that had none of the rascal's charm she'd loved so well, and all of the pirate's menace that he'd shown to the world.

The sleeves of his shirt were shoved over his forearms, and across his chest he'd slung a wide leather belt with two long-barreled pistols tucked into the front. With a scraping whisper of steel, he swept his cutlass from the scabbard at his waist, idly flourishing the blade before him in a deadly arabesque.

She'd never seen him look like this, thought Miriam with a shiver of fear. She'd never even dreamed he *could.* Yet, perversely, the sight of him like this reminded her of those long-ago days on their island. Poised there on the branch, with the cutlass in his hand, he was the flesh-and-blood embodiment of every fantasy and game they'd ever played out, on the beach or in their little shelter of tangled vines, and now, when she shivered again, she realized it wasn't fear but excitement, wicked, sinful, and entirely wrong, that was making her palms turn damp and her heart race.

"God in Heaven have mercy on us," babbled Chilton. "Have mercy, I beg you!"

Gently Miriam put her hand over Chilton's to calm him, and herself, too. She couldn't let Jack and his twirling cutlass make her forget that Chilton was the man she'd promised to marry.

"You don't scare me, Jack," she said as defiantly as she could, which, considering the way her voice was shaking, wasn't particularly defiant at all. "*And* you've no right to be spying on Chilton and me like this, anyway."

Chilton stared at her with fresh horror, his fingers tightening convulsively around hers. "You are acquainted with this outlaw, Miriam? How is it that my innocent bride can know such a scoundrel by name?"

"Of course I know him," she said defensively as she glared up at Jack. If he pounced on that unfortunate 'innocent bride,' the way she dreaded and the way only Jack could, then she'd never, ever be able to explain herself to Chilton. "Everyone in Westham knows Jack, and knows the kind of trouble he is liable to create, too."

"Ah, Miss Rowe, how you shame me!" murmured Jack, his voice a purring caress that had no shame in it at all. "You've never had need to fear me before. I don't see why you should now."

"Then begone with you, sirrah, begone at once," demanded Chilton imperiously, waving the lantern as if shooing away an unruly stray. "Do as I say directly!"

"Impatient little bastard, aren't you?" said Jack mildly as he parried the cutlass at an invisible foe hovering somewhere over Chilton's head. "For your sake, Mirry, I hope this lover of yours knows the pleasures of taking his time, else he'll never bring *you* any pleasure at all."

"Base, impudent rogue!" sputtered Chilton. "I shall

report you to the constable the minute we return to Westham, the very minute!"

"As you please." Jack's slow smile was sly and knowing, enough to send Miriam's heart to racing all over again. " 'Tis your right as an Englishman. But before you do, I must ask you to oblige me first, and turn over to my keeping the one thing you hold dearest."

Chapter 9

"MY DEAREST POSSESSION?" CRIED CHILTON WILDLY. "Then you are no better than a thief, and a cowardly one at that! But I won't let you rob me, no, sirrah, I shall not!"

He jerked his hand free of Miriam's and instead pressed it protectively over his own belly, to the right of the buttoned front of his waistcoat.

"Oh, Chilton, please, don't!" said Miriam urgently as she reached out to stop him from standing upright in the wobbling boat. Not only was he going to topple them both into the water, but what was worse, she *knew* he was going to make a total and complete fool of himself before Jack, a disastrous sight she'd no wish to see. "Mind the boat, Chilton, I beg you, please!"

But Chilton only brushed her hand impatiently from his arm, determined to take his stand against the thief, no matter how unsteady—and brief—that stand might be.

"You will never get your greedy fingers on this timepiece," he declared grandly, one hand over his watch and the other still holding the lantern. "I bought it myself from the greatest master horologist in London before I sailed to this savage land, as an especial reminder of a more civilized world, a world that your kind would never recognize. *That* is my dearest possession, and I will not let it become yours!"

"Your watch?" Jack leaned forward from the branch and frowned down at the other man, clearly mystified. "Why the hell would I want your watch?"

"You said my dearest possession," said Chilton doggedly. "You said—"

"I know what I said," growled Jack. "And I know I never meant your damned *watch.*"

He plunged the cutlass back into its scabbard, and swiftly, before Miriam quite realized what he was doing, he'd swung himself down from the branch and into the boat. Chilton's eyes rounded with astonishment as Jack's elbow landed squarely in his chest. For a fraction of a second Chilton flailed his arms to keep his balance, then toppled backwards out of the boat and into the water with a spectacular splash that drenched Miriam. The lantern flew from his hands and *kerplunked* into the water, too, dousing the candle with a hiss that left them all in murky near-darkness.

"Chilton!" shrieked Miriam, leaning over the side where he'd fallen. "God in heaven, where are you?"

"Where he should be," said Jack, raising his voice over the sound of Chilton gasping and swearing in a thoroughly uncivilized manner as he thrashed in the water. "Though to my mind he deserves someplace much hotter, the river will do for now."

"But Jack, wait—*wait!*" cried Miriam as she felt the boat begin to glide forward through the water. Unlike Chilton, Jack knew exactly how to row a boat, and fast, too. "We cannot leave him here to drown!"

Jack snorted with disgust. "He won't drown, Miriam. If he'd stop behaving like such a panicky jackass, he'd realize the water scarce comes to his waist. If he follows the path along the north bank, he'll reach Westham by daybreak."

"I will take this to the royal governor himself!" sputtered Chilton. "I will see you hanged and gibbeted for the thief that you are!"

"Ah, but I left you your watch, didn't I?" called Jack over his shoulder. "And when you speak to the governor, be sure to tell him that all I took from you was Miriam."

Miriam gasped. He'd found his rhythm with the oars, and now that they were free of the overhanging branches and into the deeper channel of the river, they were moving so rapidly that she had to hold on tightly to each side of the boat to keep from falling overboard herself. Part of her was aware that she should be frightened, that Jack was dangerous, reckless, and armed to the teeth. But the other, less cautious part of her argued that Jack had always been reckless and dangerous, and as for the pistols and the cutlass—well, those were far from the worst weapons that Jack could employ with her.

She lifted her chin, determined to look outraged even if she had to peer from beneath the drooping, sodden brim of her hat to do so. "You haven't taken me anywhere."

"Not yet, no," he said, and in the darkness she was certain he was grinning. "But I mean to."

"Then you've added kidnapping to robbery!"

"Kidnapping?" He chuckled. "Your schoolmaster's going to have a hell of a time making that stick when everyone in town knows how fond we were of each other."

"Not any longer, Jack, not when—"

"Not nothing, Miriam," he countered. "Consider how sweetly you came clear to Hickey's to see me this morning. And here tonight you greeted me by name, you didn't fuss when I joined you in this boat, and I didn't have to use one lick of force to make you come along with me. Even now you're not exactly leaping into the water to rejoin your pitiful, piss-poor intended. I didn't kidnap you any more than I stole than infernal watch of his."

She hated it when Jack became logical like this, hated it all the more because he used that logic so sparingly, to catch her by surprise the way he had just now. *She* was supposed to be the sensible one, not him. Now that the river had widened around them and they were in the open moonlight, she could see the white teeth of his smile in the shadowy outlines of his face, an infuriating smile at her expense. She felt the splashed river water trickling from the brim of her hat down the back of her neck, and suddenly, at this moment, it all seemed more than she could bear. With a muttered oath of her own, she ripped the wet straw hat from her head and slapped it furiously across Jack's arm as he leaned toward her at the oars.

"Chilton *loves* that watch!" She smacked the hat across his other arm, the straw flopping in limp, damp protest. "That watch *is* his most treasured possession, just as he said, or at least it was until you ruined it in the river!"

"Falling overboard is scarcely a capital offense," said Jack as he dodged to avoid the hat. "Even in Massachusetts."

"Then perhaps you should try Purgatory, which is where you belong!" She slapped the hat across his arm again and heard the oar scrape in its lock as his stroke went awry, making the boat lurch clumsily to one side.

"Damn it, Mirry," he growled. "Stop that before I heave your hat over the side next!"

But instead of stopping, she smacked him again, hard enough to dislodge one of the pistols tucked into the belt across his chest. The gun clattered into the bottom of the boat, and with a squeal of concern Miriam jerked her feet and petticoats to one side.

"For God's sake, it's not loaded," said Jack in exasperation. "I'm not so great a fool as that."

"So *you* say." Miriam plucked the pistol from the bottom of the boat and hurled it out into the river, where it landed with a thoroughly satisfying splash. "There. Now you and Chilton are even. You ruined his watch, and I have ruined your gun."

Stunned, Jack stilled his oars, staring out at the radiating ripples on the water, all that remained of the pistol. It wasn't the loss of the gun that bothered him—

the pistol had been an old, battered relic that he'd chosen for the ominous length of its barrel rather than for shooting accuracy—but the way things were going with Miriam. He'd planned on her being relieved, even grateful, to be rescued from her swinish ninny of a lover, especially after the cowardly, self-serving performance the man had put on in the water. What woman could have any use for him after witnessing *that?*

But to Jack's amazement, Miriam was still determined to defend Chuff. What was worse, she didn't seem at all interested in entering into the spirit and adventure of her abduction, the way Jack remembered she would have as a girl, the way he'd expected her to now. He'd wanted to be dashing in her eyes again, daring, even dangerous. He'd wanted to make her eyes shine with excitement and hear her laughter bubble merrily across the river.

Instead, he was failing. Again. Hell, could he never do anything right in his life?

Maybe Miriam really *had* changed, as Zach said. And maybe, thought Jack with growing despair, he'd come halfway around the world for nothing.

"You still don't understand, do you?" he said, his elbows resting heavily on the oars as he leaned toward her. He'd resolved not to touch her, not here in the boat, but the temptation to sweep her into his arms and *make* her understand was powerful indeed. "Chuff cares more for a watch that he'd gotten from some master whoremonger than—"

"A horologist, Jack," she corrected primly, as if the dowsing in river water hadn't made the linen kerchief over her breasts practically transparent in the moonlight. "Not a whoremonger. Chilton told me that a master horologist sells timepieces, not trollops."

"He can sell more trollops than the Grand Turk himself for all I care," said Jack, disgusted as much with himself as with Chuff. "Mirry, weren't you listening? The thing your future *husband* holds dearest is a blasted pocket watch!"

"You asked Chilton, and he answered you truthfully. I don't see what else you expected from—"

"I meant you, sweetheart," said Jack gruffly. "If you'd promised to be my wife, you'd be the single greatest treasure in my life. I'd do anything to keep you safe. Still would. I thought Chuff felt the same."

"Ohhhh," she breathed, a drawn-out, thoughtful syllable that betrayed considerably more uncertainty than she realized. "Oh, Jack, you shouldn't say such things to me, not—that is, I'm not sure what Chilton feels. He is too much a gentleman to be ruled by his baser passions and impulses."

"Like I am," said Jack. "Like you, too, as I recall."

"Oh, yes." She sighed unhappily, twisting the damp ribbons of her hat around her fingers. "I cannot seem to govern myself at all."

"Maybe you should stop trying." With her sitting less than an arm's length away, Jack, too, was finding self-government a challenging task. He shifted uneasily on the bench, praying she wouldn't glance down at the proof in the front of his breeches. "Before you find yourself caring more about pocket watches than people, too."

"Don't meddle," she said, but her downcast eyes and sad half-smile took away any of the scolding sting. So she truly hadn't realized how badly Chuff had slighted her, then. Jack could hardly believe it. Yet as unhappy as it made her, it was better that she learn now, before she married the selfish bastard. But why the devil did *he* have to be the one to tell her?

"There now, lass," he said awkwardly. "I'm sorry."

Forgetting his resolution, he reached out and gently cupped her cheek in his hand. He meant it as a touch to ease her hurt, more of a wordless show of sympathy than a caress. But to his surprise she turned her face into his palm, the warm, soft tenderness of her lips grazing across his rough skin to show she'd understood, and was grateful for it. That was all: hardly enough to be called a kiss, and done almost before he'd realized it.

But after she'd moved back on her bench, the mark of her lips burned on his palm like a brand, and the single silent gesture had told him more than any words ever could.

More, but still not enough.

With a sigh she settled the battered hat back on her head, leaving the wrinkled ribbons to trail over her shoulders as she avoided the question in his eyes, instead staring past him to the shore.

"Jack," she said softly. "We're drifting."

He nodded and began to pull on the oars again. They *were* drifting, in a larger, more challenging sense as well as along the river, and he wasn't sure what would come next. What was happening to the dashing, daring adventure he'd planned?

Yet though the silence that fell between them now made him uneasy, it wasn't unpleasant. Companionable, even. It had always been that way with Miriam, ever since they'd been children. Countless times he'd imagined them making a long voyage together, just the two of them together with the moon and the sea, and this evening had the feel of those impossible, improbable dreams. He wanted to make her happy, and he wanted to keep her safe—good, noble goals for any man, and likely the only noble ones Jack had ever had.

But not all his goals were so chivalrous. He wouldn't deny it, nor would his body. When he shifted his legs and his knee brushed accidentally against her thigh, he could feel the tension rippling between them, warm and thick with those ungentlemanly passions and impulses, and, he was sure, a good share of unladylike ones, too. Barely stifling a groan, he ordered himself to concentrate on his rowing instead.

By the time they reached Westham, his shirt was plastered to his back and arms from the heat and exertion. Thank God they'd only a bit farther to go, he thought wryly, else he'd be too exhausted later for anything but falling dead asleep on the sand.

"Mama *would* still be awake," said Miriam unhappily, "and Father, too, by the look of it."

Along the bank, the small cluster of houses and shops that made up the town were dark for the night. All, that is, except for the Green Lion, where candlelight still beamed cheerfully from the tavern's windows. An off-key, bellowed chorus of *The Colonel's Bold Daughter* came through the windows, proof that the company inside was most definitely still awake.

With a sigh, Miriam stared at the tavern, tugging her damp kerchief higher over her shoulders. "You've been very bad this night, Jack. Wicked, dreadful bad. Heaven knows what I shall tell Mama and Father about Chilton and this—this *disaster* you have made for me, and what I shall say to Chilton himself—mercy, I don't begin to know."

Jack did, or at least had a good idea of what he'd like her to say, but decided for once to keep his opinion to himself.

She sighed again, more forlornly. "First I suppose you must return Father's boat. He'll raise the very devil when he finds you took his property at all, and besides, he'll need it to send someone after poor Chilton. Then, if you've any brains or conscience, you'll go as fast and as far from Westham as ever you can, before Zach thrashes you within an inch of your life."

"And leave you behind, sweetheart?"

"Jack, don't, not again." She grimaced, the kind of wearily resigned face her mother made when Henry misbehaved. "Now set me on the dock, there, if you please."

"But it doesn't please me," said Jack evenly, steering the boat toward the mouth of the river and the sea beyond. "Never will, either. Why the hell would I go through all the trouble to steal you away from Chuff only to turn you over to your parents?"

"Because this is only a jest, a prank, more foolishness to vex me," she said quickly, so quickly that he guessed she was trying to convince herself more than him. "Like that wicked seashell you wrapped up in the silk. Isn't that so, Jack? Jack?"

He grinned, delighted that he'd been able to surprise her so completely. "No foolishness at all," he said as the boat glided past the dock. "You're coming with me."

"But I can't!" she cried indignantly. "*You* can't! Jack, I have to go home!"

He shook his head. "I'm afraid not, Mirry. I'm not welcome in your home, and I'm too much a gentleman to let you go ashore unattended."

"You're not a gentleman at all!" Furiously she twisted around in the boat, gazing back at the tavern behind them. "I'll scream, I'll shout—help me, someone, help me here!"

"Scream away, lass," said Jack pleasantly, "though I doubt anyone will hear you, especially over that jolly racket from your father's taproom. Mind, though, if you keep thrashing about like that, you'll land in the drink the same as your schoolmaster lover. Unless you wish to swim to shore?"

She froze, her back toward him ramrod straight. "You know I can't swim," she said, panic rising in her voice. "I'm a woman, and women don't swim, and the channel here is too deep for either of us to stand. Not that I could count on you to save me any more than you saved poor Chilton."

"Of course I would, Mirry," he said softly. He'd only meant to tease, not to frighten her, and he wondered uneasily if he'd botched things with her again. "I told you before. You're my treasure, and I'll not let any harm come to you."

She didn't answer, and the stiff, unyielding line of her back didn't change. "Where are you taking me?"

"Carmondy," he said. Where else, really, could he have taken her? "Our island, Mirry."

"Carmondy." Her voice trembled. "My God, Jack. I'm ruined."

Chapter 10

RUINED.

As the boat cut across the waves and into the bay, the single word hung between them, unanswered, uninvited, and thoroughly unwelcome. But for Miriam no other word could so perfectly describe her situation, and her future as well. What had happened at Tockwotten could perhaps have been explained or excused away, a misadventure that, if she groveled enough, Chilton could forgive. She could still become his bride, still have her little flower garden behind their house in Cambridge. She could still be a gentleman's lady-wife.

But disappearing with Jack to Carmondy Island at night was beyond forgiveness. She *would* be ruined, not just in Chilton's eyes, but on the gossiping tongues of every man and woman along the north shore. A pirate's doxy, the willing partner in mischief to a known rogue like Jack Wilder! Respectable people would believe it their duty to scorn her. Her friends would melt away, fearful of her taint. She'd never marry now, for no decent man would have her, and as for Jack—Jack would never marry anyone. If the talk turned ugly enough, her own father would banish her to the kitchen, where her trollop's reputation wouldn't sully his business in the front rooms. She would die a spinster, unloved and unwanted, without a husband or children or a house of her own.

And it would all—*all*—be Jack's fault.

She was so miserable that she scarcely noticed when the boat bumped ashore, and she didn't move from her seat as Jack jumped out into the water to push them up onto the beach. After the gentle motion through the water, the sand stopped the boat with a hard, jarring thump that reminded Miriam of the crash of her own future.

"Here you are, your highness," said Jack gallantly as he held his hand out to help her from the boat. "You're home to your island kingdom at last."

Miriam shook her head, keeping her hands tucked firmly beneath her folded arms. "You still don't understand, do you, Jack? What you've done, bringing me here—it's just a game to you, isn't it?"

He kept his offered hand outstretched to her. Though he'd shed his boots and stockings to wade ashore, he hadn't bothered to roll up the legs of his breeches, and the wet fabric outlined the muscles of his thighs, unfortunately close to her eye level. "What is there to understand?"

She raised her chin, striving to look defiant even as she sat huddled in the boat. "After tonight, Chilton won't marry me."

"Good." Jack grinned, and shook his dark hair back from his face. "That's what I wanted."

"But not what *I* wanted!" cried Miriam plaintively. "Not at all!"

"You don't know what you want," countered Jack, "leastways that you'll admit, even to yourself. Did you ever tell your schoolmaster about us?"

"There wasn't anything to tell," she said quickly, though at once she felt her cheeks flush at such a glaring untruth. "That is, anything that it was his affair to know."

"Oh, no, no, no," boomed Jack, sweeping his arm

through the air as if to clear away any stray doubts. "Why shouldn't he believe you're still a virgin?"

"He wouldn't have known!"

He rested his hands on the side of the boat, leaning his face close to hers. "Sweetheart, men *know.* Especially men expecting to find a sweetly untutored bride in their beds. Though given Chuff's preference for pocket watches over women, maybe he's the one man who wouldn't notice."

Before she could answer, he'd hoisted the straw hamper with her mother's supper from the boat and begun down the beach, whistling the same raucous song that they'd heard coming from the Green Lion.

"Come back here with that!" shouted Miriam crossly, swinging her legs clumsily out of the boat to follow. "Mama fixed that for Chilton and me, not for you!"

"I've already stolen Chuff's bride," called Jack without turning. "Might as well hang for taking his supper, too."

Barefoot, he walked through the edge of the water, his swaggering stride loose and long over the packed sand. But Miriam, in her best leather shoes, thread stockings and petticoats, was forced to follow across the upper beach, where the sand was soft and slow and her heels sank deep with every step. The last time she'd been on the island, she'd been barefoot, too, but then Jack had been at her side, not thirty paces ahead. She raised her skirts to avoid a soggy pile of seaweed, and when she looked up again, Jack had vanished.

"Jack?" she called as she hurried along. "Jack, where are you?"

To her surprise, the island was still the same small, unruly place she remembered, where beyond the beach lay a murky tangle of wildrose vines and purple pokeberries, scrub pines and large rocks patched with gray-green lichens. Scattered across the island were deep, weedy pits yawning like open graves, left by disappointed treasure hunters years before. The only sizable tree, a gnarled oak with a thick, jutting branch, still stood sharp against the night sky. Though the exposed roots of the oak had served as her princess's throne, legend said the branch above had been used as a gallows by Avery's crew who'd hanged three traitors there, and this was the superstitious reason why the tree had never been cut for firewood. At least, that had been Jack's explanation, and considering that his father had been among those doing the hanging, as a girl Miriam had never questioned it.

Nor, really, did she now. As much as she wanted to stay angry at Jack, as grim as her situation would be with Chilton, she found herself unconsciously being drawn back into the island's mystery, and when she looked up at the moon through the gallows-oak before her, the same shiver of excitement that she'd felt as a child beside Jack and her brother tickled up her spine.

"Jack?" she called again as she made her way around to the east side of the island, the side that faced the open sea. "Jack, where—*oh!*"

Four years and more disappeared in an instant. He'd led her unwittingly back to their special place, a small rise above the sand and between the rocks, beyond the dusty miller and marram grass, where the overhanging branches and vines wove together into a natural shelter overlooking the ocean. The vines were thicker, the branches taller, but nothing important had changed.

Nothing, yet everything, and her heart twisted at the difference.

"I knew you'd remember the way, princess," said Jack. He'd pulled off his shirt and the gun belt, and, bare-chested, he sat cross-legged in the sand, coaxing a small driftwood fire to life. Behind him was the open hamper, the contents already spread invitingly across the old coverlet her mother had packed with the food. "It's your own palace, after all."

Her palace, and his, too. No, *theirs,* and the temptation of all he was offering—and what he wasn't—made tears sting her eyes. She wanted nothing more but to join him there, yet still her battered, bewildered conscience held her back.

If only she'd been able to build the same store of memories, the same shared past, with Chilton that she had with Jack, then she would not be here now. If only she'd been content to be wooed with words alone, and not missed the kisses that Chilton had been too gentlemanly to offer, then she wouldn't have melted like butter when Jack had kissed her again. If only Chilton could *understand* the way Jack did, understand everything about her, the way he had in the boat earlier.

If only she'd loved Chilton the way she still loved Jack . . .

"It was just that one time, Jack," she said, desperation making her return to their earlier conversation as if there'd been no break. "Just that once before you left. Nobody else knew. It wasn't as if I'd—as if we'd—"

"As if I'd gotten you with child?" The little fire began to glow, its light washing up across his face to show how his first grin had faded into something far more serious. "Do you know that when I first met little Henry on the beach, I thought he was ours?"

"Henry's too old," she said swiftly, fighting the rocking jolt of her own emotions. "He's nearly eight."

"Oh, I realized that soon enough," he said, prodding at the fire. "But I wanted to believe we'd had a son, Mirry, more than I can tell you."

He didn't have to tell her, because when he'd left, she'd wanted it, too. Even as she'd fearfully counted the days until her courses came, part of her had longed for his child, a piece of him that would be hers to keep forever. In a way she wished it still. To discover that they'd been wishing for the same thing was one more shared secret, another bond that tugged them inextricably closer together.

Oh, Lord, Jack was right: why couldn't she even admit to herself what she really wanted?

"Look, Mirry." He'd sat back on his heels and was now holding something up on a plate for her to see. "Even your mother knew I'd be the one, not Chuff. She made us orange cake again."

"She knew nothing of the sort." Miriam sniffed back her tears. Better to concentrate on cake than on babies. "Mama bakes orange cake for every guest who dines at the Lion."

"Ha, I don't believe it." He broke off a corner with his fingers and popped it into his mouth, winking at her as he relished the taste. "Heaven, Mirry, pure heaven. Come, here with me now, before I eat it all myself."

"You wouldn't dare." She *was* hungry, and thirsty, and he looked endlessly more comfortable up there on the coverlet beside the fire.

"Damnation, Miriam, you know better than to dare me to do anything." He smiled wickedly as he stood, licking the last crumbs from his thumb, then reached for and raised the cutlass, sweeping the blade to point in her direction. His bare skin gleamed with a faint sheen in the firelight, every muscle defined and accentuated as he toyed with the long-bladed weapon. "Now, princess, must I come fetch you myself, or will you come of your own will?"

She met his gaze over the blade of the cutlass and sighed. She'd never known anyone with eyes the color of Jack's, or any with the power to bewitch her the way his could. All he had to do was smile at her as he was smiling now, and she felt her heart race and her palms grow damp, even her blood quickening with anticipation. It was more than enough to make her forget being a lady with a house and flower garden in Cambridge, and being second in value to an ugly old pocket watch. In a way, she supposed that Jack had done her a favor. For as respectable as Chilton was, how could he—or any other man under heaven, really—how could he possibly ever compete with Jack when he looked at her like this?

She was as good as ruined already. She might as well

have something to remember for it, and Jack was the one man she wanted with the memory.

She bunched up her skirts in one hand and began scrambling up the hill.

"I'm coming because you've no right to eat all that food yourself," she said breathlessly, "and not because you're waving some silly sword in front of my face. Besides, it's probably no more sharp than your pistols were loaded."

In one fluid motion he turned and slashed the cutlass through the stunted wild cherry tree behind him. Leaves and twigs showered down, and a branch as thick around as Miriam's wrist sliced off neatly to drop to the sand.

"Mercy." Miriam stopped and stared at the trembling branch, remembering how Jack had used the cutlass to toy with Chilton. She'd only sensed the unpredictable danger in him then; now she'd seen the proof.

"I warned you not to dare me, didn't I?" He slid the cutlass back into its scabbard and held his hand out to help her. "Take your place, my princess, and let me serve you however you please."

She ignored his offered hand, instead sinking down on the coverlet on her own, thankful that he wouldn't know how weak her knees felt beneath her. Briskly she turned to reach into the hamper, pulling out two bottles her mother had swaddled in damp cloths to keep chilled.

"The perry was meant for Chilton, but I suppose it's yours now," she said as she handed the larger corked bottle to Jack. "The other's lemonade for me."

Jack wrinkled his nose with distaste. "Perry? Pear milk, fit for old maids and nursing babes? No rum?"

Miriam shook her head.

"Perry. Lord." Jack sighed as he uncorked the bottle and handed it back to Miriam. "You drink first, princess. Perry's sorry stuff, but I won't have you sipping lemonade."

She hesitated just a moment before taking the bottle and tipping it back. He wasn't going to be the only one accepting dares. Though the syrupy liquor was sweet, like the fruit, the alcohol in it burned down her throat. She coughed with surprise, wiped her mouth, then drank again, and when she handed the bottle back to Jack, her triumphant little smile was backed by a pleasant, growing fuzziness in her head.

"Good lass," said Jack, his voice sliding low. "Never anything priggish or overnice about my princess. But how, I wonder, will that perry taste on your lips?"

As he took the bottle, he reached out to brush a stray drop of the liquor from the corner of her mouth. The drop vanished, but his fingers remained, tracing her lower lip in a leisurely path with his thumb. He didn't pull her into his arms, or slide his hand around her head to tangle in her hair, or tip her chin to kiss her the way she expected. No, the way she *wanted,* if she were honest. Yet there was only his silver gray eyes, heavy-lidded as they watched her respond, and his thumb, rough and callused, moving gently across the cushion of her lower lip, teasing her until she closed her eyes in dizzying defense, her mouth finally slipping open with a little groan of frustration.

Even then she could feel him shift closer, feel the heat of his body next to hers as his thumb eased from her lip to cradle her chin.

But shutting her eyes only seemed to awaken her other senses further, her whole body growing infinitely aware of so much beyond that touch of his thumb on her yearning flesh: the summer-night breeze that was almost chill on her skin as it came in from the sea, balanced by the heat and scent of the little fire, the sugary sweetness of the perry, the rush of the waves as they rolled and broke on the beach, the shrill, endless drone of the sand locusts in the grass.

It was a rich and complicated place, this island kingdom of hers so dear to her heart, and in the center, where it seemed he'd always been, where he'd always belonged, was Jack. The rightness of it was so overwhelming that she shuddered, her breath coming out in a little flutter of joy against his finger.

"Ah, Mirry," he said, a rough whisper on her cheek. "Didn't I tell you not to dare me?"

Chapter 11

THIS, THEN, WAS WHAT JACK LOVED MOST ABOUT HER.

Even with her eyes closed, her grin was slightly lopsided, slightly challenging as she stretched toward him, and her lips glistened wetly from the perry that she hadn't licked away. He remembered when she'd pulled off her hat, but somewhere else she'd lost her demure little cap, too, as well as most of her hairpins, for now her hair spilled freely over her shoulders, tousled and wanton. Her neckerchief had come untucked and she hadn't bothered to put it back to rights, leaving him with a voluptuous view of her round, full breasts above her lacing.

He'd pulled off his shirt in the boat, and this was how she'd answered him. He'd offered her the pear liquor and she'd drunk her fill. He'd touched his thumb to the plump cushion of her lip as a preamble to a kiss, and she'd openly savored the touch, inviting more. She'd never been a coward, not his Princess Miriam, and she wasn't going to become one now.

He'd seen enough of the world to understand that, anywhere else, this would have been called seduction, mutually pleasing and agreeable. But here on their island Jack knew it was simply one more dare, the same kind of daring that he and Miriam had done to each another as long as he could remember. Yet this time the dare wasn't as simple as who could race faster along the sand to the boat, or even who would lean forward and kiss the other first. This time, this night, there was so much more at stake that for the first time in their shared life, Jack shook his head and sat back on his heels.

She heard him sigh with regret, and when he did not kiss her, she suspiciously opened one eye, then the second. "Jack Wilder," she said. "I vow, if you intend to torment me like this the entire night, why, then, I shall—"

"I cannot do it, lass," he said sorrowfully. "Not to you, and not like this."

"You have not done much of anything that I've noticed." She sat back, too, her skirts rustling beneath her as she folded her hands in her lap and studied him with wary unease. "Except the kidnapping part, of course."

"Then your memory is either very short, or very forgiving." The little fire popped, and he jabbed another piece of driftwood into the flames. "By bringing you here, I've ruined you for any kind of decent life. You said so yourself. I haven't laid a finger—well, yes, maybe that one thumb—upon you, and yet I've ruined you just the same."

"Oh, Jack." Instantly her expression lost its wariness, her smile wobbling and her eyes shining so brightly by the firelight that he feared she'd begin to weep. "I know I said that, but if I'm to be honest, you ruined me years ago."

"Aye, but it wasn't as willful as this. When we sat beneath the dock together that night, I hadn't planned on anything happening, leastways not the way it did."

"Maybe you didn't plan," she scoffed, "but I will wager you *hoped,* just like you're hoping tonight. Don't forget how well I know you, Jack Wilder. But when I said you ruined me, I meant that after you, no other man would seem so—so right for me."

"Ah, Mirry, don't be going on like that," he said

uncomfortably, poking at the fire again as he tried not to think about the velvety shadows that were playing across the valley between her breasts. After four years with only thieves and blackguards for company, he was having a very difficult time being as honorable and noble with her as he wished now to be, and as she deserved. He took a deep breath and began again.

"I love you, and I'll always love you," he said as firmly as he could. "There's no secret to that. And because I love you, I'd never wish you any harm. But look at me, Miriam, just look at me, and tell me I'm not the greatest load of harm that's ever come your way."

She gasped, her eyes round with indignation. "That's not true, not a word of it!"

He rose to his feet instead of answering, turning his back on her to stare out at the open sea with his hands knotted into fists at his sides. The weather was changing; there'd be rain by morning. Away from the fire the breeze off the water was cool, or maybe the chill on his skin came simply from leaving Miriam.

"Look at me, Mirry," he said, despair rising up within him. "Look at me true, not as you want me to be. I'm twenty-four years old and I've yet to do one single thing in my life that's worthy of you. I'm a bad man, lass, and you're the only one in the world that would dare say otherwise."

"Please don't do this to yourself, Jack, please—"

"I'll do what I damned well please, sweetheart, because I always do." He laughed bitterly, his mood growing darker by the moment. Because he loved Miriam, he had to tell her the truth. But the irony of it was that once he did, she'd never be able to love him again.

"I told you I hated those bastards who were my father's friends, and aye, at first I did. But the farther we sailed from here, across the Atlantic and down the Guinea coast and around the Horn, the more those two black-hearted men—Long Will Stevens and Asa Paton—became my friends, too. They were my mates, and when they told me tales of my father, I could see him as a flesh-and-blood man. They made him real to me, Miriam, and for the first time in my life I knew who I *was.* I was one of them, and I liked it. I liked it just fine."

He had, too. The *Dasher* had been the largest ship he'd ever sailed in, and Captain Ellis had been a better master than many of the respectable Christian captains he'd known. He liked seeing lands so different from Massachusetts. And once they'd reached the Indian Ocean and began taking prizes, he'd discovered he liked that, too, the excitement of the chase and the dangerous challenge of the capture, of being tested in battle against wild-eyed men as desperate as himself.

"I was a true pirate at last, Mirry, the same as my father, but it wasn't like the games you and Zach and I played here on Carmondy. Pirating's only a fancy word for being a thief; I know that now. But then I kept thinking of you, sweetheart, how proud I'd make you by coming back a rich man with real treasure, the kind we'd always dreamed we'd find here. But I couldn't even do that right."

"You don't have to be rich, Jack," she said behind him, and from the way her voice broke he could tell he'd made her cry—one more sorrow he'd brought her. "That isn't why I love you."

But he shook his head again, and he didn't turn around because he didn't deserve the comfort of her sympathy. The hardest part to tell was next, the part that still haunted him, awake and asleep and in between, and always would.

"I could have been a rich man, Mirry, rich enough to buy all of Westham with jingle left in my pocket. I could have made you proud of me at last." He hunched his shoulders low, unconsciously bracing himself against the shame of the past. "It was off Madagascar that we fell in with two small ships. Some great mogul's treasure ships, they were supposed to be. The first, when we took it, was filled with gold and ivory, more than any Englishman can fancy. But the second had only the mogul's wives and daughters and their poor servants. Our captain was wicked unhappy, declaring they'd lied to us, and now must pay."

He took another deep breath, knowing he must finish. "I—I couldn't do it, Mirry," he said, his voice cracking beneath the burden he'd shared with no one else. "I couldn't follow those orders, not for all the gold and ivory under Heaven."

He would never forget the terrified screams of those Indian women, or their wails of grief when the ones who'd survived were cast adrift in their empty ship, without a crew to guide them. Captain Ellis called it merciful not to have slit their throats to silence them, but Jack knew the real horror had been in letting them live.

He was shaking now and could not stop, and when Miriam's arms slipped around his waist and held him tight, her skirts fluttering against his legs and her face pressed against his back, he could feel the heat of her tears on his skin. Blindly he felt for her hands, covering them with his own as he bowed his head.

"They thought I'd gone daft, Mirry," he continued, his voice now scarcely more than a rasping, raw whisper. "How could I be Johnny Wilder's son? They laughed at me, but when I tried to help those poor, weeping creatures, they locked me below like a madman. Then they damned me for a coward, for a traitor and worse, and only my father's name kept them from killing me, too. But I knew then I was done with pirating. Never again, Mirry. Never, do you hear? The hour we touched shore again, I ran, and I left them and all their cursed treasure behind for the devil himself to claim. I ran, and I didn't stop until I reached you."

Her fingers twisted and curled into his, all the gentleness and solace his battered soul craved there in her little hands.

"You're home now, Jack," she murmured. "Everything else is done, finished, and now you're safe home with me."

"But that doesn't change what I am, Miriam. I've nothing to give you in return, not one blasted thing that's worthy of you."

With infinite care, Miriam slid around to face him. She had never seen him like this, never seen this bleak, haunted emptiness in his eyes, and it broke her heart to know how much he must have struggled to keep the demons locked within, to keep up the bluff, brash face that had fooled the rest of the world.

She could barely imagine what he'd suffered, and only guess at everything he hadn't told her. Yet when she remembered how much his unknown father and the stories about him had meant to Jack, she understood with poignant clarity how he could have been seduced by the excitement of his father's outlaw existence—and how fortunate he'd been to escape before he'd shared his father's death.

"Oh, Jack, you great oaf," said Miriam softly as she lifted her hands to each side of his face, his beard rough upon her palms as she drew him down. "Why can't you believe that all I ever wanted was you?"

When they'd kissed before it had been from desire, from pleasure shared, but now when their mouths sought and found one another the passion that burned between them was raw with a different kind of longing. She *needed* to be his, to belong to him in every possible way and prove to him the depth and the breadth of her love. With this kind of love, the horrors of his past could be healed and recede, and with love they could begin to find their way through whatever came next.

Her lips parted for him at once, yielding to his hunger as she cradled his face. She felt his hunger in his touch, too, his hands sliding over her, scorching her through the layers of her clothes as he pulled their bodies closer together. She braced her hands across his bare chest, relishing the textures of hair curling over warm skin, skin over taut muscle. She found the puckered scar that sliced across his chest, another mark of how he'd suffered, and another way, too, that she could mark him as her own, her lips tracing a hot, teasing path along the cruel seam to the top of his hip, to the edge of his breeches.

But it couldn't begin to be enough, and as the fever grew hotter between them he began to pull at her clothes, yanking at the laces and knots and ribbons that barred his way. She broke away from the kiss to help him, her fingers trembling as first her bodice slipped from her shoulders, then her petticoat fell from her hips.

He had no patience with her stays, and she grinned, too, when he snapped the cord in the back and the whalebone and buckram fell away from the fine linen of her shift. He filled his hands with her newly freed breasts, murmuring lover's nonsense to her as he kissed her lips, her chin, her throat, before at last he tugged at the drawstring on her shift, lower, lower, until his lips could suckle on her nipples. She gasped as the pleasure swept through her, bowing her head over his as her fingers clutched convulsively at the hard muscles of his shoulders.

His fingers spread to cover the swell of her hips, gliding down the outside of her thighs until they reached the hem, shoving aside the fragile linen. She shuddered as he moved higher along the inside of her legs, easing them apart to touch her intimately with the same thumb that he'd rubbed across her lip. She gasped, swaying into him for support, and gently he rocked her backwards, into the hollowed nest of the coverlet over the sand.

As he tore away his breeches, she watched him with eyes heavy-lidded with desire. Before there'd been no time to admire him for the beautiful man that he was, to see his maleness like this, hot and powerful and gilded by the glow of the fire.

But desire gave them little such time now, either, and as she pulled off her shift to be the same as he was, he joined her, his weight welcome on her body. She kissed him again, and when he lifted her hips and entered her, her cry of joy was lost in his mouth. She gasped as he began to move, driving into her with a rhythm she was quick to answer, and pleasure whirled them higher with every stroke. Her body tightened and arched, frantically seeking the release that could only come from him, and as she cried his name one last time it did, sweeping them both along in its path and leaving her trembling and spent beneath him.

"You're home, Jack," she whispered as she held him tight, and kissed away what could have been a tear from his stubbled cheek. "You're home to stay, and so am I."

Chapter 12

"WAKE UP, SWEETHEART."

Miriam smiled sleepily at the sound of Jack's voice, but she didn't obey. Why should she, when she'd never in her life felt this contented and blissfully happy? Instead she yawned and wriggled closer against him, relishing the warmth of his body against hers and the way his arm curled so protectively around her beneath the coverlet.

"I'm sorry, love," he said softly, "but I need you awake."

With a sigh she opened her eyes, and grinned up at his face over his. How could she argue with being needed by him? But though he kissed her as she'd hoped he would, when he drew back she saw at once how serious his face had become, his expression taut and watchful. And not only had he pulled on his breeches while she'd still slept, but at his waist once again hung the cutlass in its scabbard.

"What's wrong?" she asked as she pushed herself up onto one elbow, instantly, completely awake.

"Nothing, I hope," he said softly, pressing one finger across her lips as a warning to be more quiet. "But I do believe we have guests, princess."

"Here?" Immediately she rolled to her knees, shoving

her hair back from her face as she scrambled to search for her clothes. She didn't stop to question why, for Jack's instincts for self-preservation had always been remarkably keen. The little fire had long ago died down to embers that gave no light and the moon that had guided their way on the river had hidden itself in the clouds, and she gave a small hiss of frustration as she groped vainly through the shadows.

" 'Tis not your father or Zach, lass," said Jack, "nor is it Chuff, either, if that's what's worrying you. But whoever it is, I'd rather they didn't find us first. Here now, hurry and put this on."

"But this is *your* shirt!"

"It's all I could find," he said sheepishly. "God knows what's become of your things, but we haven't time to hunt for them now."

She was already pulling the shirt over her head. The hem hung nearly to her ankles and the sleeves flopped over her hands, but at least the linen was coarse enough to cover her sufficiently.

"I'm ready," she said breathlessly as she tugged her hair free from the collar. She wasn't frightened as much as excited, the same as if this were another of their long-ago games. She wasn't completely convinced it wasn't—until she caught the faint gleam of Jack's remaining pistol in the glow of the embers.

"What are you doing with that?" she asked, though even in the half-light it was clear enough that he was wiping the gun's flintlock dry with well-practiced efficiency. "I thought you told me it wasn't loaded."

"It wasn't then," he said evenly. "It is now."

Their glances met over the pistol in his hand, neither speaking the single question that hung in the air between them. Yet even so, Miriam's heart cried the answer: he'd promised there'd be no more piracy, no more thievery, no more fighting, and because she loved him, she'd believed him. Yet what other meaning could there be to a loaded gun in his hand?

"Be easy, sweetheart," he said, though of course she was anything but. "Trust me, and I swear no harm will come to you."

She wanted to shout that she didn't want his protection, or his assurances, either—it wasn't herself she feared for—but instead all she did was nod in miserable silence. If he saw no harm or contradiction in his actions, then nothing she could say would do any good, anyway.

He made sure the lock wasn't cocked as he hooked the pistol onto his belt, then held his hand out to her with his usual gallantry. "Come, lass," he said. "Let's see to our visitors."

Despite her unhappiness, she joined him, and together they quickly edged along through the tall grass, deeper into the shadows of the scrub pines. Across the water lightning flashed through the clouds, and the wind that ruffled uneasily through the branches over them carried the heavy, wet scent of the storm from the sea. Gently Jack pulled Miriam down beside him, where they could see the beach and not be seen in return. In the next moment a small boat with two men at the oars appeared from behind the rocky point.

"Damnation, I was right about the voices," whispered Jack. "But why in blazes would anyone else row out to Carmondy on such a night?"

Miriam didn't care so much about why as who. She peered at the small boat pushing through the currents as it drew closer to the island, trying to recognize the two men by the lantern in the prow. They were not young men; they were too old to have rowed this distance on some youthful lark, and from the deft way they handled the boat as well as from their well-worn clothing Miriam knew they were sailors, sailors she'd seen before.

"Those two were in the Lion's taproom all afternoon," she said slowly. "They kept to themselves, mostly, and Father wasn't happpy that they made their rum last so long and ordered nothing to eat with it. I didn't catch their names, but if—"

"Will Stevens and Asa Paton," said Jack, his whispered voice oddly flat. "They're my father's old mates, Miriam, and mine, too, from the *Dasher.*"

"Oh, Jack, no." Her chest squeezed tight with horror as she watched him methodically pull the pistol from his belt, the easy way it settled in his hand. Stevens and Paton were the same men that had nearly destroyed his life before, and they could end it now without a thought. And there were two of them, while in Jack's hand there was only one gun with one ball loaded to fire, and worse, one promise he'd made to her.

One man raised his hand to point in the direction of the old gallows-oak behind them, his long gray hair streaming in the wind, and raised the lantern high to see better. Candlelight spilled into the boat and over the small, golden head of a third person huddled on the forward bench. Miriam gasped, and grabbed Jack's arm.

"Oh, dear God, look," she whispered in terrified disbelief. "They have Henry."

Jack saw, and he swore, quietly and violently, and she felt his body coil and tense even more beside her.

"Henry must have been boasting in the taproom about knowing you," she babbled, unable to help herself or keep the tears from her eyes, "and that you always came to Carmondy, and they must have thought he could lead them to you."

"It's not me they want," said Jack. "It's my father's share of Avery's gold."

As they watched, the two men jumped from the boat and dragged it onto the sand. The storm rumbled closer, the lightning flashing more brightly now behind the blanket of clouds, the water dappled and driven by the rising wind, but Stevens and Paton were too intent to notice. As Jack had guessed, they'd brought shovels with them, but they also wore cutlasses and pistols much like Jack's own. Stevens, the one with the trailing, grizzled mustache, reached into the boat and grabbed Henry, hauling him roughly by one arm over the side and onto the sand. The boy yelped with pain and fear as he struggled to keep pace with the two men as they half dragged him up the beach. Even at this distance Miriam could tell he was crying, and it took all her will not to run to him.

"They're hurting him," she said, her own tears streaking her cheeks. "Oh, Jack, he's still only a little boy!"

Yet when Jack looked at the boy held tight in Stevens's grasp, he saw more than Miriam's little brother. He saw the future and the children he wanted so desperately to have with her, the woman he loved more than his own life. But he also saw the grimmest part of his past, the weeping, terrified Indian women he hadn't been able to save. His future and his past now twined together, neither possible to ignore.

Rapidly he began unbuckling the belt with his cutlass. This was *his* island, his and Miriam's, not Stevens's or Paton's or even his father's. He still knew it better than anyone, and if he could just get Henry away, he knew they could vanish into the island's secret places and be safe. Carefully he set the pistol on the ground before Miriam, and the cutlass with it.

"What are you doing?" she asked frantically. "Oh, love, where are you going?"

Gently he touched her face, brushing away her tears with the tips of his fingers. He couldn't begin to tell her how dear she was to him, but maybe, this way, he could show her. "Stay here, Mirry, where you'll be safe, and I'll fetch Henry. Whatever happens, don't let them see you, mind? Promise me that, Mirry. Don't let them find you."

She nodded, understanding the danger, even as her eyes overflowed with fresh tears.

"Wait," she said, and leaned forward to kiss his cheek. "For luck."

He smiled, and kissed her on her forehead. "For luck, and for love."

Slowly Jack crept through the tall grass and the shadows. The two men had pulled off their coats and cutlass belts and begun to dig into the sandy soil not far from the oak, their backs to Jack.

"Would've been like Johnny to hide his gold with dead men to watch it," said Paton with a glance up at the gallows-like branch that had given the tree its name. "You can almost hear him a-laughin' at us now."

Stevens's only answer was to curl his fingers into a sign against the evil eye and tap his forehead before he spat and concentrated again on digging.

A few paces away Henry squatted where he'd been ordered to stay, his arms folded tight around his little body and his misery. The wind gusted again, and this time with it came the first splatter of raindrops plopping dully into the sand, but Stevens and Paton kept digging, grunting with exertion.

Jack frowned, wondering how best to get the boy's attention. He couldn't risk calling to him, but he also didn't want to expose himself any further in the open. An owl's sudden agitated hooting startled him enough that automatically he whipped his head about, half expecting to see the bird swooping down upon him. But there was nothing except the scrubby pines and weeds where he'd left Miriam, and his grin spread as suddenly as the owl's call had come.

Clever lass, he thought with unabashed adoration, his clever, clever lass, and when he looked back toward Henry, the boy was now staring directly at him. At least *he* had recognized his sister's wild-owl call. When Jack beckoned, Henry came running, a flash of lightning showing his arms pumping and his round-cheeked face alight with relief and the same excitement that Jack so loved to see in Miriam.

But as the boy ran, his toe snagged in a knot of dried seaweed and he cried out as he pitched forward. Without thinking Jack lunged forward, catching Henry around the waist to carry him to safety. But he was only halfway up the dune when he heard the unmistakable click of a flintlock being cocked.

Not now, he thought desperately, *not when we're so close.* Still he stopped, the boy in his arms, and after one endless moment, turned slowly to face Stevens's pistol.

"Look'ee, Asa, it's Little Jack, the cowardly bastard," said the man with a cackle as his finger played idly around the trigger. "Come back to cheat us one more time, have you, laddie?"

The gunshot rang so close that Jack jerked to one side, convinced he'd been hit. But instead it was Stevens who was staggering backwards toward the oak and screaming with pain as he clutched the shattered pulp of his shoulder, his arm now dangling broken and useless and his gun in the sand. Behind him Paton snatched up the fallen pistol and aimed the long barrel not at Jack, but at the child in his arms, and automatically Jack twisted away, shielding Henry as best he could with his own body.

This was not how he'd wished it to end for any of them, not for Henry or Mirry or himself. At least he could die knowing he'd done right for her after all, that he'd proven he could be a good man worthy of her love. But dear God, why did he have to die to prove it?

The brilliant flash seared his eyes, a white-hot ball of flame that zigzagged from the sky to the oak. The explosion hurled him backwards into the sand, blinding him, surrounding him with the sounds of splintering, cracking timbers and the pungent scent of singed wood. Beneath him the ground shook as the oak's great roots ripped from the soil, and when the trunk toppled to the beach, the crash was louder than the thunder overhead.

Then Miriam was screaming his name, over and over, and he felt something soft and warm wriggling impatiently to be free beneath him. Dazed, he rolled over and shook his head to clear it. With an effort he opened his eyes, a thousand tiny sparks darting through his vision.

He squeezed his eyes shut, letting the cool rain wash over his eyelids. He couldn't remember when the rain had begun, but he was grateful for it now. Carefully he opened his eyes again, and this time there were no sparks or flashes, only Miriam's dear, wet, worried face, with Henry—that wriggling mass that had been beneath him—now clutched tight in her arms.

"You're all right then, Henry?" he asked, his voice sounding thick and distant in his ears. "Nothing amiss?"

The boy shook his head, but his gaze was fixed on the great tree lying across the beach. Trapped beneath the trunk and the tangle of broken branches were one of Stevens's legs and Paton's right arm, all that remained uncrushed, and with a gasp of horror Miriam turned her brother's face away and into her hip.

Unsteadily Jack rose to his feet, his knees wobbling beneath him. Every muscle in his body ached, every nerve seemed stretched and beaten, but the wild joy he felt at still being alive made him forget everything else.

Except, of course, for Miriam. She was hanging back with Henry, hesitant, her hair in sodden tangles over her shoulders and his rain-soaked shirt sliding to one side as it clung to her body, and in her hand she still clutched the pistol she'd used to shoot Stevens.

She had never looked more beautiful, he decided, nor had he loved her more.

"Oh, Mirry," he said, his words still slurring softly as he frowned at the pistol. "Must I make you promise to give up pirating, too?"

She gasped, then laughed, and before she wrapped her arms around him she tossed the empty gun over her shoulder.

But instead of thumping in the sand, the pistol landed with a ring of metal on metal. With Miriam's shoulder tucked neatly beneath his arm to steady him, they crossed to where the pistol had dropped, into the hollow beneath the arching web of the oak's roots. Although the worst of the storm had already passed, lightning flickered and flashed one more time, over a long-buried lattice of rotting wood, a rusted padlock, a ransom of gold and silver coins with the likenesses of a dozen different kings and queens.

His father's treasure.

Chapter 13

"AHOY," CALLED HENRY IMPORTANTLY, STANDING ON the fallen tree as he pointed out into the pink sky of the new dawn. "There's a ship."

With a groan, Jack straightened and turned to look out to sea. They'd spent most of the night shifting the gold and silver coins into Mrs. Rowe's supper basket, their incongruous but useful makeshift treasure chest. The last thing he wished now was any more "visitors" to Carmondy, especially any like the earlier ones. But not only did a ship lie on the near horizon, as Henry had reported, but the captain had lowered a boat, which was even now nearly on their beach.

"Oh, hell," he said wearily as Miriam joined him. "Tell me I'm not really seeing what my eyes say I am."

"Why not, when it's true?" she asked cheerfully, wiping the mud from her hands on the side of his now filthy shirt. "And why wouldn't you wish to see Zach, anyway?"

"I don't really wish to see anyone other than you, sweet," he said, bending to kiss her. Though the evening certainly had turned out well enough, there were still parts of it he'd rather have missed. "And what makes you think it's your brother, anyway?"

"Because that's his ship," she answered, her cheeks

pink after being kissed before Henry. "Well, not quite *his* ship, because he's only the first mate, but his cousin Samson Fairbourne's ship, the *Morning Star*. I'd recognize it anywhere."

"Would you." Jack sighed. He'd almost rather be visited again by Stevens and Paton than any of Zach's high-and-mighty Fairbourne cousins. And why, he wondered suspiciously, had Zach decided to come bustling over to Carmondy on this particular morning? That hadn't been part of their plan at all.

But whether it was or not no longer mattered, because Zach himself was splashing through the shallow water, ready to hear all about the pirates and the storm and to marvel at the newly discovered treasure.

"What the hell are you doing here, anyway?" asked Jack crossly when he had the chance to take Zach aside. His friend was looking particularly proper and prosperous this morning, newly shaven and with a clean, pressed shirt and a well-brushed coat that infuriated barefoot, bare-chested Jack all the more. "I thought we'd agreed that Miriam and I would be left here alone for at least a day and a night."

But Zach only smiled blandly. "I thought it best to check on you after the storm, and a good thing I did, too. You can't fault me for looking after my sister's interests, can you?"

Jack couldn't, not even when Zach swept them all off the island and on board the *Morning Star* with the wicker treasure chest carefully hoisted up the side with them. And he couldn't object to the splendid breakfast in Samson Fairbourne's cabin, either, or the hot coffee that spread its warmth through his exhausted body, or the way that Miriam set her chair so close to his that she was nearly sitting in his lap, her hand resting fondly on his knee. She still wore his shirt, too, though with her mother's coverlet tossed over it as a shawl for modesty's sake.

"Now," declared Samson Fairbourne as the last of breakfast was cleared away. He was a large man, enough like Zach to be a brother, and when he declared things, everyone listened. "Are we all ready to begin the wedding?"

Jack felt all that splendid breakfast and coffee he'd consumed rising up to choke him.

"What wedding?" asked Miriam in a tiny voice. Her back had grown straight and stiff, and with concern Jack noted she'd turned as pale as his shirt. "I know I was to wed Mr. Chuff shortly, but I believe that is, ah, not to happen now. Unless . . . oh, Zach, whatever mischief have you done now?"

"No mischief, muffin," said Zach with enough heartiness to make Jack long to throttle him outright. "But considering the circumstances, I thought you and Jack would wish to wed here, with Sam as captain to do the honors, and without the bother of waiting for the banns to be read on land."

"But a wedding, a marriage—this is something Jack and I have not discussed!" she cried, so plaintively that Jack swiftly rested his hand over hers to reassure her. "We've never spoken of it, not—not even once!"

Zach cleared his throat. "Then perhaps you should be speaking of it now. What shall you say, Jack?"

"I say that you're a meddlesome, traitorous idiot," snapped Jack, slipping his arm possessively around Miriam's waist and pulling her closer. "I say that for someone who pretends to care so much about his sister, you're showing damned little concern for her feelings now, shaming and bullying her like this before strangers!"

"Then perhaps it's high time she had someone else to look after her welfare, someone who'll do a better job of it," said Zach, tapping his knuckle lightly on the table. "You've always told me you'd make Miriam happier than any other man alive, and you came clear around the world to do it. You've more than enough money to support her now. And you certainly seem, ah, devoted to her. You agree, don't you?"

"Aye," said Jack soundly. For Miriam's sake, he

wouldn't dream of hesitating. "It's all true. And more: I love her, Zach, I love her, and I don't care who the hell knows it."

Zach nodded solemnly, and turned toward his sister. "And what do you have to say for yourself, muffin? Do you love Jack, too?"

"Yes," she said as she turned to face Jack, her expression so dear and melting soft with emotion that he was afraid he'd cry himself, just from looking at her. "I do love him, and I always have. And *I* don't care who the hell knows it, either, as long as Jack does himself."

"Well, then," began Samson again. "Are we all ready to begin this wedding or not?"

And this time, to no one's surprise, they were.

Miriam and Jack decided not to keep house like other husbands and wives, but instead built an elegant little sloop with a cabin as grand as any front parlor for displaying her collection of shells, and a bedchamber in the stern with windows so they could watch the sun rise without rising themselves. They sailed wherever their fancy took them, best friends and lovers, and in time their little crew included three large, boisterous sons and one small but equally boisterous daughter. And pirating of any sort was strictly forbidden.

Others said the secret of the Wilders' happiness was the treasure they'd found on Carmondy Island, and when Jack and Miriam heard that, they'd smile at each other, their secret safe between them. For they *had* discovered their love there, a treasure more rare than any gold or silver.

And they didn't care who the hell knew it.

With more than two million copies in print worldwide, Miranda Jarrett's bestselling books are enjoyed by readers from Singapore to Poland to Australia. Her critically acclaimed novels of colonial America featuring the unforgettable Sparhawk family have now been joined by her newest series for Pocket Books, featuring the equally memorable Fairbournes of Appledore: *The Captain's Bride, Cranberry Point,* and *Wishing.* Her most recent book, *Moonlight,* gives Zach Fairbourne, Miriam's meddlesome older brother in "Buried Treasure," the heroine he deserves.

When Miranda is not sitting huddled on the aluminum bleachers in the ice rink where her two children skate, she enjoys spending long summer days on Cape Cod, the home of the Fairbournes. Unfortunately, none of her family have uncovered any long-buried pirate gold—yet.

Miranda is a graduate of Brown University with a degree in art history. A two-time RITA Award finalist, she is the recipient of many awards and honors for her writing, including the prestigious *Romantic Times* Reviewers' Choice Award for Best North American Historical Romance. She loves to hear from readers, and can be reached at P.O. Box 1102, Paoli, PA 19301-0792 (an SASE is appreciated), or by e-mail at MJarrett21@aol.com.

Swept Away

Mariah Stewart

For the girls of summer—Cathy, Malena, Carolyn,
Eileen, Linda, Bonnie, Ann (did I miss anyone?)—
who still haunt the dunes on Pompano Beach.

Forever young.

Chapter 1

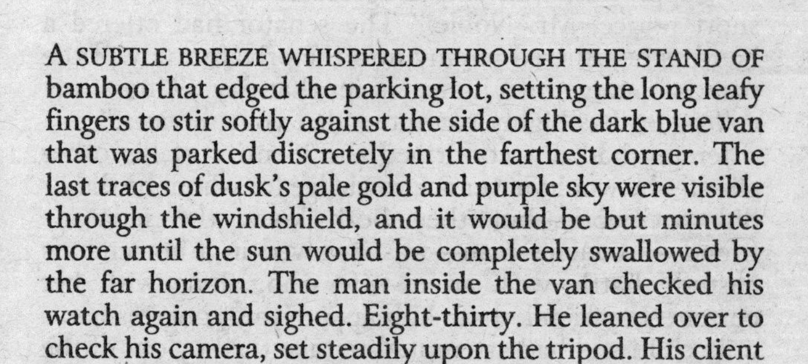

A SUBTLE BREEZE WHISPERED THROUGH THE STAND OF bamboo that edged the parking lot, setting the long leafy fingers to stir softly against the side of the dark blue van that was parked discretely in the farthest corner. The last traces of dusk's pale gold and purple sky were visible through the windshield, and it would be but minutes more until the sun would be completely swallowed by the far horizon. The man inside the van checked his watch again and sighed. Eight-thirty. He leaned over to check his camera, set steadily upon the tripod. His client had wanted both still photos and video. Jeremy Noble, of Noble and Dawson Investigations, would give the good senator what he paid for.

A small, older model foreign car slowed at the corner, then made an easy right into the lot and drove straight to the first row before stopping. The car sat at idle for a long minute or so before the engine was turned off and a door opened. A dark-haired young man got out and looked up and down the rows of cars. Apparently not finding what he was looking for, he patiently leaned back against his car, his hands in his pockets.

With the aid of small but powerful binoculars, Jeremy focused on the license plate. Satisfied that this was one of the two parties for whom he was being paid to watch, he took a few cursory shots with the Nikon of the young man leaning against the car. He then turned his attention to the video camera, focusing the lens on the small black car with the Georgetown University sticker on the back window.

Through the eye of the video camera, the investigator could see that the man was even younger than he'd initially supposed, maybe twenty-two or twenty-three. He was handsome, dark-haired, with good clean features. The senator's daughter had chosen a fine-looking man to lose her heart to. It was a shame that her father was intent on making sure that the relationship never went any further.

"I appreciate that you've agreed to meet me on such short notice, Mr. Noble." The senator had offered a hand as he ushered Jeremy into the private study of the palatial Georgetown home earlier that day. "One of my colleagues has highly recommended your services."

Jeremy had not confirmed the identity of his other client—he would never acknowledge for whom he did or did not work—but they both knew the senator's friend—a congressman—was involved in a horrendous custody battle with an ex-wife who, along with her current boyfriend, had kidnapped the congressman's only child and had attempted to take the boy out of the country. Only quick thinking and quicker action on the part of both Jeremy and his partner had prevented the child from disappearing from his father's life. Thanks to Noble and Dawson, the boy was now back with his father where, it was hoped, he would remain.

"We have a bit of a domestic matter that my wife and I feel needs to be attended to immediately," the senator confided, offering Jeremy a chair as he himself sat in a dark green leather wingback. "For the past several years, our daughter has been involved with a young man whom we feel is totally unsuitable. You see, we have long held the hope that she would marry into the diplomatic circle. Why, the son of the ambassador from Greece is head over heels for her. Good boy, good family."

The senator's cigar punctuated the air.

"Now, she tells me that she's not seeing this other boy anymore—he's a teacher. Can you imagine a child of mine living on a teacher's salary? Her mother and I certainly cannot. Anyway, she tells us that *that* relationship is over. Her mother's buying her story, but I'm not. I have it on good authority that she's been secretly meeting him"—the senator handed Jeremy a piece of paper—"at this address. The boy's license plate number is there, too, and the number of my cell phone. I want photographs. I want videos. I want her to see that she cannot lie to me, that there's no place she can sneak off to where I cannot find her."

Jeremy took the slip of paper, glanced at it before tucking it into his pocket.

"I want you to call me when the boy arrives. And I want to know when my daughter gets there."

"Why don't you just wait for her yourself?"

"I'm expected to attend a reception at the British Embassy. Besides, a man like me—a United States senator!—can't very well be lurking about in vacant lots hoping to catch his twenty-one-year-old daughter in a lie. You'll call me at the number on the card. I'll take it from there."

The senator stood to announce that the meeting was over.

"We love our daughter very much, Mr. Noble. We only want what's best for her. We strongly believe that what's best for her is *not* to marry a teacher and spend her life in the backwoods of Kentucky. That's not the future we had envisioned for her. She's our only child. I'm sure you understand."

An uneasy feeling had crept over Jeremy then and had stayed with him for the rest of the day. He always hated jobs that involved the manipulation of someone else's life. But the senator was prominent and powerful, and could be a good ally in the suburban Washington marketplace, where surveillance and intrigue services were frequently sought and handsomely paid for.

Well, the job would be over soon enough.

Jeremy watched the little BMW convertible zip into the parking lot and cruise for a place to park. The exuberant driver hopped out and all but danced across the macadam to her waiting lover. She spun into his arms, settled momentarily for a long, deep kiss, then danced back toward the BMW, pulling the dark-haired young man with her. Jeremy leaned into the video cam and brought them into sharp focus.

The senator's daughter was not a natural beauty—her features were just slightly too small, her eyes just slightly too far apart—but clearly, her young man was totally captivated. Adoration was written all over his face.

Jeremy watched as they walked to the back of her car, watched as the young man turned her to him and touched her face gently, watched as the young woman looked up at him with eyes filled with love and lifted a hand to smooth his hair back tenderly, as if to reassure. He said something to her that caused her face to crinkle with soft laughter, her eyes glowing and alive with promise and trust.

Filled with a hot, sudden shot of envy, Jeremy tried to remember when a woman had last looked at him with such loving eyes.

It had been, he conceded, a very, very long time.

Something in Jeremy's gut wrenched as he recalled that his instructions included calling the senator as soon as the young man had arrived. One hand reached for the cell phone, the other into his shirt pocket for the scrap of folded paper containing the number. He looked back at the couple in the parking lot, so filled with each other, so unaware that their happiness was one brief phone call from coming to an end.

The young woman reached into the trunk and pulled out a dark green gym bag, which she swung over her shoulder. Slamming the trunk, she turned again, and in the light of the nearby lamppost, Jeremy could see her dreams, aglow with promise, reflected in her face.

They're running away, Jeremy realized as she locked the car and took the young man's hand.

The small, slim phone lay heavy in his own.

He suddenly recalled another early summer night when the face of another young woman had been caught in lamplight, just so. He'd been a junior at Princeton that year, and had had the world by the tail. He and his date for that weekend had strolled off campus to Nassau Street, down Witherspoon to a coffee shop that was open late and served great sandwiches. On their way back to campus, they had stopped beneath a street lamp and kissed. From behind them had come a sigh, and, startled, they had broken apart. An elderly man, dapperly dressed and leaning on a cane, apologized for having frightened them.

"I'm so sorry," he'd said softly to Jeremy, "but you're so young, and she's so beautiful. Hold fast to nights like this, son . . . they pass so quickly. Hold fast to it all . . ."

The old man had stepped closer and kissed Jeremy's date, right at the corner of her pretty young mouth, then stepped away, nodded to them both, and disappeared back into the night.

It had been years since he'd thought of it—or the young woman, whose name and face had been lost to time—but the words came back to Jeremy now.

"Hold fast to it all. . . ."

Jeremy watched the young lovers walk across the parking lot, and he put the phone down. He pulled the film from the Nikon, exposing it, then packed up the video cam.

"Good luck, kids," he said quietly as the small foreign car sped from the parking lot and disappeared into the night.

He took the long way back to his townhouse. He pulled up slowly in front of his garage, parked the car, and contemplated what he'd done. Jeremy had never scuttled an investigation before, never given less than his best on any job, regardless of the difficulty. And this client would be a particularly unhappy man. Well, it was too late to change his mind now. He'd made his decision back in the parking lot, and now he'd have to play it out. The senator would have an easy enough time finding someone else to wreck his daughter's life. But at least it wouldn't have been Jeremy's call that had taken the sparkle from those young eyes.

Jeremy glanced at his watch, then picked up his cell phone and dialed the number he'd been given.

"Senator. Jeremy Noble. I'm afraid I've had a touch of bad luck . . . my car broke down on 95 outside of College Park. I'm afraid I won't be able to keep that appointment after all . . ."

Jeremy unlocked the front door, chuckling as he pictured the distinguished statesman whispering angry curses into the tiny cell phone while in the midst of an important gathering in the oh-so-very-elegant British Embassy.

Whistling, Jeremy punched the message button on the answering machine as he went into the kitchen and turned on the light. Half listening to the messages, he opened the refrigerator door and hunted for something that hadn't expired or grown some life form of its own. Unsuccessful, he checked the freezer. Nothing there either. He poked around in a cupboard until he found a can of soup. That would have to do.

The messages were still running, but so far he'd heard nothing important enough to interfere with his quest for food.

It occurred to him then that he hadn't had a meal at home or a day off in over five weeks. While there was definitely something to be said for steady work, tonight's little episode had reminded him that there were other, more important things in life. He dumped the congealed soup into a pan, then added a little water. It looked disgusting.

Nothing at all like that cream of she-crab soup he'd had at the Bishop's Inn on the Maryland coast back in June. Pale as moonlight, with chunks of crab and delicate traces of herbs. Jeremy's mouth watered just to think of it.

And not just the soup, his tired mind poked at him playfully, *the chef was pretty mouthwatering, too . . .*

Ah, yes, Jody.

Jeremy set the pan of soup on the burner and turned the flame on low.

Jody Beckett. Jody with the light brown hair and the long, lanky body and the wizard's touch in the kitchen.

He sat on one of the hard kitchen chairs, pulled another out from under the table and propped his legs up on it, thinking back to the days he had spent at the Bishop's Inn in the beginning of June. He'd been working on a big case that involved Laura Bishop, the owner of the inn, and when it had concluded, she'd invited him to stay on for a few days as a guest, a little bonus for his part in bringing the matter to a successful conclusion. Because of his work schedule, he'd been able to spend only two days and nights there, but every minute had been a treasure. Sun, sand, fishing, great conversation with the inn's other lively guests, incredible food.

And Jody.

If he closed his eyes, he could see her. Clear skin, eyes the color of pale amber, a pert nose that wrinkled when she laughed, a sweet mouth that curved up on one side. Great legs, too. Long and shapely . . .

It wasn't, he acknowledged, the first time he'd seen that face—or those legs—in his mind's eye. More than once over the past few weeks, something of Jody had seemed to be floating around inside his head, like a snippet of a song he'd yet to learn all the words to.

Hold fast to it all . . .

Perhaps it was time to take Laura up on her offer to spend a week at the inn.

Jeremy pulled his briefcase across the table and opened it, searching for his appointment book. Things looked pretty tight, he grimaced, trying to figure out which jobs he could switch around or postpone, and which he could pass off to his partner.

If he worked like a demon this week, he might be able to make it by the last week of July.

If his partner pitched in, he could make it in less.

He reached for the phone, wondering just what payment his partner, T. J. Dawson, would extract in return. Whatever it was, it would be worth it for a week at the Bishop's Inn. Long enough, he rationalized. There was something about Jody that had been circling around in the back of his mind like a lazy hawk on a summer morning. Maybe it was time to find out if it was more than just her cooking that was keeping her there.

Jody Beckett leaned against the white porcelain sink that was shaped like a big scallop shell, hoping to bring her face as close as humanly possible to the mirror that hung behind it. Narrowing her eyes, she studied the skin around them, searching for some outward sign that in one short day—just twenty-four more hours—she would turn thirty.

The big three-oh.

Gray hairs and sagging and wrinkles, oh my.

She squinted a little more, wondering if *that right there* was the start of crow's feet. Crow's foot, she corrected herself, since there appeared to be only one. Turning her face this way and that, she realized that what she had first thought to be a line was merely shadow, the play of early morning light from a nearby window. Jody sighed deeply. She just wasn't ready to be old when it had been years since she had felt really young.

Jody brushed back her hair—summer streaked and just a shade or two from being mousy—and caught it in a yellow scrunchie. A glance at the clock assured her that she needn't hurry, since it wasn't likely that anyone else would be awake just yet, but hurry she did. She liked the tranquil lull that lay about the Bishop's Inn—her home and place of employment for the past three years—at the earliest hours of the day. Pulling on a pair of faded denim shorts and a tee-shirt the color of cornflowers, she slipped her feet into Adidas sandals and tucked the key to her suite of rooms into a pocket. Closing the door behind her, she eased down two flights of steps, the second of which widened into a sweeping curve to the lobby. Once downstairs, she paused and cocked her head, listening, but hearing no telltale sounds of running water or doors closing or feet moving on thick carpet.

Good. She loved having the inn to herself, if only for a little while.

Once in the kitchen, Jody started the coffee—she'd use the big pot today, since they were booked almost to capacity—and turned her thoughts to the breakfasts she would prepare. As the inn's chef and self-proclaimed kitchen queen, she was responsible for working with the owner, Laura Bishop, to plan menus and cook the meals as well. Although Laura employed extra help in the summers and on peak weekends throughout the year, Jody preferred to do most of the work herself. She took great pride in all of her work, but particularly her exceptional regional cooking, which reflected Maryland's history and bounty. There were those who swore her cream of she-crab soup had been devised through magic alone, and others who made trips to the inn several times throughout the season in search of her crab cakes and her beach plum cobbler. Her Lady Baltimore cake had become somewhat of a legend. Over the past eighteen months, more and more happy couples had come to Bishop's Cove to tie the knot there in the lovely gardens of the historic inn, drawn, many claimed, as much by Jody's catering as by the beautiful, romantic location by the sea.

Humming happily, Jody glanced over the worksheet she had prepared for herself the night before. There would be sixteen at breakfast this morning. The Walkers' (the Rose Room) and their friends, the Calhouns' (the Chinese Room), had booked a charter boat for the morning and would be stopping by for a quick cup of coffee only, since the day trip provided a light breakfast on the bay. Jody reached into an overhead cupboard and pulled out a small silver thermos. Gordon Chandler, a long-term guest who was attempting to salvage cargo from a sunken ship off the coast of Bishop's Cove, would be going out early, and he always appreciated the extra cup of coffee that Jody sent with him. He was planning on diving that morning with his crew, she'd heard him mention the night before, and while Jody hummed, she tried to imagine what it would be like to dive into the dark, unseen depths of the ocean, to encounter . . . who knew what?

She shivered slightly. There had been a time, long ago, when she had been more adventurous, when she would have jumped at the opportunity to dive, to explore a sunken ship and seek its treasures. The passage of time and a total devotion to her job had seemed to banish the thoughts of such daring pursuits from her life's itinerary.

Not completely, and maybe not forever, she told herself as she removed a stainless steel bowl of pale brown eggs from the refrigerator and set it on the counter next to a square tray stacked with bundles of spring-green asparagus. *One week from now, I will be stretched out on a blanket on the beach at Ocean Point, New Jersey.* Of course, that little trip couldn't compare with the thrill of deep sea diving, but still, it would be a week away from the same old, same old.

She'd planned the trip at the urging of an old high school friend, Natalie Evans, one of the crew with whom Jody had spent many a blissful summer afternoon lying on the beach, greased and oiled and ready to tan. Natalie, who had turned thirty in May, had thought it would be fun to plan a reunion of sorts on their old beach, and had assured Jody that she'd line up the old crowd and they'd spend a long, happy weekend reliving old times. No spouses, no kids, just a bunch of thirty-year-olds who had spent much of their teen years together. Jody smiled just thinking about seeing everyone again. It had been so long . . .

Of course, it would have been even more fun if she'd been able to rent the house her family used to stay in every summer, but a room in that brand-new motel right there on the beach would be fine, the perfect choice for her first trip back in fourteen years. And there would be other advantages to staying in a motel, she rationalized. She wouldn't have to clean or cook. And as much as she loved cooking, she was taking this long-awaited vacation to get as far away from her real life as she could.

When her father's job transfer to Nebraska midway through her junior year of high school took her from the central New Jersey home where she'd grown up, Jody had been certain that the best years of her life were behind her. Finding it difficult to make friends so late in the year, she found herself spending more and more time at home with her mother and her grandmother, a recent widow, who had come for an extended stay with her only daughter. Grandmother Jenny Rose, a true daughter of the South, was an exceptional cook, and was more than happy to teach her granddaughter everything she knew. By the time she graduated from high school the following June, Jody had discovered that she had more than just a casual knack for cooking.

Scrapping her plans for an accounting degree, Jody enrolled in The Restaurant School in Philadelphia, and it was soon clear that she had made the right choice. She stayed in Philadelphia and went to work with a world-class chef, at first as a low-level assistant, and later, having learned all from him that she could, moved on to what would be her last job in the city. Robert Orloff, the owner of the trendy new restaurant, Flora, took Jody under his wing, where she had remained for several years.

In time, Jody had had enough of the cold, icy Pennsylvania winters. She'd thought to drive south, maybe to Savannah or to Atlanta. Someplace warm. Besides, she'd grown to love Southern cooking, having learned so much from first her grandmother, then from Robert, who'd grown up in the area of Virginia that sat at the very end of the Delmarva peninsula. What would be more natural than a move south? Almost twenty-seven that year, Jody packed up her belongings and her résumé, the glowing recommendations to several premier chefs provided by Robert, and the fat file of recipes she had developed over the years, and set out to find adventure—or, at the very least, a place to hang her hat and her pots.

A serious summer storm had forced Jody to seek shelter just as she crossed from Delaware into Maryland, and the shelter she found was the Bishop's Inn. And the rest, as they say, is history. When the inn's cook was unable to make it through the storm to get to work, Jody offered to cook dinner for the small crowd of fellow travelers who were similarly stranded. Laura Bishop had been so impressed with Jody's creativity on such short notice that she had offered Jody a job that very night. When she threw in a suite of rooms on the third floor of the lovely old inn, Jody jumped at it. She had always loved the beach, and the chance to live year-round so close to the ocean had appealed to her. Not that she had much time to spend lounging on the sand these days, but at least she could carve out an occasional afternoon run or early evening stroll along the water's edge.

And come this time tomorrow, I will be on my way to my all-time favorite beach, where I will spend a glorious week. She grinned as she poured cream into a spatterware pitcher for the breakfast buffet. *Finally, after all these years—Ocean Point, New Jersey, here I come!*

Chapter 2

"I LEFT FROZEN DOUGH IN THE BIG FREEZER," JODY WAS saying as she stashed her two suitcases and a shoulder bag into the trunk of the sports car—convertible, of course—that she had rented to drive to her destination.

No big, clunky Buick for this trip.

Fearing that her twelve-year-old sedan would not make it to Dewey Beach up the road, never mind all the way to New Jersey, Jody had decided to rent something more reliable for the next two weeks and hang the cost. Live a little, a small voice inside her had pleaded when she arrived at the agency's lot, which had been lined with zippy little numbers, their tops down, their leather new, their chrome shiny enough to see your face in.

The urge to feel young, to feel carefree and adventurous, took over her normally sensible nature.

Yesterday morning, she had rented the convertible.

Yesterday afternoon, she had her hair highlighted with subtle blond streaks.

Last night, she bought two bikinis and a little red silk dress that looked like a slightly longer version of the ever popular tank top.

"You got the body for it, babe," Marlene at Dede's Boutique had crowed as Jody stepped from the dressing room in the dark blue bikini. " 'Bout time you showed it off."

And then somehow Marlene had talked her into the red dress.

"Hey, you're going on *vacation,*" Marlene had nodded her head, her beehive hair swaying to and fro. "You might as well live a little. Kick up your heels, Jody. Besides, that dress will look great with a tan."

It was certainly different from anything she'd ever owned in her life. It was feminine. It was sexy. It fit her like a glove, albeit a somewhat snug one.

The practical, workaholic Jody returned the dress to the sale rack and turned her back on it, but still, her little inner voice had pricked at her like a thorn.

This was a dress for a woman who was adventurous and unafraid to take chances. A woman with long, sun-streaked hair who drove a convertible and who had the time to indulge herself with days spent lounging on the beach, soaking up the late July sun. A carefree, confident woman like the one an adolescent Jody had intended to grow up to be.

The Jody who just that day had had her hair highlighted and rented a convertible added the dress to the pile on the counter.

"Jody, we'll manage just fine," Laura was saying as she opened the door of the slick little sports car. "After all, I am a decent cook. Our guests will be well fed. Maybe not quite as well as you might do it, but no one will feel cheated. I promise. Go and have a wonderful time. Visit with your old friends and get reacquainted. Have a life. Have a fling." Laura tucked Jody behind the wheel and slammed the door. "Just don't forget to come back."

"You have the address and phone number of where I'll be staying . . ."

"I do. And if anyone threatens not to pay their bill until they've had some of your exquisite flan, I'll call." Laura leaned over and kissed Jody on the cheek. "Otherwise, just for one sweet week, I want you to forget that the Bishop's Inn exists. Enjoy yourself. You're long overdue . . ."

"I am, aren't I?" Jody nodded as if the idea had only just occurred to her.

"Most definitely." Laura stepped back to permit Jody to make a U-turn across Sea View Avenue.

Jody waved as she sped off past the inn, slid her sunglasses on, and headed north.

Sea breezes filled the car every mile of the way along the coast drive, and she reveled in the feeling of freedom, of anticipation.

Life should hold more times like this, she told herself. *All work and no play has made Jody a very dull girl. Well, not for the next seven days. From this moment on, I will kick up my heels. I will soak up the sun. And maybe, just for a little while, I will be that exotic creature I used to dream of being . . .*

And oh, to be returning to Ocean Point, after all these years!

She grinned, thinking back to her last summer there, the year she had turned sixteen.

Life began at sixteen, by unanimous decree of parents and Ocean Point tradition.

At sixteen, you could date for real. At sixteen, you could wear a bikini—only the "fast" girls wore them at fifteen, and Lord knew you didn't want to be called *that.* At sixteen, you could go to Docker's Amusement Pier after 10 P.M., when it would close to the "younger" kids, and you could ride the roller coaster, where you'd sit close to the boy next to you and cling to him like a terrified monkey. At sixteen, you could stay out till midnight every night of the week if you felt like it, maybe even later on the weekends. At sixteen, life had been wonderful, magical, endless fun, full of promise.

Young faces of friends, some she hadn't thought about in years, now appeared so clearly in her mind's eye. What, she wondered, might they look like now, after fourteen years had passed? Other than Natalie, she'd not really kept in close touch with anyone, though over the years she had wondered what had become of those girls she had shared her adolescent dreams with. Well, soon she would find out, would spend an entire weekend catching up.

Jody leaned on the railing of the ferry as she made the crossing from Lewes, Delaware, to Cape May, New Jersey. Off the bow, a gull circled downward to the surface of the bay and emerged with a small fish in its black beak. Several hundred feet away, a small flotilla of sailboats swayed gracefully in the wind, and beyond, the power boats cut choppy grids in tic-tac-toe fashion across each other's wake. Farther out toward the Atlantic, larger boats headed to sea. Straight ahead lay Cape May, and farther up the coast, her destination. Sighing, she turned her face up to the sun to catch its warming rays, to let the sweet salty bay breezes swirl around her.

I wonder if The Osprey is still on the corner of West Bay and Corbin's Lane, if their chocolate milkshakes are still the best on the New Jersey shore . . . if Carney's General Store is still selling Playboy *magazine with plain brown covers . . . if you can still buy plastic sandals and rough-textured beach towels and garish lipsticks at the drugstore . . . if the rides on the pier are still as scary as they used to be . . .*

As the ferry began to dock, she pulled a map from her shoulder bag and checked her route for about the fiftieth time in the past two days. Satisfied that she could indeed find her way, she refolded the map and tucked it away. If all went well, she would be in Ocean Point in less than an hour. A tickle of anticipation rippled through her. Having come this far, she was anxious now for the journey to end.

The first thing that Jody noticed as she drove over the old drawbridge that led onto the island was that new marinas had popped up everywhere along the bay side of the town. Driving those first few streets into Ocean Point, it became apparent that the sleepy little seaside village of her childhood memory had been *discovered.* Developers had strung a line of new townhouses overlooking the marshes and constructed a house on every open lot they could get their greedy hands on. Coming to the intersection of West Bay and South Avenue, she pulled to the side of the road and just sat while she got her bearings.

If this is West Bay, the old firehouse should be on that corner, she reasoned, *and if that is South Avenue, there should be a park with swings and slides right there.*

No firehouse, no park, though the sign clearly announced the street names.

Well, it *had* been fourteen years . . .

Jody eased back into the travel lane, took a right, and cruised down Bay to Ocean Boulevard in search of the Sea View Motel, her home for the next week.

As promised, her room overlooked the ocean. She dumped her luggage on the king-sized bed and drew back the curtains, opened the sliding glass door, and stepped out onto the small, railed balcony to drink in the sight. Directly below her window, round tables shaded by tropically colored umbrellas were placed here and there around a glistening pool of pale blue water the same color as the sky overhead. Beyond the motel's stucco wall, the boardwalk separated the shops, houses, and restaurants from the beach. And the beach itself, well, that was pure New Jersey, with sand slightly darker and just a little coarser than that found on the Maryland shore. Even with the recent years' erosion, the expanse of beach was deeper than the beach in Bishop's Cove, allowing more happy vacationers to lay their towels and blankets side by side and end to end for as far as the eye could see. Here and there the lifeguard stands rose above the crowd, two figures upon the benches where only one had sat in the days of Jody's youth. More bathers, more lifeguards . . .

And Lord knows, there are more bathers, lined up like sardines in a can, she marveled, shaking her head at the sheer number of people on the beach.

Stepping back into the room and closing the screen behind her, Jody debated what to do first. Natalie and the others would not arrive until later in the day. Her hungry stomach decided for her. She would walk on the boardwalk and find a place to have lunch.

The air on the boardwalk felt close and hot, being trapped, as it was, between the buildings on one side and the sea on the other. With the stagnant land breeze came nippy little green-headed flies, and more than one person strolling past was swatting at the back of a leg or the top of an arm. Two blocks down, Jody found herself heading into a delicatessen just to escape the ferocity of the flies. She took a seat at the counter rather than wait for a table, and turned toward the doorway to watch the tourists pass by.

While waiting for her turkey sandwich, she picked up a copy of the local newspaper that someone had left on the seat next to her and skimmed through it. Advertisements for bathing suits and restaurants outnumbered the ads for local amusements, but not by much. Fascinated, Jody realized that Ocean Point now boasted not one, but two movie complexes that showed ten films at a time. Years ago, there had not been enough people in town to fill one such theater.

And pizza parlors! There were ads for a dozen or more.

Whale and dolphin cruises on the ocean, a cruise around the island, a cruise to Cape May. Seems as if one could cruise to just about anyplace.

Kayaks, jet skis, wave runners, sailboats, bicycles, inline skates, surfboards—all for rent at convenient locations along the boardwalk.

Fishing tournaments, deep-sea charters, sailboat races, summer basketball and baseball leagues—both male and female—bingo games and buses to the casinos in Atlantic City.

Oyster bars and salad bars, dock bars where one could sit and watch the other patrons arrive in their boats, all the while enjoying dinner and calypso music.

Jody shook her head. What had happened to the peaceful little town she remembered?

She finished her sandwich (a little on the dry side, the

bread a commercial brand loaded with preservatives to give it that soft and squishy feel) and side order of so-so cole slaw (too much mayonnaise, not enough onion) and frowned. You'd never get such fare at the Bishop's Inn, but then again, this being a boardwalk deli and the Bishop's Inn being, well, the Bishop's Inn, perhaps, she reminded herself, comparisons were unfair. She folded the paper and left it on the stool where she'd found it, paid her check, and walked back out onto the boardwalk. She'd take a walk, then maybe stretch out on one of those lounge chairs near the pool for a while, the beach being too crowded. Besides, she wanted to be around when Natalie arrived.

Jody had intended to confine her walk to the boards, but finding herself at the very end, decided to venture into town. She was anxious to see some of her old haunts. She went straight down Ocean Boulevard to Townsend, to the corner where the old drugstore once stood. Hands on her hips, she stood on the sidewalk outside and watched the steady flow of tourists as they flocked through the electronic doors of the block-constructed discount store. She wondered if Carney's General Store had fared any better. She headed down the street to the first traffic light and around the corner. Wonder of wonders, the old place still stood intact.

The same weathered brown shingles outside, the same bell over the door inside, the well-scuffed wooden floor underfoot. The old Formica counter where groups of girls gathered to sip sodas and gossip, the neat rows of produce from local farms, the small stationery department, two aisles of hardware, a meat counter, beach toys . . . oh, it was all so much as it had remained in her memory that for a long moment she thought perhaps she was dreaming.

"Are you being helped?" A young man of about twenty asked.

"Oh . . ." His voice had stirred her from her reverie. "I was looking for . . ." she glanced around for something she might need, then, spying the long rack of paperback books at the front of the store, said, ". . . something to read."

"Right up front," he pointed.

"Thank you," she smiled.

Jody thumbed through this book and that, looking for something that would strike her fancy, all the while pleased and amazed that this little piece of Ocean Point had remained intact while so much else had changed.

"Who owns this store now?" She asked as she paid for her selection, the latest romance by a favorite author.

"The Carney family still owns the store," the pleasant young man replied as he counted out her change.

"Really? Still?"

"Yes. It's been in the family for over eighty years," the boy said proudly.

"Which members of the family are still here, if I might ask?"

"My dad, Steve—I'm Steve, too—and my aunt Beth own it now."

A sudden image of Steve Carney, at nineteen the dream man of all the girls who were sixteen that last year, invaded Jody's memory. He'd been such a handsome thing, and wild, a real daredevil and a great athlete. Steve had been the only one who could swim out to Heron Island and back, no mean feat.

"Did you know my dad?" The young man was asking.

"Umm, sort of," she replied, wondering if daydreams counted. "We used to summer here, a long time ago. My family did, that is."

"Yeah, lots of people come back. They all stop in."

"I was almost surprised to see that Carney's is still here. Everything else seems to have changed."

"We've had a lot of offers to sell, but my dad and my aunt aren't interested. My brother and I figure that someday we'll be running it with a cousin or two." Steve Junior handed her the bag that held her purchase.

"Then I'll have to make it a point to stop back in about twenty years and see how you're doing." Jody smiled and turned toward the door, wondering what

Beth looked like these days. She'd been a short, bubbly chatterbox when their paths had last crossed.

Once outside, Jody debated her options. She could check out that new outdoor mall of shops near the marina. Or she could walk over to the bay side and out onto the old piers and watch the fishermen, or she could grab a towel and see if she could find a vacant spot on the beach. Or she could head back to the motel and soak up a little sun on one of those comfy-looking lounges by the pool.

She tapped her foot, debating, but not for long. It was too hot to shop, too hot to walk to the bay, she reasoned, and the beach had been overly crowded by noon. She'd opt for the motel pool. Tomorrow, she'd venture out early with Natalie and Lindsey and Mary Anne and the others and stake a claim for a prime section of beach where they'd sun themselves on blankets. Right now she had a great new book to read, a brand-new bikini to slip into, and enough of the afternoon left to enjoy both while she waited for her friends to arrive.

Chapter 3

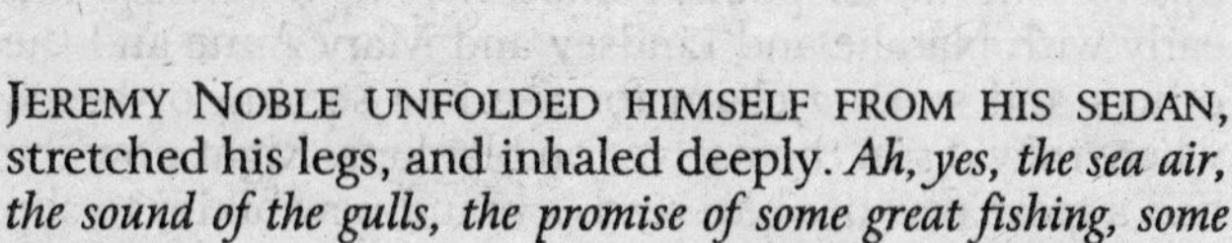

JEREMY NOBLE UNFOLDED HIMSELF FROM HIS SEDAN, stretched his legs, and inhaled deeply. *Ah, yes, the sea air, the sound of the gulls, the promise of some great fishing, some great meals, some great nights on the beach with the woman whose memory had drawn him here. Who could ask for more?*

He smiled to himself as he swung his bags from the trunk of the Maxima. He'd packed light, thinking he'd need little more than casual clothes—perhaps a jacket for dinner one night—and a few good books. And a healthy appetite. Ever since he'd made the decision to book a room at the inn, he'd been dreaming of Jody's cream of she-crab soup, her broiled sea trout, her flan.

Or had it been her face, her legs, her laugh?

"Jeremy!" Laura Bishop met him in the inn's spacious entry. "You're right on time. We've just finished getting your room ready."

"Hello, Laura," he accepted her hug and offered one in return. "How are things?"

"Very well, thank you. I'm so glad you decided to take me up on my offer and spend your vacation with us."

"Well, I really did need to take some time off. I couldn't think of anyplace I'd rather spend a week."

"The fishing's been great this summer, and the ocean's been warm. The weather's been perfect, and they're predicting more of the same for the next few days. You picked the right week." She walked to the reception desk. "Let me get someone to take you up to your room. I'd do it myself, but I'm a little busy right now."

"The room number's on the key," he said. "I can find my way."

"Are you sure you don't mind? I'm afraid we're a little short-handed this week, and we've had some unexpected reservations for dinner tonight."

"I don't mind at all." Jeremy took the key and smiled, thinking about tonight's dinner, wondering what might be on the menu.

He was sorely tempted to ask what was planned for the evening's fare, then decided he'd rather be surprised. Anything that Jody was making would be food fit for a king. And after dinner, he'd ask her to sit with him on the front porch where, over a glass of wine, they could pick up where they'd left off weeks ago. Then maybe tomorrow night they could walk on the beach, or drive out to Pierson's where a blues band played weeknights.

Humming happily, Jeremy took the carpeted steps two at a time, thinking perhaps he'd take a walk on the beach or maybe a stroll around town while he awaited the dinner hour and the opportunity to savor the soup and woo the chef.

"Will you be dining alone?" The young hostess asked when Jeremy walked into the crowded dining room that evening promptly at seven.

"Yes," he nodded.

"Then perhaps you'd like a seat by the window, where you can watch the osprey," she suggested. "There's a family nesting there on top of the telephone pole. Three babies," she said as she led him to his table.

"Thank you." Jeremy took the seat next to the wall where he could watch both the osprey and the room. He frequently dined alone, and watching other diners helped to pass the time. Not that he was in a hurry to conclude this meal.

"Hi," the perky waitress seemed to pop up from thin air. "May I bring you a drink while you look over the menu?"

"All I need to know is the fish of the day," he grinned.

"Red snapper," she replied.

"That makes it easy enough. I'll start with the she-crab soup, and go on to the snapper."

"Ah, you've been here before." The waitress nodded knowingly. "Everyone comes back for the crab soup. Now, can I interest you in a glass of wine to go with that?"

"Absolutely."

"I'll be right back with it."

While he waited, Jeremy amused himself by studying the table manners of a rambunctious three-year-old several tables away. His wine arrived at just about the same time that the harried mother decided that her fellow diners would enjoy their meals more if she and her son took theirs on the porch. She smiled an apology at the waitress as she left the room. Jeremy idly wondered where the husband/father might be. He'd never been either, but he couldn't imagine sending his wife and son off to a lovely old inn on a beautiful, romantic stretch of coast without him along to share the holiday with them.

The waitress appeared with a small white bowl of creamy liquid of the palest yellow. Jeremy dipped a spoon in, raised it to his lips, and tasted heaven. He sighed with contentment, eating slowly, making the most of the experience. He similarly sighed his way through his entree and his dessert. He accepted a second cup of coffee, which he carried with him into the kitchen to pay homage to the cook, the anticipation of seeing her again flickering inside him like fireflies. With luck, she'd be free later in the evening. He wanted to walk with her on the beach, watch the ocean breeze rustle her hair . . .

"Jeremy," Laura called from behind the long stainless steel counter, "how was your dinner?"

"Wonderful." He enthused, his eyes darting this way

and that, scanning the room for its customary occupant. "Fabulous. I just stopped back to thank the chef."

"You're welcome. I'm glad you enjoyed." Laura smiled and went back to seasoning the fish she had just placed in the baking dish.

It took a minute for Jeremy's brain to process this information.

Laura. In the kitchen. Preparing a dinner. And Jody was . . . where?

"Jody . . . ?" He asked.

"Oh, Jody's not here." Laura waved a hand and bits of dill flew here and there.

"Not here?" Jeremy frowned.

Jody not here? But the soup . . . the perfectly seasoned fish . . .

"She's on vacation. Thankfully, she made up several batches of she-crab soup and froze them to tide us over till she got back, and she left me with jars of her special seasoning already mixed for the fish. I hope I don't run out before she gets back." Laura raised her head, and saw the look of disappointment on Jeremy's face.

It was clear that he'd been hoping to do more than give compliments to the chef about her fish.

Laura smiled to herself. Of course. It would have been Jody that brought Jeremy back to the inn. She'd thought she'd sensed something running between them the last time he had been there. Laura brushed off her hands, slid the fish into the broiler, and motioned for him to follow her to the old rolltop desk at the back of the kitchen.

"There's a piece of paper under the right-hand edge of the desk blotter that has the phone number on it if you want to call her," she told him. "Would you mind getting it yourself? My hands are covered with herbs."

No, he realized, he did not want to *call* her. Talking would not be enough. He wanted to *see* her, wanted to be with her.

Laura peered over his shoulder as he lifted the small slip of paper, then said, "Yes, that's it. The Sea View Motel in Ocean Point, New Jersey."

Jeremy's insides twisted and clenched as if struck by a forceful blow, and his chest constricted tightly. One big hand reached for the edge of the desk and clutched it for support. The fog that filled his mind clogged his senses, and for a moment he could neither see nor hear nor feel.

Ocean Point, New Jersey.

"Jody will be there through next Saturday," Laura continued. "You may not be familiar with Ocean Point—I hadn't heard of it, either—but Jody said it's a small town on one of those little islands off the coast. She used to spend summers there when she was a child. Some of her old friends from high school were having a sort of reunion there over the weekend, and she's meeting up with them. She really did need a vacation, and this seemed like a fun idea. You know, getting together with old friends, looking back on your teen years. I think her girlfriends were staying just for the weekend, but Jody is staying through the week."

Only Jeremy's eyes moved, following Laura as she returned to her task.

Jeremy knew all about looking back. He had spent much of his adult life looking back on his own teen years, wishing he could reach back in time and change things.

Ocean Point, New Jersey.

Jeremy studied the slip of paper, committed the address to memory, and after thanking Laura, left the kitchen through the back door. His legs still slightly wobbly, he paused under the wisteria arbor, then followed the brick path that led around the side of the house to the front walk. As if in a trance, he crossed the street and stood atop the steps that led down to the beach, listening to the crash of the surf. He followed the sound and tried to sort through his options.

He could, of course, wait here until Jody came back.

Or he could leave and go back home, work out the week, and reschedule his vacation for the following week, then come back to the inn when she returned. Equally easy. Equally pain-free.

Jeremy's fingers closed over a large clamshell, and he flung it toward the sea. Of all places for her to have gone!

Ocean Point, New Jersey.

His mouth had gone dry, his lips parched. Jeremy sat down on the sand. He'd sworn he'd *never* go back. And in all these years, he had not. It was all too vivid in his mind's eye, the colors and sights and smells of that night where, in a matter of a few brief hours, Jeremy's entire world had been tossed upside down.

He squeezed his eyes closed to shut it out, but once it started, the whole thing played through. The argument with his stepfather over taking the car. Leaving home that night with his cousin T.J. Heading for the boardwalk in Ocean Point. Walking the boards and flirting with the pretty girls. Having one of those girls flirt back. Taking her hand and heading off for the amusement pier, where they rode the roller coaster until their throats were raw from screaming. Sitting on the beach watching the fireworks. Slipping off alone to a deserted stretch of beach where the eager young lady had taught him a thing or two.

Then later, searching for T.J. on the boardwalk, and not finding him, debating whether to call home and risk his stepfather's wrath when he was awakened from a sound sleep, or just walking the twenty-seven miles in the middle of the night and hoping to ease into the house before anyone had realized that he'd been out all night.

Jeremy had stood under a street lamp, jingling change in his pocket, then headed for the phone at the corner. His stepfather would be livid, but at least his mother would know where he was and that he was safe. He glanced at his watch as he listened to the phone ring on and on. It was ten past one.

Odd that no one had answered.

He had called again, just in case he had misdialed the first time, but there was still no answer.

Strange, the thought had niggled, that no one had

picked up the phone, as if they had all somehow just disappeared.

Distracted, he had stepped out of the phone booth and into the path of a late-model Pontiac. The driver blasted one short beep on the horn as the car swerved around him, then stopped and backed up. After loudly berating Jeremy for scaring him witless, the driver had offered him a ride, taking him as far as the first of the dirt roads that marked the entrance to the Pine Barrens, where outsiders rarely went and only a native would risk going on foot in the middle of a dark night.

Jeremy remembered listening to the night sounds, the shrieking of owls and something somewhere screaming a protest at having been caught in jaws or in talons. He remembered hearing a rustling now and then behind him, recalled an occasional finger of fear tapping his shoulders as his imagination conjured up the Jersey Devil, even though his intellect knew it was nothing more than a raccoon or a fox.

And back, far back, behind the trees, an orange glow had begun to spread.

Even now, sixteen years later, he could recall every detail of that walk through the pines, and the exact moment when he realized that somewhere deep in the forest, a fire was raging. Smoke began to fill the woods and filtered through the dry undergrowth like a heavy fog. A prick of alarm tickled the back of his neck, but fires in the Pines were common enough events. Didn't every good summer storm set off one or two? But there had been no storm that night, no lightning. And the blaze that rose above the pines and reached into the glowing sky was right about where his family's home would be, a mile or so as the crow flies.

Jeremy shook his head to clear it of the images that arose to haunt him, of the cabin burned almost to the ground by the time he got there, out of breath and his chest hurting from running the distance through the dense smoke. The line of volunteers—uncles, cousins, neighbors—manning a bucket brigade to bring water from the nearby stream in an attempt to put out the fire, for deep in the Pines there were no fire hydrants and no fire trucks.

The young man had not needed anyone to tell him that no one had survived the blaze. His mother, his younger brother, his stepfather . . . all gone in the blink of an eye.

Jeremy had never really been able to forgive himself for being out having fun that night while his family, overcome by smoke, had been swallowed by fire. He'd been convinced that if he'd stayed home that night, it never would have happened. He would have saved them.

He would have smelled the smoke. He would have put out the fire. They'd still be alive, he was certain of it.

If only he'd stayed home that night . . .

How could he go as far as Ocean Point, and not complete the journey to Crismen's Well?

He'd once believed that no power on earth could get him back. Yet here he was, sitting on a Maryland beach watching the day fold away, contemplating the very real possibility of doing just exactly that. He leaned back on his elbows and watched a heron cross the horizon on its flight back to its nesting place in the trees somewhere behind the dunes. Unconsciously his fingers traced little circles in the sand, and he tried to think it through.

If he spent the rest of the week at the inn, he could use the time to do some deep-sea fishing. Catch up on his reading. Maybe rent a boat and do a little crabbing out in the bay.

The easy way.

He sighed and thought about just how much the easy way had cost him over the years. An aunt had died, and he had resisted attending the funeral, because it would have meant going back. His old high school had invited him to a special ceremony honoring their star athletes, and he had declined, because it would have meant going back. He thought of those who were still there, back in the Pines, those who, over the years, had remembered him for weddings and christenings, and fought back the feeling that he had run out of excuses to stay away.

And yet, hadn't he somewhere, deep inside, suspected that the day would come when the time would be right and he would, in fact, go back?

Jeremy lay back on the sand, his arms under his head, watching the night turn on the overhead lights as one by one the stars became visible, and wondered if that time was now.

Chapter 4

JODY SLIPPED HER FEET INTO TURQUOISE RUBBER FLIP-flops and peered into her beach bag to make sure she had not forgotten anything. Sunscreen, a soft blue-and-white blanket, a beach towel, a small radio, a thermal mug of ice water, a package of crackers, flavored lip balm, the book she had purchased the day she arrived and had yet to finish. The long awaited weekend was over. She swung the bag over her shoulder and, locking the motel room behind her, set out for her first full day on the beach in many years.

It was early, not quite ten, when she descended the few short steps from the boardwalk to the sand—early enough that she would get a prime spot on the beach, late enough that the surf fishermen had taken their buckets of bait and disappeared till later that afternoon. She slipped off the flip-flops, wiggled her toes into the warm sand happily, and smiled. The sun was already blazing overhead, and a shift in the wind had banished the flies. She was going to enjoy every minute of this vacation.

Humming as she crossed the beach, she debated her options. Too close to the lifeguard stand and there'd be love-struck girls kicking sand on her as they jockeyed for the optimum positions to be noticed. Too close to the ocean and before noon, she'd be surrounded by toddlers. Selecting a spot that was just the right distance from both ocean and lifeguards, she spread her blanket on the sand and proceeded to make herself comfortable.

First the sunscreen, which she lathered on all those body parts left exposed by the bikini—which had somehow appeared to be more conservative back in Marlene's shop—and on her face. Her fair skin was already pink from the previous two days in the sun, and she didn't want to take any chances. Rolling the beach towel into a tubular pillow, she placed it behind her head, lay back, closed her eyes, and rested for a few minutes.

It was far too quiet. Yesterday and the day before there had been eleven of them there on the beach, laughing and chatting and becoming reacquainted. It had been great fun.

She turned on the small radio, found a classic rock station, and settled back down, thinking back over the weekend. How many of the girls had stayed the same. How many of them had changed. Sharon had gained forty pounds—ten pounds with each child, she had laughed self-consciously, waving several inches' worth of baby photographs under Jody's nose. Lindsey, their favorite ditzy blonde, had fooled everyone by not being quite so ditzy after all, having started her own interior design business right out of college and becoming wildly successful. Carla had fulfilled her dreams of law school, Julie had dropped out of college in her sophomore year to marry a navy man and moved to California where he was based. This one had stopped smoking, that one had started. Over the course of the weekend, Jody had waded through endless envelopes of photographs—weddings and babies, mostly, and everyone there had seemed to have a significant other.

Everyone but Jody, that is.

She squirmed a little, repositioning her hips and digging her heels into the sand.

Well, it wasn't that there hadn't *ever* been anyone in her life. There had been men, now and then, but there had always been something missing, somehow, no matter how handsome or interesting or attractive they had been.

She had tried to explain it to Natalie the night before. It just seemed that, all her life, the men she met had lacked that special *something* . . . that spark that made the difference between interesting and irresistible. Between handsome and to die for. Between attractive and I'll-follow-you-anywhere. Between sexy and sensational.

Natalie had laughed and said that Jody was too picky for her own good.

Jody had tried to explain that what she wanted—what deep in her soul she knew she needed—was a man who could turn her knees to jelly, a man who could make her bottom lip quiver with just a smile. A man who could turn her inside out by merely walking into the room. She'd had infatuations, she'd had one or two short-lived affairs that had left her knowing that there was something more, something bigger, deeper. She wanted passion. She wanted a man who could sweep her off her feet. She wanted to be swept away.

"You want *From Here to Eternity,*" Natalie had nodded knowingly. "We all wanted that, once upon a time. Unfortunately, most of us have had to settle for something less."

"I don't want to settle," Jody had shaken her head. "I've waited too long. I'm not going to settle."

"You could be very old before you meet a man like that," Natalie cautioned.

"I think I already did." Jody had sighed.

"What?" Natalie grabbed Jody's arm. "Where? When?"

And Jody had proceeded to relive that moment when Jeremy Noble had first walked through the big front door of the Bishop's Inn. A few inches over six feet tall, broad shoulders, a lean, athletic body. Brown hair that fell over his collar like fringe, deep blue eyes in a face more rugged than handsome. As a private investigator, Jeremy had walked into the chaos that followed Laura

Bishop's disappearance and had taken charge, commanded order, and surveyed the facts quickly and efficiently. With the help of Laura's brother and a family friend, Jeremy had led the search for Laura, had assisted in locating and returning her within twenty-four hours. Jeremy had been a rock, had never hesitated for a moment, had never doubted for an instant that Laura would be returned safely to her family.

Right then and there, Jody had decided that she wanted a man like Jeremy Noble. But then again, what woman wouldn't?

Jeremy, of the easy smile, the quick wit, and the sharp intelligence. Jeremy, who was brave in the face of danger, whose mere presence in the inn had made for several sleepless nights back in June when he'd stayed for a few days after Laura was found and brought home. Jeremy, who was as close to being a real hero as any man Jody had ever met.

Jody's fingers, sifting through the sand to the right of her blanket, located a broken piece of scallop shell, and absently, she began to make little roads with it in the hot sand.

If she'd been a different sort of woman, she'd have made an obvious play for Jeremy that week. But things had been so jumbled, the terror following Laura's abduction, then her rescue from a house that had been set afire, well, it just hadn't seemed like the ideal time to make a major move on one of the rescuers. It would have seemed, well, *tacky*. Inappropriate. Opportunistic, under the circumstances.

Although Jeremy *had* seemed interested in her.

Of course, that could have been the crab soup. Or the flan.

Jeremy had loved her flan . . .

To her left, a small band of teenage girls were claiming their turf, that very spot near the lifeguard stand that Jody had earlier rejected. Their laughter floated across the beach on a brisk sea breeze, and from the distance she watched their antics as they set up their multicolored towels, helped one another apply sunscreen, tossed one another paperback books or magazines.

Jody dropped back on her blanket and closed her eyes. The past weekend with "the girls" had brought back memories of summer days they had shared so long ago. From across the years, snatches of conversations drifted with such clarity that she opened her eyes and looked around to make certain that somehow she had not been thrust back in time.

The scent of Coppertone and the sounds of summer blaring on radios all across the beach had remained the same, though the anthems that year had been varied. That last summer they had baked in the hot sun to Springsteen's "Dancing in the Dark," the Pointer Sisters' "Jump," Steve Perry's "Oh Sherry," and Rod Stewart's "Infatuation," Huey Newton and the News' "The Heart of Rock and Roll," Madonna's "Borderline," and Lionel Richie's "Hello." Tina Turner's "What's Love Got to Do with It" was getting a lot of air time as the season had drawn to an end. Jody closed her eyes and drifted off, trying to remember the words to Cyndi Lauper's "Time after Time."

An hour or so later, disoriented from dreams filled with faces, snatches of conversations, and songs long forgotten, Jody sat up slowly. Yes, she was in fact there, alone, on the beach at Ocean Point. From her beach bag, she drew out her water bottle and took a long sip. The nap had relaxed her, had brought back that old, languid feeling of lying too long in the sun, oiled and content and having no particular place to go, nothing important to do. Jody had forgotten just how good that feeling was. She'd make it a point to take more time to sun herself when she returned to Bishop's Cove. She'd been spending entirely too much time in the kitchen and too little time on the beach.

Laura had often offered to hire someone to help Jody in the kitchen, but Jody had always resisted. Maybe she should give in and have Laura do just that. If it freed up even an hour or so each day, it would be worth it. She'd definitely discuss it with Laura when she went back. Right now, her body having absorbed all the sun it could tolerate, she would stroll down to the water and perhaps take a dip.

While she slept, the temperature had skyrocketed and the beach had filled in around her with bathers and sun worshippers of every size, shape, and age. She picked her way carefully through the noisy rows of towels and blankets that littered the beach, stepped around the sand castles built by busy children, made her way to the water's edge, and walked into the ocean without hesitation. It was colder than she'd anticipated, and she turned her back to the cresting wave that was just about to break. A second, unexpected wave slapped her from behind and she lurched forward. Turning back to face the sea, a third, larger wave broke over her without warning, spinning her around and dragging her out and under. She emerged with a mouthful of saltwater and the top of her bikini half filled with sand. She sought the cooperation of the next wave to wash out the sand and help her back to shore.

"That's some undertow," noted the middle-aged man who stood about three feet behind her, holding the hand of a six- or seven-year-old girl.

"You can say that again," Jody mumbled as she casually attempted to extract her legs from the ocean's clutches while at the same time seeking to salvage some dignity by pulling up the wayward top of her bikini.

She'd forgotten what it felt like to have the water pull at her like that. Next time she'd be more cautious and wouldn't just rush in.

"Ouch!" She exclaimed as a sharp pain sliced through the bottom of her right foot. Balancing on the left, she lifted the foot for inspection and found a gash almost two inches long, running blood. She must have stepped on a sharp piece of shell. As she dipped the foot into the water to clean it off, the little girl behind her yelled, "*No!*"

"What?" Jody asked.

"Sharks! If you get blood in the water, sharks will come!" The girl began to hop up and down.

"I think it takes a little more blood than . . ."

"Daddy!" The girl continued to shriek. "Make her stop! She'll make the sharks come!"

"She was watching the shark special on the Discovery channel last night . . ." Daddy smiled sheepishly, but did nothing to quiet the child.

Jody merely nodded and limped back to her blanket, trying her best to avoid getting sand in the offending cut that left a trail of red splotches across the beach. Plunking her butt unceremoniously on the blanket, she grabbed her water bottle and poured out careful drops to wash the sand away from the jagged wound in the bottom of her foot. Rummaging in her beach bag, she found a tissue, which she held against the cut until the worst of the flow ceased. She took a drink of the now warm water and lay back against the blanket again. Her short battle with the ocean had left her with the ball of her foot throbbing and an irritating sprinkling of sand under her bikini. She shifted uncomfortably and closed her eyes.

The sounds from the blanket to her left—those of a young mother inspecting the morning's collection of shells with her toddler—brought back memories of Jody's last summer as an only child, the summer before her brother Jack was born. Jody had been five that year, and the vision of those days on the beach with her mother returned now with crystal clarity. Jody had had a big yellow plastic bucket, and every morning right after breakfast, she and her mother would comb the beaches for pretty shells and interesting pieces of driftwood that had washed ashore during the night. At the beach, her mother's long, thick, dark brown hair—usually worn loose to fall in unruly curls around her pretty face—would be twisted into a long, casual braid that hung down the middle of her back. Jody had loved to sit behind her mother's beach chair and play with that braid, wrapping it around the back of her mother's head in big concentric circles or just holding on to it to feel its weight, tracing lines down her arms with the fat curl at the end.

It had been a long time since she'd thought about that, Jody realized as the warmth of the sun began to lull her once again. What, she wondered sleepily, had become of all those shells they had collected over the years . . .

A blast from a passing radio startled her, and she sat up, not quite sure how long she'd been reminiscing, but knowing it must be close to lunch time. Jody debated her options. She could walk up onto the boardwalk and grab lunch—assuring that she'd lose her prime spot on the beach if she vacated it for too long—or she could eat the crackers and drink water. Opting for the crackers, she munched and washed them down with the now *very* warm spring water. Finishing her snack, she decided to read for a while, turning onto her stomach and opening the book. She missed the chatter of her friends, and wished that one of them had stayed an extra day.

Last night they had gone en masse to the House of Crabs for seafood, where they had sat for hours laughing and talking. Tonight Jody had plans for a gourmet dinner at the highly touted Joanna's—reputedly the best restaurant on the island—at the end of the boardwalk. It was said that Joanna's chef had trained in Paris and made a roue like no other. Like all professionals who excel at their craft, Jody couldn't resist comparison, and planned to order one of his specialties tonight.

At least she'd have a great dinner, she sighed. Of course, after dinner, she'd end up back at her room—alone—where she would probably read until she fell asleep with the book in her hand.

Right now, what she really wanted was to cool off. A swim would be perfect, but a second trip to the ocean with its wicked undertow held little appeal. That left the motel's pool, only a short hop away across blistering sand. Gathering her things, Jody dug her flip-flops from the bottom of her bag and started a slow trek, favoring her cut foot, to the steps. Once back at the motel, she brushed off the irritating grains of sand that clung to her since her dip in the ocean and eased herself into the pool, which was surprisingly empty.

The water was cooling, soothing, and Jody floated easily for a few minutes, leaning her head back to allow her hair to fan around her. She began a languid lap the length of the pool, all the while trying to remember the last time anything had felt better than the water that flowed around her body. Soon she found a natural rhythm, and it carried her back and forth, back and forth. Reveling in the easy motions that took her from one end of the pool to the other, Jody swam until her arms began to ache. When she'd had enough, she walked to the shallow end and up the concrete steps. Grabbing her towel from the lounge where she'd left it, she leaned forward to dry off her hair when she sensed that she was being watched.

Jody glanced around the pool area, noticing that most of the other motel patrons seemed to be sleeping in the shade or engrossed in reading their books or magazines. Shaking off the sensation, she dried her legs, then spread the towel over the lounge. She would sit in the sun and allow it to dry her off while she too read. She slipped on her sunglasses, leaned back against the cushion, and opened her book.

She'd read no more than three pages when she felt it again, the feeling that someone's eyes were on her. This time, however, when Jody looked up, there was a man walking toward her. He was tall with dark glasses and brown hair, exactly like the hero she'd been reading about in her book. A shiver went up her spine. Surely he was a hallucination, a mirage born of sun and heat on the smoldering concrete around the pool. It would have to be so, because he looked exactly like . . .

"Jody?" The mirage stopped at the foot of her lounge.

Later she would recall thinking that, for a mirage, its voice was awfully deep and rich, much like the hot fudge on the sundae she and Natalie had shared the night before.

"Jody?" Her hallucination repeated, and she smiled, thinking how wonderful fiction was, how it could take you away and almost make you believe that . . .

The mirage grabbed her by the toe and gave it a tweak. She slid her glasses down onto her nose and looked up.

This had to be a dream.

"Aren't you going to say hello?" He asked, looking mildly amused.

"Jeremy?" She gasped. "Jeremy Noble?"

"Ah, so you do remember me. I was beginning to get a little worried there for a minute." He grabbed a nearby chair and swung it around so that he could sit next to her. Which was, in his estimation, preferable to standing there and looking down on that long, lean body.

Whatever had made him think that Jody was all angles? In her little bikini, she was all curves.

Jeremy sat.

"I hope you don't mind if I join you . . ."

"No. Of course not. I'm just so surprised to see you."

Had she said *surprised?* Perhaps *dazzled* said it better. Or possibly *incredulous* . . .

"What are you doing in Ocean Point?" Jody forced a nonchalance she wished she felt.

Jeremy leaned forward, his clasped hands falling between his knees, and he wondered if he should tell her the truth, that he had followed her. Just then she sat up and removed her sunglasses completely, and those amber eyes seemed to swallow him whole.

"I'm on vacation," he told her. That was the truth.

"Why, so am I!"

If she blinked, would he disappear? Was he in fact really there? Were her fellow loungers at this very moment exchanging nervous glances as she leaned forward and addressed what was, in reality, an empty chair?

"And it's been years since I've been to the New Jersey shore . . ." Also true.

"Me, too. I spent every summer growing up in Ocean Point."

"So did I."

"Why, that's unbelievable! Did we talk about that at the inn?" She frowned. Surely she would have remembered that, even in the midst of the craziness that had colored his stay there in June.

"No, we didn't. I just found myself with a few days off, and I decided to spend them at the inn." He stopped, feeling awkward. "Actually, the truth is that I just wanted to see you, Jody. Laura told me where I could find you. I hope you don't mind that I followed you here."

"You *followed* me here?" Had he really said that?

"I'm sorry, maybe I should have called you first. To see if it was okay with you. To see if maybe you had other plans. If you don't want me to stay, I can . . ."

"No. No. No other plans. Of course you should stay. Why shouldn't you stay?" She was totally flustered at the thought that this man had followed her from Maryland. "You should definitely stay."

"Great." He smiled and her heart did a flip-flop. "What are you doing for dinner?"

Chapter 5

IT WAS ALMOST EIGHT O'CLOCK WHEN JEREMY KNOCKED on Jody's door.

"I'll just be a minute," she told him.

Just until my hands stop shaking and I figure out a way to keep my knees from knocking together.

It had taken Jody almost an hour to decide what to wear. The red silk didn't seem appropriate, so she'd had to run out to one of the stores along the boardwalk and find something suitable. She hadn't planned on having to dress for dinner with the man of her dreams. The short blue sundress that she found at one of the little boutiques had been just right.

I wished him here, she thought, and the possibility filled her with a sort of power she'd never felt before. *I willed him here.*

One last glance in the mirror had her feeling like Cinderella about to set out for the ball on the arm of her prince.

"Hi," she said as she opened the door. The look in his eyes made her feel all the more like a princess.

"You look beautiful," he said simply, making her feel that it was true.

"Thank you," she blushed under her makeup and bit her tongue to keep from adding, *So do you.*

"Your hair . . ." He reached out a hand to touch the long curls that bore a pale shade of moonlight and drifted around her like a halo.

"I had it highlighted," she nodded, as if he couldn't see that for himself.

"It looks great." He slid his hands into his pockets, the urge to crush those soft ringlets was so strong. He cleared his throat. "Joanna's is just down the boardwalk, isn't it?"

"Yes." She grabbed her purse and checked to make certain her room key was inside, then stepped through the door that he held open for her. "I called and changed my reservations to a table for two. The receptionist here at the motel told me it was only a ten-minute walk."

It was a pleasant stroll along the boards to Joanna's and a picture-perfect night. Gulls cried here and there as they raced each other and the tide for the bits of marine life that landed unceremoniously on the shore, dumped by one wave, carried back out to sea by the next. Tanned children raced by, their parents hot on their heels, anxiously trying to keep them in sight lest they fade into the crowd and disappear before they reached the amusement pier at the opposite end of the boardwalk. A sunburned couple strolled by, their faces looking red and uncomfortable.

"Cute shop," Jeremy nodded to the storefront where large shells and all manner of kitschy things crowded the windows.

Jody glanced at his face to see if he was kidding.

"Might have to stop there on the way back and pick up something suitably hokey for my partner." He grinned.

She stopped in front of the window. "Is he the tacky tee-shirt type or the ceramic mug with obnoxious saying type?"

"Both," Jeremy nodded.

"Ah, well then. I'd say you're in luck. They have a bit of everything in there."

"I kind of like that little rubber hula dancer over on the side there." He leaned a little closer.

"The one that says 'I danced my grass off at Ocean View Beach'?"

Jeremy's laughter flowed through her like warm molasses.

"It's perfect," Jeremy nodded, taking Jody's hand. He doubted he'd find anything better—or worse, depending on how one looked at it—to take back to T.J., who after much protest had agreed to take over that last investigation that Jeremy hadn't been able to get to.

Well, of course he had. Just as Jeremy would have done for T.J. After all, they were almost brothers, weren't they? More or less . . .

Joanna's was a perfect wedding cake of a house, with a tower overlooking the ocean and a wraparound porch, all set upon pilings that raised the house far above the beach. The underside of the structure was open, which accounted, Jeremy noted, for the fact that the structure had been able to withstand the many storms it must have seen over the years. They took the stairs hand in hand and stepped through a screen door, heavily detailed with fretwork, into the relative cool of the handsome reception area.

"This definitely has atmosphere," he mused as he peered beyond the lobby into a small dining room where round tables were set to overlook the ocean.

"It's also supposed to have the best chef on the island."

"Do you have a reservation?" the hostess, in a white skirt and short-sleeved shirt and sporting a red plaid bow tie, asked.

"Yes," Jody nodded, giving her name.

The hostess scanned the list of reservations.

"Ted," the hostess signaled a passing waiter. "Table three in the Marina Room."

The waiter led them through one lovely room to the next to a table overlooking not the ocean, but the opposite side of the island where, before too much longer, the sun would begin to set over the bay. Having seated them and given them each a menu, he took their drink orders and disappeared.

"What are you having?" Jeremy asked after he had scanned the menu.

"Grilled Chilean sea bass," she told him, "and I'm toying with the idea of trying their crab soup."

"That sounds good. I think I'll have the same." The waiter reappeared with their wine at the precise second they folded their menus, and Jeremy ordered for them both.

Jody looked across the table and fought the urge to pinch herself.

"I still think it's the most amazing coincidence that you used to come to Ocean View," she said. "It's not as if it's a well-known resort."

"Actually, I grew up not far from here."

"Where was that?"

"Just a small town inland a bit."

"Oh? Which town?" She persisted.

"Crismen's Well." Just speaking the name aloud after all these years all but stopped his heart from beating.

"Do you have family there?"

"No," he said softly. "Not anymore."

"Your salad, madam," the waiter appeared, offering a welcome interruption. "And yours, sir. Another glass of wine, sir?"

Jeremy nodded dumbly.

"How long are you planning on staying?" She was asking, mercifully changing the subject.

"Till the weekend." He willed his pulse to return to normal, his palms to stop sweating.

"What are you planning on doing for the week? You don't look like the sunbathing type."

"You're right about that. I never could just lie there on the sand and bake. I thought I'd do some deep-sea fishing one day. The motel desk clerk said you can sign up for a charter down at the marina with just a day's notice. Do you fish?"

"I have, but it isn't something I'd do on my summer vacation. I'm more inclined to bake on the beach."

"Your skin is so fair," he commented, "you must burn easily."

Jody grimaced. "I do. I have to be really careful. I actually got a little more sun today than I'd have liked."

"Are you telling me that you'd spend a whole week at the beach just lying on the sand?"

"And that would be a mistake because . . . ?"

He laughed. "Don't you get bored? Aren't you motivated to do other things?"

"Other things such as?"

"Jody, Jody, Jody," he shook his head slowly. "One would think that, as a veteran shoregoer, you would know that the Jersey shore is more than sand and surf."

She laughed softly, the sound of it burying itself in his gut and digging in.

He smiled and continued. "I could stay here for weeks and never spend so much as an hour on the beach and never do the same thing twice."

"Okay, tomorrow, then. What do you have planned?"

He'd actually not thought to plan anything in advance, but once pressed, he responded easily. "Whale watching."

"Whale watching?" Her eyebrows rose in interest.

"Ever been?"

"Once, in Maryland."

"Did you see any whales?"

"Actually, no, we did not."

"Why not join me?"

"Sure. Maybe we'll even see some whales." She grinned as the waiter brought their soup. "And you're right, there are other things to see. Actually, I can't believe how much the area has changed. I wish I had time to see it all."

"To see what all?"

"Oh, everything. You know, there used to be some small islands out toward the marsh, on the bay side.

We—my friends and I—used to go over there, two to a canoe, and have lunch. I wonder if they're still there."

"You want to see it all, do you? The whole island?"

She nodded as she took a taste of the soup.

"It's wonderful," she sighed.

"Did you taste the little herb rolls?"

"Umm. Excellent."

It was all delicious, the chef living up to his reputation. To end their meal, they shared a slice of perfectly tart mile-high lemon meringue pie and sipped excellent coffee and watched the sun drift into the picture-perfect arms of a harlequin sky reflected in the tranquil bay. When the sun had finally set, Jeremy paid the check and held the back of Jody's chair for her, asking, "How does a walk on the boardwalk sound?"

"Great." She nodded.

Once at the bottom of the outside stairs, she bent over, saying, "Wait . . . just one minute . . ." and removed her shoes.

"I cannot tell you how good this feels." She sighed as she swung her shoes over her right shoulder.

Jeremy laughed. "You could have slipped them off in the restaurant, you know. I doubt anyone would have known under that long tablecloth."

"I'd never have gotten them back on. I cut my foot on a shell in the ocean today and it's killing me."

"You should have said something," he told her. "We could have done chili dogs and fries in shorts and bare feet tonight."

"And missed that incredible dinner?" She shook her head. "I don't think so."

"How 'bout some boardwalk fudge?" Jeremy pointed to the little wooden stand overlooking the beach.

Best Sweets on The Boards, the sign over the door announced.

"I couldn't eat another thing," she told him. "I may not eat again until Thursday."

"I'll have to buy some later in the week"—Jeremy pointed back to the fudge shop as they strolled past—

"for Mrs. Dane. And she'll probably be expecting some saltwater taffy, as well."

"Who's Mrs. Dane?"

"She's our secretary, T.J.'s and mine."

"Who's T.J.?"

"T.J. Dawson . . ."

"Ah. The *Dawson* in Noble and Dawson." Jody nodded. "What's he like?"

"T.J.?" Jeremy slowed his pace while he debated how best to answer, how best to describe the man who was not only his cousin, but his best friend since second grade, who had stood beside him through the worst of times, whose parents had opened their home to Jeremy when he'd had no home to go to, who'd made him part of their family when his own family was gone . . .

How do you describe a man like that and do him justice?

You didn't. You couldn't.

Jody would meet him, one of these days, and then she'd know. For now, all Jeremy could think to say was, "He's a great guy. You'll like him."

Their hands swung easily between them as they meandered down the boardwalk.

"Oooh! A palm reader!" Jody exclaimed. "Let's have our palms read!"

Jeremy laughed and allowed himself to be pulled by the hand to the open storefront where a woman in her mid-forties with teased red hair of a shade not found in nature sat at a card table filing her nails.

"Have a seat," she said without looking up. "I'll take the lady first."

Jody sat opposite the woman at the card table and dropped her handbag on the floor.

The woman tucked the nail file into a side pocket of her short shorts and pulled a pair of black-framed glasses from a worn cloth case. Slipping the glasses onto her face, she turned to Jody, reached across the table, and, without ceremony, asked, "May I?"

Jody placed both hands on the table, and the woman took both of them in her own.

"I am Anna," she told them. "And if you're expecting me to tell you that I am a descendant of gypsies, you'll be disappointed. But I do have a gift, and I'll share it with you."

For a price, of course, Jeremy mused, but said nothing. As a private investigator, he'd once been involved in breaking a ring of fortune-tellers who were fleecing elderly residents of several small communities in the Baltimore suburbs, and was only mildly curious about the boardwalk palm readers. After all, they were all the same, weren't they?

Anna turned Jody's hands over several times, then concentrated on the left palm.

"It is said," Anna told them, "that the left hand will show what was intended in your life, and the right will show what you have done with what you were born with."

She tilted Jody's hand toward the light.

"You have long hands," she said softly. "They tell me you have tact and sensitivity. The palm and the fingers are the same length, telling me that your instincts and judgment are balanced. Your hands are strong, you work hard, you have a great deal of energy."

She examined Jody's thumb and fingers, and nodded, saying as she went from one digit to the next, "Again, energy, an energetic will. You are ambitious. Prudent. You bring a certain artistry to your work."

You've got that right, Jeremy nodded imperceptibly. *Jody's flan is an art form unto itself . . .*

". . . and you love your work; you're very good at it and take great pride in your accomplishments. I see that you are independent; you enjoy the freedom to express yourself that you are allowed. You work for someone who encourages you to experiment, do you not?"

"Yes." Jody laughed a tad nervously. "Actually, I do."

"She . . . it is a woman, I see that . . . relies heavily

upon you. You enhance her business. She admires your creative spirit, your industrious nature."

Jody smiled and glanced up at Jeremy, who raised an eyebrow.

"Now, let's see what else there is here . . ." Anna's glasses slid onto the bridge of her nose and she pushed them back up with her index finger. "A touch of shyness, I see. Idealistic. A believer in romance, ah, yes, in love at first sight. And you are capable of great passion . . ." Here she glanced up with a half smile and said softly, ". . . as yet untested, but it is there. Now let's look at the lines . . .

"Long life, good character. A heart to be cherished, since it will be given completely but once." Anna lifted Jody's right hand and peered intently into the palm. "You have used your gifts well, you have exceeded your own expectations."

Anna folded Jody's hands, one atop the other, whispering as she did so, "You are entering into a new phase, with new challenges. Trust your heart to lead you, and you will not be disappointed. All you need is within your reach. You need only to take it."

Jody smiled and wondered if Anna really knew what she was talking about.

"And now, sir, if you would have a seat . . ." Anna gestured to the chair Jody was vacating.

"Oh, I think I'll pass," Jeremy waved Anna off. "Thanks anyway."

Anna smiled. She knew a skeptic when she saw one. Well, then, it would be his loss. "That will be twenty dollars for the lady's reading."

Jeremy pulled a twenty from his wallet and handed it to her. He took Jody's arm and steered her toward the narrow doorway.

Still, Anna couldn't resist.

"Your journey home is nearly at its end."

Her words stopped Jeremy in his tracks, as she had known they would.

"Before the week has ended." She whispered so that only he could hear. Then she nodded toward Jody and said, "For her sake, you'll go."

Jeremy forced a patronizing smile and saluted Anna as he turned back to the door, forbidding himself to dwell on her words. A lucky guess, nothing more. Isn't that the way the fortune-telling game was played? He tucked Anna's comments into a corner of his mind where he kept things he'd rather not think about.

Anna stood in the doorway and watched them walk away, mildly amused. Before the week was over, he'd see . . .

Jody slipped her hand through Jeremy's arm and asked, "What did she tell you there at the end?"

"Oh, just the kind of stuff they always tell everyone so that you go away thinking that they have some kind of psychic gift."

"I thought she was pretty good," Jody continued. "She certainly had my job situation pegged pretty well."

"Well, you play the odds often enough, sooner or later you'll hit one right on the money," Jeremy nodded, and having decided that a change of subject was called for, asked, "What would you like to do now?"

"Hmm, let's see." She stood in the center of the boardwalk, looking first to the left—toward the big amusement pier with its killer roller coaster and the water slides—then to the right and the more "gentle" rides, the ones suitable for children and adults who have recently had a large meal.

"Shelton's Pier?" She asked hopefully.

"Shelton's Pier it is." Jeremy smiled and took her hand.

Leisurely they strolled to the white picket fence that surrounded the amusement park.

"Oh, Jeremy, look!" Jody grabbed his arm and pointed off to her left. "Teacups! I remember riding the teacups with my mother when I was little. And look there, there's that little boat ride."

Laughing, he allowed himself to be led to the short metal fence that closed off the narrow waterway from spectators. Tiny passengers, strapped into tiny seats, held tightly to the sides of the miniature rowboats as they floated along, dragged by a pulley under the water to keep all moving at the same rate of speed.

"Oh, I remember riding in those little boats! I thought I was such big stuff, because I got to ride alone. You must have ridden in them lots of times, living just down the road."

He shook his head.

"How 'bout the merry-go-round?" She asked. "My mother and I used to go on together. It would always be our last ride. Then we'd stop for cotton candy on the way home. Did you use to ride the merry-go-round, Jeremy?"

"Once or twice."

"Ferris wheel?"

"Only until I became too cool for anything less than the big, nasty rides."

"Wait here," she told him.

Jody returned shortly with a string of multicolored paper tickets.

"We need three each for the merry-go-round, five each for the Ferris wheel." She held up the tickets. "Unless, of course, you're still too cool . . ."

Jeremy laughed and took her hand, leading her to the line for the big wheel.

Ten minutes later, they were strapped into a canary yellow gondola and watching the park patrons on the ground grow smaller and smaller.

"Look, from here you can see the lights from the marina," she said.

"And the lights from the roller coaster." He pointed to the south. "That's one wicked-looking machine, isn't it?"

"Oh, I saw it on Saturday night. A few of my friends went on, but I just couldn't bring myself to get on it."

"I'm game, if you are."

"After that dinner, I don't think so." She laughed.

"Maybe tomorrow night."

"Maybe. Look, there's the center of town. Three streets over from that red neon sign, on the bay side, is the house we rented when I was little. If it was daylight, we could probably see it from here. What a fun thought, to see the entire island from up above it all."

"Hmm," he rubbed his chin. "There's a thought . . ."

"When I was little, I used to think that you could touch the stars from the top of the Ferris wheel." Jody said when the ride came to an end and began its gradual release of passengers, giving each car a minute or so stopped at the very top of the wheel.

Her face was so near, tucked as she was into the crook of his arm, and her mouth was so close, that he never thought about kissing her, he just did. Her mouth was warm and sweet and still bore the slightest trace of lemon mixed with sea air. She tasted so good that he kissed her again, parting her lips with his tongue and tracing the contour of her mouth. Deeper and deeper, seeking more and more of her.

Had any woman ever been sweeter to taste, softer to touch? Had he ever suspected that it would be otherwise?

With her hands on either side of his face, she drew him back to her when she thought he would pull away. She'd never been kissed quite like that, and she didn't want him to stop, pure and simple, and so she kissed him until their car was making its last little swing to the platform where they'd get off.

They wandered around the amusement park, holding hands, but not speaking, until finally, on their third pass of the merry-go-round, Jody said, "There's a big black horse draped in scarlet and gold that's calling my name. Want to ride with me?"

"Sure."

Jeremy helped her to the platform when the ride had

stopped, walked with her through the crowd of children and young lovers who were threading their way through the handsomely painted mounts.

"Here's my horse," she said as she climbed atop the black horse to sit sidesaddle. "Are you going to ride? There's a pretty mean looking dragon over there that might suit."

Jeremy laughed and nodded in the direction of the bright green beast.

"I'd hate to have to fight an eight-year-old for him. I think I'll just stand here with you, if that's okay."

The music started and the carousel began to turn slowly.

"Ah, that must be the legendary gold ring," he said as they passed the wooden post where the ring hung from a small dowel. "I'm going to have to go for that, you know."

Lights twinkled on and off, the mirrored back of the carousel reflected the gaily decorated animals as they pranced past, faster and faster until the reflection was little more than a blur of color. As the ride began to slow, Jeremy walked to the edge, and holding onto the nearest post, waited to pass the wooden pole. Jody never did see him reach for the gold ring, but as they hopped off the ride, he slipped it onto the middle finger of her left hand.

"I'm afraid it's a little big," he apologized.

"Oh, you got it!" She laughed, delighted that he had done so. "I never thought that anyone ever actually got one of these things!"

"Beginner's luck." He shrugged, gratified that she was so pleased with so small a trinket. "I spent a lot of time on the boardwalk as a teenager, but I never spent much time riding the carousel horses."

"Not macho enough?"

"Not by a long shot. The Rattler, the Twister, the Sea Serpent—those were manly rides."

"Then I guess the spinning teacups were out."

He laughed and drew her close to him as they walked

past the arcade where boys in baggy pants and tank tops fed an endless supply of quarters into the machines.

"Now, how about that cotton candy you were talking about? Isn't that what you said you used to end up your nights on the boardwalk with?"

Jeremy purchased two paper cones of the spun-sugar confection, and handing her one, said, "You have to wonder just who thought up this stuff."

"It's awful," she said as nibbled.

"Umm. Disgusting." He agreed.

"It's so *summer,*" she sighed. "Cotton candy and boardwalk fudge."

"Saltwater taffy and snow cones."

"Boardwalk pizza."

"Boardwalk fries."

"With cheese."

"Uh-uh. Old Bay seasoning."

"Ooh, that sounds good, too."

"Maybe tomorrow night we should just do boardwalk for dinner," Jeremy said as they arrived back at the motel. "And later, we can take on the roller coaster."

"Not after a meal of boardwalk food."

"Hmm, good point."

"Oh, look. People are swimming in the pool there. Want to join them?"

He glanced at his watch.

"Not tonight," he told her. "I have to get up early tomorrow. And so do you."

"I do?" She frowned. "Why?"

"Because there's something we want to do."

"There is?"

He nodded.

"How early?"

Jeremy appeared to be calculating something.

"Well, if we want breakfast first, we should probably meet at the coffee shop here in the motel by about five."

"And if we don't want breakfast?"

"Five-thirty should do it."

"Are the whales up that early?"

"Whales? Oh, no, that's not whale-watching time. That'll be later in the day. This will be something else. Something special."

"What?"

"It's a surprise," he told her. "You'll just have to wait till the morning to find out."

They stopped in front of Jody's door and she handed him her key when he reached for it. He pushed open the door with one hand and turned on the lights for her.

"So. You game? Five A.M.?" He asked as he gathered her in his arms.

"Yes," she told him as his mouth lowered to meet hers. "I'm game."

He kissed her until something inside him told him he'd better stop while he still could.

"I'll see you at the coffee shop at five," he said, closing the door behind him.

Jody dropped her shoes on the floor and sat on the edge of the bed and held up her hand. The thin band of mystery metal on her middle finger gleamed like the finest gold. She lay back across the bed, dazzled from kisses she could still feel, right down to her toes, and wondering what incredible surprises tomorrow might bring.

Chapter 6

"AH, THERE YOU ARE." JEREMY COULDN'T HELP BUT grin as Jody half stumbled into the lobby at 5:35 the next morning wearing gray shorts and a hooded sweatshirt of the same color.

"Here's part of me, anyway." She covered her mouth to yawn. "The rest of me is still sleeping peacefully back in room three seventeen."

He handed her a tall cardboard cup and said, "You'll be wide awake in a few minutes, I guarantee it."

"Is that coffee?" She sniffed and sighed. At that moment, it smelled like heaven. She could have wept. "Bless you. I need this. You're a prince, Jeremy Noble."

"I am indeed." He took her elbow and guided her through the door and into the parking lot.

"It's still dark out. You know, back at the inn, I'm up every day by at least this hour. But for some reason, I just haven't wanted to get out of bed all week."

"That's 'cause you know you're on vacation and you think you should be sleeping late. But trust me. This will be worth getting up early for." He opened the door to the Maxima and stepped back so that she could slide in.

She could have told him that she'd gladly get up at five any morning, just to look at him. Instead, she asked, "What's *'this'?*"

"You'll see." He grinned and turned on the ignition.

They drove through quiet streets, those same streets that just the night before had been teeming with life. Jody sipped at her coffee, grateful for his thoughtfulness, and tried to guess what surprise he might have come up with.

She hoped it wasn't deep-sea fishing.

"We're almost there." He glanced over and added, "You might need that hood. It might be a little cool."

"Give me a hint."

"Too late. We're there."

He rounded a deep bend in the road and pulled off to the side, to a clearing where several other cars were parked on a sandy lot lined with a narrow row of scrub pines.

"This way," Jeremy motioned to her, and in the growing light she could see that his eyes were dancing—with mischief or pleasure, she wasn't sure which.

Jody followed him down a path leading through the sparse stretch of trees, her curiosity piqued.

"I know. We're going to watch the sun rise." She caught up with him and tucked her arm through his, still holding her coffee cup in one hand.

"Yes." He grinned, and stopping at the end of the path, he pointed straight ahead. "From a slightly different vantage point."

Jody stopped, drop-jawed, in her tracks, and stared at the brightly colored balloon that rose fifty feet above her head.

"It's a . . . it's a . . ." she stuttered and pointed.

"Hot-air balloon," Jeremy grinned, taking her hand. "You said you wished you could see the entire island from up above. Well, this morning you'll get your wish."

"From the air," she whispered, horrified as she stumbled along behind him. "I'm not sure that I really meant that I wanted to see it from the *air* . . ."

He laughed and squeezed her hand.

"Alan Dember?" He called to the tall, thin man inside the balloon's basket.

"Right." Busy checking something near the burner, the man responded without turning around.

"Your ad said first come, first served."

"You're the first," Dember called back over his shoulder. "Climb aboard."

"Climb aboard," Jody repeated dumbly.

"Just swing your leg over. Here, like this," Jeremy demonstrated and helped her over the side.

"We'll be ready for takeoff in just a few," Dember told them.

"You're the pilot?" Jody asked anxiously. "Are you certified or whatever it is you have to be to fly one of these things?"

Dember laughed. "Certified by the FAA, just like an airplane pilot. The balloon is regulated by the FAA, too, so it's subject to inspections and has to meet certain standards, just like a commercial jet. That make you feel any better?"

"Not really," she said under her breath.

"Well, then, if you're ready, I'm ready," the pilot told them, a bit too cheerfully, Jody thought.

How could anyone be that cheerful about going up into the air in a basket held aloft by a balloon?

Jody looked up above her head to where the enormous balloon seemed to fill the sky. It looked like a party balloon. A very large party balloon, but a party balloon all the same. She was just about to tell Jeremy that she'd wait for him on the ground when Dember yelled to the crew, "Untie her. We're going up."

"We're going up." Jody clutched at Jeremy's arm.

"Wait till you see the sun coming up over the water, Jody. It's like nothing you've ever seen, I promise."

"I've seen it from the beach," she said. "I liked it from there."

There was a whooshing sound from the burner, and she felt the basket begin to rise slowly. Panic began to overtake her, and she grabbed the edge of the basket, then made the mistake of looking down, rather than out or up. Below her feet, she could see lights from the cars below.

"Jeremy, we're in a basket," she told him. "You can see through it."

"It's okay, Jody, it's perfectly safe."

"Baskets are for flowers, Jeremy. Potted plants. Newspapers and magazines. Baskets are not for climbing into and flying over the ocean." Jody's eyes were closed, her hands clammy with fear, and it was then that Jeremy realized she was truly afraid.

It had never occurred to him that she might be afraid. He put one arm around her and drew her to him, and with the other brushed her hair back from her face.

"Jody, it's okay. It's safe, I promise."

"Where exactly are we going?" She asked, still not looking beyond Jeremy's chest.

"Wherever the wind takes us," the pilot nodded happily.

"Any idea where that might be?"

Dember laughed. "It isn't quite as random as you think. I get reports on wind speed and direction before each flight."

"Wind direction. Speed. Can't those things change?" she muttered.

Their pilot nodded. "They can. They do, at varying altitudes."

"How do you control this thing?"

"By adjusting the altitude of the balloon," he told her, and realizing that his passenger was more than just a little scared, took her arm and turned her to the burner. "Now, if we need to rise above an air layer, we heat the air inside the balloon a little. If we want to come beneath a layer of air, we vent it, let a little of the air out to drop the balloon. We use liquid propane gas, by the way, just like a barbecue. It burns quickly, to heat the air inside the balloon quickly, which allows me to make it ascend or descend as quickly as I need it to go. It's safe, I promise. I do this every day. I've never lost a passenger yet."

"That's reassuring." She nodded.

"Here now, hold on. We're going up just a little higher."

"More good news . . ." Jody squeezed her eyes closed.

"Jody, look," Jeremy said gently. "Look at the sky. Did you ever see anything more beautiful? Colors more glorious?"

She peeked out around his shoulder, and in spite of herself, an "Oh!" escaped her lips.

"It's . . . it's like floating up into heaven," she exclaimed. "Oh, Jeremy, look at the clouds. And the ocean looks so *blue.* It looks bluer from here. And look at the boats out there . . . oh, it's amazing."

Jeremy smiled. He'd hoped that one look would make her forget her fear, and it had.

"And look down there, at the way the waves curl toward the shore . . ."

Jody was really loosening up.

"Can we go back over the town, over Ocean Point?" She asked the pilot.

"We will, on our way back to the launch pad. My intention is to go on down to the end of the island, then swing back inland a bit, then try to get back to where we started. If the wind cooperates, that's what we'll do. If it doesn't, then our chase crew will meet up with us at another landing site."

"How will they know where to find us?" She frowned.

"Radio," he pointed to the floor where the radio sat between his feet. "But so far, the winds have been good. Spectacular sunrise, would you say?"

"Definitely," she sighed.

"Feeling better?" Jeremy asked softly.

"Much," she nodded, and turned in his arms to look into his eyes. "Thank you. This was a wonderful surprise."

"I'm sorry that you had a few bad moments there. I should have asked you first how you felt about hot-air balloons."

"I'm glad you didn't ask. I'd have said no and I would have missed this and I'd never have known what it felt like to watch the dawn over the ocean from the *air*. It's glorious, Jeremy. Everyone should see this, just once. Thank you so much for sharing this with me."

"You're welcome." He slipped both arms around her and nudged her into leaning against him, thinking that there was so much more he wanted to share with her. So much more he *would* share with her.

"And over there, off to the left, you can see all those trees there," their pilot was saying above the whoosh of the burner. "That's the start of the Pine Barrens. Of course, most folks around here call it the Pinelands, or just the Pines, since they know there's nothing barren about the area, which covers over a million acres. In 1983, the United Nations designated the Pines as an International Biosphere Reserve, 'cause there are species of plants back in there that are endangered or extinct every place but here. If we were to get close enough, you'd be able to see that the Pines are crisscrossed with a number of slow-moving streams of fresh water. You have your swamps back in there—cedar swamps, mostly American white cedar. Water the color of tea. Sphagnum moss everywhere. It used to be a big business, gathering sphagnum moss to sell. Still is, in some parts."

"You know a lot about the area," Jody turned to the pilot.

"My mother was a Piney," he told them. "Used to be a certain stigma attached to the word *Piney,* but these days, people are more proud than ashamed of the term."

"Why's that?" She asked.

"I suspect it's just a matter of coming to understand and appreciate the culture for what it is. Ethnically, the people here are a wonderful mix. German, Scottish, Irish, Swedish. Some Quaker, some Catholic. Russians. New England fishermen who came south to follow the whales before New Jersey was even a colony. I've heard even Hessian mercenaries who deserted after the Battle of Trenton came to lose themselves in the wilderness. Some still speak the dialect, back in there." Dember turned to Jeremy, who had been silent during the pilot's recitation, and asked, "You ever been?"

Jeremy had not expected the question, and his eyes drifted over the endless acres of green that now spread out below them like a fan. "Yes. Yes, I have. But not in a very long time."

"Beautiful, don't you think?" Dember's eyes were shining. "It's still wild. People too often think of New Jersey as being, you know, one overpopulated, polluted city after another. If they could only see this, the miles of forest . . ."

The pilot's voice droned on and on, extolling the virtues of the Pines and its history. And all the while, Jody was watching Jeremy's face.

His eyes followed the sea of green below even when Dember had switched course and had headed back toward the island. His face seemed touched by melancholy, his smile gone, his mouth taut, and he was, for an instant, a million miles—or a million acres—away.

". . . but right now, we're over the bridge leading to Ocean Point. You see the bay there, and off to the left you can see the yacht club, the marinas . . ."

"Jeremy," Jody tugged on his sleeve, "where did you go?"

He looked down at her, a sadness in his gray eyes, and said simply, "Home, Jody. Just for a minute, I went home."

She wanted to ask him where home might be and why the thought of it disturbed him so. Maybe, before the week had ended, she might learn.

"Now, right there's the park . . ."

"Oh, and Jeremy, look! Down there. Right down there. There's the street where our old rental house was. The third street in from the bay! The house was right in the middle of the block, the seventh one . . ." She counted the rooftops. "There! That one! Back then, the roof wasn't *blue* . . ." She tried to bring him back. "Do you see?"

"Yes," he nodded idly, still looking back over his shoulder to the blur of green that was diminishing in size as the balloon headed in the opposite direction.

Later, when the balloon had landed and they had thanked their pilot for a wonderful ride, as they sat in a diner—all chrome and glass—and waited for their breakfast to be served, Jody sensed that he was still not completely with her.

"Seeing the sun over the ocean like that, the colors . . . that may have been the most unforgettable moment of my life," she said, hoping to draw him back.

He nodded and said, "Good."

"What was yours?"

"My what?"

"Most unforgettable moment."

He stared at her for a very long time, and she began to regret having asked the question when he replied quietly, "I'm hoping it hasn't happened yet."

Jeremy leaned back as the waitress set down a white plate from which an enormous omelet threatened to overflow. "Maybe it will be this afternoon. You up for a little whale watching?"

And just that quickly, he had put it aside—whatever it was—and kept it hidden through the rest of the afternoon.

"This is incredible!" Jody shouted to Jeremy above the loud hum of the boat's engine. "It's been so long since I've been out on the ocean, I'd forgotten how much I used to love it."

Jeremy smiled and pointed to the left of the bow where a dozen or more dorsal fins broke the surface of the water, all at the same time.

"Oh, look at them!" Jody cried, leaning over the side of the boat to trail her hand through the water.

"Miss, try not to touch the dolphin," the weathered

old guide told her. "Sometimes we humans have substances on our fingers that can cause skin irritations for them."

Jody removed her hand, but the rest of her remained as it was against the railing. The dolphin swam so close to the boat that she could have touched them, would have, had it not been for the warning. Much to the delight of the passengers on the boat, the dolphin leaped from the water, splashing their audience and playing with gleeful abandon for ten or fifteen minutes before swimming off. Jody turned to watch them, realizing for the first time just how far they were from shore.

"It's only a mile," Jeremy shrugged.

"I feel better when I can actually see land," she told him, looking down into the dark blue green of the ocean and wondering just how far below the bottom might be. Then again, she told herself, there are some things we are better off not knowing.

"There's a whale off the bow!" The shout went up, and all forty passengers rushed to the left side of the boat.

"Maybe now might be a good time to go up to that second level," Jody said nervously as the boat seemed to list to one side.

Jeremy laughed as he took her hand and led her up the narrow steps.

"There, now," he said once they reached the top. "Feel better now?"

"I do. It just seemed a little too crowded for comfort down there. Oh, Jeremy, there's the whale! Look at it! It's as big as a bus!"

"Bigger," he nodded, admiring the creature's agility, in spite of its size, as it turned and dived. "Look, there's a second."

Her eyes followed his finger to the right of the large mammal, where a smaller one had surfaced. In awe, they watched the two enormous creatures frolic before disappearing beneath the dark waters and appearing again some yards away, over and over, until finally they were farther out to sea than Jody wanted to be. She was grateful to hear the boat's engine as the captain prepared to turn the vessel about and head toward shore.

Overhead a gull swooped low to the water, searching, she guessed, for a mid-morning snack. The sun had burned away the rest of the clouds, and she wished she had worn a hat to keep the sun from her face.

A boy of about ten ran across the deck and stood atop the back of the bench seat.

"I don't think that's a very good idea," Jeremy told him calmly. "If the boat lurches, you could get tossed over the side."

"So what? I can swim." The boy said rudely over his shoulder.

"Think you can outswim him?" Jeremy pointed toward the water, and the boy's line of vision followed his finger to the dark fin that had just broken the surface of the water.

Jeremy stood to grab the front of the boy's shirt to pull him down onto the seat and to safety. The child landed with a plop, his face white and his eyes as big as saucers. "That's a shark," he said dumbly.

"That sure is." Jeremy agreed.

"Bobby, there's a shark," the boy called to the thin, dark-haired boy who poked his head out from the doorway.

"A real shark?" Bobby ran to the railing to see. "Hey, everybody, a shark! A shark!"

"So much for tender moments," Jeremy grumbled as the shark circled around and came back towad the boat.

"Hey, mister! How big is that shark?" The boy in the striped shirt asked.

"Maybe fifteen, sixteen feet long. He's a big one," Jeremy told him.

"Wow! If I had fallen in . . ." his eyes widened even more at the prospect.

"Shark bait," Jeremy nodded.

The two boys exchanged an anxious glance, then

headed for the steps and made a noisy decent. Jody laughed. "You scared the bejesus out of them."

"There are some risks not worth taking," he told her as he pulled her closer, mindful of her sunburn, "and there are some that are. You, Jody Beckett, are a risk worth taking."

"What risk . . ." she managed to ask before his mouth, ever so gently, reached her own.

It was more caress than kiss, more a gesture of longing than fulfillment, but beneath its tenderness there was a promise of something more, something deep and powerful and *total.* Jody wondered how long she would have to wait before its promise would be kept.

Chapter 7

"I CAN'T REMEMBER WHEN I HAD MORE FUN," JODY laughed as she unlocked the door to her motel room. "But, oh, man, that roller coaster is a demon! I thought I was going to pass out."

"That's why they call it the Jersey Devil," Jeremy closed the door behind them.

"Oh, but the worst was the Serpent! Who ever dreamed up that ride should be tortured unmercifully!"

"I could tell you hated it," he grabbed her by the arm and pulled her to him. "That's why you had to go on it four times."

Jody's face was still flushed from that last roller coaster ride, her eyes still sparkling from the excitement of that last downhill spiral, her lips still touched with the last bit of pale pink cotton candy. Jeremy could not resist the urge to remove that trace of spun sugar from the corner of her mouth. He licked at it with his tongue, until she turned her head just slightly and parted her lips to meet his tongue with her own and to invite him to taste deeper and deeper.

Jody's arms had found their way to his chest, then to his shoulders, then to the sides of his face. His hands slid down her body, then back again, sending warming waves of keen sensation to ripple through her. Everywhere

Jeremy touched her, she seemed to melt, skin and bones. When his mouth moved to her throat and traced a hot sweet line to her shoulder, the warmth shot straight to her belly and lower. She drew his mouth back to her own and drank him in. Jeremy's hands sought and found the soft swells of her breasts and grazed them once, twice, three times, each successive passing lingering a little longer to tantalize her eager flesh. She took one slow step backwards, then another, then another, until she felt the edge of the bed behind her. His hands slid down to her hips, drawing her body tightly against his own, his mouth possessing hers.

"Jody . . ." he whispered into her neck. "Jody . . ."

"Don't stop, Jeremy." She pulled him onto the bed with her. "Please don't even think about stopping . . ."

In a heartbeat, he was everywhere, his mouth was everywhere, his hands were everywhere, and Jody was lost on a turbulent sea that spun her around and around and turned her inside out. She shed her clothes, item by item, and Jeremy hungrily devoured every inch of newly exposed flesh. Every bit of her ached with wanting him, every fiber of her body craved him. A soft moan escaped her lips, and she arched her back, demanding yet still more of him, more of the hot sweet rhythm that spurred her on. When his mouth found her breasts, she all but screamed. When finally, he slid inside her, she took him in eagerly. When he began to rock inside her, she urged him on impatiently. And when he had shattered inside her, she wanted him all over again. Jeremy, being a gentleman, did not make her wait.

The alarm on Jeremy's watch went off at four-thirty. A sleepy hand slapped at the top of the bedside table, seeking the source of the irritating sound.

"What time is it?" Jody muttered, her eyes still closed.

"Four-thirty," he told her.

"Didn't we just go to sleep?" She grumbled.

"About an hour and a half ago," Jeremy laughed.

A few minutes later, she asked, "Why?"

"Why what?" His hand stroked her arm gently.

"Why did the alarm go off at four-thirty?" She snuggled into his arms, completely at home there.

"Because I have to run back to my room and change my clothes, then get myself to the marina before five. I have a date with Captain Helmet." He kissed the tip of her ear. "It isn't too late, you know. You can still come with us."

"Captain Helmet," she muttered. "Oh. The deep-sea thing. No, no, thank you. I'll just relax on the beach while you and Ahab chase the giant white tuna or whatever's running this week."

He passed a loving hand over her thigh as he swung his legs over the side of the bed.

"I should be back by early this afternoon," he told her as he stood up and stretched.

"If you catch fish, what will you do with them?" She sat up and opened her eyes. "Keep them in ice in the bathroom sink?"

"Helmet will have your catch cleaned, frozen, and packed in ice when you're ready to go home. That's part of his service."

"That Helmet thinks of everything." She flopped back on the pillow, her hand reaching out to the warm spot next to her where he had been.

In the dark he pulled on his jeans, and in the faint light from the balcony she could see him sliding on the shirt he'd worn the night before.

"Be careful," she said softly. "Don't fall overboard."

"Not a chance." He leaned down and kissed her solidly. "I'm just beginning to really enjoy this vacation."

"Me too."

"Good." He kissed her again. "I'll see you later."

When Jody awoke several hours later, she was humming.

She rolled over, a smile on her face, and ran her hand

across the pillow where Jeremy had laid his head. The smile widened as she thought back to the night before.

Endless kisses, endless pleasure, endless joy.

Had that really been her, Jody Beckett, behaving in so mindlessly wanton a fashion, doing things she'd once blushed to merely read about? What in the world had come over her?

Jeremy.

Sweet, gentle Jeremy, who had made love as much with his heart as with his body.

Passionate, sexy Jeremy, whose inventiveness and exuberance had kept her up almost all night.

Jeremy, who had stunned her with the intensity of his ardor, captivated her with the depth of his tenderness.

And it had all been so right, so natural.

Well, she grinned as she sat up and stretched her arms over her head, she'd wanted to be swept off her feet, and she had been. Completely. Miraculously.

She glanced back at the clock. Nine-thirty. Jeremy said he expected to be back from his fishing trip by early afternoon. She'd have a leisurely breakfast by the pool, then soak up some sun until he returned. Still humming, she went into the bathroom, wondering if tonight—if any other night—could possibly be as wonderful as last night had been.

The water in the pool had been warmed by a blazing sun until it felt more like bath water, but still, it was wet and much closer than the ocean that lay at the other side of the burning sand. Jody took her second dip of the morning in a futile attempt to cool off, then returned to her lounge to lie on her stomach and read her book. The big clock on the wall that surrounded the pool had told her it was now eleven. Jeremy wouldn't be back for a few more hours.

The next time Jody looked up from her book, the clock said noon. She grabbed a yogurt and a fruit salad from the poolside vendor and tried to resume reading, but the midday heat was stifling. She set the book aside, then walked into the pool again, where she floated aimlessly on her back, her face to the scorching sun. She ducked her head under water several times to cool off a little before she got out of the water and flopped back on her lounge. It wasn't yet one o'clock. She closed her eyes and, lulled by the sun, fell into a deep sleep. Jeremy would wake her when he got back. Which should be soon . . .

"Hey! Sleepy-head!" The voice seemed to float freely through her dream.

"Jody, wake up."

She opened her eyes to see Jeremy leaning over her.

"Oh." She smiled and stretched languidly. "You're back. Did you catch anything?"

"Big tuna," he grinned and moved her legs to one side of the lounge to make room to sit beside her. "Lots of big tuna. It was an incredible day, Jody. The tuna were running like I've never seen them run before. That's why we're so late coming back in. No one wanted to leave. Helmet said they should all be cleaned and ready to be picked up by tomorrow. I'm thinking we'll ask the chef at the restaurant here"—he gestured to the motel—"if he can bake a piece of it for us tomorrow night. Then maybe we'll take the rest back to the inn. We can share it with Laura and her guests. What do you think? Helmet says I should have about a hundred and twenty pounds after it's cleaned and cut up."

"I think it sounds wonderful." She raised a hand to shield her eyes from the sun. "I just happen to have an incredible recipe for tuna."

"Somehow, I knew you would." Jeremy leaned forward to kiss her. "Now, what would you like to do for dinner tonight?"

"Whatever," she took his hand in hers. "Whatever you want to do. We have hours to decide."

"Not so many hours," he told her. "It's almost five."

"Five!" She shot up to a sitting position. "How could it be five?"

"Now, don't tell me that you lazed the day away," he teased.

"I must have slept all afternoon," she said, a touch of confusion in her voice.

"Well, then, you must have needed the sleep." He leaned down and kissed her again. "And my guess is that you'll be up late again tonight, so it's a good thing that you got lots of rest today."

"What about you?" She draped a lazy arm around his neck.

"I'm used to keeping erratic hours in my work, so it doesn't bother me so much. But I think I will go back to my room, take a cat nap and get a quick shower. How 'bout if we plan on six-thirty, seven, for dinner? One of the other guys on the boat today was telling me about a great seafood place a few blocks into town."

"Sounds great. That will give us lots of time to walk off our dinner afterward and maybe still sneak in a roller coaster ride later on."

"Nah, tonight we're taking on Nessie." His eyes twinkled with mischief.

"What's Nessie?"

"A brand-new, state-of-the-art, guaranteed-to-terrify new ride down in Ocean City. I thought maybe we'd take a ride down after dinner and check out their boardwalk."

"I haven't been to Ocean City in a million years. But wait." She grabbed his arm. "Is Nessie one of those rides where you stand up and get strapped into a harness—"

"Yup." He leaned forward and kissed her mouth. "Upside down and backwards."

Jody collapsed back onto the cushion and groaned.

"We'll save Nessie for the end of the night," he laughed, "and you'll have the drive back to the motel to recover."

"I don't think that the human body was intended to hang upside down and spin around at a high rate of speed, Jeremy. At least, I don't think that mine was."

He laughed again and kissed the end of her nose, then stood up to leave. He seemed to stare at her for a long moment, then removed his sunglasses and appeared to take a second look.

"Jody, how long have you been out in the sun today?"

"Since about ten or so."

"Did you use sunscreen?"

"Yes. I put it on before I even came out. Why?"

"How many times during the day did you reapply it?" He leaned closer and touched a finger to her leg.

"I don't know." She shook her head, trying to remember. She had reapplied it after coming out of the pool, hadn't she?

"You look really red, Jody."

She looked down at her chest. She could see white under the top of her bikini, but she *had* been in the sun every day for the past few days.

"I had a mild sunburn from yesterday," she told him, not particularly alarmed. "I think I'll just take one quick dip in the pool, then I'll go in and clean up for dinner."

"I'll stop by your room in an hour or so."

"Great. I'll see you then."

Jody watched him walk across the concrete patio that surrounded the pool and sighed. Jeremy looked great from absolutely every angle.

She dove into the deep end of the almost deserted pool and surfaced halfway down the length of it. The water felt cooler now, and she floated, drifting for a few long moments, then hoisted herself out of the pool, pondering what she'd wear that night.

Rousing herself from the water, she towel-dried her legs, noticing for the first time that her skin had taken on an ominously deep shade of pink. How many times during the day *had* she put on sunscreen?

She reached in her beach bag, searching for the sunscreen. Suddenly she recalled lathering herself with the white cream while she was in the bathroom earlier that morning. In her mind's eye, she clearly saw the tall brown bottle resting on the side of the bathroom sink, right where she'd left it.

Jody stuffed her belongings back into the bag, then followed the patterned carpeting from the poolside lobby to her room, mentally berating herself for being so careless.

I hadn't expected to be out there for so long, and I hadn't intended on falling asleep, she reminded herself as she went into the bathroom to hang up the wet towels. *I thought Jeremy would be back earlier . . .*

The sight of her own face and body in the mirror made her head swivel around in surprise. Was her skin really that red? Or was the skin that had been covered by the bikini really that white? She leaned closer, not believing her eyes. Could she have gotten *that* much sun today?

Maybe on her way back from dinner she'd stop at the drugstore and pick up something for sunburn. She hummed as she showered, hummed as she washed her hair. The humming stopped when her skin seemed to tighten as she began to towel-dry it.

Every fiber of cotton seemed to abrade, as if the towel were made of sandpaper, and she finished drying by patting the towel on her skin. She didn't panic until she looked back into the mirror and saw just how red she was.

Lobster red. Crayon red. Fire engine red.

I must have something with me, she muttered, rummaging in her suitcase for something, body cream, lotion . . . something that might help.

Jody found a jar of skin-care lotion and soothed a wide white swath onto her arms, but it only seemed to make the skin feel more taut.

Swell, she muttered as she blow-dried her hair. When she finished, she turned her back to the mirror and looked over her shoulder, trying to gauge how badly she was burned on the flip side. Had she even applied sunscreen to her back?

Jody winced as she drew her bra straps over her

shoulders. The thin satin straps lay like rough burlap on her tender skin. She ignored the discomfort as she pulled a white top over the bra, then slipped on a short skirt. It took only about thirty seconds for Jody to recognize the truth of the situation. The skirt tightened like a vise around her waist, the pressure more than she could stand. She took off the skirt, the shirt, and the bra, and tossed them on the bed in disgust.

Well, this is a nice kettle of fish, she mumbled, standing in the middle of the room in her panties. *How can I go out to dinner if I can't put any clothes on?*

Her eyes drifted back to the closet inside the motel room door to where the red silk number was pinned to its hanger.

With a sigh, she slipped it off the hooks and over her head. It skimmed her skin like a whisper. And a short-sleeved shirt would provide a little cover, hiding the obvious fact that she was wearing very little under the dress. She slipped her feet into high heels and groaned. Between the still-sore gash on her right foot and her sunburned soles, her feet hadn't fared much better than the rest of her.

Here she had little choice. She had her heels, her running shoes, and her flip-flops. The heels it would have to be. Jeremy said the restaurant was just a few blocks away. She should be fine. And if her feet hurt when she got there, she could slip her shoes off and no one would be the wiser.

Jeremy did a triple take when Jody answered the door. The red silk dress was soft and alluring, feminine yet sexy.

It was also the same color as her face. And her arms. And every other inch of skin that wasn't covered.

They stopped at the corner across from the motel, waiting for the light to turn green so that they could cross. Jeremy's eyes narrowed and he leaned forward. Were those blisters on her nose?

Jody, meanwhile, was trying to ignore the fact that her skin felt like glowing embers and her lips felt as if they were beginning to swell. Inside the high heels, her feet protested every step.

"Jody, that burn looks really painful."

"It is." She bit her bottom lip.

"Did you put something on it?" He touched her arm and she flinched.

"I didn't have anything in my room. I didn't expect to be stupid enough to have something like this happen. I thought we'd stop at the drugstore on the way back and pick up something for sunburn. I'll bet they see lots of sunburn down here."

"Are you sure you want to go out to dinner?" he asked.

Jody nodded. "I'll be fine."

She hoped she'd be fine. She *would* be fine. She'd waited a life time for a man like Jeremy. She'd *have* to be fine.

There would be a twenty-five-minute wait for a table, they were told when they entered the restaurant.

"Want to wait at the bar?" Jeremy asked. "It looks as if there are a few stools left there on the end."

"Sure." Jody took Jeremy's hand, and leaned heavily on it as he helped her onto the tall, high-backed bar stool.

Jody leaned against the hard wooden back, then shot forward with a lurch.

"Jody, are you sure you're all right?"

"My back is a little sensitive, that's all." *And the soles of my feet are on fire, and my thighs are melting under my skirt. Other than that, I'm perfectly fine.*

Jody bit her bottom lip, wondering if she'd be able to sit through an entire meal without spontaneously combusting. Unconsciously, she ran a knuckle across her chin.

Jeremy took her hand away and peered closer. "Jody," he told her, "your face is starting to blister."

"Damn, are you serious?"

He leaned closer still.

"I think your nose is blistering." He traced her lips

with one gentle finger. "And it looks like your bottom lip is swelling."

She searched in her handbag for a mirror. Finding a compact, she opened it and found herself peering at a creature with lips as big as saucers and bubbling blisters rising up on her face like tiny volcanoes.

"Oh, no!" she cried. "Look at me! My whole face is starting to swell up!"

"Calm down, Jody, it isn't that—"

"I look like I've had a run-in with killer bees!" She held both hands in front of her face, as if to shield what she perceived as a hideous visage. "Jeremy, look at my lip. I look grotesque."

Jeremy tilted her face to the light. It wasn't his imagination. The blisters were getting larger. Visibly larger.

"Look, how 'bout if we skip dinner, and we'll go find a drugstore right now and we'll get something to take the sting out."

"There's a pharmacy two blocks in that direction." She pointed in the opposite direction from the motel. "I saw it on Saturday."

"Okay, so we'll walk . . ." He paused. She was clearly on the verge of tears. "What?"

"I can't walk two blocks. I'll be lucky to make it back to the motel," she told him miserably. "The soles of both my feet are burned."

"Okay, then, I'll go to the drugstore. You wait right here. I'll be right back." Jeremy signaled to the bartender. "Another club soda—lots of ice, please."

He turned to Jody and said, "Keep sipping the soda and let the ice rest against your lips. It'll help a little."

She nodded and watched him disappear through the crowd around the front door.

Was this the worst luck in the world? She couldn't recall ever having had a sunburn this bad. It hurt to move. Her feet hurt unmercifully.

And here she was, with the most incredible man in the

world. If he touched her tonight, she'd die of pain. If he didn't, she'd die of regret. She prayed he'd find something mighty potent at that drugstore, a wonder drug that could totally anesthetize only the nerves that controlled pain while leaving the pleasure center intact . . .

Within minutes, Jeremy was striding back into the bar, a plastic bag bearing the name of a chain drugstore swinging from his left hand.

"Aloe," he told her, holding up the bag. "How do you feel?"

"Like I stood too close to a volcano," she told him, adding, "and at the same time, I'm freezing from the air-conditioning."

Jeremy took off his jacket and slid it gently over her shoulders. "Is that better?"

"A little. Thank you." She shifted slightly in her seat. The movement left her slightly nauseated.

"Jody, do you want to leave?"

"I just don't feel very well all of a sudden. I'm sorry."

"Stomach queasy?"

She nodded.

"You might have sun poisoning. Let's get you back to the motel and take care of that burn."

"I can wait till you've eaten."

"No, I don't think you can."

"But, Jeremy—"

"No buts. Let's go." He offered her his hand to help her down from the stool, and she took it gratefully.

She picked her way slowly through the crowd on her screaming feet. Once outside, she removed her shoes and took the steps at a snail's pace.

"You look like you're having a hard time there. Feet really hurt, do they?"

She nodded her head.

"Here," Jeremy started to put his arms around her as if to lift her. "I'll carry you."

"No, don't pick me up." She backed away from him. "My sides, my back, my hips . . . anyplace that you would have to touch me to carry me is screaming right now. I think I can make it if I walk sort of on the sides of my feet."

"All right, then, let's get you back to your room and cover you in aloe."

The one-block walk back to the motel seemed endless.

"Jody," Jeremy said as he closed the door to her room behind them, "you're going to have to get out of that dress."

"Somehow, that sounded better last night," she tried to joke about her situation.

"And it will again in a few days," he kissed the side of her swollen mouth with great tenderness. "But right now, we have to take care of this burn."

"I'll put my bathing suit back on," she told him.

She ducked into the bathroom and closed the door, leaving Jeremy holding a bag of aloe gel. She emerged a few minutes later, the bikini covering the vital parts but little else.

Jeremy sighed. That sweet body he'd loved the night before—that perfect body that had seemed to fit his like a glove—was fried to a crisp.

"So," she said, clearing her throat nervously. She'd dreamed all day of having those skillful hands of his caressing her body again, but she'd been hoping for a more pleasurable experience than she was bound for this time around. "Should I just stand here and you can pour that stuff on my back?"

"No, I think you need to get a towel and spread it across the bed. Then you can lie on the towel, and I'll pour the aloe on. You're already blistering in places. I'll just keep reapplying it."

Nodding without looking him in the eyes, Jody retrieved a bath towel from the bathroom and spread it on the bed, then painstakingly lowered herself onto it, face down.

Lord have mercy. This was Jeremy's best fantasy and worst nightmare.

So near, he sighed, *yet so far.*

"Maybe you should start with my shoulders."

Jeremy poured the cool gel into the palm of one hand and gently began to apply it to her shoulder blades.

"Sorry," he told her when she flinched.

"It's just that it's *cold.* Keep going."

He poured a little aloe directly onto each of her shoulders and smoothed it as kindly as he could down into the small of her back.

"How does that feel?" he asked.

"It's still cold, and my skin's still hot."

Jeremy spread a little over the tops of her hips and she groaned again.

"Want me to stop?"

"No."

He peered at her shoulders. The gel he'd applied had totally soaked into her skin. He reapplied the cooling substance over the entire area.

Jeremy dribbled a few drops of aloe across the backs of her legs, then gently began to rub it in. Jody moaned, and his mouth went dry. Torture. Sheer torture.

"Don't worry—the aloe should help a lot. My grandmother was a great believer in natural remedies. When we were little, it was aloe for sunburn, poison ivy, any skin abrasion, really."

"Who's we?"

His mouth went a little drier as he pondered an answer.

"My brother and I."

"You have a brother?"

He paused before responding.

"I had a younger brother," he said softly.

" 'Had'?" She shifted onto her elbows and looked over her shoulder. "What happened?"

"He died a long time ago."

"Oh, Jeremy, I'm so sorry . . ." She made a movement to turn over and he stopped her from facing him. He just couldn't go into it right then.

"It was a long time ago," he repeated. "Anyway, my grandmother had no faith in modern medicine. Saw a doctor once in her life, when she had pneumonia and my aunt took her to the hospital. As luck would have it, she picked up an infection while she was there and it killed her. She was eighty-seven and didn't look a day over sixty-five. Never used anything but aloe on her skin."

"Oh, well, then. Pour away. I wouldn't mind looking a few years younger."

"If you looked any younger, I'd be arrested for what I'm thinking."

She laughed for the first time since he had arrived at her hotel room earlier in the evening, and he realized then how much he had missed the sound of her laughter. In that minute he knew he would do whatever it took to drive away her pain and bring that smile back to her face.

"Are you feeling better?" he asked.

"A little. My back and shoulders aren't quite as tight."

"Good." Jeremy dribbled a bit down the back of her leg to the calf, and she shivered under it. With sure hands, he rubbed the colorless remedy into the skin, marveling at the strength and shape of the legs right there under his nose.

Purgatory, he thought. *This must be what purgatory is like.*

"Okay. Flip side." He tried to force a lightness he did not feel into his voice. How to touch her and not want to make love to her again?

"I think I can take it from here." Jody rolled over and sat up. "Thank you, Jeremy. I'm beginning to feel less like a burnt offering and more like a human being."

He didn't bother to protest.

"I'll just do your shoulders and your face," he told her, "and you can do . . . well, you can do the rest of you."

He watched silently as she eased the liquid onto her arms, onto her chest, onto her abdomen. She had just reached her hips when he decided he couldn't watch anymore.

"I'm going to run back to my room to get a few things," he told her. "And I'm going to stop in the restaurant and pick up some cool drinks, some ice, and some hot water and tea bags, then I'll be back."

"What's the tea for?"

"Are you aware that your eyes are half closed? If we don't do something tonight, they might be swollen shut by tomorrow morning. We may be able to avoid that if we pack tea bags on your eyes now. And I'm going to stop back at the drugstore. One bottle of aloe is not going to be enough."

He paused, looking down at her, then added, "I'm not sure that we shouldn't make a trip to the nearest emergency room."

"For a little sunburn? No, I'll be fine tomorrow. But Jeremy, you don't have to stay here tonight," she told him, although she wished that he would. "I'm afraid I'm not much company."

"I promise to let you make it up to me." He kissed the top of her head, about the only spot on her body that wasn't glistening with aloe.

"You're very good to me, Jeremy." She watched, through swollen eyelids, as he unlocked the door.

"You have no idea of how good I intend to be to you. But first, let's see what we can do about this sunburn."

Chapter 8

THE NOTE ON THE PILLOW READ, *GONE FOR COFFEE. BE back in 5.*

Jody sat on the edge of the king-sized bed and wondered how she could avoid letting him back in.

Despite the fact that her face had been lathered with aloe all through the night, her mouth was still swollen, her chin was still blistered, and her eyelids, while not swollen shut, were puffed. She'd shrieked when she'd caught a glimpse of herself in the mirror. How could she face Jeremy with her face so distorted?

The doorknob rattled and she ducked under the pillow. There was no way he was going to see just how ugly she was.

"Jody?" he asked softly.

"Go away," she grumbled miserably into the mattress.

"Jody, what's wrong?"

"I look like a ghoul. I'm not leaving this room. Ever. Go away."

"Sooner or later, you're going to get pretty hungry, you know."

"Promise me that, if I starve to death, you'll make them cover my face before they bring the body out."

"Jody, it's not as bad as all that."

"Yes, it is. I thought you said that the aloe would fix it."

"I said the aloe would help it heal. If your skin was already badly burned, it can't reverse that. What it can do is help it to heal quickly. Open the door," he said patiently.

"No. I can't let you see me like this, Jeremy."

"I already did."

"You didn't!"

"Sorry, but you were right there, next to me in the bed when I woke up this morning."

Jody got out of bed and padded on bare feet to the door to let him in.

Jeremy placed the bag down on the dresser and began to unload its contents. "Coffee, orange juice, an English muffin, and some cantaloupe."

"Jeremy, this is very sweet of you," she said, trying to keep her head down.

Was it possible to eat with your head at such an angle? How did one drink coffee without raising one's head?

With the fingers of one hand he tilted her face up to his. When she tried to turn away, he stopped her, saying, "We might as well get this over with now." He peered closely. "My, my, those blisters are really impressive. And I didn't expect that the swelling would be quite so bad this morning; too bad we didn't get the aloe on earlier."

She pulled away and averted her eyes.

"The blisters will heal, Jody, and with any luck, the swelling will be down by the end of the day," he told her gently, hoping he was right.

"I look hideous."

"If you say so." He turned his back and opened one of the bags. Handing her a cup of coffee, he asked, "Would you rather have breakfast out by the pool? There are a few tables in the shade, so you won't have to worry about getting more sun."

She put the cup down, wanting to protest. She'd never

felt uglier in her life. But here was Jeremy, holding out his hand to her.

"I can't believe you'd want to be seen in public with me."

He shook his head. She was, in his eyes, beautiful, the blisters and puffy eyes inconsequential. How did you make a woman understand a thing like that?

"And I hurt. I really hurt." Tears welled in her eyes. "I never knew that sunburn could hurt so much."

"Jody, if you are still in that much pain, I think you should go to the nearest hospital."

"Jeremy, this is sunburn. I'd feel like an idiot going to the hospital for sunburn."

"You'll feel like a bigger idiot if you get really sick, Jody. And people do get really sick from sunburn. You could have sun poisoning."

She sat up and looked at him through slightly swollen eyelids.

"I really think you should let me take you."

Reluctantly, and with the greatest of care, Jody swung her legs over the side of the bed. She gathered elastic-waist shorts and an old, oversized tee-shirt from her suitcase, and walked to the bathroom.

As she closed the door, she said over one shoulder, "Just give me five minutes to get dressed."

The day was overcast, the fog thick as they went from her room to his car, and Jody was thankful for the fact that she needn't fight the sun's rays that morning. She slid cautiously into Jeremy's car, wincing as her sensitive thighs met the leather seat.

They followed the signs for Island Memorial Hospital, just four blocks away. As the sedan rounded the corner to the emergency room entrance, shrill sirens split the morning calm, and Jeremy stopped to allow an ambulance to precede him into the parking lot. He pulled into the nearest parking spot just as the first ambulance was followed by a second, then a third.

"What do you suppose that's all about?" Jody shifted

in her seat to watch the last of the ambulances pull into the line that had formed at the doorway to the emergency room.

"Stay here," Jeremy told her, "and I'll find out."

He was back in minutes, his face white.

"There's been a really bad accident out on the Garden State Parkway. A tractor trailer jackknifed, and there was a six-car pileup because of the fog. Apparently there were a lot of severe injuries. You can't get near the emergency room right now. I think there's another hospital farther up the coast, though. We can try that one."

"I'll bet they're jammed, too. There are only three ambulances here, Jeremy. There must be others on their way to every hospital within miles." She nodded her head in the direction of the ambulances that were lined up, and the flurry of activity that had erupted. "Compared to *that,* a little sunburn seems pretty insignificant."

"Jody, what you have is more than just a little sunburn."

"There's no way that I would expect anyone to tend to me in the midst of what those people must be going through. Let's just go back to the motel, Jeremy, and try a little more aloe." Jody shifted uncomfortably in her seat and tried to smile.

One possibility nagged Jeremy all the way back to her motel room.

It nagged him as he watched Jody walk across the room on swollen feet and smile at him ruefully as she eased onto the side of the bed.

It nagged him as he watched Jody try to sip coffee between swollen lips, and his insides twisted, knowing that she was in pain.

It nagged him as he bit his bottom lip pensively, knowing he had a choice to make, right here and now. Jeremy had hoped that the visit to the hospital would have provided relief for her discomfort, but now, with the hospital personnel concentrating on patients with more immediate, more critical concerns, Jeremy had to face the fact that he had one option left.

Help was less than an hour away, if he was man enough to take that one giant step backwards into his past.

His heart turned over in his chest, and he knew that there was, after all, really no choice to be made. She was hurting, and there was only one person that he knew for certain could help her.

Miz Tuesday, the older-than-the-hills healer from deep in the Pines, could heal wounds in a fashion that never left scars. In his youth, Jeremy had seen Miz Tuesday set bones and cure everything from pneumonia to snake bites with concoctions that had been passed down through generations of healers.

Surely, Miz Tuesday could treat Jody's sunburn, could take away her pain.

Assuming, of course, that Miz Tuesday was still alive.

And if his own wounds were opened, well, he would just have to deal with it, as he always had.

The drive was not a long one, but Jeremy was numbly aware of every mile, every turn in the highway. It wasn't until he pulled off the main road onto the first of the more narrow country lanes that his senses began to come alive. Sights and sounds, smells, some long forgotten, all but overwhelmed him. Forced to slow down once he hit the dirt roads, he found himself surrounded by a half-dozen varieties of pine and as many of oak. Here and there he stopped momentarily to look around, but never spoke. Jody sat quietly, watching his eyes, knowing that wherever he was taking her, he was paying a toll that she had yet to understand. She suspected that before the day had ended, she would learn.

"We're going into the Pines," she said finally as the forest deepened around them.

"Yes." He nodded.

"There aren't as many trees as I would have thought,"

Jody said. "I always imagined the Pines to be thick with trees and densely overgrown."

"Fires are very common here," he said, sounding detached. "Plants that can't adapt, don't survive. That's why there is so little diversity of plant life here. Some are structurally better insulated from heat than others. Some are better adapted genetically to the conditions. Some seeds germinate more quickly when heated or when they fall onto the bare soil left behind after a fire. Some produce root sprouts that grow more quickly after being exposed to intense heat. Several of the pines that thrive here—the pitch pine, for example—have thick bark and can send up new shoots from the base if the top of the tree is killed."

His voice had taken on the flat monotone of a tour guide who had recited his lines a time or two too many, but she let him continue, since talking seemed to be distracting him from whatever it was that he was trying to avoid thinking about.

"The hot-air balloon pilot said there were lots of streams back here."

He nodded. "There's a whole network of them farther in, back in the swamps. I used to know the streams like I know the streets in D.C. now. Like the back of my hand."

"You grew up back here."

"That's right."

They drove in silence for a very long five minutes.

"How does a boy from the Pines get to go to Princeton?" she asked.

"It's a very long story, Jody," he answered without looking at her.

She was about to ask when he'd be telling her that story, when they rounded a bend in the road that broadened into a clearing, beyond which stood an ancient cabin of wood that seemed to grow out in all directions from a central square.

All Jody could think of was Hansel and Gretel.

Jeremy stared ahead at the cabin for a long, quiet time,

his left hand on the door handle. Jody kept waiting for him to open the door, but he did not. Finally, from around the side of the cabin, an old woman appeared, her Brillo-like gray hair partially hidden by the dark blue scarf around her head. A faded brown dress that must have had a belt at one time hung on her slight frame. She leaned on a thick walking stick of white birch.

Jody's eyes widened. Hansel and Gretel indeed!

Upon seeing the car, she stopped and stared intently at them, her eyes seeming to dismiss Jody's presence as she appeared to focus solely on Jeremy.

"Who is that?" Jody whispered.

"That's Miz Tuesday," he said softly.

"Miz Tuesday?" she repeated.

"My stepfather's great-grandmother." Jeremy pushed open the car door and stepped out without waiting for Jody and walked slowly to where the old woman stood.

Jody opened her own door, and forgetting the bubbly appearance of her face, followed behind.

"Jeremy." The old woman said. *"Jeremy."*

He nodded slowly, and they eyed each other without speaking.

"'Bout time." The old woman turned toward the house and pointed the stick in Jody's direction without turning to look at her. "Bring your friend."

Jody touched Jeremy's arm. He looked back over his shoulder at her and said, "She hasn't changed in sixteen years. She hasn't changed at all."

"Are we going inside?"

"Yes."

He held the door for Jody, and she stepped into a darkened parlor. The shapes of furniture loomed here and there around her, but there was no light. Jeremy led her through the dim room into the kitchen, where the light was only slightly better.

"Miz Tuesday, this is my friend, Jody Beckett." Jeremy said as they crossed the worn threshold.

The old woman nodded to acknowledge the introduction but did not turn around.

"I'm makin' you a dish of tea." The old woman told them as she placed a few short pieces of wood into the big woodstove that dominated one whole wall.

"Thanks, Miz Tuesday."

She nodded that they were welcome.

"You ever get electricity, Miz Tuesday?" Jeremy asked.

"You been away a long time." She turned and smiled slyly. "Even stump jumpers got e-lec-tricity these days."

Jeremy laughed for the first time that day.

"How've you been, Miz Tuesday?" Jeremy's face softened as he watched the old woman fill a teakettle with water from the spigot of an old porcelain sink.

She nodded her head briskly. "Pretty middlin' smart."

"I'm glad to hear that."

The old woman pointed to the wooden chairs that sat around the old round table in a corner of the room.

"Set there," she told them as she cleaned the dust from mismatched teacups, long unused, and placed them on the table.

He sat where he was told to and said, "You haven't changed much, Miz Tuesday."

"Not much do back here." She nodded. "Roads been science'd, some 'em. 'Bout all. You bein' a Clam Towner, wouldn't know."

"I don't live in Tuckerton anymore," Jeremy told her. "I haven't lived there in a long time."

"Then where?"

"Outside of Washington, D.C."

Her eyes widened. "All that far?"

He nodded.

"Lotsa folks going from here, but me, I beant going nowhere." She sat and leaned back in her chair. "Our Martha, she bent down to Mays Landing, and her son John, he bent all the way to Trenton, to a school to learn to be a teacher. I always figured him for a weighty man. Like you, Jeremy Noble. You grown up to be a weighty man? A schoolteacher? A bookkeeper, maybe?"

"I'm an investigator. I don't know that what I do

makes me 'weighty,' Miz Tuesday, but I guess sometimes you have to be smart enough to find people who don't want to be found."

Her eyes narrowed and she studied his face.

After a long minute, she turned and leaned over to cup Jody's face in her hand.

"You're here for a curin'," she said, and underneath her sunburn, Jody blushed.

Drawn in by the unknown drama unfolding around her, she had forgotten just how awful she looked.

Self-consciously, Jody raised a hand to cover the blisters on her chin.

"Aloe." Miz Tuesday pronounced.

"Tried that."

"Where'd you find aloe in D.C.?" She pronounced the letters as if they were in quotation marks.

"Not in D.C. In Ocean Point. In the drugstore."

"Boughten?" She raised her eyebrows. "From a store?"

"Yes. They sell it in bottles."

"Fancy that." She shook her head. "Next thing you'll be saying they sell turpentine and Jersey lightnin' too."

Jeremy laughed.

Miz Tuesday stood up and went to a cabinet that hung from the wall next to the stove.

"Turpentine and Jersey lightnin'?" Jody whispered. "And what the hell's a 'stump jumper'?"

"Stump jumpers are the backwoodsmen." He grinned. "Turpentine, in one form or another, has been the traditional treatment of choice here in the Pines for any number of conditions. And there are some that maintain that Jersey lightnin'—homemade applejack whiskey—can cure just about anything. If, of course, it doesn't kill you."

Miz Tuesday shuffled back to the table with several small vials in her hand. After reinspecting Jody's face, she turned her attention to the shoulder burns, then to those on her chest. She nodded to herself, then went to the sink, refilled the teapot, and turned the burner back on.

"First thing you need is to get out of that dress. Then you soak in the tub in flower water . . ."

"Flower water?" Jody mouthed the words silently.

". . . then you have salve, then later, some pure aloe." Miz Tuesday gestured for Jody to follow her through a doorway to the right, muttering under her breath, "Boughten aloe. Hmmph!"

"Jeremy, you can cut me some short pieces for my woodstove." She pointed to a woodpile about ten feet from the back door. "And you can stack 'em right here, near the door."

"Yes, ma'am," Jeremy stood, an amused expression on his face. The lost look he'd had all day seemed to have faded slightly.

"I'll be findin' you an old something of Martha's to put on," Miz Tuesday was telling Jody. "The marigolds might stain your clothes."

"Marigolds?" Jody asked.

"In the flower water." Jeremy heard the old woman say as she closed the door behind them, shutting Jeremy out and leaving him alone here for the first time since he was fifteen years old.

Miz Tuesday wasn't the only thing that had not changed. The old cabin remained exactly as he remembered it. One room had been tacked on to another until the small house was five or six rooms deep or wide. The room where Miz Tuesday had taken Jody had been added two years before Jeremy left, and boasted an old claw-foot tub that John, Jeremy's stepfather, had salvaged from a boardinghouse that had been torn down in Waretown. Jeremy could close his eyes and recall every detail of the day they had brought that tub into this house. It had taken six of them to carry it in and put it in its place in the newly constructed room off the kitchen. Miz Tuesday had been very pleased with her new bathroom.

He walked to the back door and looked through the carefully mended screen to the small herb garden a step or two to the left, around what they called the door yard back here in the Pines. He pushed the door open and walked outside and drew in a deep breath. The overwhelming scent was, well, *pine.* Oh, there were flowers that grew wild in the nutrient-poor sandy soil—mountain laurel and wild indigo, sweet goldenrod and goat's rue, and farther down along the waterways, sweet pepperbush with its fragrant white flowers. But it was pine, above all, that saturated the air. The smell of it brought back a flood of memories from a lifetime ago.

A trail worn in the gray sand parted the shrubs and wound deep into the forest, and without choosing to do so, Jeremy followed it to its end, three quarters of a mile away.

Chapter 9

"NOW, WHAT'S THIS?" JODY SNIFFED AT THE FRAGRANT lotion that Miz Tuesday was applying to the blisters on her shoulders. The bath had been pleasant enough, and she could almost feel the blisters begin to shrivel under Miz Tuesday's gentle ministrations.

"Flax seed, plantain, maybe. Red clover. Some others. Maybe."

"Maybe?" Jody raised a questioning eyebrow.

Miz Tuesday shrugged. "Sometimes one, sometimes another."

"Umm, not that I doubt that you know what you're doing, of course," Jody looked down at the pale yellow tincture that was being smeared onto her shoulders, then held still while Miz Tuesday patted some on the blisters on her face and tried to be tactful. "But shouldn't it *not vary?"*

Miz Tuesday just smiled and held up a worn cotton shift.

"This won't rub on your blisters."

"Thank you." Jody took the dress, in style akin to a hospital gown without the back opening, and slipped it over her head. "I really do feel better, Miz Tuesday. Thank you."

"He be the one that bringed you."

Miz Tuesday opened the door and stepped into the kitchen. She was not surprised to find the house empty, nor did she expect to find Jeremy still chopping wood. Neither did she wonder where he had gone. She knew.

He was, in her opinion, long overdue.

Jody watched the old woman return her vials of herbs to the cupboard and asked, "Miz Tuesday, how do you know what herbs to use for what ailments?"

"You just know, sometimes." She shrugged. "My mother and her mother and *her* mother were healers. They taught me as they did."

"Is that what you are, a healer? Like a doctor?"

Miz Tuesday shook her head. "I don't know about doctors. But I can heal, all right."

Jody was about to ask if Miz Tuesday grew all of her own plants when she glanced out the back window and realized that Jeremy wasn't there.

"Where do you suppose Jeremy went?"

Miz Tuesday rinsed out the small bowls she had used to mix her lotions and debated whether or not to tell her. How might Jeremy feel, after all these years, once he arrived at the end of the path?

She watched Jody out of the corner of a cloudy eye. The young woman must mean a great deal to Jeremy. After all, it was only to seek help for her that he had, finally, come back. Once here, he would deal with all that had been left behind, Miz Tuesday was certain.

She turned to Jody and said, "There's a path through the woods there, out back. It ends in a clearing. He's there."

"And if he's not?"

"Follow the path back here."

But there he'll be, she could have added, watching Jody cross the yard.

The forest spread out indefinitely on either side of the narrow path that was little more than a sandy trail. The trees themselves were spaced somewhat far apart, but the dense shrub layer below made it difficult to see beyond several feet off the trail. Feeling a bit uneasy in the unfamiliar surroundings, Jody picked her way quietly on sandaled feet, wondering if maybe she should have waited at the cabin for Jeremy instead of setting out through the woods like Red Riding Hood.

And she wondered, too, if maybe she should have stolen a peek in that old mirror hanging over the sink in Miz Tuesday's bathroom before going out to find Jeremy. Lord knew just how bad she might look, in the cotton shift, her hair pulled up in an elastic, and her face dotted with Miz Tuesday's ointment, which was, gratefully, pale in color and hopefully would not eat the skin off her face.

Jody had sensed a change in Jeremy the minute they had crossed Miz Tuesday's threshold, a quiet resignation, as if he'd finally exhaled a breath he'd been holding for a long, long time. There was no question that something here was the key to doors that were long ago locked, and instinctively, Jody knew that, if they were to share more than a few fun-filled days at the beach together, Jeremy would not only have to unlock those doors himself, he'd have to share whatever waited behind them with her. She wondered if he could.

The path ended abruptly, and the gray sand with its sparse covering of poor grass spread out around her in a wide clearing that bore signs of fire from sometime in the past. Fifty or so feet away from the charred remains of a house, Jeremy sat, still as a stone, his back against a fallen log. From the end of the path, Jody waited and watched for some movement on his part, but he appeared to be in a trance.

Jody walked to the log and sat behind him, wrapped her arms around him protectively, and waited.

Finally, he said, "There's nothing left."

"What was here before, Jeremy?"

"My home. My mother. My brother. My stepfather."

"Did you lose them in a fire?"

"If I'd been home that night, I could have saved them."

"How do you know that you wouldn't have been trapped inside with them?"

"I could have saved them," he repeated sadly. "There was no one here to save them."

He leaned back against her, and let her rock him gently, side to side, and he told her what had happened that night, long ago, how he had left home a cocky fifteen-year-old hell-bent on enjoying a wild Fourth of July at the beach with his friends, how he had returned to find that his world had been destroyed and replaced by a nightmare of flames and smoke.

Then, abruptly, he fell silent. It had been so long since he had put his memories into words that he seemed stunned by them.

"Then what happened, Jeremy?" Jody asked to draw him back. "After the fire, where did you go? Where did you stay?"

"I went to live with my aunt—my father's sister—and her family in Tuckerton."

"What happened to your father?"

"He was killed in a boating accident when I was two. My mother remarried about three years later. My stepfather had lived in the Pines all his life. When he was growing up, he picked blueberries in the summer, harvested cranberries in the fall. And he carved decoys—ducks, geese, loons. Mostly, he supported his family by building Barnegat sneakboxes—small rowboats that he'd sell to hunters or fishermen—but he was a real artisan when it came to carving. His decoys were in great demand, the colors and the carvings were so exacting, so beautiful. Whenever I think about him, I remember that he worked very hard. And that he loved my mother very, very much." He cleared his throat, then continued. "Anyway, my aunt had married a high school teacher. They had a son my age, T.J.—"

"Your partner."

"Yes. We'd been close since we were little kids. After I moved in with them, we grew even closer. My aunt never forced me to come back here, and I never did."

"Jeremy, I'm so sorry."

His right hand dragged through his hair. "They never did determine what caused the fire. I have relived every detail of that night a thousand times in my head, trying to piece it together, trying to figure out just what happened. I never really did. Not even after several years of investigative training."

"You mean, training to become a private investigator?"

"No, I mean when I joined the FBI."

"You were in the FBI?" Jody hadn't meant to let her jaw drop, but there it was, almost to her chest.

"I was recruited right out of Princeton."

"May I ask how you managed to get *there?*"

"T.J.'s father's brother was one of the assistant football coaches there. He came to watch T.J. and me play several times in high school. Our grades were very good, our SAT's were high . . . and we both applied. I didn't expect to get in, but . . ." He shrugged. "Anyway, we both graduated and we both joined the FBI."

"This must have haunted you, all these years." Jody said softly.

He nodded. "Every day. I think about it every day."

"But you never came back."

He shook his head. "There really was nothing here for me, Jody, other than some very painful memories. I never wanted to stand in this spot again."

"But you're standing here now."

"You needed Miz Tuesday," he said simply.

He had traded her pain for his own, pure and simple. The knowledge of how much he had paid for Miz Tuesday's floral bath and herbal ointment all but knocked the wind from her lungs. Jody sat back down on the fallen log and waited while he poked here and there about the remains of the house. She watched as he sifted through ashes in the fireplace that stood along what had once been an outside wall. Occasionally he would pick something up and examine it, sometimes pocketing whatever it was that he found, but most often just dropping the object where he'd found it.

Finally, after close to an hour had passed, he looked over to where she sat and said, "There just isn't anything here, Jody."

She went to him and took his hand. "Well, at least you finally came back, Jeremy. You can't tell me that you're not glad to be back."

"No. I can't say that I'm not." He sighed and looked overhead to the tall pines that stretched above him. "I never realized how much I still miss this place. I never imagined how much like *home* it would feel, how familiar it all would be even after so many years."

A bird trilled melodically from a nearby branch, bringing a smile to his face. "That's a pine warbler. I haven't heard one in years."

Jody looked up and followed the small buff-yellow bird as it hopped from branch to branch overhead.

"Are you ready to go back to Miz Tuesday's?" she asked.

Jeremy nodded and took the hand she held out to him. "I guess I should have prepared you for her."

Jody smiled. "I don't know how you could prepare anyone for Miz Tuesday."

"She's one of a kind, all right. How does the sunburn feel?"

"Much, much better." Jody shook her head. "I don't really know what was in the bathwater, and I'm not sure about what's in the ointment. I almost think I'm better off *not* knowing. But whatever it is, it's taken the fire out of my skin, and I've all but forgotten that I have blisters."

He peered down at her. "They haven't disappeared," he told her, "but they do seem to be drying up a little."

"Maybe I'll get lucky and they won't scar," she said as they walked from the clearing to the path without having decided to do so.

"Well, that was the whole idea."

"You're quite a man, Jeremy Noble," she told him

when they had reached the edge of the path and he had stopped to look back at the remains of his childhood home. "I know it wasn't easy, coming back here. I'll never forget that you did this for me."

Jody leaned up and kissed him very lightly on the tip of his chin. It was the best her swollen lips could do at the time. She would, she promised herself, make it up to him later. As often as he would let her.

"How old do you suppose Miz Tuesday is?" Jody asked as they followed the path through the woods.

"Oh, over one hundred."

"You think Miz Tuesday is more than one hundred years old?"

"Sure. I know she is. She was old when I first met her. Old the last time I saw her. And she'll live forever." He grinned. "Everyone in the Pines knows that."

"She's pretty savvy for a woman that old."

"Miz Tuesday is savvy for a woman of any age," he assured her. "I've never met anyone like her. She's a legend around here, you know. When I was little, there was a story going around about how she fought the Jersey Devil over in the cedar swamp and won."

Jody laughed. "Who's the Jersey Devil?"

"Not 'who,' darlin,' what. According to local legend, a Mrs. Leeds, who lived somewhere in Atlantic County—the exact whereabouts depends on who is telling the story—had twelve children. When she learned that she was expecting yet another child, she was said to have proclaimed angrily, 'I hope this one is a devil.' And sure enough, she got her wish."

"She gave birth to a baby devil?"

"So they say."

"And what exactly does this 'devil' look like?"

"Let's see, I think it had the face of a horse—with horns, of course—and a body that sort of resembles a kangaroo. Wings, like a bird. Cloven feet, like a pig. A forked tail."

"And how big is this thing? Just so I don't confuse it with any other horse-pig-bird-kangaroo."

"Well, that, too, depends on . . ."

". . . who's telling the story. Gotcha." She laughed. "And people claim to have seen this thing."

"On and off for the past two hundred years."

"Must have been that Jersey lightnin'."

Jeremy laughed and squeezed her hand.

"What's Miz Tuesday's real name?"

"That is her name, as far as I know," he said as they came to the end of the path, where the subject of their conversation was leaning into her garden and gathering a blossom here, a leaf or two there. "I've never heard her referred to any other way."

"You find what you were looking for, boy?" the old woman asked without turning around.

"I think so," Jeremy told her.

She continued clipping her plants. "Then you'll be going. I'll be giving her"—she nodded in Jody's direction—"some for her bath, some for to keep on the blisters."

"Thank you, Miz Tuesday." Jeremy said softly.

"You won't stay away as long next time. You'll be back twice before Christmas," she told him.

"Will I, now?"

"Yes. The second time, she'll be with you." Miz Tuesday turned toward her cabin and added slyly, "No scars, she'll have."

"If Miz Tuesday says it's so," Jeremy said to Jody as they followed Miz Tuesday down the path of crushed oyster shells, "it's so."

Miz Tuesday handed Jody a small container and said, "This for the blisters. This"—she held up a small bag—"for the bathwater."

"Thank you, Miz Tuesday. I'm very grateful." Jody tucked everything into her shoulder bag. "I don't know how to thank you." Jody reached out to touch the old woman's arm.

"Bring the boy back again." The old woman almost smiled. "Just bring the boy back."

Chapter 10

THE EARLY EVENING SKY HAD REMAINED CLOUDY AND A bit of a breeze had picked up by the time the Maxima pulled back into the parking lot of the Sea View Motel. Jeremy had been silent for most of the drive back from Miz Tuesday's. Clearly, for him, the trip to his childhood home had been both emotional and cathartic. Jody reached for his hand as they walked to the end of the concrete path that led from the parking lot to the boardwalk. Beyond the nearly deserted beach, choppy waves doused the sand with white foam.

Jody squeezed his hand and asked, "How does a walk on the beach sound?"

He looked off in the distance to where a storm was just beginning to gather and nodded. "I think it's a good day for it."

Jody wasn't sure if he was referring to a walk or to a storm.

"I think I'd like to stop back at my room first and change, though. It was sweet of Miz Tuesday to let me keep Martha's dress, but I think that a pair of shorts and a tee-shirt might be more apropos."

"Mr. Noble," the pretty young desk clerk called to him as they entered the lobby. "A Mr. Dawson has been trying to get in touch with you all day. He said it's urgent that you call him as soon as possible."

"Thank you," he said, then turned to Jody and frowned. "I wonder what that's about. I better stop back at my room and call him."

"I'll go on to my room and change. I'll meet you out by the pool and we can take that walk."

"Okay," Jeremy nodded tersely, already contemplating any number of possible emergencies as he headed up the steps. "I'll see you in a few minutes."

A few minutes turned out to be closer to thirty. Jody was just beginning to think that perhaps she should call Jeremy's room when she looked up and saw him making his way around the pool. In his right hand was his suitcase, in his left, the bag from the shop on the boardwalk where he'd bought T.J.'s tacky gifts.

"Jody, I'm really sorry. I have to leave." His jaw was tight and his eyes guarded.

"Leave?" she repeated.

"There's a case I worked on . . . something has come up. Sometimes things come up and . . . I'm sorry, I can't go into detail, but I have to go *now.*" He dropped his bag on the ground and took her into his arms and kissed her.

She stood on her tiptoes and drank him in, savored the curve of his mouth and the taste of his lips.

"I'll call you when it's done." He skimmed the side of her face with his thumb.

"What do you mean, when it's . . ."

He kissed her again. "I'm sorry, Jody. I can't tell you anything else. I have to go. I promise I'll be in touch as soon as I can."

And in less than the blink of an eye, he was gone.

"Well." She took a deep breath, still trying to understand exactly what had just happened. "That was short and sweet."

Folding her arms across her chest, she stood at the top of the steps leading down to the sand. Only a few souls remained on the beach, and those were now shaking out their towels and blankets and gathering their belongings, heading for the boardwalk, hoping to keep ahead of the rain. Fat plops of water began to pelt the ground, lightning cracked across the ocean, and thunder rattled the sky. Feeling defeated by even the weather, Jody turned back to the hotel and returned to her room.

Dressed in a wide-brimmed hat to shelter her face from the sun, Jody walked the beach close to the wrack line early the next morning. She'd barely slept the night before, wondering if her days with Jeremy had really happened at all. He'd left so unexpectedly, with so little explanation, that she almost felt as if she'd been struck. What could have been so important that he'd leave at the drop of a hat?

Was there really an important job that he needed to tend to?

Maybe he'd just been overwhelmed by his trip back into the Pines and didn't know how to handle it. Maybe whatever it was that had been happening between Jody and him seemed, well, *insignificant* in comparison to standing in the spot where his family had died.

Maybe he just wanted to be alone.

Jody kicked a piece of driftwood and tried to roll a clamshell with her toes. Finding a dry spot on the sand, she sat down and viewed the wreckage left on the sand by the storm the night before. *The beach looks the way I feel,* she sighed, *tossed and confused and devastated.*

Overhead a hot-air balloon drifted, and Jody closed her eyes, remembering how it had felt to ride the wind in an oversized basket, wrapped in Jeremy's arms, and to gaze down on the early morning sea.

Maybe some breakfast, she thought, having forgone dinner the night before. After Jeremy left, so had her appetite. She wandered into a small luncheonette on the boardwalk and surveyed the menu, but nothing seemed to appeal. After ordering a coffee to go, she bought a newspaper and took both in search of an outside table where she could sit and read and stare at the beach. Twenty minutes later, the cardboard coffee cup empty and the paper having been scanned, she dumped both into a nearby receptacle and strolled aimlessly down the boards. She stopped at a newsstand and perused the new paperbacks, but nothing seemed to entice her.

Next, she poked into a series of shops that were just opening for the day, thinking to find souvenirs for Laura and Ally, Laura's daughter, but everything looked the same. Sighing, she kept walking until she found herself at the end of the boardwalk. She followed wooden steps to a sidewalk that led to the main street and walked into town without noticing where she was going.

It was almost noon by the time Jody decided that Ocean Point, without Jeremy, was just another vacation spot, and a very lonely one, at that.

By two, Jody had seen everything there was to see in town. She'd walked to the park and watched young mothers push their little ones on the swings or wait at the bottom of slides to catch the toddlers when they reached the bottom. She'd walked past the house her family had rented, years before, and smiled at the little girl who sat on the front step trying to tie a baby bonnet onto the head of a cooperative dog. Reaching the bay, Jody had gone all the way to the end of the old fishing dock and stood, hands in her pockets, watching the charter boats return from their day at sea. Not knowing what else to do, she sat down on the weathered boards and took off her sandals and dangled her feet over the water. Barnacles grew on the piles of the dock, and if she looked closely enough, she might see a small school of tiny fish darting just under the surface of the water. She just didn't feel like looking for them. She didn't feel like doing much of anything, now that Jeremy was gone.

"I can't even sit in the sun," she grumbled as she rolled down the sleeves of her cotton shirt. "Not until this sunburn heals, anyway."

Jody stood up and slipped her feet back into her sandals. She didn't fish and she didn't crab. She couldn't lie on the beach or swim in the pool. She couldn't do much of anything down here that didn't make her miss

Jeremy. She might as well go back to Bishop's Cove. At least there she had work to do. People to talk to. Things to do.

Might as well, she concluded as she headed back toward the other side of town, thinking that at least she'd had a few good days here.

Who am I kidding? They were great days. Maybe the best days of my entire adult life. Jeremy Noble is the best man I've ever known, and even if I never see him again, I'll never forget . . .

Unthinkable. She shook her head as she walked along, her pace quickening. That couldn't happen. *He said he'd call, and he will. He will!*

There had been too much between them in all too short a time, too much left to explore, too much left unsaid. When he was finished with whatever it was that had taken him away, he'd come back. And he'd know right where to find her.

Certain of it, Jody returned to the motel, packed her bags, and checked out.

"Mommy, will you take me for my dancing lesson now?" Ally, Laura's six-year-old daughter, flew into the kitchen through the back door.

"Is it time already?" Laura frowned.

"Yes. See"—the little girl pointed to the big clock over the stove—"the little hand is on the one, and the big hand is on the twelve."

"So it is, sweetie. Go get your dancing things and meet me out by the car."

Ally cheered and ran like a rabbit up the back steps of the inn.

Laura turned to Jody. "Do you need any help here?"

"No, I'm fine," Jody smiled absently. "Kevin will be here any minute now. He's been a big help. Hiring a couple of students for the summer was a great idea. I don't know why I resisted it for so long."

"Do you have everything you need for dinner? Any last-minute things I can pick up for you?"

Jody grinned, one of the first real smiles Laura had seen since Jody had arrived back at the inn from her vacation several weeks earlier. "I have everything under control, and you know that I always have everything I need before I start to cook."

"Just checking." Laura smiled back.

It was good to see Jody's good humor starting to return. She'd been far too somber when she'd arrived at the inn, several days before Laura had expected her. Jody had sported a wicked sunburn, but Laura couldn't help but think there was more behind Jody's listlessness than a few blisters. Other than to say that her reunion with her friends had been fine, Jody had barely responded to Laura's attempts to discuss it. Whatever had happened during Jody's stay at Ocean Point, it had left her distracted and saddened.

Just the night before, Laura had paused in the kitchen doorway and watched as Jody had chopped onions, constantly wiping her eyes on her sleeves. Somehow, Laura suspected that it was more than the onions that caused Jody's eyes to tear.

And of course, it would have something to do with Jeremy Noble.

That much had been clearly established when Laura asked if she had bumped into Jeremy and Jody had merely nodded in response and changed the subject. Something in her eyes had warned Laura not to pursue it, and so she had not. Still, Laura hated to see Jody so unhappy, and it encouraged her to see a bit of the old Jody flash in that brief smile.

"Mommy, I'm ready!" Ally hopped off the bottom step and, waving to Jody, bounced immediately out the back door.

"Have fun, Ally," Jody called over her shoulder as the screen door slammed.

"We'll be back well before dinner," Laura said as she searched her handbag for her car keys. "Kevin should be here soon."

"Okay." Jody nodded.

The kitchen fell silent except for the hum of the ceiling fan and the *chop chop chop* of Jody's knife as it ate its way through carrot after carrot. Jody welcomed the quiet, welcomed the solitude. She'd had so little to say to anyone over the past few weeks that it was a relief not to force conversation.

She'd stopped straining her ears to listen every time a phone rang and was answered, stopped thinking that *this* call would be for her. At a loss to understand why he had left so abruptly in the first place, how he could have forgotten her in three short weeks, Jody tried her best to convince herself to chalk it up as that summer fling she'd never had. It had seemed like so much more than that at the time, but, well, maybe that's how summer romances were. Maybe they all seemed like the real thing.

It was the real thing, she protested. *It was.*

Well, she sighed, she'd wanted to be swept off her feet, just once in her life, and she had been that. Totally. Completely. Incredibly.

There had been a time when she thought that that would be enough. She had been wrong. One night with Jeremy had not been enough. A lifetime with Jeremy might not be enough . . .

Jody wiped weepy eyes on the short sleeve of her tee-shirt.

"Hey, Jody," Kevin swung the back door open, startling her. "Since when have we used frozen fish?"

"What?" She frowned.

"Frozen fish." Kevin went straight to the refrigerator, looking, no doubt, for a cold drink. "There's a guy outside, says he's got one hundred and twenty pounds of frozen tuna to deliver."

Jody froze in mid-chop.

"What did you say?"

"I said there's a guy outside with . . ."

"One hundred twenty pounds of frozen tuna," Jody whispered.

"Yeah."

"One hundred twenty pounds of frozen tuna," Jody repeated.

"Umm . . . Are you all right, Jody?" Kevin leaned tentatively toward her. Jody's eyes had taken on a strange sort of glow.

"One hundred twenty pounds of frozen tuna!" She ripped the apron off over her head and flew out the back door.

The Maxima was parked next to her old Buick, its trunk standing open and its owner leaning against the driver's door.

"You!" she yelled as she took the steps two at a time. "Where the hell have you been?"

Jeremy stepped forward and caught her in his arms as she hit the bottom step.

"I had a job to do."

"And I suppose there were no phones on this job?" She sought—half-heartedly—to disengage herself.

"No. There were none." He'd taken off his sunglasses, and gray eyes now bore into her own.

"Where were you that there were no phones? There are phones everywhere, Jeremy."

"Have you been watching the news these past few weeks?" he asked patiently, refusing to let her go.

Jody paused.

"Did you watch the news yesterday morning?"

"Yes . . ."

"What was the big story, yesterday morning?"

These past few weeks the news had been dominated by the kidnapping of a congressman's only son by the boy's mother, who had fled to the Canadian Rockies, taking the child with her. The story had had a happy ending just yesterday, when it was announced that the toddler had been found and returned to his anxious father by Canadian and American law enforcement officers. The rescue team had been led by two unidentified investigators hired by the family to track the child into the wilderness.

"You helped find that little boy," she said softly.

He nodded as he drew her closer. This time, she did not protest.

"I'm very sorry, Jody. I couldn't call. But I came as soon as I could."

"After a quick trip to Ocean Point," she noted, "to pick up your fish."

"Well, yes, but I wanted to drop off some aloe for Miz Tuesday."

"*Boughten* aloe?" Jody leaned back and stared up at him. "You took *boughten* aloe to Miz Tuesday?"

"I did."

"What did she think of it?"

"She appeared disdainful at first, but when I told her I'd return it, she wouldn't give it back."

"Was it easier, going back the second time?" Jody asked, watching his face.

"Maybe a bit." He nodded. "There's still a lot I have to work through."

I'll be there with you, every step of the way, she wanted to say. Instead, she merely said, "I'm glad you stopped to see Miz Tuesday."

"So am I. She asked about you. I see the blisters are gone," Jeremy noted as he lowered his mouth to hers for one very satisfying, very long overdue kiss.

"I missed you, Jody. Every day." He kissed her again. "Every night."

"I missed you, too, Jeremy. I was beginning to think that maybe . . ."

"Don't." He stopped her. "There are no maybe's. I should have explained to you that sometimes I have to go at the drop of a hat, and stay until the job is finished."

"Well, you did *say* that," she allowed. "I just didn't know that *finished* could mean weeks."

Jeremy ran his hands up and down her arms, just to feel her skin. She would never know how much he had ached to do just this.

"Do you think Laura has a room for me?" he asked.

"Gosh, I'm sorry." Jody shook her head. "I heard her say just this morning that she was booked to capacity."

"Any thoughts on where I might find a bed for a few nights?"

She slipped her hand into her pocket and pulled out her key, which she held up between two fingers before pressing it into the palm of his hand and closing his fingers around it.

"How many nights?" She leaned into him.

"Well, I thought I'd take the rest of that vacation." He bit at her bottom lip. "The one that was cut short a few weeks ago. I was just starting to enjoy myself."

"Some of us might have to work this week. At least, during the day," she reminded him.

"Well, that's okay, since I'll be busy while I'm here."

"Busy with what?" She frowned. "I thought you said you were on vacation."

"Well, it's sort of a working vacation." He leaned back against the car and took her with him. "See, Anna thought it would be a good idea if I . . ."

"Anna?" Jody frowned.

"The palm reader from the boardwalk." He nuzzled the side of her face.

"You stopped to have your palm read while I was languishing here in Bishop's Cove?" She fought an urge to smack him with one of his own frozen fish.

"Well, she had been right about everything else, about me being near the end of my journey and going home for your sake and all that. I thought she should know that, that she had been right. And I thought I'd see what else she had to say."

"And?"

"She said T.J. and I should think about expanding our business, open another office. She thought a small town on the ocean might be a lucky move."

"Really." Jody grinned. "What else did she tell you?"

"Nothing I didn't already know. That I just couldn't wake up every morning so far away from the woman I love."

"The woman you love . . ." Jody's eyes went misty.

"Right. Anna told me if I had any sense at all, I'd drive right down here and give you a fitting peace offering."

"You mean the fish? That's your idea of a *peace offering?*"

Jeremy beamed and nodded happily.

"What ever happened to flowers?" Jody tapped her foot, trying to decide if she was amused or insulted. "Chocolate? Jewelry? What kind of man brings a woman one hundred plus pounds of frozen tuna?"

Jeremy gathered her into his arms. "A man who plans on spending a lot of time with that woman. After all, how long do you think it will take us to eat all that fish?"

"Oh, a long time," she whispered as she lifted her face for his kiss. "A very long time."

"That's pretty much what I thought," he dipped his head to hers and chuckled. "Besides, how can you argue with a boardwalk psychic?"

Mariah Stewart is the award-winning author of seven contemporary romances and two novellas, all for Pocket Books. Recently nominated by *Romantic Times* magazine for a Career Achievement Award for Contemporary Romance, she has been called "one of the most talented writers of mainstream contemporary fiction in the market today" (*Affaire de Coeur*). Her work has been described as "multi-layered novels that appeal to fans of romance, mainstream fiction, and family sagas" (amazon.com). The *Philadelphia Inquirer* calls her books "Delightful. Totally charming and enchanting." Her titles include *Moments in Time, A Different Light, Carolina Mist,* and the popular Enright family saga: *Devlin's Light, Wonderful You,* and *Moon Dance. Priceless,* her seventh book, was released in June of 1999.

A native of Hightstown, New Jersey, Mariah Stewart lives in a century-plus Victorian country home in a Philadelphia suburb with her husband of twenty years, two teenage daughters, and two golden retriever puppies. Presently at work on her next book, she divides her spare time between her daughters' field hockey and lacrosse games and her perennial garden. Drop her a line at P.O. Box 481, Lansdowne, PA 19050.

Catch up with love...
Catch up with passion...
Catch up with danger....

Catch a bestseller from Pocket Books!

Delve into the past with *New York Times* bestselling author
Julia London
The Dangers of Deceiving a Viscount
Beware! A lady's secrets will always be revealed...

Barbara Delinksy
Lake News

Sometimes you have to get away to find everything.

Fern Michaels
The Marriage Game
It's all fun and games—until someone falls in love.

Hester Browne
The Little Lady Agency
Why trade up if you can fix him up?

Laura Griffin
One Last Breath
Don't move. Don't breathe. Don't say a word...

Available wherever books are sold
or at www.simonsayslove.com.

17660